Baptization

Path of Lazy Immortal Book 3

A.P. Gore, Patricia Jones

Sign up for my Wuxia Sect to get latest update, and sneak peeks and an extended epilogue of the other books.

Patricia's Cultivation Sect

Contents

Chapter 1

Prologue

A servant named Shrug watered the rapidly withering Celestial Mayflower, caressing it with his soft whistle. But even after pouring a drop of Heaven's Pure Water on it, its sharp purple petals turned dull gray, then withered into ashes. Twenty breaths later, only a stem remained, telling the story of one thousand deaths.

The east wind blew away the unpleasant smell the withered mayflower produced and set Shrug's dark-green robe fluttering when it blew past.

Shrug frowned, making more creases than his tiny forehead could sustain.

This was the thousandth time he'd used Time Law to bring the Celestial Mayflower back to life, and a different method to grow it rapidly. His lord wouldn't be pleased when he saw Shrug failing after just ten days. He had brought this flower from T3540, a world he had recently created to grow some celestial plants for his lady interest.

What should he do?

Unknowingly, Shrug floated over the garden, staring at the other gray mayflower that reeked of a thousand deaths as well. Listening to the sound of spring, he turned backward and looked at the floating palace where his lord spent time with lord's current lady interest. She was his lord's fifth one in the last one year, and he continuously created universes to grow more treasures, flowers, or fruits to please her.

Studying the large palace floating in the distance, he sighed. For once, he didn't know when he would finally greet his new lord's lady. It had been millennia since his lord's wife went missing in one of his own creations, and since then his lord rarely looked at his creations and rarely created new experiments.

Considering his next action, Shrug floated into the Paramount God Palace where his lord hosted his inventions. If the Celestial Mayflower could grow on T3540, then there must be a low-level treasure formed there. That would help Shrug find out the properties of the treasure and borrow a similar one that could withstand the celestial energy roaming through the Paramount God Palace.

Yes, that seemed like a good idea. After spending millions of years with his lord, some intelligence had rubbed off on Shrug. Once he continued down this path, he would find a path to serve the lord in the best way.

While walking toward the T3540 status screen, Shrug's gaze lingered on T120 status screen. The last time his lord had asked him to check on what was missing from here, he had used his celestial energy to create the item called as AI Chip in local language of T120 that had vanished with the soul he moved to T2460.

However, the original AI Chip was still growing on T2460 with that reincarnated soul.

That as an issue.

If his lord found out Shrug had messed up some things behind his back, his lord would be unhappy. And other than withering plants, Shrug hated it the most when his lord became unhappy.

Should he destroy the AI Chip by sending celestial energy? No, that might trigger imbalance in the entire universe of T2460. But he couldn't leave it wandering there, or else his lord would definitely find out about his mess, and that would make his lord unhappy.

A better option would be to use a native lifeform to destroy that object.

Enlarging the T2460, he vaguely discerned the place where the soul with AI Chip fell. The Mortal Realm. Picking a very low-level creature, Shrug sent a bout of celestial energy into the creature's dark body and then commanded it to destroy the object that had been stolen away from T120.

"This should be enough." He smiled, feeling freed up from the guilt that had weighed down his heart. Once the soul that stole the AI Chip from T120 died, it would follow the proper reincarnation path.

Yes, that would be the best outcome as he wouldn't have to do anything else to solve the issue.

Chapter 2

Two Girls One Man

In a lone courtyard built at the base of a lone mountain, a girl with long black hair stood alone, staring at a boy wrapped in white bandages and lying on a bedroll. Ki Fei's heart shook, and tears flew when she looked at him. He was Li Wei, her young master.

Her small fingers curled in a fist as she looked upon his poor condition, and when she fumed inside, the atmosphere around her heated up and the life energy turned gloomy.

A woman with a high chin and a beautiful face walked in, holding a bucket of water and a bowl of soup filled with fragrant herbs. Ki Fei had tasted it earlier, and it would suit her young master's taste buds. He liked sweet things.

"Fairy Fei, if you get angry, it will affect your cultivation," the woman, Tang Sia, said. "I promised you, I'll take care of him, but you can't go back on your promise and ignore your cultivation."

"Senior Tang, please don't worry. I'll keep my promise, but you must keep your promise too and not let my young master suffer even a little. He has gone through a lot for me, and I want to serve him wholeheartedly."

Tang Sia's eyes flashed with disgust for a moment before calming down.

Ki Fei sighed in her heart. These people didn't understand what young master Wei meant to her. He was her world, and she would never let him suffer. These people were only asking her to cultivate and break through. What was difficult in that? All she needed to do was eat pills and cultivate, and she would break through the new layer. She had already reached layer eight in the Foundation Realm, and she had touched the layer nine boundary.

"Don't worry Fairy Fei. Sect Master has already settled things with Destiny Mirror Sect, and he will be safe as long as he is in Divine Fragrance Palace," Tang Sia replied in a calm voice. "You should head to the peak of the mountain and cultivate in Pure Lotus Water. You can't come out before reaching Bone Baptization Realm. Do you understand?"

Ki Fei sighed, audibly this time. This was all because of her young master who had waged a war with Destiny Mirror Sect. But she was proud of him for killing someone much higher than his own cultivation level. Her young master was awesome. When he wore the clothes she sewed for him, he was invincible.

"Okay. Please give him this set of clothes I sewed for him. He loves my clothes." She smiled and then turned away. If she was going to protect her young master, she had to be as powerful as him.

That was her drive for cultivation. To serve young master Wei.

For young master Wei.

In a dark place behind the State of Zin's royal palace, a girl wearing a black dress sat on a stone bench, studying the metal bars that separated her cell from the lunatics and frenzied criminals. The air was dark, and with the killing intent exuded by everyone, it was hard to breathe. But she sat cross-legged and revolved her qi as per the qi path mentioned in the Wood Monarch's Embrace. It was difficult to move from spear to sword, but she would do it. She would undergo the baptization of sword.

"In this prison, my will, will be my sword and my heart will be my master." Whispering, she got up and moved into a sword stance.

"Wood King's Sword level one."

Five hours later, sweat ran down her head and turned her lips salty, but she didn't stop. If she'd been in her own chamber, maids would have rushed to wipe her forehead, but there was no one here. Other than the darkness and the horrific shouts from frenzied horny males, there was only her steadfastness.

Then again, she also had the treasure given to her by senior Xue Qi to accompany her, to guide her on this dark path.

When footsteps sounded from the entrance of the tunnel that connected to her prison cell, she stopped and went back to her stone bench. It was her chair, her bed, and her practice bench.

With the hem of her dress, she wiped her face and lay on the stone bench, appearing normal by the time the visitor arrived.

"Nuan, are you still not going to answer?" A sharp sound rang through the prison cell, followed by the clinking of golden jewelry. It was Sun Kiyari, the current queen of her father. She was a bitch, and as soon as Destiny Mirror Sect had raised a single complaint, she'd had Sun Nuan thrown in prison.

But knowing this would happen, Sun Nuan had sent her sister, Hua'er, away. Their mother had vanished too. However, thanks to the pill offered by senior Xue Qi, her mother had recovered from the strange illness that had plagued her and broke into the peak of Marrow Cleansing Realm. Once she recuperated, she would come free Sun Nuan from this prison.

Sun Nuan just had to put up with it until then. Thinking about her mother, she felt proud. Once, her mother was the queen, the strongest female warrior in the entire State of Zin, but a mysterious illness had changed her fate. That illness had changed everyone's fate.

"If you don't give me that bitch's whereabouts, I'll kill you like I killed your sister." She threw a bloody pendant toward Sun Nuan.

Sun Nuan caught it, and her eyes shone with a strange light. This was Hua'er's pendant, but how did it come to be in the queen's hands? Whatever. She knew her sister was fine because they shared a deep connection that allowed her to peek into Hua'er's life whenever needed. By giving this pendant to her, the queen had actually done her a favor. Unbeknownst to the queen, this pendant could let her save Hua'er once—and only once—but it could also act as a one-time escape card as well. With it, she could travel once to Hell's Eye Bloodline Forbidden Ground. It was a last resort, but it was something.

She might not even need it. She had sent Hua'er to Divine Fragrance Palace, closer to big brother Wei. Without telling her about their mother, she had asked Hua'er to stay with big brother Wei. He would protect her. Sun Nuan believed in him. She had seen his fate with her own eyes, and it was magnificent. And after hearing about his heroic deeds in killing Destiny Mirror Sect's elder Wen Shang, her trust in him deepened. If she didn't have the treasure from senior Xue Qi, Sun Nuan would have followed him everywhere. In fact, she went to Old Martial City after she heard about the Devil Cicada Challenge, but before she entered the city, queen Sun Kiyari had captured her.

It was troublesome.

"Okay, I haven't killed your sister yet. But let that bloody pendant be a warning to you. I've got people inside Divine Fragrance Palace," the queen shouted. "Everyone is on my side, and soon you'll hear about your little sister's death. Brace yourself for it."

Sun Nuan's eyes flashed with a strange light. Queen Sun Kiyari's words shook something inside her mind. Brace yourself.

This word triggered a new thought in her mind. It belonged the skill set name of Destiny Mirror Sect. Wood Monarch's Embrace.

This was it. She had found the answer to her question. Suddenly, the shackles that bound her from reaching the peak of the Wood King's Sword level one broke, and she saw the path in front of her.

If big brother Wei could defy all odds, why couldn't she?

For her sister Hua'er. For big brother Wei.

Chapter 3

Awful Things

A stone gate stood in front of Li Wei, practically reaching the sky. This was a marvel in the Mortal Realm, where cultivation boundaries were stuck at the Houtian Realm. Standing in front of the gate, he wondered who'd had so much free time to build this behemoth. Even with his divine sense sent out as a beam, he couldn't reach the top of the gate. It was said that Divine Fragrance Palace's first sect master had found this gate and built a sect behind it. But even after a thousand years' inheritance, no one could open this gate anymore, so the sect had built two smaller gates in the stone walls connecting to the giant gate.

Many disciples bustled around the gate. A couple even tried to sell him minor healing pills that smelled like failed products. Seeing those pills, he couldn't forget the bitter taste of the medicine Tang Sia had made him drink for the last five days so he could recover from his injuries quicker. It was torture, and if he could have, he would have relied solely on his physical body's recovery attributes. But it had been a month since he'd fought in the Devil Cicada Challenge, and as per Tang Sia, he had to move his ass out of Fei'er's courtyard. And then meeting that bastard Li Sua had added more to the bitter taste in his mouth. He was an asshole, as usual. But what was he doing at his grandfather's grave?

Anyway.

Placing his hand on the giant black metal door with a cauldron engraved on it, Wei tried to probe it with his divine sense, but it couldn't penetrate the door. It was same with the other door, a golden one with a huge five-leafed herb engraved on it. No one knew the meaning behind the symbols marked on the doors, but the sect had constructed their internal system based on these symbols.

Lifting his feet, he walked toward the small open door on the right of the stone wall. Soon the marble-paved road turned black, like the cauldron on the door, and a rampant fiery aura washed over his face. A ten-foot-tall black cauldron welcomed anyone who walked through that door. An Undying Gladiator beast's fire continuously fired the cauldron; the fire was one of the famous treasures of the Divine Fragrance Palace, and it helped a cultivator to ignite their qi fire. Beyond the other door, the one engraved with the five-leafed herb, lay a precious plant that had a mind-calming effect on the cultivators walking through that door.

Of course, those were replicas of the original treasures, and their effects were subpar at best. But each of those symbols, the cauldron and the leaf, marked one of the three internal factions that controlled the Divine Fragrance Palace. The third faction didn't have a door, but it was the worst faction and he didn't want to join it. Thanks to Tang Sia, he had learned more than enough information about the Divine Fragrance Palace in the last few days.

When he moved closer to the door, his heart thumped wildly. Even after two hundred years of life, he became anxious, the same way he'd felt when he joined the Heavenly Firmament Sect in his previous life. This anxiousness was all because of his dream of becoming an alchemist and living a lazy and comfortable life. Walking through this door was the first step he'd taken on the dao of laziness. That was also one of the reasons he'd decided to join the Black Cauldron Faction, which specialized in pill concocting. The other faction, the Five Leaf Faction, specialized in herb growing.

Walking toward the small door on the right, he wondered if he should redecorate his outer sect courtyard that sect would provide to him to match his own shabby room, or if he should wait until he was promoted to inner sect disciple. Damn that Destiny Mirror Sect. While he was passed out, the Divine Fragrance Palace had recruited him as a core disciple, but he was demoted because he'd killed one of the Destiny Mirror Sect's elders.

Maybe he should remain in the outer sect, walk on his path of lazy dao, and redecorate his courtyard to match his shabby room from Old Martial City. That way, he could be as lazy as he wanted inside that room. When someone had nothing to protect, they could be lazy.

That was a new thought, and he noted it down in his Dao of Laziness Diary he had started with the help of the system while he recuperated for a month after his fight with the Du clan, Tiang Fu, and Wen Shang. The diary had two rules now.

1) Never cry. It takes you on the path of revenge, and you have to work hard to do that. Instead, eliminate anything that can make you cry.

2) Make everything shabby. Having nothing to protect means you can be as lazy as you want to be.

That was nice.

"Wei Lin, what are you doing here?" A soft voice struck him from behind, and when he turned, a short immature girl stared at him with two shiny brown eyes.

"Sun Hua, why are you here?" he asked the girl in the fiery red dress looking at him disdainfully.

A burly youth jumped forward. "Impudent fool, how dare you call a princess by her name. Are you tired of living?"

Wei frowned. Girls always brought trouble, and this burly youth was just that.

"You scoundrel!" Sun Hua said. "You bewitched my sister to fight the Destiny Mirror Sect, and now she is detained by the order of our lord father." She stomped her foot and flared her nostrils like he had bullied her. "How are you going to compensate me?"

Wei frowned. "Compensate?"

"Princes Hua, who is this guy? Is he bothering you?" A huge smelly guy with a big mustache stepped forward and crossed his arms over his chest. He smelled like he had applied a thick medicinal paste to his body, overpowering the girly fragrance exuded by Sun Hua.

"Brother Xin, you have to help me seek justice." Sun Hua shaded tears, but he knew they were fake. "This guy has wronged my sister, and she may not take a step out of her courtyard because of him."

Wei gasped hard. What nonsense was this? Did she even think twice before spurting such nonsense? "Sun Hua, watch your words."

Seeing her crying, many disciples crowded around them.

"What a beast. He did something to Princess Nuan," someone from the crowd shouted and glared at Wei.

"You—what awful thing you did with Princess Nuan?" Xin pointed a finger at him.

Wei hated it when someone pointed a finger at him, so he grabbed it and twisted.

Xin cried in agony.

Suddenly a knife appeared at Wei's neck, and he twisted at the waist to avoid it. A sword flashed in his hand, and it almost cut through the attacker's throat. But seeing the fair skin below his sword, he paused. It was Sun Hua. She had sneak-attacked him. He drew his sword back. "If it wasn't for Sun Nuan, you'd be dead now."

Her face flashed with fear, and she dropped onto her ass, crying out loud.

"Look, he agreed to the accusation. He has done something to Princess Nuan. Now he wants to silence Princess Hua. We must not allow this," someone shouted, and the crowd went into an uproar. Everyone looked at him as if they would attack him anytime.

His fingers wrapped around his sword hilt. If they dared to attack, he might be in a big trouble.

Chapter 4

Growing Troubles

The situation got worse when Sun Hua dropped on the black-paved road, in tears. Numerous disciples roaming outside of the Divine Fragrance Palace entrance gathered around her, giving Li Wei murderous glares.

"You! What did you do to my sister?" Sun Hua slapped the ground, attracting more people that looked at him like they wanted to eat him alive. Her red dress fluttered, and many people gulped.

This wench. Was she trying to get him killed in broad daylight? And couldn't she show some manners, for being a princess? If she wasn't Sun Nuan's sister, he would have slapped her already.

She suddenly started wailing like he had killed her husband.

"You! What did you do to her?" many people shouted.

"He is trying to silence her," someone else from the old bunch of fools commented.

Li Wei sweated profusely even on the chilly winter day. This mess was getting out of control, and the intense medicinal smell coming from some people made him dizzy. He hadn't even taken a step inside the sect, and trouble had come looking for him.

Wei glanced at the small open door and the black cauldron looming beyond it, lit with the Undying Gladiator beast's fire, and then looked at the surrounding crowd. Although the door was only one hundred feet away, it seemed like an eternity away.

"You beast! What did you do to junior apprentice sister Hua?" A girl wearing the Divine Fragrance Palace's black gown stepped forward and pointed at him. She had a round face and flat body, but she wore an overbearing scent that overpowered every nasty smell in the surrounding area. But her fragrance wasn't pleasant to start with.

With all his might, Wei suppressed the urge to break her finger.

"Senior apprentice sister Yungun, please save us from this monster. He did something to the princess, and now she is locked up in the imperial dungeon," Xin shouted, still crying, looking at his broken finger.

"Senior apprentice sister Yungun," someone else said, "he also did something to Princess Hua. Look at her, crying her heart out. I bet he harassed her."

"What a beast!" someone else shouted. "He's got eyes on two sisters, and princesses at that. Does he even place heaven in his eyes?"

Wei almost rolled his eyes. What the hell? In just a few breaths, things had taken a 540-degree turn. He had turned from a normal guy into a wicked criminal. Was there any justice, heavens?

"Bastard! You are courting your death by harassing a disciple of the Divine Fragrance Palace," Yungun shouted. "As a senior apprentice sister of my junior brothers and sisters, I ask everyone to beat this man black and blue and then take him to the Disciplinary Hall."

In response, every disciple raised their hands and attacked him.

Wei's eyes turned cold. If these people wanted to play hard ball, he wouldn't stay his hands anymore. The girl Yungun had peak qi

Foundation Realm cultivation, but that didn't arouse any interest for him.

"Mad Elephant Stomp." He lightly stomped his feet on the ground, and a physical force swept from his legs into the ground and then into everyone around him. People fell like cabbages, and soon the whole crowd around him was crying and wailing. With his layer one qi Foundation Realm and layer six body Foundation Realm, these were nothing but flies—except Sun Hua, who had jumped away and had a nasty smile plastered on her face. Everyone else was on the ground.

His face hardened as he glared at her, but she kept taunting him with her eyes, mocking him for falling into her trap so easily.

Compared to her sister, Sun Hua was a disaster ready to explode. He had to be careful around her unless he wanted to move out of his lazy path.

Ignoring her, Wei rushed toward the small door. Although he had recuperated for a month, his blood pearls hadn't fully replenished yet, and he didn't want to attract too much trouble. All he wanted was to concoct a few Foundation Expanding Pills and cultivate quietly.

"Senior, please direct me toward the Disciple Administration Hall." He placed the light brown metal token he had received from Tang Sia on the counter built inside the wall attached to the gate where two disciples checked people going in and out of the sect.

"Junior." A senior with a small cut on his left cheek took his brown token and handed him a jade slip. "Take this to the fourth building on the path that heads north. You'll meet Elder Jun, and he will help you settle from there." He coughed and looked around. "I'll give you one piece of advice. Stay away from Miss Yungun. You'll only bring trouble to yourself if you clash with her."

"I'll thank senior for your advice." Wei nodded and grabbed the jade slip to head toward the Disciple Administrator Hall. As per Tang Sia, this hall took care of new disciples joining the sect.

Five minutes later, he reached the Disciple Administrator Hall. It was a large single-floor stone structure with a long counter occupying most of the front hall. A few disciples moved behind the counter, carrying various things, and a few disciples were lined up in front of various counters. There was one old man with a long beard who sat on a chair behind a counter. Eyes closed, he seemed to be in a deep dream.

"Elder Jun, disciple Li Wei is here to enroll in the outer sect." He placed the jade slip he had obtained from the gate room on the brown wooden counter.

Elder Jun opened one large eye and glared at him and cursed. "You bastard, why did you wake me up?"

Wei was taken back by the sudden curse. Had this old fool gone mad? "Elder Jun, disciple Li Wei is here to enroll in the outer sect. Here is my entrance token." He pushed the token forward, suppressing his anger.

Elder Jun got up on his feet and slapped his hand on the counter. "Are you nuts? Can't you see so many disciples here doing the same, and you wake me from my seclusion? Do you know the punishment for disturbing someone else's cultivation?"

Wei frowned and was about to reply when a commotion arose from the door. Yungun stormed in, pointing at Wei. "Elder Jun, please help me. This bastard harassed me outside of the sect door."

Chapter 5

Serious Accusation

"Sexual harassment?" Elder Jun glared at Li Wei before slamming his hand on the wooden counter. "Call Disciplinary Hall members here and arrest this lunatic," he shouted at a disciple standing in a corner.

Li Wei turned to face the woman with the overbearing scent that irritated him. Even in the thousand-foot-wide Administrator Hall, her scent made him feel stuffy. Seeing her left a rotten taste in his mouth, and his palms turned sweaty. This was a trap. A trap bigger than he'd thought.

"Miss Yungun, don't go overboard and sputter nonsense. When did I harass you? Do you have proof?" He shifted his weight on his other leg, and the girl stepped back with a twisted face, her gaze stuck on his legs.

"Elder Jun, he is threatening to kill me," Yungun screamed and ran behind the other disciples standing nearby.

"You bastard!" Elder Jun turned on him in a frenzy. "You're trying to kill a disciple in front of me. You're courting death." He raised his arm and sent a palm attack toward Wei, killing intent flashing through his big watermelon-shaped eyes. With his layer five Bone Baptization Realm cultivation, he had used a profound attack, and brown wood qi swirled around his palm.

Pulling a cold metallic sword out of his storage ring, Wei raised it in the air to defend himself. Simultaneously, he activated his Blood Force Earth shield, and a red aura radiated around his body, enveloping him completely.

Their attacks met in midair, and it blasted Wei toward the back wall. He crashed into the wall, and his body slid down it to the floor. The attack reopened a few old injuries that his body hadn't fully healed yet, and it made his vision turn black for a moment.

No, he couldn't pass out now. That would be troublesome.

When he focused his eyes, he saw everyone in a daze, staring at elder Jun whose hand was pierced. White bone was visible through a large cut.

"You dared to attack an elder in Administrator Hall? You are courting your death." Elder Jun composed himself and conjured a red light behind his head. It was his Bone Manifestation, and the bone was illusory. Although it didn't match the nearly real bone image Tiang Fu had cultivated, it was still substantial, and Wei knew he would have to go all out once again if he wanted to defeat this bastard. And if he went all out, he would kill this old bastard.

But was that a good choice? Well, he wanted to kill this old man and the bitch who continuously provoked him, but he wasn't a fool to kill an elder within the sect itself. He wanted to be lazy, not a crazy person leaving trails of blood everywhere.

He wasn't strong enough to go against the whole Divine Fragrance Palace. So, he crushed a signal talisman given to him by Tang Sia. This situation was beyond redemption, but he didn't want to flee. Not that he was worried about getting trapped, but if he ran away the Li clan might end up in a predicament they wouldn't be able to get out of.

A minute passed, yet everyone remained in their positions. No one dared to move.

Other than Yungun's continuous sobbing, everything remained calm.

"Where is the rapist?" Two elders, old folks stormed in and looked around. They both had a black cauldron marked on their shoulders, and that meant they belonged to the Black Cauldron Faction.

Wei almost threw up blood. He had turned from an assaulter into a rapist in a mere few breaths within a mere few minutes of entering this sect. Was it the right decision to enter this sect?

Maybe not.

"Elders, he is there." Yungun dropped to the ground and started crying. Looking at her pitiful condition, even Wei believed he did something to her for a moment.

"You bastard. You dared to force an external disciple of the Divine Fragrance Palace? Even death is not a harsh enough punishment for you." One of the newly arrived elders raised his palm and attacked him. He had layer seven Bone Baptization Realm cultivation, and if Wei didn't go all out, he might suffer a severe injury.

"Senior Tang, are you going to hide there and watch this happen?" Wei shouted, and a woman wearing a pure white dress appeared from a corner. She had arrived right after he had crushed the talisman, but she'd hidden in the corner watching everything. But with Wei's divine sense, how could she hide from him?

"Elder Tang." Everyone bowed, including the three elders who were trying to kill Wei.

Tang Sia stepped in front of Yungun and seized her for a moment. "Wang Yungun. When did he harass you?"

Wei's eyes turned cold. Now he realized why this Yungun girl had accused him of this serious crime. She was part of the Wang family, and he had recently nearly annihilated Du clan that had relationship with Wang family. Someone had said it right. Enmity didn't finish until you removed even the weeds around your enemy's house.

The Du clan tribulations weren't over yet. It had just shifted to the Wang clan tribulations.

He rubbed his face. This was stupid. All he wanted to do was cultivate peacefully, and trouble just kept arriving.

"Elder Tang, this guy assaulted me right outside of the gate. You can ask anyone." Wang Yungun sobbed hard.

"Did he touch you inappropriately?"

Wang Yungun nodded and broke into a long cry.

"Do you have proof?" Wei asked in a stern voice.

A grim-faced Sun Hua walked in, followed by a bunch of guys, and that stupid fellow Xin was one of them. "I'll vouch for her. I saw him assault elder apprentice sister Yungun."

Other people vouched for her.

"Elder Tang, I apologize for interfering, but this matter is as clear as daylight." One of the elder with a black cauldron on his shoulder spoke. "We must execute this guy and cleanse the sect."

Tang Sia frowned and looked at Wei with complex emotions.

Wei chuckled in response. This was awesome. He hadn't realized it at first, but this was a big plot against him. Everything grew clear in his eyes.

Chapter 6

Waste Disposal Faction

Sun Hua sneered in her heart when everyone vouched against Li Wei. The bastard had finally been caught in their act, and now there was only one way out: his demise.

Seeing his listless expression, her heart rejoiced. He more than deserved this. How could he do what he'd done to her sister? He'd forced her to go against the Destiny Mirror Sect, and now she was trapped in the dungeon, left to rot for eternity by their imperial father. Of course, she didn't dare say it out loud. Sun Nuan was a princess, so no one could know her true condition. Even their mother had been demoted to a palace maid position. Hua could only imagine how bad the other concubines were treating her. If it hadn't been for a favor owed to her mother by the sect master of the Divine Fragrance Palace, Hua would be rotting in a dungeon too.

Tears rolled down her cheeks, and she reached instinctively for her neck. Someone had stolen the pendant her mother had given to her. Her sister was rotting in the dungeon, and when she was asleep, she could feel her sister's loneliness inside her heart. From birth, she'd had this connection with Nuan'er that allowed her to sense her emotions and premonition even when they were hundreds of miles apart. Sun Nuan could even switch their consciousnesses, but their mother had warned them not to do it ever.

"Princess Hua. Please don't cry. We will get justice for senior apprentice sister Yungun," Xin Pu shouted from next to her, and everyone shouted their agreement.

Yes, Li Wei had destroyed their lives, and he would pay with his life. That bastard had even lied to them and told them a fake name. Only after hearing about the Li clan's fight with the Du clan had she realized his real name was Li Wei.

But why was this bastard laughing suddenly? Had he gone mad with despair? That would be better, because that way he would experience what her mother and sister were facing right now.

Suddenly, she wanted to cry and run back to the imperial capital. But she was bound to this city's boundaries. If she took a step out of Fragrance Herb City, she would be captured and put in a dungeon by royal guards. Going forward, she had to live inside the Divine Fragrance Palace's compound while her mother and sister suffered calamity.

How could she?

It was all because of this bastard, so he had to die. But she couldn't do it by herself. When Wang Yungun had approached her, she'd said yes without giving it another thought. Only when she saw him die would she feel satisfied. And only after being satisfied could she work on her alchemy to become a high-grade alchemist and change the destiny of her mother and sister.

"Elder Jun, please bring justice to senior apprentice sister Yungun and kill that blasphemer," she cried, pointing at Li Wei.

"So, you all say that I assaulted her and touched her improperly, right?" Li Wei asked, his fierce eyes gazing over everyone present in the Disciple Administrator Hall.

A chill passed down her legs when his deep blue eyes stared at her before moving away. In that one glance, she felt like he had boiled her in thousand-degree hot oil and then skinned her alive. He was too terrifying. That's why her sister had acted like a fool and fell into his trap.

But she was pulled out of her shock when everyone around her shouted at him. The Wang clan had offered a ton of benefits to all of them, so they had to nod and blame him for everything.

"Wang Yungun, do you also say that I assaulted you and touched you improperly outside of the sect gate half an hour back?" Li Wei pointed at Wang Yungun.

She nodded before breaking into another round of sobbing.

Sun Hua couldn't help but appreciate Wang Yungun's acting ability. Wang Yungun was the best at it. She herself was nowhere near her.

"Then let's see my indecent actions again." He pulled a small metal chip from his shoulder and threw it in the air. A water bubble appeared out of the metal chip that started displaying the events that took place right before Sun Hua appeared in front of Li Wei.

Wang Yungun's face darkened, and she threw her shoe at the metal chip floating in the air. But her shoe passed through the water bubble and nothing happened. The bubble continued displaying images with sound.

Sun Hua gulped. This was a Water Image Storing Talisman used by elders to capture important lectures from higher realm cultivators, and only elder-level figures had access to them. How did Li Wei get his hands on one?

And seeing everything happening again, what would happen to her and Wang Yungun now?

This was bad. Very, very bad. Their whole plot had flipped upside down.

Li Wei sneered inside his heart. Did these people take him for a fool? Even before stepping out of Fei'er's courtyard, he'd known something like this would happen, so he'd a long chat with Tang Sia. The Wang clan was one of the integral clans in the Divine Fragrance Palace, so they were bound to clash. There was no other choice. Tang Sia had suggested joining another sect, but he'd declined. Other than the super-sects, the Mortal Realm only had a few good alchemy sects, and he wouldn't go to the Destiny Mirror Sect at any cost. Joining any other sect would be a waste. In this life, he wanted to walk on the path of alchemy, and he wouldn't steer away from that goal. No matter what.

Seeing his determination, Tang Sia had given him a Water Image Storing Talisman. Although there was an array that could do the same thing, he could not carve it with his current cultivation, so he'd borrowed the talisman from Tang Sia. In the future, he should keep a few of these always with him.

It had paid off on day one. Many people had fallen into his trap, and he realized his days in the sect would be lively. But considering the scale of the trap the Wang clan had set up for him, he was impressed. If he hadn't had the talisman, he would soon be rotting in a dungeon or on his way to the yellow spring.

However, one thing had defied his expectations. Sun Hua. Why was she targeting him like they had a blood feud between them? Was Sun Nuan really in trouble?

He had an uneasy feeling about this. He ought to check on Sun Nuan. But, for now, he had bigger fish to fry.

His gaze fell on the dark faces of the elders and disciples. "Wang Yungun, do you have an answer for this?" Wei asked as the images replayed up to when he'd executed the Mad Elephant Stomp and rushed away from the crowd.

Wang Yungun shivered, and her face turned grimmer with every passing second.

"Elders, do you've anything to say?" he asked arrogantly. These bastards were trying to blame him for something awful, something he hadn't done, and he would not let it go.

"This proves that you attacked Divine Fragrance Palace disciples in the open," one of the elders with the black cauldron on his sleeves refuted, but he lacked any confidence in his voice.

"Yes, and that's a grave crime," the other elder said and looked at Tang Sia.

"The question is whether he sexually harassed her or not," Tang Sia said calmly, but there was cold intent in her voice that sent a shiver across many people's bodies.

"He attacked our disciples. Isn't that enough proof?" This time it was elder Jun who tried to refute. "He dared to do so even before becoming a disciple of my Divine Fragrance Palace. This is a grave crime. We can't let him walk away from this."

"Who said he isn't a disciple already?"

Smirking, Wei pulled a dark brown emblem out of his storage ring and displayed it to everyone. He had obtained after he opened his eyes in Fei'er's courtyard. Tang Sia had personally delivered it.

One of the black cauldron elders clenched his fist and roared. "So, you colluded with a disciple to strike against my Wang clan?"

"Do I need to collude with a disciple to take action against your Wang clan?" Tang Sia roared, her face flashing red. "If I want, I can annihilate your clan in one go."

Everyone went silent. Deathly silent. The elder supporting the Wang clan grew pale.

"Wang Mang, don't provoke me unnecessarily. I wanted to see how brazenly the Disciple Administrator Hall and Disciplinary Hall would act to deal with a little fellow in the Foundation Realm. Elder Jun, as you dared to attack a new disciple without even listening to his side, you're stripped of your position at the Disciple Administrator Hall. Go to Ten Deathly Winds Valley to receive your punishment immediately." She then turned to face two elders from the Disciplinary Hall. "You are relieved from your posts for three months. You can meditate on the wrong thing you did today."

Wei sneered inside his mind. Having an elder as backup always proved useful. The Divine Fragrance Palace had multiple elders. Those below the Marrow Cleansing Realm were called elders, while those in Marrow Cleansing Realm were called great elders. Then Boiling Blood Realm cultivators were grand elders and then came overseer and sect master who were in Heart Blood Realm. This was a layer weaker than Heavenly Firmament Sect.

Tang Sia turned to Wang Yungun.

Wang Yungun dropped on her knees, and then bowed her head to the ground. "Great elder Tang, please show mercy and spare me."

Wei was shocked by her words. Great elder? When did Tang Sia become a great elder? He had been calling her senior Tang for the last month. He had a feeling he was in trouble.

“You’re expelled from the Divine Fragrance Palace along with all others that colluded with you.” Tang Sia moved her gaze to the bunch of people who had followed Wang Yungun. Then her gaze stopped on Sun Hua.

Wang Yungun suddenly spoke, her eyes shining with a resolute expression. “Great elder Tang, I swear on my life that Princess Hua has nothing to do with this. I manipulated her to do this task. Please don’t punish her.”

What had gotten into her? Why was she saving Sun Hua?

“Sun Hua.” Tang Sia sighed. “Given the conditions, I can’t let you go unpunished. You’ll work in the Waste Disposal Faction going forward.” She then looked at Wei. “Li Wei, you’ve attacked fellow disciples in the open, and you’ll work in the Waste Disposal Faction as well.”

Wait what?

Before Wei could get the question out, Tang Sia was gone, leaving everyone dumbfounded.

What was that? Why had she just thrown him into the worst faction of the Divine Fragrance Palace? Was this revenge?

Joining this sect was a mistake. A real mistake.

Chapter 7

Heavenly Wind Cloud Beast Array

A small, dark courtyard welcomed Li Wei. No, calling it a courtyard would be an insult to the word itself. It was a single room attached to a small backyard that opened to a black river overflowing with stink. That was all it was. Even labor disciples in the Heavenly Firmament Sect, his previous life's sect, had had a better place than this. If there hadn't been fragrant incense burning inside the room when he stepped in, he might have died of the stuffiness already.

"Li Wei, I'm going to kill you!" A scream echoed from the next courtyard over. Sun Hua had been assigned an adjacent courtyard by the Waste Disposal Faction, apparently.

Rubbing his forehead, he cast a glance at the next courtyard, bathed in moonlight, and sighed hard. This was a sigh of regret. Regret for joining this sect, and regret for having Sun Hua as his neighbor.

He scanned the ten-by-twenty room with wary eyes. A thick layer of dust covered the small table in the corner, and when he sneezed, he noticed there was a blue or gray—he couldn't decide—prayer mat placed on the table. It must have been around for at least a thousand years. It wasn't in good shape, and some holes exposed the dust-laden wooden table's uneven surface.

Even his shabby room at the Li compound was better than this, and the surroundings left a bitter taste in his mouth. On top of that, Sun Hua lived next door. Soon, he would be facing assassination attempts in the night. But considering the dark and gloomy atmosphere, he wondered if he could sleep peacefully inside this room at all.

He ran his fingers along the stone wall, removing a thick layer of dust. It seemed that no one had lived here for years.

"Li Wei, I'm going to kill you!" White moonlight illuminated Sun Hua with her hands on her tiny waist. Black patches covered her face and her messed hair. If someone saw her, they might think she had rolled in a pool of mud on the way here.

"You already said that," Wei replied calmly.

"Did I?" She scratched her neck, then looked at her dirty hands in horror.

Screaming, she ran toward her courtyard, but then she suddenly stopped and came back. "Li Wei, come and kill that thing in my courtyard." Her small body shivered a little.

"Why would I help you?" Although he didn't beat this girl for her role in getting him here, he hated her in his bones. For her sister, he maintained some sanity or else he would have slapped her until her teeth were knocked out of her mouth. "Don't you want to kill me? Then why are you asking for my help?"

Stomping her feet, she turned away. However, when she gazed at her courtyard, she turned back again. "You have to help me kill that thing. I took you inside the Alchemy Comprehension Tower, and you haven't repaid your debt to me."

He arched his brows. "Didn't I pay you with Two Colored Poison Repelling Flower? We traded fairly, and your s—" He bit his lip. There was something wrong with Sun Nuan, and he didn't want to trigger that subject right away. First, he had to gather some information about her. "Just get lost. I don't have time to talk with a stupid girl."

Her nostrils flared, and even in the dim light, he could see her ears turning red. Tomato red. "You—" She pointed her finger at him, and he fought the urge to break it. If she wasn't Sun Nuan's sister, he would have broken that finger already.

When he didn't react, she grabbed the only chair in the room, blew the dust away, and sat on it. "I'm not going back until you kill that thing in my courtyard."

Wei sneered and ignored her. He didn't have time for a little girl like her. He had so many things to do, and one of them was to practice the Five Elemental Weapon Art he'd gained access to after waking up. It was strange. Technically, he should have gotten access to it when he reached the qi Foundation Realm in the Five Elemental Way Qi Cultivation Art, but he hadn't. It might be related to him reaching layer zero of the qi Foundation Realm by using the Essence Burning Art, a forbidden technique, to fight Tiang Fu. Yes, it had to be that.

Anyway, first thing first, he had to make this room habitable.

Reaching the middle of the room, he cleaned a small circular portion before taking out a bottle of beast blood and a bristle brush he had bought from old man Wu's store back in Old Martial City. Observing their weathered state, he made a mental note to buy the best brush and beast ink available in Fragrance Herb City. Although he could carve arrays with this trash, he might fail because of the quality. Even the quality of his arrays would diminish once he began carving Gold Grade arrays. From Gold Grade onwards, arrays would have grade, tier, and rank, and every tier would have five ranks starting from first rank and going up to fifth rank. Also, the efficiency of two similar arrays would be measured by their ranks. A common brush could downgrade his array ranks by two.

Anyway, this was what he had right now, so he had to go ahead with them.

When the floor became clean enough that his beast blood marking could be carved, he drew two circles first.

"What are you doing?" Sun Hua asked after a while. "Is that an array?" She moved closer and peeked over his shoulder.

Ignoring her, he first drew a small diagram of a cloud beast. It was a Heavenly Wind Cloud Beast. Found only in the Martial Realm, it was famous for its wind-based attacks, and it always lived in clouds. This array used it as an inspiration to connect with heaven and earth to generate wind attacks. Arrays were mysteries of heaven and earth and many of them were inspired by different elements of nature to do wonders for the users.

"It's so simple. Can I try it?" She pulled the chair next to him and kept peeking at his process.

In the dim moonlight, he wondered how she could see what he was doing, but then he remembered her hereditary power was related to eyes.

"Shut up and let me focus. And you'd better get out of my courtyard if you don't want to die." Scolding her once, he focused on his strokes.

"But I want to draw arrays too. They look so easy."

Wei rolled his eyes and continued with his strokes. This stupid girl was acting like a new array school student. The uninitiated always thought arrays would be easier to draw because they were based on some natural entity or a tangible object. But that thought was far, far away from reality. People only saw the end product. They never thought about intricate complexities working under the hood. Every single line of an array was formed by numerous tiny lines arranged in a specific way. Even a low-tier Bronze Grade array was comprised of hundreds of different tiny lines arranged in a sequence. All the intricacies were impossible to grasp before one reached the Foundation Realm, and one could only grasp the basics then. Real array cultivation started after one reached the Houtian Realm and got their hands on the Earth Grade array. Before the Houtian Realm, one wouldn't have the divine sense, qi, and comprehension to draw thousands of tiny lines in a particular sequence. Although Wei had a strong divine sense and heaven-defying comprehension due to reincarnation, he still lacked enough qi to draw anything beyond high-tier Silver Grade arrays.

"What's the difference between arrays and talismans? I'd seen one talisman with nearly the same symbol carved on it," Sun Hua said.

"I'm warning you again. Get out before you regret it." Saying this, he focused back on his array. For this array, he was using his abundant wood qi, and he could feel the easiness of drawing with wood qi.

"You're a jerk. Talismans are much better than these shitty arrays," Sun Hua complained.

Wei chuckled inside his mind. Talisman creation was another branch of the Mystic Arts of Heaven and Earth, and it too required one to draw diagrams on talisman papers, but they differed a lot from arrays. Compared to arrays, talismans were much simpler. But their might couldn't be underestimated. Many times, they overpowered the same grade arrays by a large margin, and they were easy to use. One could use talismans with a single strand of qi, and they were used in many battles. The Wood Shield Talisman used by Tiang Fu was one good example. Anyone from the Foundation Realm to the Houtian Realm could use one.

Arrays were complex, and they had a wide variety of applications. Another difference between them was that arrays had source points and power points. For example, the part between the inner and outer circles might have twenty power points. These points would release the might of the array outside. This was only a mid-tier Silver Grade array, so it only had ten power points and five source points located in the beast's eye.

It was called a Heavenly Wind Cloud Beast Array, and its sole purpose was raising strong winds.

After half an hour, Wei finished drawing the full array, emptying half of his wood qi reserve. If he didn't have an abundant amount of wood qi, he would have failed to carve this array. After lifting his brush and putting it back inside his storage ring, he raised his head to look into Sun Hua's shiny eyes. "I'm warning you again. Get lost." Her eyes reminded him of Sun Nuan. He hoped she was okay.

When Sun Hua didn't move, he pulled a Qi Stone out of his storage ring and tapped it on a source point before jumping backward. This was going to be fun.

Chapter 8

Blasting a princess

As soon as Li Wei landed near the door, he turned and leaped outside of the courtyard. A calamity was about to happen, and the farther he was away from it, the better he would be.

After reaching a hundred feet's distance from his courtyard, he stopped and turned back.

Howling winds surged out of his courtyard, sending gales everywhere. Along with the gales, a muffled cry and lots of dust flew out. A thin cloud of dust clashed against his face and even entered his mouth, making his judgement of the array's power futile. Everything in the area turned dusty, and the howls suppressed the roaring sound of the river flowing next to the backyard. It was a good thing that all the nearby courtyards were empty, so no one came after the commotion.

Pulling a blue cloth out of his storage ring, he wiped the thin layer of dust from his mouth, then rinsed it with clear water from the soft leather skin. He had only used one source point to charge the array, and yet it had created an impact that could be felt one hundred feet away. If he had been standing inside the courtyard, he might have been buried in dust. Thank the heavens he had checked the walls and roof before triggering the array. Despite looking disgusting and small, the courtyard was built from Gray Cobble Stones, and it remained intact even after an assault of winds.

At some point, a sorry figure had blasted out of the door and crashed not far away from him.

Wei chuckled. He had warned Sun Hua multiple times, but she didn't listen. She got what she deserved. But that was fine. Although he had used a Silver Grade array, he had dampened its might by only charging a single source point so the overall effectiveness was decreased by 80%. If he had charged all five source points, the courtyard would have been blasted apart.

After five minutes, the howling sound stopped and everything grew calm, but way before the winds stopped, the dust had also stopped flowing out of his courtyard. The Heavenly Wind Cloud Beast Array was a common array used to generate winds for various usage. Some used it to temper their disciples, and some people—like him—used it to clean their own rooms. With the impact seen, he could bet his room was as clean as newly polished metal.

Of course, he could have done this with a broom in few hours, but why would he tire himself out doing these things when he had arrays like these? This was his Dao of Laziness.

Cough! Cough!

Sun Nuan struggled to rise from the thick film of dust, and after rolling for a few breaths, she crawled her way upward. "Yo—" Dust flew out of her mouth. If she'd looked like she'd fought a beast when she entered his room, now she looked like a child who had played in mud. Other than her sharp watery eyes and hints of her white teeth showing from the film of dust, she looked nothing like a pretty girl.

"Li Wei, I'm going to kill you!" Shouting, she ran toward her courtyard, but then she suddenly changed her direction and rushed inside his courtyard.

"..." Before he could protest, the door closed.

"Sun Hua, get out of my courtyard or I'll come inside and throw you out!" He fumed. What a nasty wench. How could she run inside his courtyard and lock it from the inside?

"You can't come in, I'm naked."

"And why would that stop me from coming in? Even if you're ugly as a furry beast, I don't care. I'll just throw you outside."

"Li Wei, you dare call me an ugly beast? I'll tear out your eyes and feed it to some real beasts!" she screamed like someone stepped on her throat.

What was wrong with her? Was she pissed off because he'd called her ugly?

"If you dare to enter, it would be real sexual harassment this time." Her voice rose.

He chuckled. She was falling into the same trap. "Did you forget I have . . ." He bit his lip. Even though he had an image recording talisman, if he captured naked Sun Hua, he would be doomed for eternity.

His internal organs boiled, and he really wanted to slap this girl to death. She was going overboard. "Sun Hua, get out of my house or I'll call other people and then throw you out."

"Would they believe you once they see me lying naked and wounded in your courtyard? Don't push me, Li Wei, else I'll harm myself and put everything on you."

Sweat broke over Wei's back. A chill crawled down his spine. This girl was terrifying, and he should stay as far away from her as possible. Compared to her docile elder sister, she was a she-devil. Whoever married her would be in trouble. Big, big trouble.

Taking a deep breath, he calmed himself. "Okay. What do you want?"

"Now you are talking like a gentleman. If you had done this before, we wouldn't have to get in another conflict."

"Shut up and tell me what you want, or I'll just go outside and book a room at the inn and deal with you tomorrow."

She didn't reply for a moment.

"Sun Hua, don't test my patience."

"Okay. There's a thing inside my room. Kill it and use that array to clean my room as well. This room cleaning method is much better than a broom."

Wei almost fainted on the spot. This she-devil wanted him to clean her room? She was threatening him because she wanted free labor? This was infuriating. No, this was unreasonable to the core. If other array cultivators found out that he'd used a mid-tier Silver Grade array to clean his courtyard, they would haunt him for eternity, and this girl was calling it an easy job?

"Sun Hua, you're a princess. Can't you call some servants to do this job for you?"

No reply came for a few breaths.

"Li Wei, stop mocking me and get this done. I'm holding a distress flare in my hand, and you can imagine what the Disciplinary Hall will do if I send it up." Her voice grew frosty, and he had a gut feeling that she would do as she said.

Wei gulped. "Okay. You got me. I'll get it cleaned in an hour. Just get back to your courtyard as soon as you hear the howling winds." Fuming inside, he walked away from his own courtyard. Whatever the thing was inside her room, it would face his wrath.

Chapter 9

Yin Sucking Spider

When Li Wei entered Sun Hua's courtyard, he activated the Water Image Storing Talisman. It was better to be safe than sorry. There might be a trap waiting for him inside, and right now he didn't have the strength to go against the Wang clan, so he had to be careful. Thinking about the Wang clan left a rotten taste in his mouth. The way they'd set up a trap by sacrificing the chastity of one of their own clan members. It was disgusting.

He would make the Wang clan pay for their sins. By accusing him of harassment, they had stepped on his reverse scale, and he had to retaliate in time. But ten years were not long for a man to take his revenge, so he would wait for the perfect time.

When he stepped into the ruined garden outside of the courtyard, he felt nothing. A faint smell of decay lingered around him, and a mush of unattended garden occupied his vision. Weeds had grown right up to the door of the courtyard, and he could spot small forceful footsteps on the yellowish grass. If Sun Hua had set up a trap, it was a well-planned one.

But they didn't know he had a trump card. His divine sense. Spreading it wide, he covered the whole garden, but there was nothing amiss. In fact, there was no one in a hundred-foot area around the courtyard. It was cold, dark, and dusty.

However, when he glanced at the half-open door, a strange sense of danger permeated through his backbone. Something was off about this place, and his gut was screaming of danger. But his divine sense hadn't picked up anything.

Without stepping inside, he spread his divine sense in a wave mode. Sometimes one could remain undetected by using the gaps in the divine sense, but there was no gap in the wave mode of divine sense. Every second, he sent multiple waves of divine sense outwards, considering his body as a center. It consumed a lot more divine sense than it normally would have, but this was one of the best detection methods for spotting any fluctuation.

Something moved in the area covered by his divine sense, and that something was quite small, like a tiny stone. It was a spider, but not a normal one.

A Yin Sucking Spider.

Wei's divine sense turned into a beam, focusing on the black and red spider hanging on a thin gray thread hanging from the ceiling.

Tiny legs wrapped around a thin thread of energy from the air and pushed it into its mouth. That was yin energy. With his divine sense, it was impossible to see the yin energy, but Yin Sucking Spiders had a special bloodline power that allowed them to convert yin energy from the surroundings and turn it into a form of energy it fed on.

Wei frowned. How could this place have had yin energy?

Yin energy was one of the heaven and earth's natural energies, like essence energy. It was a dark energy that represented night, ghost, and dead. It was often found in graveyards, and demonic cultivators cultivated it. But what was it doing in the Divine Fragrance Palace?

Was there something he didn't know about this sect?

Closing his eyes, Wei absorbed essence energy from the surroundings and circulated it through his hands as per the Yin Yang Liquid generation technique. Although it wouldn't work, he should feel the intensity of yin energy in the environment.

Suddenly, his eyes opened and flashed with a bright light. He had felt traces of both energies. Yin and Yang. When yin was night, yang was day, sun and male. It was positivity that balanced yin from the world.

However, the presence of both energies left him bewildered. So, when he spread his divine sense further, he spotted two small beetles, Dantian Burning Yang Beetle. But the yang energy they exuded wouldn't answer the yang energy source he felt.

Was there a natural yin-yang treasure present nearby?

If he found that treasure, he might obtain a steady source of yin yang energy. Right now, he only had a few Yin Yang Fruits remaining with him, and he had stopped using them in case he needed them urgently.

Of course, he had a bottle half-filled with Yin Yang Liquid, but that would vanish as soon as he started concocting pills for himself.

"Are you afraid of this little fella?" he asked. Sun Hua had appeared at the boundary of his divine sense. She had changed into an ocean-blue dress, and she looked beautiful.

"Yes. Kill it and clean the courtyard."

"I can run back and pretend nothing happened here." A smug smile appeared on his face. That would be the best course of action.

"Are you planning to go back on your word?"

"No, but you'd better get this courtyard changed." He pulled a Moonlight Stone that the sect had given him with his disciple badge from his storage ring. It was a peculiar stone that could absorb moonlight to illuminate one's surroundings.

"Heavens!" Screaming, she leaped out of the courtyard and stood in the outside garden, shivering. "It's a nest. Why is there a nest of those things in my courtyard?"

Stepping out, he stretched his arms. Using the Yin Yang Liquid generation technique had left him feeling a bit dizzy. It wasn't supposed to be used without a yin yang source, but he had forcefully used it.

"I don't know. Let's swap our courtyards tomorrow. I'll clear this and live here, and you can use my courtyard which I've already cleaned." Wei observed the little hole that held many Yin Sucking Spiders using his divine sense. He had a gut feeling that it would lead to the source of this energy.

She arched her brow. "Why are you being a benevolent monk all of a sudden? Do you want to scam me like my sister?"

"Do you want to or not? If you think clearing the nest will let you sleep peacefully, then do that." He shook his head and headed toward his courtyard. "Don't come screaming into my courtyard in few days when a small larva crawls out of the nest."

Her body trembled. "Will they come back?"

"Of course. You can only clean it from the outside, but only heaven knows how many are breeding inside that hole." He sneered. "On second thought, I think I'll live in my own courtyard."

Her face twisted in worry, and then she scurried like a mouse and reached his courtyard before he took a few steps. "This princess will bestow her grace on you and let you live in my courtyard. You can say thanks later." She vanished inside his courtyard, and the wooden door closed tightly.

Wei chuckled. This girl was too naïve. She didn't notice, but there were only a few more Yin Sucking Spiders in the nest. In fact, Yin Sucking Spiders had a weird trait. They ate other Yin Sucking Spiders, so their nest would never have a large number of them.

But first, he had to fetch the couple of beetles that were trapped in the spider nest, and they were still alive. Those were Dantian Burning Yang Beetle, and those were nasty beetles that attacked one's dantian and formed a cocoon inside. But they were useful in couple of forbidden techniques he knew, so he was happy to find them here.

Now he was itching to find out where that hole led.

Chapter 10

Sect Master

A jade-skinned woman entered a secret chamber inside the largest mountain of the Divine Fragrance Palace. Wrapped in white clouds over the year, the mountain looked close and distant at the same time because it was a forbidden land in the sprawling Divine Fragrance Palace. It had a peculiar name: Cloud Severing Mountain.

Tang Sia's blue eyes turned solemn when she stepped in front of a shriveled man who looked like he was hanging onto this world by a single thread, but she knew how powerful he was. Even experts from super-sects feared this man and didn't dare to face him head on. If not for the injury he'd received in the Martial Realm five hundred years ago, he would have been the strongest man in the Mortal Realm.

"Disciple Sia greets sect master." She bowed. This old man was the sect master of the Divine Fragrance Palace in the State of Zin. He was also her master, but she was afraid of him, because he instilled fear in his own disciple's mind. He cultivated some strange cultivation art that made his opponent fear him until they dropped on their knees. Only after reaching Marrow Cleansing Realm could she stand in front of him without going to her knees.

However, she knew her sect master was soft at heart.

"Speak."

"Master, Fairy Fei has reached half-step of the Bone Baptization Realm and I seek your permission to allow her to cultivate under the Holy Bodhi Tree." It meant her cultivation was ready to breakthrough anytime, and she was comparable to a Bone Baptization Realm cultivator.

He shook his head, and a deep wrinkle appeared below his eyes. "The Holy Bodhi Tree has stood for my sect for eight hundred years, but after that fight, it has sustained a wound and there is not much vitality remaining in it. If we want to remain a first-rate sect in the State of Zin, we have to preserve our guardian tree."

Tang Sia's face turned darker. "Master, can't we ask our parent sect to send a Divine Healer to treat its injuries?"

The old man's eyes dimmed. "The parent sect won't bother with a tiny sub-branch like us. They have their own difficulties. Gatekeepers are making things difficult for every sect. Let her drink a drop of Divine Nether Rector instead. She has a Verdant Wood Constitution and a Human Grade Spirit Root, so any wood type natural treasure she consumes will increase her cultivation by leaps and bounds."

"Disciple will obey master's command," Tang Sia muttered, feeling jealous inside her heart. A Human Grade Spirit Root was an abnormal one, rare even in the Martial Realm. The worst part was that little lass was devoted to that boy with all her heart. She'd even fought with her to shield him from the Destiny Mirror Sect. She just didn't realize how futile this was. Chasing after a man wasn't worth the effort. They all betray in the end.

"What about that boy related to her?"

"Master, I probed his conscious using a secret art, but there is no sign of him acquiring any inheritance from the Alchemy Comprehension Tower."

"No?" He sighed in disappointment and stroked his long white beard. "How about his constitution? Anything special about it?"

"No master, I've checked his Spirit Root but it's only a Silver Grade Spirit Root. It's attributeless, but he cultivates some unknown cultivation art that lets him use wood qi. I had no means to check his Physical Root, but I suspect it would be Silver Grade as well. So, despite him cultivating in body cultivation, I doubt he will go any further in that aspect."

The old man's face turned dark like he had lost a chance to grasp heavens.

"What a disappointment. Without an Earth Grade Spirit Root, he won't have any chance of becoming a Holy Son and save the parent sect. Leave it. Keep your focus on Fei'er and groom her well. I've already asked the parent sect to send someone to fetch her in two years' time. Once she breaks through to the Marrow Cleansing Realm, she can cultivate in the parent sect."

"But master, I'm afraid that she will have negative influence if we keep her hear. If other sects find out about her constitution, they might try to assassinate her."

The old man shook his head. "With Gatekeepers guarding the ascension door, two year is the earliest parent sect can send their envoy."

"Those bastards." She clenched her fingers. "Master, that guy reached level six in the Alchemy Comprehension Tower, so he might be good at alchemy. He has also killed a Marrow Cleansing Realm elder from the Destiny Mirror Sect."

The old man shook his head. "Sia'er. Times have changed. If it was another time, I'd be happy to foster him. But the Holy Alchemy Competition is coming up, and we have to direct all focus on Fei'er. If we let him meddle with Fei'er, I'm afraid he would affect her concentration on cultivation. If she can't break through to the late

Marrow Cleansing Realm in the next two years, then she won't survive Wood Fairy Baptization, and her wood qi quality will be stuck at Gold Grade."

Tang Sia lowered her head. This lass wasn't fostered from birth, so her wood qi quality was too low when compared to her Spirit Root. If only she had realized her potential back then, she would have brought her here a year back. What a waste.

"Master, disciple has one more thing to report."

"Go ahead."

"Despite having a trash Spirit Root, Li Wei's attunement in arrays is better than anyone I've seen. When I investigated him, I learned that he and master Wu have a very close relationship, and in his storage ring, I found two spears carved with Exploding Arrays, and they had his qi signature. Even Fairy Fei once said that Li Wei is proficient in arrays. Is there no way we can groom him a little?"

Tuck! The sect master made his distinguishing sound.

Then he sighed, a deep regretful sigh. "Master Wu must have taught him some things about arrays. But we can't foster him. The Wang family is against him, and we can't allow any internal strife right now."

"But Fairy Fei?"

"Isolate her, and tell her you are giving the best treatment to Li Wei. She is the future of our sect, and we can't let her thoughts stray away anymore."

"Disciple will listen to master's orders."

Chapter 11

Black Cauldron Faction

Inside the Black Cauldron Faction, the main building atop Alchemy Ascension Peak, two old men stood in front of another old man who sat on a high stone chair. One of his ears was cut in half, and it looked weird. But this old man had an imposing aura that made Su Pan apprehensive. No one dared to look at the ugly half ear covered by a thin black cloth. He felt like their secrets were exposed by one glance at this old man.

He was one of the great elders of Divine Fragrance Palace, Wang Jiang, and right now he was in deep thought.

The third of the three old men, Wang Tian, coughed. "Great elder Jiang, what are your orders?"

"Master, please convey them and we will follow them," Su Pan said in an earnest voice. He had been the first personal disciple of Wang Jiang when he was just an elder, and he'd remained faithful to his master all these years. Su Pan was considered the most influential non-Wang member of the Black Cauldron Faction. But he knew he was nothing in front of the Wang clan, so he always showed his royalty to great elder Wang Jiang, and he was treated well enough that he didn't feel deterred by their inner clan politics.

This old man, great elder Wang, had unprecedented authority in the Black Cauldron Faction and held an important position in the Wang clan. No one knew about his cultivation. One couldn't find opponent's cultivation until they have a high cultivation themselves. There was a rumor that he was one of the strongest in the Wang clan and had already reached Boiling Blood Realm. Only the Wang clan ancestor was stronger than this man. Even the Wang clan patriarch had to give face to this man. But Su Pan knew his real cultivation, and although he hadn't reached Boiling Blood Realm yet, but in a decade or two he would definitely break into it.

Wang Jiang opened his eyes and stared at the two of them for a brief time before withdrawing his gaze.

"Disciple Rong greets great elder Jiang." A youth with a harmonious smile on his face stepped forward and bowed deeply to the great elder.

Su Pan frowned a little before smoothing his forehead. He didn't understand what a junior was doing in an elders meeting. Did master Jiang call him?

"Rong'er. You've shown promise in recent alchemy competitions, and you're a good child."

"Great elder praises me too much." Wang Rong bowed again, but he couldn't hide his complacent smile.

"Our clan's influence on the Alchemy Board is waning, so you should get the first position as soon as possible."

Wang Rong's face twitched. "Junior will try hard next time."

"Tang Sia has bared her fangs using an insignificant brat from the Li clan who massacred my daughter's husband, Du Lufang. That brat has joined the sect."

Su Pan sighed inwardly. Master Jiang had one son and one daughter. His son was a criminal, and his daughter had taken a liking to an insignificant cultivator from a nearby city. Master Jiang had allowed them to marry, but later broke all contact with them. For many years, she'd lived the life of a nobody, but a month back her husband had vanished, and it was related to the Li clan of Old Martial City. A month later, news had come that a brat from the Li clan had massacred the Du clan patriarch, Du Tenjua. Although the Wang clan had never recognized the Du clan as their in-laws, they didn't annihilate them either. That meant they didn't look down on them. It was in fact telling the world that the Du clan was under the Wang clan's protection. So, killing them was like a slap to the Wang clan's face, and that too was done by an insignificant unknown clan like the Li clan which no one had known about until they surrendered an Earthly Fruit Tree to the sec t.

Unfortunately, before the Wang clan could take action, another great elder, the sect master's personal disciple, had taken the Li clan under her wing and everything became difficult to handle in the open. The sect master didn't permit open war between clans in the sect, so everyone showed their pretty faces in the open.

"Disciple Rong will take care of this impudent bastard who dared to kill our relatives. I'll show this criminal that the Wang clan is full of righteous people, and we won't let go of a lowly ant." Wang Rong's face filled with a righteous expression.

Wang Tian's brows twitched. "Wang Rong, did you know he colluded with Tang Sia and expelled two elders from the Disciplinary

Hall? He is sly as a fox, and you're not his match when it comes to playing games."

Wang Rong's face turned green, and he lowered his head. "Disciple has spoken without thinking. Great elder, please punish disciple."

Su Pan's forehead shifted into a bunch of black lines. This bastard had overstepped and rebutted Wang Tian by asking for punishment from master Jiang. This was nothing but saying "you don't have authority to scold me." Although he stood with the Wang clan, the internal strife made his head hurt, so he had stopped meddling in the Wang clan's internal matters many years ago. He only listened to master Jiang these days.

Wang Tian snorted, but when he was about to speak, Wang Jiang lifted his hand and stopped him.

"Rong'er. I have something else for you," Wang Jiang said.

"Great elder, please order." Wang Rong bowed his head, showing his attentiveness.

"Challenge Ki Fei in the year-end competition in a few months. I want you to win and stomp over her ruthlessly. It'd be better if you can kill her through an accident."

"Master Jiang—" Su Pan was about to complain about the plan when Wang Jiang signaled for Wang Rong to step out.

"Great elder Jiang," Wang Tian said. "If we kill Fairy Fei, our clan will attract calamity. Even the sect master will take action."

Wang Jiang grunted. "You don't have to worry about that. What you need to do is to get that brat Li Wei killed, arousing no suspicion. Although he is a sly fox, he is nothing but an ant in front of our Wang clan." He looked at the mountain peak visible from the door. "Ask Zhang'er to come and see me before you go."

"Disciple will do as you wish, great elder." Wang Tian bowed his head and then moved out of the main hall.

Su Pan pondered. Why was master Jiang calling Wang Zhang? He was a criminal, tasked to guard a secret place for the rest of his life. What had he to do with any of this?

After Wang Tian disappeared through the brightly lit door, Su Pan opened his mouth. "Master Jiang. I heard a rumor that Li Wei killed a Marrow Cleansing Realm elder from the Destiny Mirror Sect. We can't underestimate his combat capabilities."

Wang Jiang smiled, a smile he only showed when he had something terrible in his mind. After spending so many years with Wang Jiang, Su Pan knew something terrible was going to happen to whoever he was thinking about.

"Pan'er, don't worry. You should focus on your cultivation and break through to the Marrow Cleansing Realm soon. I've obtained a Marrow Forming Pill recently, and you should prepare for breakthrough."

A surge of warmth spread through Su Pan's mind and he bowed deeply. "Disciple thanks master for showing me your grace."

Wang Jiang smiled. "Assist Wang Muxi in this operation before breaking through."

Su Pan nodded. A bitter taste spread over his mouth. Now he knew why this old man had offered him a precious pill. He was clear about his action. If only he could succeed, Su Pan would get a pill, otherwise he could forget about it.

"Remember, use your strongest force. A lion attacks with full force, even when he is hunting a rabbit."

Su Pan bowed deeply and left the main hall.

Chapter 12

Secret Love

Bright piercing sunlight peered into his dust-laden courtyard when Li Wei opened his eyes. Squinting, he scanned the room and found the culprit. He had forgotten to close the back door that opened into the backyard. It allowed sunlight to pour in like a tidal wave, and the roaring sound of the black river flowing behind his courtyard had awakened him prematurely.

"Damn! I wanted to sleep for a few more hours." Sleep was the second most important thing in a lazy cultivator's life. Of course, food was the first.

Jumping to his feet, he brushed off the thin layer of gray soil that had settled on his sky-blue robe. Scanning the still-dusty room, he rubbed his forehead. Although it looked insanely messy for a lazy ass like him, he had no plan to clean it right away. First, he had to set up a courtyard-wide isolation array, and the Lesser Isolation Array he'd used last time wouldn't work. For this, he was planning to set up a Trifactor Concealment Array that would conceal his workings from a peak Marrow Cleansing Realm cultivator. The Divine Fragrance Palace had many cultivators beyond the Marrow Cleansing Realm, but those old fogies wouldn't sneak into a remote courtyard of a

Disposal Faction disciple. This was the most left-out faction of the sect, so he didn't have to worry about anyone too powerful intruding he re.

"Still, I should clean one corner for my sleep." His gaze flashed through the whole room while he munched on a sweet Fragrant Green Potato, he had gotten from the Ten Beast Valley. That little fox had had a hill of these things, and they were the tastiest food he had eaten in a while.

A rapid knock on the door pulled him out of his ruminations, and after closing the back door to prevent the roaring sound of the river from disturbing him, he went to the front door to check on the visitor.

As expected, it was Sun Hua, but surprisingly, Tang Sia was with her.

"Junior greets great elder Tang." He cupped his hands and slightly bowed. "What can this junior do for you?"

Tang Sia rolled her eyes and threw a bunch of clothes at him. "I'm here to deliver these. Wear faction clothes inside the sect, or you'll be punished."

Sun Hua arched her brows.

Looking at the sky-blue robes, he couldn't restrain himself from bringing them to his face and inhaling the familiar orchid fragrance. It had reached another layer of purification, and that meant she had broken through once again. "What level has she reached?"

"She has recently broken through to the Bone Baptization Realm and stabilized her cultivation. That's another reason she can't come to you."

Wei sighed inside his heart. It had been a while since he'd met that little lass, and he would be lying if he said he didn't miss her.

However, meeting Tang Sia was Ki Fei's good fortune, and he wouldn't disturb her for the sake of his emotions. "Junior understands. Please tell her to take care of herself." He wanted too say many more things, but they remained in his heart.

"Don't you want to gift her something in return?"

"Great elder, can I trouble you to give this to her?" He pulled out two hundred-year-old Green Bamboo Ginsengs. While in Ten Beast Valley, he had found them in the mystery palace garden where he'd lived for fifteen days. By using his Yin Yang Liquid, he had upgraded their age to hundred year. They had overflowing wood qi, so they should be useful for Fei'er in her next breakthrough into qi Marrow Cleansing Realm.

"Green Bamboo Ginseng, and that too hundred-year-old." Tang Sia's eyes shined brightly. "This should help Fei'er a lot in her cultivation." She jutted her neck up. "Where did you get them?"

"Outside of Black Alley Town," he said calmly.

"But they—" Tang Sia looked away and then hurriedly left.

"And you said you didn't look through my storage ring." Wei sneered inside his mind. He knew this woman had looked through his ring, but there was nothing to hide. For other people, Yin Yang Liquid looked like normal juice, and who would think of dropping it on an herb to check its effects? He had placed it in a very ordinary bottle, so no one would think to check it out.

"You cheater. You never told us you found something precious outside of Black Alley Town." Sun Hua stomped her foot.

Wei rolled his eyes. What was wrong with this girl? Did she think he owed her his life or something?

"Let's go. We should get over this courtyard swap and never see each other's faces again," he replied coldly. Once done with the courtyard matter, he had to find a way to gather the materials required for a Trifactor Concealment Array. Just using a Qi Stone wouldn't suffice here. To set up that array, he needed three different energies: Brown

Qi Bark, Thriving Wooden Grass, and Sharpened Yang Stone. They were rare treasures found in nature, but they weren't extremely rare. However, they would cost him a lot, so he had to find a way to earn some money first.

Maybe he should carve some arrays for others and get some money for himself.

Sun Hua stomped her feet. "Who wants to spend more time with a loser like you?" Then she took off toward a distant Waste Disposal Faction peak. In fact, they could be said to live at the base of the mountain. Every faction had few mountains. The Black Cauldron Faction had four mountains, while Golden Herb Faction had three, and Waste Disposal Faction had only one mountain peak. There were a few more mountain peaks, but they were used by the council of Great Elders and the Sect Master. One was dedicated to the Alchemy Treasure Hall, and one was used by the Mission Hall. So, in all, the Divine Fragrance Palace had sixteen mountain peaks.

Ignoring her, he walked at his own pace. There was no need to waste energy with mindless running. While traveling back to Old Martial City, he had run like a madman, and he didn't want to do that again. Although he would take revenge on Tiang Fu in the future, he wouldn't seek it right away. For a man, ten years wasn't long enough to take revenge. For the near future, his goal was set. Be lazy. Eat. Become fat. Concoct a Foundation Expanding Pill and power up to the peak of the qi Foundation Realm quickly.

After running for five minutes, Sun Hua stopped and then waited for him to catch up. "You brute, why are you crawling like a snail?" she asked as soon as he caught up to her.

"I'm preserving my energy. If you keep running, you'll get wrinkles all over your face."

Her eyes widened and she touched her cheeks. "Really?"

"Of course. Have you ever seen a woman running?"

She puckered her lips before shaking her head.

"Of course not. They don't. Did anyone not tell you about this?"

She shook her head as if someone had wronged her.

He sighed. "You're too naïve. No wonder you're getting some wrinkles already. Women don't run because they have these two . . ." He almost sputtered nonsense in front of an immature girl. "Wrinkles. Don't ask me why, but this is fact." He had almost gone overboard. Not that he cared about polluting her mind, but she was from the enemy group, and what if she had some recording talisman on?

She touched her forehead and cheeks, as if to feel if she had any wrinkles. She even pulled a mirror out from her pouch and checked her face carefully.

"Aiya, you're telling the truth." She extended her face toward him and pointed at her furrowed forehead. "Look, I already got wrinkles."

He shook his head heavily. "Stop running, and they may go away."

She pressed her lips together in determination. "I'm never going to run again in my life." Her face drooped like someone had insulted her family and she couldn't refute it. "I'll tell everyone I know to not run at all."

Damn! It was nearly impossible to hold in his laughter when looking at her.

"Thanks." She licked her lips, and she almost looked cute. "Why did great elder Tang give you clothes? Did you not have clothes?"

He lowered his head and moved closer to her. "If I tell you a secret, can you keep it to yourself?"

She nodded with a serious expression.

"No. You'll tell everyone and it won't be a secret anymore."

"Aiya, no, no." She waved her hand in front of her chest. "I'll absolutely not tell anyone. You can trust me on this." She patted her chest like her guarantee was enough for him to believe her.

How naïve.

"And what if you expose this?"

"I'll be a beast if I expose your secret. Tell. I'm good at keeping secrets."

"Listen." He lowered his head once again and brought it closer to her. Close enough that he could smell a mysterious fragrance coming from her body. To his surprise, he couldn't identify the fragrance. It was kind of sweet and racy, but he couldn't guess what flower it belonged to.

"Say it already." She nudged him when he didn't talk for a few breaths.

"Tang Sia likes me, and she wants to court me."

Sun Hua, who was listening intently, jumped backward and, in doing so, somehow kicked him in the gut.

"Damn you!" he cursed. Although it wasn't a powerful kick, it still hurt.

"I'm sorry. But why did you speak nonsense?"

"Do you think with her status she would launder my clothes?" Stopping, he glared at her. That Tang Sia had looked through his storage ring and even pushed him to the bottom of the food chain in the Divine Fragrance Palace by sending him to the Waste Disposal Faction, so he would take some petty revenge on her.

She puckered her lips. "I guess not. But she is a great elder. Why would she like you?"

"Because . . ." He smiled mischievously. "I can't tell you my every secret. But think about it. A woman who is like a goddess giving new clothes to a trash disciple. Does it fit in any of the wild theories your brain has come up with?"

She turned silent for the next few breaths and then shook her head. "But if she likes me, then it's possible, right?"

"Aiya, yes." She cupped her face and scanned him from top to bottom. "But you look average at most."

Wei felt like someone had stabbed a knife in his heart. Well, he knew he didn't look handsome because he had lost so much weight, but this girl, did she have to tell him that to his face?

"I told you, you won't believe. If you don't want to believe, then forget it."

She walked with him, staying quiet, but her eyes were glued to his face like he was a candy.

"If she does like you, what are you going to do? Are you going to accept her?"

"No. I declined her."

"What?" She once again jumped backward, but this time Wei had jumped backward too, avoiding her kick.

"Are you dumb? Why would you decline a fairy like her?"

He sighed regretfully. "I have, my issues. Anyway, forget it."

"Did she demote you to the Waste Disposal Faction because you declined her?"

He nodded subtly.

"Aiya, then she is exploiting you." Her face darkened. "What will you do?"

He shrugged. "I don't know. Do you know how pitiful my condition is now?"

She nodded.

"Soon she will come back again and give me more clothes." Fei'er would send more clothes to him for sure. She liked that, and she wouldn't change.

"Then whom did you give the two ginseng to?"

"That's another secret, but I can't tell you that." Wei shushed her and increased his pace of walking.

"Don't tell me she forced you to give them to her."

He said nothing.

"That's worse. How could she do that to you?"

"Nephew Wei, what are you doing here?" A familiar voice stuck his ears, and when he turned back, he saw Li Ti standing near a small building, wearing the Waste Disposal Faction's gray clothes.

Chapter 13

Pill Clone Alchemy Art

A small stone-paved road built between fields of green herbs led to the Administrator Hall of the Waste Disposal Faction. As the group of three people walked along the road, chilly winds coming from the medicinal gardens brushed against their faces, bringing a calming aroma of herbs along with them. The strong fragrant aroma left them refreshed, and for the first time, Li Wei felt like he was in an alchemy sect. His mind relaxed a bit. It had been so many days since he'd felt calm. Since reincarnating, he'd been in a constant rush to do something, fight someone, but seeing the herb fields that wrapped around the base of the mountain and vanished into the sky made him realize there was more to life than just fighting.

Seeing a few apple trees planted in between the fields, he had the urge to go and pluck a few to eat them. It had been an hour since he'd eaten the Fragrant Green Potato, and hunger had started making noises from inside his stomach.

"Nephew Wei. Did you not get your faction clothes yet?" Li Ti asked, staring at the pretty Sun Hua in her red dress.

Wei glanced at his uncle's grayish martial robe with an even darker gray plant embroidered on his right shoulder. That was an ugly robe. Then he followed his uncle's gaze that was glued to Sun Hua's slightly mature body. This immature girl had a sort of charm that had attracted his uncle, but if he knew who she was, he wouldn't brazenly stare at her like a display piece in a shop. That was insulting.

"Uncle, let me introduce you to Princess Sun Hua first." To avoid future trouble, he took the first step. Not that he cared about his uncle, but since his grandfather had left this world, he'd had a strange feeling that the Li clan's survival rested on his shoulders. Especially considering his grandfather's dying words. Grandfather had asked him to find his mother, but he didn't tell him where she was. All these years, he'd thought she was dead, and now he knew she was alive. After recovering from his injuries, he'd gone to see the Li clan in Fragrant Herb City, specifically to ask about this, but no elder knew about his mother. They all said she'd vanished one day, and grandfather had told them she'd died in an accident.

It was a mystery.

Li Ti cupped his hands. "Princess, please forgive me for not knowing your identity." He pulled his disturbing gaze away from her.

Ignoring him, she kept looking at the sprawling green herb fields occupying everything until the horizon met the blue sky.

"Uncle Ti, we are heading toward Administrative Hall to swap our courtyards and get initial supplies."

"That's a good thing, then. I work in the Administrative Hall, so I'll make things go faster for you and junior apprentice sister Hua."

"Uncle Li, is this the Golden Herb Faction's area?" He glanced at the herb fields, wondering if it had the herbs he required for Foundation Expanding Pills?

"No, these herbs are not for concocting. They are poisonous herbs raised for purifying waste material from other factions."

"System, analyze these herbs." Wei ordered in his mind.

System: Dragon Poison Plant. Nine Withering Herb. Snake Protruding Grass . . .

A bunch of names and related information popped in his mind. Some were commonly known from *Basic Compendium of Alchemy and Herbs*, and some were from the scattered inheritance he'd gotten from Xue Qi. Around seventy percent of the inheritance was still sealed up. He only had access to few Bronze and Silver Grade pills and two Gold Grade pills.

He also had access to Alchemy Cultivation Arts and some Poison Pills ranging from Bronze Grade to Human Grade. In fact, it looked like the inheritance he'd gotten for Poison Pills was very much intact, as he could see the continuity in the path of poison alchemy in the poison pills. While lying on the bed in Fei'er's courtyard, he had gone through most of the things and had found some interesting things in the Alchemy Cultivation Arts. There was incomplete information about a strange cultivation art, Pill Clone Alchemy Art. It allowed one to create a clone from pills and divine sense. One could even create a permanent clone after reaching a higher level of this cultivation art. It was a good thing it could be practiced along with his other cultivation arts.

"Why are they raising poison herbs?" Sun Hua asked in a wary voice. Looking at her gloomy face, Wei wondered if she too had a thought of touring the fields and eating a few tempting fruits from the common fruit trees planted in the distance.

"I don't know how it is used. Only elders from the faction are aware of that part."

Wei rubbed the back of his neck. "What does our department do, actually?"

Uncle Li sighed. "We collect waste, almost every type of waste, and dispose of it after purifying it through a special array."

"What kind of waste?" Wei hoped it wasn't the kind of that was excreted by humans.

Uncle Li's sigh deepened. "Pill wastage, herb wastage." He pointed at a huge stone building built on top of the mountain. "That's the Waste Disposal Building, and it has a grand array that helps us purify the waste collected from other factions. You guys will be working in it as per your shifts."

"When will we learn alchemy then?" Sun Hua asked.

"We don't learn alchemy in the Waste Disposal Department. Alchemy is only taught in the Golden Herb Faction and the Black Cauldron Faction."

"What kind of joke is this? Why can't we learn alchemy?" she asked.

Uncle Li's sigh deepened once again. "We get access to books, or attain some guest lectures. Also, if we work for two years and survive, then we can ask for faction change. Until then, we can only work in the Waste Disposal Building." His reluctant gaze moved toward the tallest building on the top of the mountain. "But I'm sure that the senior apprentice brothers won't make it hard on you, princess. They will definitely ask you to do the easiest job: taking care of the herb garden. With your status, no one would dare bully you."

She grunted, but her face held a fierce expression.

Hatred grasped his heart. Why the fuck had Tang Sia put him here? His thoughts were disturbed when two people passed them in a jiffy, and a man attracted his attention by the way he walked. It was clumsy, and he kept so much distance between his legs while walking that a tiger could pass through them.

"Brother Du, are you confident about your preparation?" A tall woman in a faction robe asked the brute next to her. She rubbed her curvaceous chest against the man's arms, but he had no change of expression. Nor did he deter her. "Brother Du, please take the challenge only if you are a hundred percent sure. This junior sister will die if something happened to you."

Chen Du only smiled back and didn't reply, but his face turned gloomy when he heard her words.

Wei knew this man, because he had seen him a few times in his previous life. He was the little brother of his good friend Chen Xiang. In fact, Chen Du looked like a little version of Chen Xiang except the color of their eyes and the sword on his back. Chen Xiang practiced the spear.

When Wei had joined the Heavenly Firmament Sect in his previous life, he'd attracted calamity after reaching the Bone Baptization Realm. But brother Xiang had saved him, and his clan had sheltered him, shouldering the calamity for him. He owed his life to them, but he couldn't pay them back at the time. After he ascended to the Martial Realm, the Chen clan vanished from the Mortal Realm, and no one knew what happened to them. Even with his supreme cultivation, he couldn't find any trace of their clan. There was a karma built between them, and he ought to look after them in this new life.

"That's senior apprentice brother Chen Du," Li Ti said after the pair of Chen Du and the woman clinging to him vanished on the horizon. "When I said you have to wait two years, that's not exactly true. After you spend six months in the Waste Disposal Faction, you can issue a challenge of alchemy to any disciple of any faction. If you win, you can join that faction, but if you fail, you will be sent into the deadliest zone of the Waste Disposal Faction, the Snake Rearing Chamber, for ten days. If you challenge anyone from the Alchemy Board, you can join the Alchemy Board. But if you lose, you'll be sent to the Snake Rearing Chamber for three months. I wonder if he can beat Wang Fantai with his layer three Foundation Realm cultivation."

Wei arched his brows. "Snake Rearing Chamber?"

"Yes, it's a deadly place where no one would survive for more than three months. Nine disciples out of ten that go in there become sick, and a few of them even die of poisoning," Li Ti answered. "I don't know what's in there, but no one talks about it." He looked in the direction Chen Du had gone as if he would never see the man again.

"What is the Alchemy Board?" Wei asked.

"That is a special reserve force that trains under the Great Elders directly. They don't belong to any faction and have their own peak to live on. You can call them elite of elites from the sect."

"Uncle Ti, is this competition today? Let's watch it. It would be fun." Wei raised his pace to chase after Chen Du. If he could do something for Chen Du, then he would do whatever he could.

But while walking forward, he couldn't guess why the Divine Fragrance Palace was working on so many poisonous things at one time. And why was it hidden from the outside world?

Chapter 14

Su Clan's Target

When Wang Rong received the news of an alchemy competition inside his courtyard on the Twin Profound Mountains—a cultivation paradise where Alchemy Board members lived—he wasn't interested in it at all. For the last few days, he'd been working on his leg muscles, and they had finally shown some improvement so they didn't look like sticks attached to a boulder anymore. He wasn't going to waste his time on a stupid alchemy competition, anyway.

Then he'd heard the names of the competitors and his sense of disgust deepened. Wang Fantai and Chen Du.

Suddenly he remembered a note from great elder Jiang he had received a couple of days ago. Was this the same Chen Du?

The note instructed Rong to kill someone in the sect named Chen Du—discreetly—and said that in return the Su clan of Heavenly Firmament Sect would hand over a low-tier Gold Grade beast flame—Flood Dragon's Roar—which they had found in some ancient ruins.

A Gold Grade beast flame.

Conjuring his own beast flame, a mid-tier Silver Grade Salamander's Oath, Wang Rong stared at it. Just a glance made disgust roil in his stomach. He wanted to wipe it out from his dantian. This flame was utter trash. For a dragon like him, only Flood Dragon's Roar would suit. It was the best flame for him. With that flame, he would trample over Ki Fei's corpse and show the world that he was the best.

"Yes, I should first aim for the beast flame. With the beast flame I can easily defeat Ki Fei," he muttered to himself.

Ten minutes later, he stood in the crowd with his face covered by a black cloth and a few layers of pants wrapped around his legs so they looked meaty. This way, no one would identify him.

The competition was meaningless as usual, and he didn't even glance at the trash Wang Fantai's face. Chen Du held his full attention, but when he looked at him, all he saw was the Flood Dragon's Roar beast flame that would be his reward.

"This is my chance. I must kill him in the open, so no one will suspect me." Without thinking too much, he pulled the Conscious Erasing Talisman out and pointed it at Chen Du. With his background in archery, it was easy to target Chen Du precisely. This talisman had been given to him by great elder Jiang, and it was useful for killing low-level ants like Chen Du without alerting anyone. He'd had plans to use it on Ki Fei, but the beast flame was more important to him. Great elder Jiang would be angry, but once Rong got on his knees and begged, he would let it go and give him another talisman.

However, right before he crushed the talisman, someone swiped it from his hand like a wind devil.

Wang Rong looked around and noticed a young man with long black hair smirking at him. The bastard. Why was he laughing? Did he see someone steal the Conscious Erasing Talisman from Wang Rong's hand?

Impossible. Even he, who had held the talisman, hadn't seen the thief. How could a youth like him see them?

But before Wang Rong could take action, a hooded girl stabbed the young man with her sword. He frowned. It was Shadow Twelfth, and if she'd stabbed him . . . that meant the youth was Li Wei. Well, he wasn't smirking anymore.

What useless trash. From the way everyone else described him, he was a super powerful fighter, but a weak girl had just stabbed him easily.

What a bummer. Now he wouldn't have the chance to kill Li Wei himself.

Either way, he was pissed. He'd lost great elder Jiang's attack talisman without using it. How could he kill Chen Du and get the reward from the Su clan?

This was infuriating. His many plans depended upon that reward, and he wanted it right away. If it wasn't for that, he wouldn't have come to this shitshow. Wang Fantai, the joker, besmirched the Wang clan's name by fighting with a non-alchemy clan disciple.

It was a slap to the Wang clan's face, and soon he would teach the bastard Wang Fantai a lesson. He deserved a beating.

Chapter 15

Alchemy Challenge

Two stone tables were set across from each other at a bustling square near a stone tower. Two shiny black metal cauldrons were set up on the tables, and three sets of herbs were placed in separate jade boxes. Two people stood behind the tables, one inspecting herbs with a gloomy face and the other talking with a cute girl standing next to him.

The guy with the gloomy face was Chen Du, and he too had a girl next to him with an average face and an exquisite body, but he was busy with his herbs. With his broad shoulders and a face like a stone tablet, the brute Chen Du didn't look like an alchemist.

Li Wei stood among the crowd, observing Chen Du's actions. He didn't remember which sect Chen Du had joined in his previous life, but he never thought it would be the Divine Fragrance Palace. The Chen clan was one of the prominent support clans of the Heavenly Firmament Sect, and it was unlikely someone from them would walk the path of alchemy.

Well, exceptions always happened.

"Do you think senior apprentice brother Chen Du stands any chance of winning this challenge?" Someone from the Waste Disposal Faction asked from the crowd.

"No way. If he had challenged someone weaker than him, there might be a chance, but he challenged senior apprentice brother Wang Fantai. I heard senior apprentice brother Wang reached layer seven Foundation Realm last month, and he can even control a mid-tier Bronze Grade Ten Tendon App's beast flame. Even his Nine Lotus Alchemy Art has reached initial completion. I heard he boasted about his fifty percent success rate of any Bronze Grade pill in a nearby inn."

The face of the one who'd asked turned serious. "That's too bad. Senior apprentice brother Chen didn't have time to practice his alchemy, and the beast flame he controls is only a low tier Bronze Grade Three Fire Crawler Ant's beast flame. That's subpar when compared to his opponent."

"Did you forget with senior apprentice brother Fantai's alchemy art reaching initial completion, his wood qi grade would be a tad higher than Chen Du? It will affect the quality of processing."

"I thought I'd see a good fight, but I don't think senior apprentice brother Chen has any chance. But why did he challenge a strong opponent, and that too from the Wang clan who controls the Black Cauldron Faction?"

"Don't take the Chen clan for a weak clan," the other one continued. "So what, they don't have influence in the sect. They have many connections in the Heavenly Firmament Sect."

"Are the Wang clan and the Chen clan opposing each other? But how come? They have an amicable relationship."

"It's because of a girl. I heard senior apprentice brother Wang Fantai took a liking to a girl from the city, and she likes senior apprentice brother Chen Du and they fought openly."

Wei rolled his eyes. How could a girl like a brawny fellow like Chen Du.? He even had a girl following him right now, and she was all over him.

Wei's gaze unknowingly jumped to Sun Hua, who was glaring daggers at him. How could an ugly fellow like Chen Du have two girls following him while a fat, handsome fellow like him had assassins lurking behind him?

Damn, this world was too cruel.

"But issuing a challenge you can't win is foolishness," the second person continued. "Even if he dies in the Snake Rearing Chamber, what can the Chen clan do to the Divine Fragrance Palace? I heard senior apprentice's brother wanted to join the Black Cauldron Faction, but the Wang clan used their influence to send him to the Waste Disposal Faction. It's too pitiful to see a genius dying like this."

Everywhere in the crowd, a similar discussion happened, and with his divine sense, Wei listened to everything. So, there was enmity between Chen Du and Wang Fantai. Well, even if there wasn't, he would have helped Chen Du.

From observing the crowd's discussion, he found out the nature of the challenge. They were concocting a Bronze Healing Pill. It was a mid-tier Bronze Grade pill used by common practitioners, but it was a tricky pill as it involved processing four different herbs and required fine control of wood qi and beast fire. Xue Qi's inheritance also contained a method to concoct this pill, and it differed from what he overheard from the crowd.

This was going to be interesting, but Wei wasn't sure how could he help Chen Du.

Then he chuckled, and everyone looked at him with frowning expressions.

"Li Wei, are you going nuts?" Sun Hua glared at him.

Shaking his head, Wei controlled his evil chuckle. Helping Chen Du would be easy. Easier than anything he had done. He just had to make Wang Fantai fail, and that was easier than he thought. All he had to do was mutter some words with his divine sense, and Wang Fantai would fail. The Mortal Realm was an exiled land of cultivation, and other than some high-level cultivators, none knew about divine sense. If someone heard a sound in their mind, what would they think?

Wouldn't it be easy?

"Li Wei, are you laughing at me?" Sun Hua stomped her foot on his shoe.

"Damn you girl," Wei shouted and everyone turned their attention toward them.

"Everyone." A man in his fifties came forward and everyone turned silent. Wei and Sun Hua disappeared from their attention as they turned to focus on that man. "I'm elder Fu Moi from the Golden Herb Faction, and I'll preside over this competition. I'll announce rules now. Every competitor has three sets of ingredients for concocting a Bronze Healing Pill, and they have three hours to complete a pill. Whoever creates a higher ranked pill will win."

The two contestants nodded. Like arrays, every pill went from first rank to fifth rank, and the higher the rank, the better the efficacy of the pill.

"But as per the challenge rules, the challenged disciple can amend or change an existing rule." Elder Fu turned to look at Wang Fantai. "Junior Wang, do you want to modify a rule? Remember, you can't disqualify your opponent and declare yourself a winner. You can only ask for something that is in acceptable boundaries."

Wang Fantai stared at everyone. "Junior apprentice brother Chen, I won't make it difficult for you, but I'll add a condition that you'll only have one hour to concoct the pill, and if you fail, you lose the battle."

A commotion took place in the crowd, and Wei's face turned darker. In this challenge, by default, both competitors had three chances each, and if all failed they would lose. So, even if he made Wang Fantai fail, if Chen Du failed once, he would lose. This would be difficult, but not impossible. What he had to do was to make Wang Fantai fail quickly, before Chen Du could disqualify himself.

Elder Fu nodded. "This is acceptable. Both of you can start now." He waved his hand, and the crowd retreated a bit so the two of them could have a peaceful competition.

"Li Wei, let's go back and finish our transaction." Sun Hua tugged his sleeve.

This girl, she really lacked any manners. "Wait a bit. Wang Fantai is going to lose this match soon."

Suddenly Wei's gaze fell on a heavyset youth with thin legs who pulled a talisman from his clothes and pointed it at Chen Du.

"Conscious Erasing Talisman." Wei felt a headache coming on. This was a rare talisman and shouldn't be in a disciple's hand. It was a peculiar talisman that could target one's conscious and erase it for some time. If a soul-recovering medicine wasn't given swiftly, the target would suffer a heavy blow to their conscious and may never be able to cultivate again.

However, when it was used on low-level cultivators like Chen Du, it was most often fatal. Why was this bastard using such a talisman?

Wei couldn't let Chen Xiang's brother get injured, so he rushed forward and snatched the talisman from the youth's hand and dropped it into his storage ring.

The bulky youth looked confused before he fixed his eyes on Wei.

Wei smirked, but suddenly a sense of danger rose—too late. Even before he turned, a woman cried out and stabbed him with a sword, and Wei couldn't do anything but let her.

Chapter 16

Pill Ghost

Wang Fantai looked at Chen Du in disdain. That mongrel bastard had challenged him to a match when he didn't even have a mid-tier Bronze Grade beast flame. This was more than laughable.

Today he would show the whole sect who was the boss here.

A flame revolved through the meridian of his right arm, flickering a little. It was loaned flame, so he couldn't control it like his own flame, but it was enough to defeat Chen Du.

With a high-tier Bronze Grade beast flame with him, he would trample this bastard Chen Du and win Bao'er's heart. Just because this bastard had known Bao'er for a few years, Chen Du had smeared his plans to make a good impression on Bao'er.

How hateful.

"Junior apprentice brother Fantai, you have to win today and show those bastards from the Waste Disposal Faction that no matter what they do, they can't win against us. Don't lose face for my beast flame," the cute girl standing next to him spoke in an enchanting way.

"Senior apprentice sister Kai Kai, this junior brother won't let your help go to waste. I'll crush this bastard and make you proud." He smiled at the girl, but in his mind he cursed a mouthful. This bitch had been pestering him since he'd asked to borrow her high-tier Bronze Grade beast flame, Fire Cat's beast flame. In return, she'd asked him to put a good word in for her with his cousin brother Wang Rong, one of the so-called prodigies of the Wang clan.

How hateful. What prodigy, Wang Rong was just a cripple in his legs and he won't be able to satisfy Kai Kai. Only he could do it.

After this competition, he would delay the return of her beast flame and use a secret art to subdue the flame for himself. Why would he let go of a good flame? With a high-tier Bronze Grade beast flame, it would be easier to join the Alchemy Board and then defeat Wang Rong in the future.

"Junior apprentice brother, you can't go back on your word. I just need you to introduce me to senior apprentice brother Wang Rong, and this favor will be called off."

How hateful. Once he won this challenge, he would drug this bitch and turn her into a plaything. How could she ask him to talk with that bastard Wang Rong?

Something happened in the crowd, and two people fought a brief battle. A woman from the Waste Disposal Faction attacked a youth in a sky-blue robe. But the battle was suppressed by elder Fu instantly.

"Juniors, you can start concocting." Elder Fu Moi signaled them to start after he finished quelling the scuffle. His forehead had a deep furrow, and his mood didn't look good.

Wang Fantai opened the jade box on the table and looked at the ingredients placed neatly inside.

Underground Sun Grass. Pure Liquid. Red Ginseng. Three Leaf Dark Grass. All four ingredients had been grown for five years. Sufficient for concocting a rank two pill if everything was prepared meticulously. And with the high-tier Bronze Grade beast flame, Fire Cat's beast flame, he had sufficient confidence in bringing out the best of the herbs and completing the concoction.

Collecting Pure Water in a glass beaker, he poured a strand of wood qi into it using Nine Lotus Alchemy Art. This alchemy art purified his wood qi and enhanced it to process herbs effectively. Under his gaze, the Pure Water soon took on a white hue. This was a common process to turn Pure Water into Qi Water that would be used to process Underground Sun Grass and dispel its impurities. Underground Sun Grass was the main herb of the pill that defined the rank of the final pill.

"Hey junior, what are you doing? Why are you mixing a cream into the liquid?" Someone spoke in his ear, and he almost lost his concentration and stopped pouring wood qi into the glass beaker.

Calming himself, he rectified his mistake and replenished the qi supply before looking around. His gaze landed on the bastards in gray robes with a darker gray plant symbol embroidered on their shoulders. Those bastards almost succeeded in breaking his concentration. How hateful.

"Senior apprentice sister Kai. Can you take care of these Waste Disposal Faction disciples from near me? They are trying to disturb me." He spoke in a calm tone, hiding his wavering tone somehow.

"You bastards, you dare to disturb my junior brother?" Kai Kai pulled a sword out and slashed at the disciples from the Waste Disposal Faction.

"Senior apprentice sister Kai, what is the meaning of this?" Two of them jumped backward, startled by the sudden attack from Kai Kai.

Wang Fantai smirked and focused on the beaker in his hand.

"You bastard, why are you diluting my liquid with your waste? Stop it already, else I'll call a pill tribulation upon you." The same voice echoed in Wang Fantai's mind, and this time the beaker in his hand shook and everything was ruined.

"Who the fuck is disturbing me?" he roared and looked around. But there was no one around him, as Kai Kai had started beating people with her sword.

"Junior Fantai, what happened?" Elder Fu walked forward, his forehead breaking out in black lines.

"Elder Fu, these Waste Disposal Faction disciples are messing with me. Just now someone broke my concentration."

Elder Fu looked around and ordered everyone to go further away from the opponents before turning back to face Wang Fantai. "Junior Fantai. In concoction, mental fortitude is the most important thing. If you let your concentration break by some random words from trash around you, then you won't go far on the road of alchemy."

Wang Fantai lowered his head in shame. Elder Fu was right. He should have done better than this.

"This junior will keep elder's words in heart." Then he opened the second batch of ingredients and poured Pure Water in another glass beaker.

"You bastard, you're wasting a second set of my drinking water. I'm going to blast you this time into smithereens." The same voice struck his mind, and this time he realized it wasn't from someone in the crowd.

"Why are you looking around, bastard? I'm a pill ghost, and I'm going to haunt you forever for ruining my drinking water. See how I play with you now."

Suddenly, a commotion took place, and a girl from the Golden Herb Faction pulled out her sword and pointed at senior apprentice sister Kai. "You bitch, you threaten to cut my manhood and feed them to a dog? Come, and I'll show you who is stronger."

Li Wei gasped hard. The girl he had just fought with was far stronger than he'd expected. A single attack from her had thrashed his stomach meridian and left a residue of cold energy inside his body. If he hadn't had Blood Essence Body to heal his meridians quickly, he would have been bedridden for at least a month.

And that bitch had vanished as soon as she attacked him. "Uncle Li, did you see who that girl was?" he asked, looking in the direction that girl vanished.

Li Ti shook his head. "No. I haven't seen her in the faction hall. How are your injuries?" He glanced at the bloody patch on Wei's stomach.

"I'm okay. It's just some blood." Wei had burned some blood pearls to speed up his healing. It was going smoothly, but he couldn't guess why she'd attacked. And as soon as she'd attacked, she'd targeted his stomach. Anyway, with his Blood Essence Body, he didn't have to care about minor injuries like these, so he focused on the competition. All he had to do was to startle Wang Fantai, and he would fail.

And that went smoother than he imagined.

When he talked with Wang Fantai using his divine sense, Wang Fantai messed up his ingredient on the first try. And soon he was blabbering some nonsense. Wei even managed to incite some girls that were looking at the small girl named Kai Kai standing next to Wang Fantai with jealous eyes. All he'd had to do was speak a few provoking words toward them using Kai Kai's body language as the source, and those fools believed that Kai Kai had insulted them with some vulgar words.

That was fun. Using Divine Sense like this, he could mess with anyone who hadn't reached the Houtian Realm.

However, when he glanced at the flickering wood qi Chen Du was pouring into the glass beaker, Wei's expression turned grim. Although he had practiced no alchemy except what he'd done inside the dream space in the Alchemy Comprehension Tower, he still had some knowledge about processing Qi Water. And there was a huge difference in the quality of wood qi poured by Chen Du and Wang Fantai in their respective glass beakers. As per the description in the alchemy inheritance he could still access, processing Qi Water from Pure Water was a very important factor in the success of a Bronze Healing Pill.

Then there was the issue of Chen Du's concentration. With his quivering fingers, he would fail to concoct the pill in the end.

In summary, Chen Du would lose even if Wei made Wang Fantai waste all his ingredients. The challenge only looked for the pill quality, and if the challenger couldn't even concoct a pill, then he would definitely fail.

Wei looked at the pill recipe from Xue Qi's inheritance, and he judged if he could help Chen Du change the steps on the fly. There was a certain danger that Chen Du might fail because of the unfamiliarity of the recipe, but he had to take the risk.

There were no ifs in the world of cultivation.

Chapter 17

Divine Sound

"Holy heavens." Chen Du tapped on either side of his chest and looked at the sky before taking a deep breath. He was about to start the pill concoction, and he wasn't as confident as he would like to be.

Chen Du's hands shook, and he almost dropped the glass beaker when a commotion arose on Wang Fantai's side. A fight broke out among a few girls, and when Chen Du looked over, he saw four girls fighting amongst themselves. No, three other senior apprentice sisters were beating senior apprentice sister Kai Kai.

What was wrong with them?

Ignoring them, Chen Du focused on his processing. Converting Pure Water into Qi Water was a very important step, as he would use the Qi Water to boil the Underground Sun Grass for ten minutes in the cauldron and dispel impurities from it. But the issue was his wood qi from his Nine Lotus Alchemy Art. Having been thrown into the Waste Disposal Faction, he hadn't had enough time to reach early completion of his Nine Lotus Alchemy Art, and that meant his wood qi wasn't as pure as it should have been.

“Chen Du, if you want to win this competition, you can’t process the Qi Water like that.” Someone spoke in his mind, and he almost jumped away.

“Brother Du, what happened?” Chi’er asked in an intimate voice.

“Did you hear something just now?” he asked, confused.

“No.” Chi’er looked around. There were not many people around them. Everyone had gone to watch Wang Fantai’s herb processing, because they all thought they would learn something by watching him. They could have been right, but they didn’t know that Chen Du had chanced upon a mid-tier Bronze Grade beast fire recently, Flaming Rabbit’s beast fire, and he had subdued it to make it his own. Only because of this had he dared to challenge Wang Fantai. The reason for the challenge that people talked about was bullshit. He knew Kang Bao, but she wasn’t the reason he would fight against Wang Fantai. Bao’er was just a friend, and all his thoughts resided with Chi’er, his childhood sweetheart.

“Brother Du, please focus on the concocting. I’ll die if you’re thrown into the Snake Rearing Chamber.”

“Chi’er. Don’t worry. I’ll succeed this time.” His eyes turned sharp, and he focused back on revolving his Nine Lotus Alchemy Art. This was his only option to survive. Because of the fight with Wang Fantai in the city, he would be punished or expelled from the sect soon, so he could only challenge Wang Fantai and win a place in Alchemy Board.

This battle was inevitable.

“Do you realize your wood qi is not pure enough to convert the Pure Water into Qi Water completely? If you continue like this, your Qi Water will have 34% impurities in it, and you will at most create a rank one pill.” The same voice struck his ears, and this time he looked around but no one had uttered a single word to him.

Was there a ghost?

A chill rushed through his legs, and his knees nearly buckled.

"Are you shivering in fear?"

"Mr. Ghost. Please leave me alone. I'll burn some paper money for you. Please leave me alone." Sweat poured from his forehead, and it dropped into the glass beaker, instantly wasting his efforts. But who cared about that when he was besieged by a ghost?

"Brother Du, what's wrong? Who are you speaking to? Is someone disturbing you?" Chi'er pulled her sword out and pointed at the air.

"Chen Du, are you nuts? If it wasn't for your brother, Chen Xiang, I wouldn't help you at all. Why are you calling a perfect man a ghost?"

Chen Du's face hardened, and his eyes became focused. "How do you know my brother Xiang?"

"That's not important. You still have two sets of ingredients. Why don't you try processing one with my method? Worse case, you'll fail. But looking at your current wood qi and Wang Fantai's wood qi, you're going to fail anyway."

Chen Du had a complex emotions in his mind. When he looked at Wang Fantai, he saw a golden-brown stream of qi entering his glass beaker. That golden brown color couldn't be faked. Only after reaching initial completion of the Nine Lotus Alchemy Art could one achieve it.

If Chen Du's Qi Water had any impurities, he could concoct a rank one Bronze Healing Pill at best, and he would lose. After reading so many books on alchemy, he knew the importance of alchemy arts. They make or break the pill concoction.

"What is your method?" If he was going to win, he had to take drastic measures. Even if it meant trusting a stranger. And to save his place in the sect, he would do anything.

"Use your mid-tier Bronze Grade beast flame to heat the glass beaker to forty degrees while pouring your wood qi into the Pure

Water. This way you'll vaporize the impurities in the Qi Water. Although you'll lose some quantity, you can overcome it by processing the second set of ingredients in the same way."

"Are you mad?" A thick film of sweat formed over Chen Du's back. Qi Water was a highly flammable substance. Without a thick metal cauldron separating the fire from the Qi Water, it would burst into flame. Glass was a flimsy separator. "Wait, how do you know I have a mid-tier Bronze Grade beast flame?"

"Brother Du, what's going on? Who are you talking to?" A panicked expression covered Chi'er's face, and she looked around with vigilant eyes.

"What does that have to with your current predicament?" the voice in his head said.

"Brother divine sound, are you sure this will work?" Chen Du steeled his heart. In his current state, Divine Sound didn't have to do anything for him to lose the competition, so he could only trust it. Worse case, he would lose one set of ingredients. Either way, he was going to face the Snake Rearing Chamber, so why would he fear other things?

"Do it."

"Holy heavens." Chen Du took the second bottle of Pure Water, poured it into the second glass beaker, and started imbuing his wood qi in the glass beaker from the top while heating it at the bottom with his new beast flame.

Dark orange fire leaped out of his left hand and struck the bottom of the beaker. With a flicker of his left hand, he reduced the flame and maintained a constant heat of forty degrees using his Nine Lotus Alchemy Art. By fusing his wood qi with the beast fire, he could control the optimal temperature of the heat he produced.

Everyone around him grew silent, deathly silent, when they spotted the dark orange flame.

"What is he doing?" someone asked.

"I don't know, but that's a Flaming Rabbit's beast flame. When did Chen Du get it?"

"He hid himself well. I think we will see a good competition," another one spoke.

For a moment, Chen Du relaxed. This reaction wasn't beyond his expectations. Nobody would have thought that a Waste Disposal Faction disciple could get his hands on a mid-tier Bronze Grade beast flame, but he'd done it anyway. After beating Wang Fantai, he would wash away the disgrace he'd brought on his family by thrown into the worst faction of the sect. They were already unhappy about this, but if he could win a place in Alchemy Board, they would be proud of him.

"No way. That brute is heating Pure Water while turning it into Qi Water? Has he gone insane? Did he forget Qi Water is highly flammable? Is he going to frigin explode his own face?" someone shouted, and everyone started looking at him.

Chen Du's heart sunk. Had he made a mistake by trusting this brother divine sound?

"Look, the Qi Water is breaking down. Chen Du must have gone insane and is trying to kill himself by blowing up his face," someone shouted, and Chen Du's heart flipped inside his chest.

Suddenly, a crackling sound came from the beaker, and heartache squeezed his sunken heart. Was he going to fail and become a laughingstock?

Chapter 18

Great elder arrives

Everything was going smoothly, and as Li Wei expected, the brute Chen Du picked up the second portion of Pure Water from the stone table containing the ingredients. A sweet fragrance wafted over the chilly air when Chen Du poured the Pure Water into a clean glass beaker.

Wei licked his lips in anticipation. This would be the first time he watched Xue Qi's inheritance knowledge being used. Considering the heaven-defying Foundation Expanding Pill Sun Nuan'd created, he had high hopes for this previously unknown method. His heart was already drumming inside his chest, and his index finger brushed against the smooth metallic surface of his storage ring that was now concealed by a small concealing array carved on the surface. He was so focused that he forgot to keep instigating the four girls fighting behind Wang Fantai's table.

However, his mood dampened when orange fire leaped out of Chen Du's hand. Wei couldn't restrain himself from cursing the brute inside his mind.

Everyone around them grew silent at the display of fire touching the glass beaker, but Wei had the urge to shout and smack the brute's head with his leather shoe. Was he trying to ruin things even before starting?

A crackling sound came out of the glass beaker, and disgusted whispers emerged from people around Chen Du. They were belittling Chen Du for playing a prank on them.

They were right. Chen Du was joking. Now even Wei wondered if the brute had a brain inside his skull, or if only air filled it.

Another crackling sound came, and the liquid turned semi-white.

Everyone shook their heads in disappointment, including elder Fu.

Fuck! That was infuriating, and it left a sour taste in Wei's mouth.

"Chen Du, are you trying to mess things up? I said forty degrees, not a degree less nor a degree more. Why aren't you using the temperature-sensing talisman on that beast flame of yours?" Wei sent a divine message when things grew worse.

Chen Du's face darkened. "Brother divine sound. I don't have a temperature-sensing talisman. I only have a few defensive talismans."

Wei frowned, a deep frown. Taking a deep breath, he drew on his divine sense and formed a cocoon around the glass beaker in Chen Du's hand. With his divine sense, he measured the exact temperature of the flame, and it was forty-five degrees.

"Reduce the power of your flame by a few degrees."

"But I think temperature looks good."

"Looks good my foot. Shut up and listen." Wei had no patience to debate with a muddlehead like Chen Du. What kind of alchemist didn't bring a temperature-sensing talisman to an alchemy competition? At least Wang Fantai was better than this muddleheaded brute. As soon as Wang Fantai checked his ingredients, he had set out a temperature-sensing talisman. It was a reusable talisman everyone knew about.

Chen Du didn't reply, but the temperature of his flame lowered, and Wei sighed in relief. But soon the temperature dropped to thirty-two degrees, and Wei wanted to smash Chen Du's head with a brick lying next to his shoe. He started to squat down to pick it up, but a sudden bout of pain emerged from his stomach and he stopped himself.

"Increase the intensity a little. A little." He sent a divine sense transmission while addressing the pain in his stomach. After burning a couple of blood pearls, it subsided.

After two or three rounds of to and fro between them, Chen Du finally managed to sustain the temperature. But another issue appeared when the Qi Water turned a muddy brown color.

Wei poured out more divine sense and checked the wood qi quality. It was inferior. Qi Water had to achieve a pure white color to be potent, else the processing would fail.

"Chen Du. Reduce your wood qi a little and monitor the Qi Water. It should remain pure white." Wei sent another divine sense transmission.

"Why isn't the beaker exploding?" someone whispered in the crowd, and Chen Du's face turned unsightly.

"Just wait and watch the fun. This muddlehead is playing with his own life," another one sneered.

"Look at the Qi Water in Chen Du's hand. It's turning whiter with every second," someone from the crowd shouted, and everyone looked at the glass beaker in Chen Du's hands. After Chen Du started heating the Qi Water, many of the people from Wang Fantai's side had come to his side to watch Chen Du blowing up his face, but they didn't know what was going to happen.

They were going to slap their own faces instead.

Wei smirked and continued monitoring every minute change in Chen Du's Qi Water. Soon it turned whiter than Wang Fantai's Qi Water. That meant this technique mentioned in Xue Qi's inheritance was better than the one used commonly.

"Wow, he didn't blow up his Qi Water. But how is this possible?" someone exclaimed from the crowd.

"You bitch, stay away from bother Du and don't disturb him." The average-faced girl from Chen Du's side turned vigilant and stopped all those who tried to get close to Chen Du. Seeing her protective actions, Wei's initial impression of her improved slightly. Maybe she wasn't just a flimsy sucker, and she might genuinely care about Chen Du.

Elder Fu also walked closer to Chen Du, and with one glare from him, everyone stepped backward.

Wei noticed the slight change happening to the Qi Water. It had transformed at the core level, and although he couldn't guess what that transformation was, he knew it was something good.

"Stop the fire and wood qi infusion, and dip the glass beaker in water to maintain the optimal temperature." Wei sent a divine sense transmission to Chen Du.

Nodding, Chen Du stopped his processing and pulled a wooden crate filled with normal water closer to him.

"Junior Du, wait." Elder Fu said, his eyes glued to the glass beaker in Chen Du's hand.

"Elder Fu, is there a problem?" Chen Du asked, his face turning a shade of gray.

"No, there's no problem. I wonder if you can let me test the purity of your Qi Water?" elder Fu asked. Before Chen Du answered, he pulled a pitch-black stone out of his pouch and extended it forward, giving Chen Du no choice. That pitch-black stone was peculiar, and light scattered around it; as if it sucked up every strand of light that fell on it.

"This junior agrees." Using a small glass spoon, Chen Du collected a few drops of his Qi Water and then dropped them on the stone in elder Fu's hand. Sharp light emitted from the stone, and the entire stone shone with a bright white light before vanishing from it.

"Eighty-six percent purity," elder Fu muttered to himself, his voice shaking.

"What?" a couple people from the crowd shouted as if someone stole their brides. "How is that possible? With the Nine Lotus Alchemy Art method we can get sixty-nine percent purity at most."

Wei searched through his memories and realized that this stone was a Purity Testing Stone. As per *Basic Compendium of Alchemy and Herbs*, the basic recipe for converting Pure Water into Qi Water only provided seventy percent purity at max. There were a few other methods, but those required costly catalysts and some other herbs. Comparing the cost to benefit, wasting so much money on Qi Water wasn't worth it. One could buy seventy percent pure Qi Water in any alchemy shop. When Wei had concocted the Golden Meridian Healing Pill, he'd directly conjured ninety-five percent pure Qi Water, as it was a dream space and he didn't have to process it himself.

"Elder Fu, why did you send a sound transmission?" An elder with a long white beard walked out of the shadows. "Is someone causing you trouble?" The newcomer had an old face. An aged face if one had to describe it correctly.

"Look, great elder Moi has arrived," someone whispered, and everyone went silent.

"Elder Fu. This better be important, else you can forget about getting a Soul Ascension Pill," great elder Moi said in a stern voice.

Wei was startled by the reference to this pill. How did a Mortal Realm sect know about Soul Ascension Pills?

A sharp pain shot through his stomach, and he realized his internal wound had opened up. If he didn't go back to his courtyard and heal it with some pills, this might prove difficult.

Chapter 19

Trouble at the Capital

In a large hall inside the Tang clan mansion in Bloodshed City, the imperial capital of the State of Zin, a man sat on a high chair placed at the end of the hall. A black patch covered his right eye, and a matching martial robe made his demeanor oppressive. The white beard hanging on his chest contrasted with his clothes. His finger constantly tapped on the metal arm of the high chair, but it didn't attract the attention of the three other men sitting on nearby chairs, wearing black martial robes themselves.

A young man in his twenties stood politely in front of the four men, his gaze glued to the marble floor. In a tight-fitting black martial robe, he looked like a warrior with chiseled muscles, but his baby face belied his overall impression.

Light shone from the crystal chandelier overhead and fell on the face of the old man sitting on the high chair. It illuminated the black patch, giving him a threatening look. That chandelier always illuminated the black patch of the Tang clan patriarch, but no one knew if it was a coincidence or done on purpose.

"Mian'er, how are your preparations?" the Tang clan patriarch asked.

"Father, this little one has comprehended late completion of the Qilin Wood Sword's third level. I'm confident in showing a good performance at the Imperial Battle Ground." Tang Mian spoke in a polite voice. He was the young master of Tang clan.

"Mian'er. You must win if our clan will survive this ordeal. If we can't create a single link with the imperial clan, our clan will fall from among the Tier 3 clans of the capital, and then the other three clans will take action and wipe us out." He sounded heavy and disturbed.

Tang Mian sighed inside his heart. Their clan ancestor was on the last part of his journey, and no one had broken into late Marrow Cleansing Realm since him. Mian's father, the patriarch himself, was stuck at layer six of the Marrow Cleansing Realm. Once their clan ancestor died, the other three great clans of the capital city would wipe them out for sure. "This little one understands the predicament. I'll definitely win a top place at the Imperial Battle Ground and attract the attention of a princess." In his mind, a figure appeared, someone he had known for many years. A princess who neither had arrogance sunk into her bones nor acted as pretentiously as other princesses he had met.

The Imperial Battle Ground was a competition held by the imperial clan every five years. Although it was to choose prodigies from the State of Zin, the imperial clan—the Sun clan—used it to find good talent and recruit them into the Sun clan by marriage. The king had one hundred and eight concubines, so he had no shortage of princesses in the imperial clan.

However, Tang Mian didn't want just any princess. His eyes were set on the cream of the crop of beauties, Sun Nuan. She was the daughter of one of the ten main concubines of the king, and she was like a fairy that had descended from the heavens to enlighten the commoners.

"If you seize this opportunity, we will get enough resources to advance to a Tier 2 clan," the patriarch said. "That would be the greatest service you can do for our Tang clan."

"Little one understands lord father's command," Tang Mian said sincerely. "I'll cultivate diligently and win the heart of Princess Nuan in the upcoming competition."

The air around Tang Mian grew heavy, and his father's oppressive aura locked on him. "Mian'er. You're not allowed to speak that name going forward. You should aim for Princess Sun Xin."

"Nephew Mian'er," said one of the other men. "Don't even ask anyone about Princess Nuan. I know you've doted on her since childhood, but she has committed a grave crime. She has been named a traitor, and if you associate with her in any manner, our clan will face the same fate."

Tang Mian looked up, his eyes wide open, ready to pop out of their sockets.

"Mian'er. Stay away from her, and Princess Hua as well. Princess Nuan went against the Destiny Mirror Sect, so it's unwise to ask about her," another man from the elder council spoke in a soft tone. "I heard the Destiny Mirror Sect has approached the imperial clan to hand her over to them, so she may be sacrificed for the country's wellbeing."

How could it be? Tang Mian's heart grew heavy. From the moment he'd first seen Nuan, he had developed a soft spot for her, and he was looking forward to winning her heart. But now it seemed impossible to do that.

But somewhere in his heart, an image remained intact, and that image matched Sun Nuan's figure.

Wang Zhang appeared outside of a courtyard on Alchemy Ascension Peak. It was the topmost location on the peak, and only great elder Wang Jiang had access to this place, so Wang Zhang had to stop outside and send a message through his Sound Transmission Talisman.

"Enter."

Wang Zhang entered the courtyard and then into a room devoid of any light. With his intact eye, he could only see darkness that clawed at his heart. For so many times Wang Zhang had entered this room, but he always found it gloomy and foul. Fouler even than the Snake Rearing Chamber, which he frequently visited.

And his father always hiding his face behind the darkness made it worse. Since the day Wang Zhang was given a punishment to guard the Snake Rearing Chamber, he'd never seen his father's face, and it had been forty years. Maybe he would see it when he completed his task.

"Zhang'er, what is the progress on your task?" Wang Jiang asked.

"Father, the orb has collected nine tenths of the sacrifices, and we should gather enough material to cut open a hole in the formation the next time we obtain sacrifices."

Wang Jiang spoke again from the darkness without showing his face. "Good. We have to cut through before the parent sect finds out about this."

"Father, about the bloodline requirement?"

A chuckle came out of the darkness. “Don’t worry about it. A discarded princess has joined the sect recently. She has what we need. Now go back and continue with your task. We’ll succeeded this time and obtain the treasure.”

“Yes, father.” Bowing deeply, Wang Zhang vanished from the courtyard.

Chapter 20

Taking the audience by storm

Closing his eyes, Li Wei burned a few more blood pearls inside his stomach. After completing his Taiyang of bladder, a water constellation meridian, his healing speed had greatly improved. A wound that normally took him a day to heal could be healed in a quarter of that time, so staying here and helping Chen Du shouldn't be an issue. He didn't want to leave his friend's brother in a difficult position.

So, he firmed his shoes on the paved ground and steeled his resolve. A calm energy rushed through his stomach as he burned the blood pearls, healing his internal wound rapidly. If his normal blood could heal an injury quicker than anyone else, then burning blood pearls quadrupled that speed. It's just that he would need more time to re-condense those blood pearls.

An old man appeared in the shadows around the stone tower that stood erect close to them. Others didn't notice, but Li Wei spotted him with his divine sense. The man stood in the same position great elder Moi had stood for a minute before appearing in front of disciples. Unlike great elder Moi, this man had a deep, unfathomable cultivation. Beyond the peak of Marrow Cleansing Realm. While great elder Moi had layer five Marrow Cleansing Realm cultivation, his aura seemed much weaker than his cultivation. It was evident that he had raised it by depending on the external things.

But the man hiding in the shadows had the aura of a king. Probing the new arrival with his divine sense made Wei felt like brushing his divine sense against a sharp sword edge. Even with the deep experience of his previous life, Wei felt danger from this old man. Although he didn't show it, he might be well into the peak of the Boiling Blood Realm.

However, he seemed to want to hide, so Wei ignored him and focused his attention back on the eccentric great elder Moi. In last few breaths he had stroked his beard so many times that it troubled Wei. A golden five leaf herb was embroidered on his left shoulder, and he smelled like a bunch of herbs smashed together. It was clear that this old man spent most of his time in an alchemy room.

Without making a sound, he glided toward the competition area before anyone noticed him. If someone saw him, they might have thought his feet didn't touch the stone paved ground, but Wei knew the man was using at least a Gold Grade martial movement skill.

This old man was filthy rich, and the storage ring shining on his left index finger screamed it. A mere Marrow Cleansing Realm expert having a storage ring meant he was a bigshot in the Divine Fragrance Palace.

"Great elder Moi, please inspect this Qi Water." Elder Fu bowed, showing no change of expression after the great elder belittled him.

An annoyed look flashed in great elder Moi's eyes before he picked up the beaker. What good acting. That old fogey had stood in the shadows for the last two minutes and watched everything Chen Du did. Yet he pretended to know nothing.

"What's so special about it? It's just little purer Qi Water," great elder Moi said in a disdained voice. He looked pissed.

"Junior Du, can you display the processing method once again?" Elder Fu asked.

"Holy heavens." Chen Du's face turned grim, and he looked around, his fingers tapping on his chest as if he was performing a ritual.

"Insolent brat. Going against an elder's order. Are you refusing to give face to an elder?" Great elder Moi snorted coldly. His attitude was clear. By continuously looking at elder Fu, he made the other person shrunk in guilt.

Wei sighed in his heart. He couldn't guess what this old fogey Moi wanted to do, but Wei wasn't afraid of him, so Chen Du shouldn't be. "Don't worry. Show it to them and slap that old fogey's face." Wei sent a divine transmission.

Chen Du shuddered for a moment upon receiving Wei's message. "Junior dares not disagree. I was shocked because of great elder Moi's arrival. I couldn't find words because of your benevolence, great elder." Chen Du bowed so deeply that he looked like he had a broken back.

Elder Moi's lips curled in a smug smile.

This fogey liked being buttered up, Wei noticed.

Chen Du lifted the third ingredient and a new glass beaker from the stone table and repeated the process with Wei's help. Although Wei thought of blowing up the beaker a couple of times when Chen Du acted muddleheaded, he suppressed his flame and let the process go smoothly. As Chen Du had already showed off, why not let him ride on the tiger's back a little longer?

By this time, everyone had gathered around Chen Du. Other than the cute girl, no one accompanied Wang Fantai. His face held a displeased look, but what could the bastard do?

When the Qi Water formed, it shone with a brighter color than the previous one because Wei had guided Chen Du to a T. The last time, Chen Du had let his beast flame burn some Qi Water, but Wei had made sure it wouldn't happen again.

Elder Fu's face flushed with greed as he poured a few drops of the new Qi Water on a Purity Testing Stone.

A commotion took place when the stone shone more brightly than the previous time.

"Eighty-nine percent. Impossible," Elder Fu exclaimed. "Great elder Moi, please take a look." He handed the old man the glass beaker.

Great elder Moi sniffed the solution, and his eyes shone with a strange light for a moment before switching back to their normal color. "Not bad. But elder Fu, shouldn't we continue with the competition?" he asked in a stern manner, but his tone had softened when compared to how he'd spoken with elder Fu before Chen Du had processed the second set of Qi Water.

"Yes, great elder. Disciple has wasted your time, so let me hasten the process." Elder Fu bowed deeply.

Wang Fantai squeezed the edge of the stone table. What kind of dogshit fortune had Chen Du eaten this morning? How dare Chen Du show off in front of him? Chen Du was an ant from the roadside, and he should remain there.

But when great elder Moi showed up, Wang Fantai grew serious. The Golden Leaf Faction always went against the Black Cauldron Faction, and one of the great elders from this faction showing up meant things were serious. If he lost now, that would bring big trouble.

Although he was panicked in his heart, he showed no ill expression on his face. He was all smiles.

"Junior apprentice brother Fantai, do you feel threatened by that bastard?" Kai Kai moved close to him. Her hair looked like a bird's nest. She had spent the last ten minutes fighting with other girls, and she looked dumb enough to laugh at. But once again, Wang Fantai controlled his emotions and smiled amiably.

"Why would I, senior apprentice sister, Kai? I've received your grace, and I'll crush him in the actual concoction. Look at his beast flame. It's only mid-tier Bronze Grade. Can it go against your beast flame?"

The girl smiled. "That's right. With my beast flame and your alchemy knowledge, you should crush him ten feet deep in the ground. So what, he found some ancient technique to process Qi Water with a fluke. Can he do it with every ingredient? There are three more ingredients, and he ought to fail."

"Senior apprentice sister Kai is right. He is nothing but a frog at the end of the well. I'll trample him and show great elder Moi that I'm the disciple he should look after." He picked up the next ingredient and tossed it into the alchemy cauldron. It was time to show off.

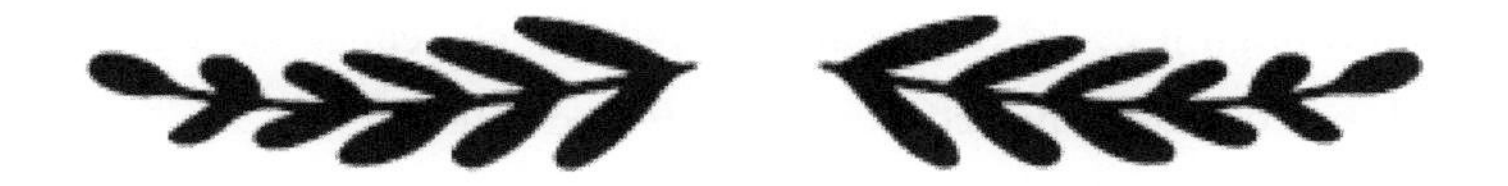

Fu Moi's eyes were glued to the junior Du like he had found his long-lost son. The others didn't understand the significance of what they'd seen, but he and great elder Moi did. What this junior had displayed was beyond their comprehension.

It could change a small part of their destiny.

Qi Water was widely used in numerous recipes, and any corner pharmacist with wood qi could make it. But they could only achieve fifty to sixty percent of purity. While sects achieved better purity thanks to their cultivation arts, they still topped out around seventy percent purity. To achieve more, one needed to use costly methods, and they would fail when one considered the big picture. If one had Gold Grade wood qi, they would also achieve more than seventy percent purity by the normal method, but only a few rare people had Gold Grade wood qi. Like that freakish girl who had entered the sect recently. Fairy Fei.

Thinking about that girl made Fu Moi's heart shiver with excitement.

"Elder Fu, keep an eye on the technique. This will be helpful." Elder Moi whispered lightly so only Fu could hear.

Elder Fu nodded, squinting to watch every single thing junior Du did. This was important to the sect. If they wanted to achieve seventy percent purity, that normally required them to buy Pure Water that cost one Qi Stone per gallon. If they wanted ninety percent purity, they would have to spend five Qi Stones worth of natural treasures on the conversion process. When using it to concoct a pill that had market value of three Qi Stones, no one wanted to use purer Qi Water, even though it could raise rank of a pill. So, alchemists only used high-purity water when concocting high-grade pills.

But people didn't know that every sect made a higher profit in low-grade pill sales as they were available in shops. High-grade pills were only sold in auctions, or to other sects only, and that reduced the profit ratio for the sects.

However, if one sect obtained a simple method of generating ninety percent pure Qi Water without spending too much effort, their pills would be superior in quality, and this would have wider ramifications in the Mortal Realm. That's why he had called great elder Moi as soon as he recognized junior Du's talent, and judging from the expression on great elder Moi's face, Fu Moi knew this had worked.

Now they just had to wait until the competition was over and pull this junior toward the Golden Herb Faction. Then they would have a great means of going against the arrogant Black Cauldron Faction.

So far, this junior Du had proved his usefulness, and he had used a rare method of processing Underground Sun Grass that allowed him to combine three stalks of the grass into one set of powder with increased efficiency, too.

The more he looked at this junior, the more he felt that their fates were entwined. Being the first one to recognize his talent would make Fu Moi's life a lot more comfortable in the Golden Leaf Faction. He could see himself drowning in the well of Qi Stones. The day wasn't far away.

Suddenly, a commotion took place, and a junior collapsed. Fu Moi frowned. This same junior had fought with a woman before the competition started, and now he dared to faint when a great competition was going on?

Insolent bastard.

Chapter 21

Heart Devouring Poison

In a hidden cave inside White Cauldron Mountain—one of the mountain peaks controlled by the Black Cauldron Faction—an old man paced around with his hands behind his back. With every turn, his complexion grew paler. His gaze kept jumping at the brightly lit cave entrance hidden by a concealing formation.

The results should be out now, but they were delayed. The poison he'd gotten from Wang Muxi couldn't fail, so he wasn't worried about it, but he was worried if the shadow twelve could succeed here. What if she failed?

A shadow appeared on the illuminated cave entrance, and then a man clad in black clothes dashed in. A thick black mask that covered everything below his nose hid his expression perfectly.

"Shadow ten greets master Su." The black-clothed man kneeled on the ground and lowered his head in front of Su Pan.

Su Pan's muscles tensed in anticipation. "Report."

"Shadow twelve has completed her mission, and then she detonated herself at the base of the Golden Herb Mountain." Shadow ten's voice held no emotion.

Su Pan gasped. It had been a decade since he'd learned about the Dark Shadow Force under his master Wang Jiang, but they never ceased to amaze him. Each of them was a born killer, and they didn't hesitate to die on command of the Wang clan. They were specially chosen from the youngsters with mutated Spirit Root with wood and ice attribute.

"Good work. Vanish from Fragrance Herb City for two months."

Shadow ten nodded once and then disappeared in a puff of black smoke. It was a strange cultivation method effect they used. It allowed them to vanish in smoke, making it hard to pursue them.

"Elder Su, can this junior ask a question?" Wang Rong stepped out of a side room inside the cave. Master Jiang had sent him to learn from Su Pan. Master Jiang wanted Wang Rong to take care of Dark Shadow Force in the future.

"Pray."

"That brat Li Wei is just Foundation Realm trash. Why did you sacrifice a shadow warrior to poison him? Heart Devouring Poison is costly and overkill for a brat like him. I think we could have used shadow ten to kill him directly and vanish for few months from the city."

Su Pan shook his head in disdain. This brat didn't even grow full hairs on his face, and yet he questioned his methods. How naïve.

"Junior Rong, did you assess your opponent before making this comment?"

Wang Rong shrugged. "What's there to assess? He is just a Foundation Realm cultivator. Even I could kill him in one blow. I saw shadow twelve stabbing him easily."

Su Pan sneered in his heart. "Do you have the confidence to fight with Tiang Fu from the Destiny Mirror Sect with all his trump cards activated?"

Wang Rong shook his head.

"Do you have the confidence to trap and kill a layer one Marrow Cleansing Realm expert from the Destiny Mirror Sect?"

Wang Rong's face turned darker this time before he shook his head in a big no.

"Li Wei did that."

"Impossible," Wang Rong roared. "Someone has given us wrong information."

"Wang Shuang from the Imperial Guard saw it with his own eyes. Don't you trust your own uncle? If you don't, then make a trip to Old Martial City and hear the same thing from other cultivators present at that time."

Wang Rong wiped a line of sweat from his forehead. "How can he be so terrified? Elder Su is right. Please forgive this junior for being rude." He bowed his head slightly.

Su Pan's lips curled upward. Not bad. This junior hadn't become arrogant just because master Jiang chose him to be his successor. Maybe this man would lead the future Wang clan in the right direction. When Su Pan had to choose a side, Wang Rong wasn't a bad option. If he could realize there was always a new heaven behind another, he might survive the upcoming turmoil in the Wang clan.

"You don't have to worry about him anymore. Heart Devouring Poison is a traceless poison that will kill him in ten days, and his death will seem natural. This is all in preparation to tackle great elder Tang Sia. If that woman becomes mad, she will harm the Wang clan by its roots. Don't forget she has support from the sect master. So, prepare hard to thrash Ki Fei."

A bloody dark light flashed in Wang Rong's eyes. "I'll humiliate her and then kill her."

"Take this." Su Pan handed him a messaging talisman. "Contact shadow thirty, and ask her to monitor the princess, Sun Hua. We have orders from the imperial clan to kill her."

Sun Hua had a complex emotions in her heart when she looked at the man lying on a bedroll inside her old courtyard. It was Li Wei. The spiders had vanished from the courtyard, but he hadn't killed them yet. But in broad daylight they didn't frighten her as much they had last night.

A sharp metal knife flashed in her hand as she struck downward, aiming at Li Wei's throat.

She stopped herself an inch above his throat, unable to strike further. She was conflicted, and Li Wei was the reason for her conflict. She hated him in her bones, and if it weren't for her fear of spiders, she would have never, ever asked for his help. All she wanted was to kill him, and now she had the chance. After he fell unconscious at the alchemy competition, his uncle Li Ti had brought him here and then went somewhere to get some herbs, leaving her to look after him. This was the best chance she would have to kill him.

Li Wei lay in front of her, unconscious, defenseless. Just a swipe of her blade, and he would bleed to death.

But Sun Hua felt conflicted because of her sister. Before she came here, elder sister Nuan gave her a bunch of things and asked Sun Hua to give them to Li Wei. In her sister's blue eyes, she didn't find any hatred or anger. Instead, she was at peace. She'd even told Sun Hua that she could rely on big brother Wei. Yes, her elder sister called Li Wei 'big brother Wei.' Her elder sister had never called anyone that. Not even their stepbrothers from the royal palace had this privilege.

But Li Wei had also made her elder sister suffer. He bewitched her to go against the Destiny Mirror Sect, and in the end Nuan had ended up in the palace dungeon. Their mother had become a palace maid, and Hua herself was a fugitive. This guy had destroyed three people's future. He deserved to die.

With determination, she lowered her knife and pushed the tip into his fair skin. A drop of blood oozed out, and he convulsed. His body spasmed violently, his throat moving across her knife. Without her doing anything, his throat pierced itself on her knife.

You can always ask big brother Wei's help. Sun Nuan's words flashed again in her mind, and she pulled back her knife. Finally, she understood the look in her elder sister Nuan's eyes. It was reverence, trust, for big brother Wei.

Hastily, she put the knife back and applied a Body Healing Paste on Li Wei's wound. The wound healed in seconds, so perfectly that no one would know she had pierced his throat.

His body eased, and she stepped back.

"Li Wei. By not killing you, I repay the debt of you not killing me a few days back. This will also settle the debt between you and elder sister Nuan. The next time I won't hesitate to kill you." Turning around, she walked toward the door. She was going to tell great elder Tang about Li Wei's condition and hand her the books sister Nuan had left for Li Wei. As his lover, Tang Sia would help him out of this predicament, and Sun Hua and Li Wei would have everything even between them.

Chapter 22

Desperation

A sharp pain woke Li Wei in the dark of the night. The pain was so intense that he felt like someone sat inside his heart and carved at his flesh with a sharp sword.

He convulsed, and the pain intensified. Rolling his body, he moved over to the ground, but he felt nothing under his back. Pain blocked everything for him. He only knew he was inside his own room, and he could smell a faint hint of dust lingering in the air.

"Aa!" he shouted. This was the worst pain he had felt so far. This was beyond the pain he'd borne when he first absorbed the Soul Stone. If he could, he would have carved his heart out and thrown it away.

A hand grabbed him. Two pairs of eyes looked at him from behind the curtain of dizziness. He was losing it again.

Biting his tongue, he regained consciousness. He might be in danger; he couldn't fall unconscious. But he didn't know he'd been unconscious for hours, and if someone had wanted to kill him, they would have done it already.

As he regained a hint of his self, he sent his divine sense throughout his body, and his eyes turned darker. He'd been poisoned, and it was a nasty one. It had attacked his heart blood, and half of it had vanished.

His own blood battled with the poison, but it was failing miserably. He had seen this before when Li Tang poisoned him, but that poison was nothing compared to the poison now inside his body.

A moonstone lit the room, revealing two faces: Tang Sia and Sun Hua.

"Drink this." A cold thing touched his lips, and a fragrant liquid entered his mouth. It too was poison, but surprisingly, it eased the pain from his heart. The poison inside his heart eased, and the newer poison surged through his body, mixing with his blood.

"Heart Devouring Poison." His eyes turned cold, and he sent a tide of his wood qi surging through his body, destroying the poison he'd just drunk. He wanted to send it to his heart meridian, but it was insufficient to be of any help.

"How do you know about this poison?" Tang Sia asked, her face full of worry. "Do you remember who poisoned you?"

A woman's image flashed in Wei's mind. A woman had attacked him before the competition between Chen Du and Wang Fantai. It was so sudden that he'd only reacted at the end, and that woman managed to injure his stomach.

That bitch. She'd poisoned him.

"I was attacked . . ." He coughed up a mouthful of blood.

"A woman attacked him at the alchemy competition," Sun Hua said. "I knew she'd injured him, but I didn't know there was poison."

"Sun Hua," Tang Sia's voice became cold. "Is this another lie? This time, even your mother's favor won't save you."

Sun Hua crawled backward. "No, it wasn't me. Trust me, great elder Tang. I don't know the girl, but she wore a Waste Disposal Faction robe."

"Why would someone from the Waste Disposal Faction attack him? Then also manage to injure him. This is not simple as it looks."

Tang Sia's voice became heavy. "Li Wei, you've been infected with Heart Devouring Poison, and sadly, there is no antidote. All I can do is to feed you some poison and reduce your pain. But it will eventually kill you."

"Poison for poison?" Sun Hua asked.

Tang Sia sighed, a sigh of regret. "I should have sent you away. I didn't think your enemies would make a move inside the sect." She tapped on his back. "I'll investigate this, but I'm unable to cure you. There is no antidote in the Mortal Realm."

Wei grew solemn as he drank some more of the poison. She was right. There was no antidote to this poison. It was a peculiar poison that affected one's heart blood and sucked it dry. If one loses all their heart blood, they would die. One could only reduce the pain by drinking more poison. But that would be complete suicide.

For the first time since his reincarnation, he had no solution for this issue. All he could do was to wait for the poison to consume all his heart blood.

Desperation struck him hard.

Chapter 23

Ray of hope

When his breathing became ragged and the pain pushed his life to his throat, Li Wei stopped crawling. The sun had risen, and two birds chirped on the ceiling of his room, a sound of warmth and hope. But his life had no hope.

Even his two hundred years of experience didn't provide him with a solution.

"A few more feet." Wei glanced at the stone wall before licking his lips to moisturize them. The sour taste of Green Poisonous Melon still lingered in his mouth. That fruit was awesome when it came to inducing poison in one's bloodstream. At least it had allowed him to crawl for the last ten minutes without his body convulsing under the effect of the Heart Devouring Poison.

Dust floated up, and thin pieces of crushed stones he hadn't cleaned up, pricked his skin through his sky-blue robe as he crawled toward the wall. He couldn't sit in a lotus position without support, so he had to reach the wall to force himself up, and crawling was the only option he had left. He could, of course, shout for Sun Hua, but he would rather not do that. Who knew if she had stabbed his heart with a knife?

Finally, he got close to the wall after some more struggle and made himself sit in a lotus position. This was the first time since waking from his unconscious state that he had a clear consciousness, thanks to the Green Poisonous Melon Li Ti had brought him.

Taking a deep breath, he calmed his mind and pondered his predicament without a solution.

But no, there was a solution. This Heart Blood Poison was ineffective against higher realm experts. If he could reach the Houtian Realm, this would be nothing.

He sighed. It was impossible to reach the Houtian Realm in a short time.

Plus, he couldn't even think of cultivating when he'd suffered so much just from moving from his bedroll to the nearest wall. He was too miserable to do anything.

An Array Master who looked down upon the world had turned into a beggar.

Heart Devouring Poison was a nasty poison. It would eat up one's heart blood, and then the person would die. But for the time he remained alive, he would feel an immense amount of pain. He would much prefer dying in a bloody fight over suffering from poison.

Wei clenched his fingers together. If he survived this, he would feed the nastiest poison pills to these bastards and make sure they would lie inside a poison pool for eternity.

Poison Pills.

"System, access Poison Pill inheritance memories." He sent a command inside his mind.

System: Redirecting some processing power for the host.

A slew of messages appeared first that he had missed before.

System: Host body is in danger. Transferring all processing power to host body analysis.

Wait, this was strange. When Li Tang had poisoned him, the system had instantly alerted him, but this time it hadn't. This last message had come in the late afternoon, hours after he'd suffered the attack from that unknown woman. Had something happened with the system?

System: Reporting to host. Host had set full processing power to Simulation of Blood Essence Body Cultivation Art using Devour Bloodline Cultivation Art. Directing all power to simulation, system had no processing power to monitor host's body.

Wei rolled his eyes. This was new. The system had answered him like a human.

"System, can you talk with me?"

System: No. System can only answer questions related to the system's activity.

Wow!

Then regret swept over him. If he hadn't used the whole system's power to simulate the next realm of Blood Essence Body, it would have alerted him about the poison right away. A single mistake might cause him his life.

He went on reading the remaining messages.

System: Analyzing new substance.

System: Substance is composed of multiple unknown ingredients, but analysis has proved it is poison. Host's internal powers cannot fight against it.

System: Host body has suffered a wound at the throat. Under the rule TQ356, system can take decision when the host's conscious is not active. Activating emergency mode to exude poison from host body.

System: Poison quantity removed 1%... 2%... 3%... 29%

System: Host body's wound is sealed.

The next message was from a half hour later.

System: Poison has entered host's heart and started attacking heart blood. System can not expel the poison. Chances of the host's survival reduced to 29%.

System: Host has lost 45% of heart blood. System will activate hibernation mode at 10% heart blood capacity.

This was insane. Even through the pain, Wei couldn't praise the system's capability of analyzing things enough. His regret doubled, no tripled, in quantity. If only . . .

But there was a peculiar thing. How was his throat cut when he was unconscious? Did someone try to kill him?

Well, whoever it was, they did him a favor. It had allowed the system to force out 29% of the poison, and his survival chances had increased because of that.

Damn, this system was awesome. Without this system, he might have died many times over. This also proved that not everything was lost. There might be a ray of hope after all.

His mind's eye moved to the Poison Pills section of the inheritance from Xue Qi. Maybe there was something there he could use.

After spending an hour going through the information, he sighed in frustration. There was nothing in there. The ray of hope he'd imagined had vanished. Everything had turned as bleak as a dark night.

Rubbing his forehead, he thought about the lost chances in his reincarnated life. Maybe he should have walked out of the State of Zin after waking up in Fei'er's courtyard. When Tang Sia had asked him to join some other sect, he'd refused her, telling her he had to be here. Now that he thought about it, he'd been seriously fucking overconfident. He'd underestimated his enemy.

He'd underestimated many things since his reincarnation. With two of the best cultivations art, he'd thought he would soar through the skies like a calf turning into a dragon. In the end, he was too weak to go against this world.

Damn, he'd even stumbled upon Xue Qi's inheritance, and he'd been looking forward to cultivating a pill clone for himself. There were so many things he wanted to do. And the most frustrating thing? He didn't even eat all the heavenly things he missed out on in his previous life. There was a restaurant that sold heavenly dishes in Fragrance Herb City itself, and he had only heard about it in his previous life.

Fuck! His dream of becoming a lazy immortal was going to vanish like this?

Wait. He remembered something. The Pill Clone Alchemy Art contained many types of pill clones, and one of them was a Poison Pill Clone.

"System, access Pill Clone Alchemy Art."

A vast amount of information floated in front of his mind's eye.

Poison Pill Clone:

Created from various poisons and divine sense, a cultivator can create a Poison Pill Clone. This Poison Pill Clone will help the cultivator while concocting poison pills by controlling the poison. From the initial completion level, the Poison Pill Clone can absorb pill toxin or injected poison from a cultivator's body. Once a cultivator reaches a high level in Pill Clone Alchemy Art, the clone can be separated from the cultivator's body and given a separate life.

Then there were a bunch of requirements for one to cultivate this art. The most difficult requirement was having the divine sense that he already had. The process required him to cut away a portion of his divine sense and use poisons to cultivate a Poison Pill Clone inside his dantian at first. Later, it could be moved to his soul space. In lower levels of this cultivation art, this Poison Pill Clone could help him perform auxiliary actions while creating poison pills, like regulating the amount of poison inserted in the cauldron.

The gist of it was, this alchemy art created two more hands that a cultivator could use to perform many activities in pill concoction. One could have a Flame Pill Clone that would control multiple beast flames or a Wood Pill Clone that would increase the cultivator's control over herbs and let him grow herbs inside his body.

But one could only have one pill clone.

Damn, this was a heaven-defying cultivation art. No wonder Xue Qi was a genius.

However, this was the lifesaving clone for Wei. If he could use the poison inside his body to create the Poison Pill Clone, he would not only get rid of the poison, he would become immune to poison in the future.

"Xue Qi, you're awesome. If you were alive, I'd kiss you to offer my gratitude."

"Human, are you sure you want to kiss a Specter?" A little fox appeared next to him and asked him earnestly.

Chapter 24

Spatial Space?

When the little brown-furred fox appeared in front of him, Li Wei was bewildered. Where did she come from, and how did she find him? Forgetting to close his mouth, he stared at her like a fool.

His back was drenched in sweat. If he wasn't wrong, this little fox had jumped out of his body. Was there a teleportation formation built inside his body that one could use to travel from Ten Beast Valley to his body?

Or it was an illusion, and his body and mind were breaking down to the poison? But how could he explain the familiar fragrance of herbs she exuded; the same one she'd carried with her before?

Pressing his back to the stone wall, he stared at the little fox with the dark brown eyes. He opened his mouth to say something, but nothing came out of his parched and salty mouth.

"Human, why are you sweating? Come, give me some Twisted Vitality Fruit quickly. I'm hungry to my bones, and I'll starve to death if I don't eat something other than Blue Berry Fruit Vines." She scratched her whiskers and yawned before looking around. "What a messy place. Clean this so this princess can sleep in peace. I was stuck in that herb garden for too long."

Wei gasped. "Little fox, is that you?"

The little fox growled, baring her small white teeth. A bout of pain emerged erupted inside him, so he had no time to enjoy her cuteness. Suppressing the pain with his willpower, he pulled a Green Poisonous Melon out and took a big bite.

"Hateful human, why aren't you giving me something to eat?" The little fox leaped at him, opening her mouth wide to take a bite from the Green Poisonous Melon.

"Wait!" he shouted with all his might. "This is poisonous." He regained his senses back with one bite.

"Then why are you eating it?"

"Because I'm suffering from Heart Devouring Poison." He sighed, taking another bite.

"What's that?" The little fox asked innocently.

"It's a killer poison. Never mind." With the pain ebbing, he grabbed a few Fragrant Green Potatoes and placed them in front of the little fox. "Eat these for now. I'll ask someone to get you some Twisted Vitality Fruits later."

The little fox stomped her front paws on the ground and sniffed the fruits. "These are trash fruits. I'll eat some more Blue Berry Fruit Vines instead. Call me when you have the Twisted Vitality Fruits in bulk."

And then she jumped inside his body and vanished.

Damn, what the fuck was going on? How could living things vanish inside his body? Xue Qi was an exception, and she was a Specter? Wait, why did the little fox call Xue Qi a Specter, and what did that mean?

He shook his head. If things started living inside his body without him knowing, he would be in trouble. Big trouble. He had to call her out and check on this.

But how could he call her out?

Scared, he spread his divine sense inside his body, but he found nothing. Nada.

A strong presence spread over his courtyard, and Wei hid his divine sense. An old man with a shriveled look appeared in front of him, exuding a strong aura that almost touched the Houtian Realm. Almost. Maybe he could fight with a Houtian Realm expert, but he wasn't in the Houtian Realm itself. But looking at his face made Wei's mind go numb, and his body shivered.

Wei's divine sense couldn't perceive it, as it was still lacking in power, but he knew one thing. If this man lifted one finger, Wei would die. Just seeing him made his mind go numb, and he had the urge to prostrate and give up everything he had.

"Junior, where is it?"

Wei coughed up some blood, partly due to resisting this old man's fear and part from his own worsening condition.

"Heart Devouring Poison?" The old man frowned and came closer and put his hand on Wei's forehead, sending a stream of wood qi into his body. The wood qi was calm and overbearing. It rushed to his heart and wrapped around the Heart Devouring Poison.

Wei felt the Heart Devouring Poison retreat in fear, but it sealed itself in a green ball and remained in his heart.

"Junior. Eat this." He pulled a lustrous red pill from the air and gave it to Wei.

Without doubting the old man, Wei gulped the pill. If that man wanted to kill him, he didn't need to use this method. He was powerful enough to go anywhere in the Mortal Realm, so Wei did not need to doubt him.

As soon as the pill entered his stomach, a stream of energy rushed throughout his body, removing all the side-effects of the Heart Devouring Poison, and he felt like his body was recovering from a deadly illness. The pill had so much efficacy that his wood qi surged by itself, and he instantly jumped to layer three of the qi Foundation Realm. That was two minor realm jumps.

So, the pill must be . . .

"Senior. This junior thanks you with sincerity for helping me. This junior will remember favor from senior." Wei bowed deeply. This man had really helped him. Although he couldn't wipe out the Heart Devouring Poison from his heart, he had sealed it and, as per his guess, it would take some days for the poison to reactivate. In this time, he could start cultivating the Poison Pill Clone.

The old man had a solemn expression on his face. "You don't have to thank me because I haven't cured you, but I've sealed that poison away for a few days. Unfortunately, in this whole Mortal Realm there are only a few people who can cure it with a poison crystal, and you don't have enough value to make them do it for you."

Wei sighed inside his heart. "Junior knows this. May I know whom senior is looking for? I might be some help."

"I sensed a Spirit Beast in your courtyard just a minute before. Where did it go?"

Wei's heart sunk deep inside his stomach. This old man must have sensed the little fox, but he couldn't give the little fox to this man. First, he wouldn't do that to a friend, and second, even if he wanted to, he didn't know where the little fox went.

"Senior . . ." He didn't know what to say.

Chapter 25

Meeting Chen Du again

Li Wei stared at the old man standing before him, his robe sticking to his sweaty back. Now that the Heart Devouring Poison was temporarily sealed, he understood the immensity of this old man's aura. Despite being a supreme cultivator in his previous life, the threat of death remained true. This old man was more powerful than the mother fox at her peak. Maybe he should give up and tell this old man everything. He was a nice person, after all.

"Where is the Spirit Beast?" The old man's eyes directly pierced into his mind, unraveling his secrets. The pressure became so strong that Wei's shoulders slumped toward the ground.

Wei rubbed the back of his neck, looking around but seeing only his courtyard, full of dust and nothing else. It even smelled damp. He'd thought no powerful person would come to this remote courtyard, but one had already arrived here, just from the scent of the little fox. If he had detected the yin yang source emitting from the hole created by the Yin Sucking Spiders, he might have been in trouble. Nothing was safe inside the Divine Fragrance Palace. If he couldn't create an array to conceal himself from a Houtian Realm expert, then there was no point of searching for a treasure. He couldn't hide anything from this man who was the embodiment of fear. Just thinking about betraying him made Wei feel like he should kill himself over and over.

Wait, what? What was wrong with him? Where did the thought of killing himself come from? He had faced worse situations in his previous life. One time he was poisoned in a secret realm, but he'd survived with his willpower and came out unscathed.

The old man paced around, searching for something, but Wei was lost in his mental fight.

He was better than this. Way better. Although he shouldn't think himself invincible just because he knew a bit of the future, he shouldn't give up on his dream of becoming a lazy immortal either. A person who feared death would never be a lazy immortal. Being lazy meant being free from everything, including death. He wouldn't steer away from his dao because of a powerful person.

Steeling his nerves, Wei straightened, shaking away the fear crowding his mind.

Just now he'd been too afraid to say anything and had wandered into dark thoughts. Being afraid wasn't his dao. So, what if his opponent was stronger than him? Would Wei remain weak for his entire life?

The shift in his thought process brought a change in his mental fortitude. Like a prisoner getting out of the shackles tying him to the wall, his mental bottleneck evaporated, and something wondrous happened inside his mind. A blue flicker emerged from the depth of his soul, and it grew. It was the fighting will, the unbending will that his soul possessed.

His soul literally grew in size, and he could sense it with his divine sense. Wait, even his divine sense grew. Previously, he could only cover a two-hundred-foot area with his divine sense if he used it in a circular radius, but now he could cover a three hundred fifty foot area.

He didn't feel the same oppressive fear from this old man anymore, either. He could raise his eyes and look at the old man's wrinkled face.

The old man's pupils widened, and he looked at Wei with interest. "Not bad, junior. My cultivation method makes everyone fearful, but for a kid like you? Not bad at all."

Wei feigned innocence, like he understood nothing the old man said. "Senior, what is a Spirit Beast?" With his soul advanced, everything became clear, clear enough to touch on the next image of his One Sword Strike. Although he had memories and experience of his previous life, he didn't have a strong soul to carry them at their peak.

System: Host's soul has advanced to a new level. Level unknown with current information stored.

Power source absorption rate has increased to 0.5. The entire power source will be absorbed in six years.

This was a pleasant surprise. For the first time, the system displayed a time period for absorption. If the system had more processing power, his simulations would become faster. Thanks to this old man who'd turned into a whetstone for his soul advancement.

"You really don't know about Spirit Beasts?"

"If senior cares about them, I don't believe I can hide them with my current power, and under the poison's influence I couldn't even walk here." His gaze darted to the crawling path he had left on the dust-covered ground.

The old man followed his gaze and then paced the courtyard, looking for the little fox. But he found nothing.

Tuck! The old man made a weird sound with his tongue. "That makes sense. You'd be long dead if a Spirit Beast came here." And then he turned to leave.

"Senior, may I know your name please?" Wei wasn't sure about this old man's identity, and he had helped Wei a lot, so he should pay back the favor in the future. He was either the sect leader or someone in a similar position. No one from the Martial Realm would come here, anyway.

"A dead man doesn't need to know my name, but if you survive, we might have a fate between us." The old man vanished in the sun, and Wei let go of his breath. A heavy pressure vanished from his heart. Although, with his soul upgrade he could hold his own against the old man's fear inducing aura, he still felt a lot of tiring pressure on his body and soul.

"You look better." Tang Sia's voice woke him up from his trance. "Did you recover?" She was wearing a bright yellow dress today, and it wrapped around her curves perfectly.

Wei shook his head. "Not yet, great elder Tang." He stared into her blue eyes. "Junior has a favor to ask."

"What request? I can't cure you, nor do I know anyone who can." She sounded helpless.

"I want to go into the Sneak Rearing Chamber."

She arched her brow. "What?"

"Great elder Tang, is that a difficult ask?"

"Not at all. I can send you there right away, but why do you want to go there? Do you even know what dangers reside inside that place?" She shook her arms in a heavy declining gesture. "You . . ." She pointed her finger at him. "Are you trying to use poison from inside to suppress your Heart Devouring Poison?"

He shrugged.

"Let me tell you something. It won't work. It will kill you faster. Why are you losing your life a few days earlier just for an elusive hope?"

"Great elder Tang, a cultivator should never give up until their last breath. By cultivating, we are already walking on a path of dao. If I let my death deter me from this path, would I have a face to call myself a cultivator?"

Her face flushed red, but she calmed down the very next moment.

"Great elder Tang, rest assured. I know what I'm doing. If I have a one percent chance of survival, then that's the only place that will provide me that opportunity. Did you forget I survived against Wen Shang?" He had a certain confidence, and it came from Xue Qi's inheritance. There were two requirements to cultivate a Poison Pill Clone, divine sense and lots of poison. Thanks to the mysterious old man, his soul had advanced so he could spare some of his divine sense, and the Snake Rearing Chamber was the best place to get lots of poison.

"But Fei'er . . ."

"Don't worry about her." He pulled a paper out of his storage ring and wrote a small letter to Fei'er. Tang Sia helping him was all for Fei'er, and he couldn't keep depending on her position. He told Fei'er that he was going on an adventure, that she shouldn't search for him for the next few years, and he would come back on his own. "Please give this to her. She may sulk about it, but she won't make things hard for you. She's a good girl."

"She is a good girl." A small smile popped up on her face. "Okay. When do you want to go?"

"Now. But I have a request. Can you give me a Silver Grade bow? And a Crafting Paper?" There was a divine art he knew he could use with bows, Giant Killing Bow Divine Art, and with his lack of usable martial skills and divine arts he wanted to have one more ability in his arsenal. He knew the first three levels of that divine art, and it had seemed promising when he'd first learned it. Fighting with fists or swords was good, and he loved it. But sometimes a situation demanded fighting at a distance, and he had obtained this divine art from Rual'er, the strongest beast archer in his previous life. She was a good girl. If only she hadn't wished to pursue him and ended up hating him in the end.

Wei sighed. He had so many regrets, and he wanted to correct them in this life. So many friends he'd lost, and so many debts he needed to pay. Chen Xiang was one of those friends he owed a lot, and he wanted to repay this debt in this life.

Sighing hard, Tang Sia pulled a small black token, and a sheet of paper from her storage ring and handed it to Wei. "This will do it for you. It also has information on the tasks you need to perform inside. But unfortunately, I don't have a bow, but a special arrow." She then pulled a silver-coated arrow out of her storage ring. "I got this from a friend, but I've no use for it. You can have it."

Wei nodded. "Thank you, great elder Tang. I'll remember your benevolence." It was a pity that he didn't get a bow, but he couldn't do anything about it.

"Just stay alive so I won't have to tell Fairy Fei the bad news." She smiled lightly. "Here are some books Sun Hua left for you before she left the Divine Fragrance Palace. They are for cultivation skills."

Wei furrowed. "She left?"

"I sent her away after someone tried to kill her last night."

"Why would someone attack a princess?"

Tang Sia emitted another hard sigh. "She is not a princess anymore." She explained to him the current situation with Sun Nuan and their mother.

Hearing how Sun Nuan had suffered because of him, a weight settled on his conscience. She suffered because of him, and he didn't like that.

"Great elder Tang, do you know if Sun Nuan is in danger? Please tell me frankly."

"Not entirely, but her situation is not good."

Determination flashed in Wei's eyes. Sun Nuan had helped him a lot, and she was a true friend. And as a friend, he had to help her overcome this predicament. "Thank you for your help, great elder Tang. I'll say goodbye, then."

Tang Sia nodded and turned to leave. Seeing her hunched over back, Wei sensed the weight she carried on her shoulders. The weight of an entire sect. But unlike him, she had no one to share it with.

Well, he too didn't have much of anyone to share his burdens with. But he still had the Li clan, and he had to take care of them. So, before heading toward the Snake Rearing Chamber, he handed a bunch of array diagrams and weapons to Li Ti that he had prepared while recuperating in Fei'er's courtyard. The array diagrams were for old man Wu, who had been living with the Li clan, and the weapons were for Li clan members. He also gave them some money he'd gotten from Wen Shang's pouch, as it could help the Li clan obtain some pills and other stuff from the Divine Fragrance Palace. Any disciple could buy pills at less than market cost, and Li Ti was a disciple now. Of course, Tang Sia had invited him in because of Wei and Fei'er. Nonetheless, Li Ti could manage the Li clan in grandfather's absence.

That was another reason he had to get stronger soon, so he could prevent accidents like his grandfather's.

After settling his affairs, he headed toward the Waste Disposal Building and the tunnel that led to the chamber, but on the way, he saw an old acquaintance. Chen Du was heading toward the Snake

Rearing Chamber too, carrying a big bottle on his back along with his sword.

Chapter 26

Array Adapt Realm

In the Li clan compound in Fragrance Herb City, Wu Xiodia stared at the array of diagrams in his hands. Those harmless black lines made him shudder with excitement, especially the lines written in cursive calligraphy on the next page. This was a high-tier Silver Grade array, Explosive Power Array, that could be carved on any Silver Grade weapon to enable the user to attack with four times the power of his martial skill. This was a highly sought-after array, and only a few sects had it.

Now he had it in his hands, and this diagram would set him on the path of becoming an Array Adapt. One had to carve a low-tier Gold Grade array to become an array adept, but they had to carve a new array given by the Array Master's Guild on the day of examination. And to become an Array Adapt, one had to become an official Three Star Array Apprentice first. When he took the exam to become an Array Apprentice, he only became a One Star Array Apprentice. To become a Two Star Array Apprentice, he had to carve a mid-tier Silver

Grade array. Thanks to master Wei, he could carve a mid-tier Silver Grade array easily now. To become a Three Star Array Apprentice, he had to carve a high-tier Silver Grade array in the examination, and no one had access to these arrays but the sects.

But now he'd had one delivered to him, along with master Wei's comprehension notes written on another parchment.

This was heaven-defying opportunity. Especially the comprehension notes by master Wei. Array cultivators would fight with him if they knew he had these notes.

A tear rolled down his cheek when he read through them.

Dao of Array. It was an elusive condition at the beginning. He had worked his ass off to become an Array Carver, but he had lost all hope of becoming an Array Apprentice in the last few years. It was impossible to get a Silver Grade array without pledging his allegiance to a high power, and doing that would have restricted his freedom. Plus, he would have had to curry favor with that power to gain more array diagrams.

It went against his nature to become someone else's dog. But it was different with master Wei. He was the real deal, and Wu Xiodia wondered what level his array realm had reached. So, when the Li clan moved to Fragrance Herb City, he'd come with them and joined them as a guest elder. With master Wei helping him, Wu Xiodia was confident in becoming an Array Adapt in the near future.

"Elder Wu." Li Ti knocked on his courtyard door.

After master Wei defeated Wen Shang, great elder Tang Sia from the Divine Fragrance Palace had gotten them this large area with a few courtyards, and Wu Xiodia had obtained one for himself.

"Come in."

"Elder Wu, the Divine Fragrance Palace, wants to collaborate with you on array carving. They want your help carving a few more Temperature Sealing Arrays."

"That's fine. Send the cauldrons to my practice chamber, and use fifty percent of the earnings to buy Purple Cream Crystals and Three Layered Inscription Papers from the market. Use half of the remaining for the Li clan and give me the remaining half." Master Wei had told them to buy Purple Cream Crystals and Three Layered Inscription Papers in bulk, so he wanted to help the Li clan do it right.

Li Ti rubbed his nose, his gaze jumping erratically as if he wanted to say something more.

"What's the matter? Speak."

"They want you to carve twenty arrays at the cost of one."

Wu Xiodia squeezed the wooden handle of the array brush in his hand. "Are they insane? Do they treat me like a joke?"

Li Ti lowered his head. "Master Wu, I think it's best to agree. Nephew Wei is injured and has been sent to the Snake Rearing Chamber. I don't think he will come back alive this time."

What a naïve fool. Did he really think master Wei would die just because of some injuries? Did he forget how master Wei had fought with Wen Shang from Destiny Mirror Sect and killed him?

Another elder from the Li clan walked in. "Elder Wu, Ti'er speaks the truth. We can't rely on a seventeen-year-old brat, right?"

Wu Xiodia shook his head in disgust. This was the same clan master Wei wanted desperately to save? After joining the Li clan, he had learned everything about master Wei, and how he'd overcome all odds to come this far in his cultivation. But even after risking his life for the Li clan, these bastards looked down on him.

Why was master Wei trying this hard to save them?

“Tell them I’m doubling the price of array carvings.” He got up and walked toward the inner chamber of his courtyard. “I’m entering closed door seclusion, and no one is to disturb me unless its master Wei.” Without looking at bastard Li Ti, he vanished into his inner chamber and shut the door behind him. This time he wouldn’t leave seclusion until he was confident he could become a Three Star Array Apprentice.

Chapter 27

Sect master's decision

Tang Sia walked into a secret tunnel hidden under the depths of Cloud Severing Mountain where the sect master lived. It led to the sect master's private chamber, and only his personal disciples and some important people had access to it.

A strong fishy smell assaulted her nose when she reached the end of the tunnel, and then she spotted an old man with a hunched back walking out of the sect master's chamber, holding a thin piece of wood cane. The man looked ancient, and no one could count the wrinkles on his face, but he had two powerful brown eyes that could stir fear in his opponent's mind. Stroking his long white beard that reached the Black Marble Stone floor, he stared at Tang Sia with a deep meaning.

"Sia'er greets Ancestor Uncle Wang." Cupping her hands, she pretended to bow.

"Beautiful." His lecherous eyes flashed before he went past her and vanished from her senses. This old man was the Wang clan's ancestor, and he had unfathomable cultivation, only lower to that of the sect master. But he had a loose deposition and loved to flirt with girls that were his great-great-great-granddaughter's age.

He was a bastard in her eyes. She hated people who loved chase skirts, even at his age.

Today he'd surprised her. He'd only said a single word when he saw her. Usually, he would try to take some cheap advantage and she would be pushed in a corner.

Was he in conflict with the sect master?

"That old man, it's getting hard to judge his secrets," the sect master mumbled when she reached the open door.

"Sect master, Sia'er seeks permission to enter." She knocked on the stone door.

"Come in," his furious voice struck her ears, alarming her.

"Master, you called me?" She bowed deeply with respect, unlike her paltry bow for ancestor Wang.

"Sia'er, I'm getting old, so I might have missed some things going around the sect. Tell me more about sect affairs." His snarky voice struck her, and a chill ran through her core. Master was angry with her, and that meant she had missed telling him something important.

But what was that? Ancestor Wang was here, so it had to be about the Wang clan. But what did she miss? The sect had been calm for the last few days, and other than Li Wei's mess there was nothing. As for Li Wei, she had already told her master everything she knew.

Unless . . .

"Master, this disciple acted without thinking." She dropped to her knees. "Please punish this disciple." She bowed her head in shame.

"A vial of Heart Devouring Poison appeared in the sect, and I didn't know about it. How shameful. I think I'm getting old and useless."

"Master, please punish this disciple." She pressed her head on the ground, ready to accept any punishment her master gave her.

"Get up. I won't punish you for a trifling matter like this."

"Master. This disciple will face the wall for fifteen days and meditate on this mistake." She didn't dare get up.

"You should do that."

When she heard the sect master's cold voice, she relaxed. Punishment was normal, and she deserved it, but she didn't like it when the master became distant with her.

Patting her heart in her mind, she got back to her feet. "Master, this disciple is useless. Someone attacked a junior inside the sect and I couldn't protect him. I even let the princess vanish." This was a real regret. If Fairy Fei learned about Li Wei getting poisoned, she might flip out.

The sect master slammed his hand on a stone table, turning it into powder. Power radiated through him that sent a shiver down her bones, skipping her skin.

"The Wang clan is growing impudent, but they have forgotten the immensity of the heavens. After Gatekeepers arrived, Mortal Realm is changed, and one can even find Xiantian in the empires. They dared to collude with the Destiny Mirror Sect just to handle one tiny junior, but they don't know why parent sect haven't sent anyone here in last two years so all their efforts in undermining me would be waste."

Tang Sia's bones froze, and her gaze jutted up to see a stone-cold expression on the sect master's old face. "Master did they really . . ."

"What other way could the Wang clan can get their hands on Heart Devouring Poison and Bone Corroding Poison?" he asked. "The Destiny Mirror Sect is presumptuous to think they can control the State of Zin. We won't allow them. So, what, my sect is little bit weaker in power. If they dare, I can fight until my last breath." His face turned red. "Take my Cloud Soaring Shuttle and visit the Sun clan to warn them. They can't hand over Sun Nuan to the Destiny Mirror Sect at any cost. I've given enough face to them by not meddling in their business when they let Sun Nuan's mother vanish from the capital and put Sun Nuan in the dungeon. Tell them not to push it too hard until it breaks."

"Master, I saw some recent activity around Snake Rearing Chamber. I've sent many disciples to investigate in pretense of giving them punishment, but they didn't find anything suspicious inside."

"Leave it for now. I know they are trying to weaken the array formation, but they don't have any means of doing that."

Tang Sia nodded.

"After you come back, carry out your punishment."

Tang Sia eased up. Punishment was good.

"Did you find any trace of the other Sun girl?"

Tang Sia's face darkened. "No. I've searched everywhere in the sect, but she vanished like she never existed. Even the marker I placed on her vanished into thin air." Sun Hua had vanished the night Li Wei was attacked. When Tang Sia checked on her, she only found a bunch of books and a note for Li Wei. At first, Tang Sia thought Sun Hua had left of her own accord, but then she found traces of a struggle and a patch of blood. No one knew where she'd gone, so it was a big concern for Tang Sia. How could a disciple vanish from inside the sect? Especially a princess who had taken refuge in the sect.

"This is another reason I must save her elder sister from death. I can't let their mother's lineage die in vain." He sighed. "Prevent any news of Li Wei reaching Fairy Fei's ears."

"Master, Li Wei has given me a letter for Fairy Fei." She handed the letter to the sect master.

The sect master's face lit with surprise when he read the letter. "That kid is more mature than I thought." He returned the letter along with a small pipe. "If he wasn't affected by Heart Devouring

Poison, I might have helped him a little, but it's regretful that we met a little late. If his fate is death by poison, then I can't stop it from happening."

"Master, did you meet him?" She placed the small gray pipe in her storage ring. It was Cloud Soaring Shuttle, a magic artifact that would allow her to fly. It was precious and a rare artifact.

He nodded. "I've suppressed his poison, but he won't live past a month."

"I doubt he will live that long. He requested to go to the Snake Rearing Chamber, and he might not make it out of there."

The sect master sighed regretfully.

Bowing once again, she left his chamber and headed to her own mountain peak. She had tons of preparation to do before she visited Bloodshed City. It had been years since she'd visited it, and she wondered if that man was still doing well.

The moment that thought appeared, she shook it away and steeled her heart. Relationship was a futile word, and she was better off focusing on cultivation rather than a man who had betrayed her. She had already gotten rid of the arrow that reminded her of that man, and now she had no connection with him. Whatsoever.

Chapter 28

Snake Rearing Chamber

The dark tunnel led into a deserted mountain devoid of any life. A deathly aura floated out of the ground, covered with black charred soil. Decades of poisoning, if not centuries, had turned the soil into a death trap.

Two men crossed the soil and stepped on a road paved in marble, every inch of it showing signs of corrosion and cracks. One of the men, Chen Du, had a gloomy face, and his gaze jumped all over the place. The other, Li Wei, walked with a bright face and lots of hope.

They had yet to reach their destination, but Wei could already sense the poison radiating in the air, corroding his skin little by little. It was a subtle effect, and he would have missed it without his divine sense as his skin repaired itself quickly.

"Junior apprentice brother Wei, once we go in, don't step off the road," Chen Du said in a heavy tone. "I hope the air inside the room doesn't taste like rotten fruit." He made a weird face that looked funny with his brutish build.

Wei nodded, and they continued. In the last ten minutes, Wei had heard Chen Du's side of the story. He'd said that because of some issues he couldn't complete the competition and lost his duel with Wang Fantai. So, he was sent here for the next thirty days. But elder Fu had made a concession. After Chen Du detailed the Qi Water refinement technique for him, he'd given him some better-quality Poison Repelling Pills.

Wei could guess what had happened, and he didn't like letting down an old benefactor. But what could he do?

Hardened blocks of black soil cracked under their leather shoes as they entered another dark tunnel. The air had turned foul, and the system had shared a warning with Wei that the air pollution was too high for normal breathing. The air only provided 44% of the essential particles for his lungs to operate, and it was poisonous.

Well, he didn't care about poison as long as the Heart Devouring Poison remained sealed up. And once he completed the pre-requisite for the Poison Pill Clone, he would get rid of it completely. There were two requirements to initiate the Poison Pill Clone. First, he had to reach layer one of the qi Foundation Realm. Second, he had to reach early completion of level one of the Pill Clone Alchemy Art.

Unlike his qi and body cultivation art, Pill Clone Alchemy Art had multiple levels and four sub-levels called completion levels. They were similar to martial skills and had early, mid, late, and peak completion levels.

At the end of the second tunnel, a man with a cauldron symbol on his robe stopped them and checked their disciple tokens. A black patch covered one eye, making him look more like an evil pirate than an elder.

With his one eye, the man scanned them thoroughly. "Juniors. Don't go near the array formation for a long period. Water the boundary trees and head back to the hut," he said, "The hut is the only place you can survive, so remain there as much as possible." He scratched his balls. "One more thing. Don't look in those nasty motherfucker snake's eyes. You'll lose your sight if you do." He lifted his eye patch, and a pitch-dark black eye stared at them.

Chen Du stepped backward while Wei gasped. It was like looking into an unending abyss that could wipe out their soul within a second.

"Junior will listen to elder." Chen Du bowed and turned away. With his action he made clear he didn't want to dilly dally talking with this terrifying elder, so Wei followed him through the tunnel's end.

The elder called after them. "Wait, take these Poison Repelling Pills. This should be enough for a week. Come back to get more. That way I can check your condition. Also, I'll keep the door open for the next two hours, so you can come back and ask if you need something. After that, the seal will open only after seven days. After twenty days, you can take a break, and I'll come myself to water the plants."

"Junior understands," Wei said. After reluctantly bowing to the elder once more, they headed through the door.

A thin film of energy wrapped around them when they walked out of the second tunnel. It was a new world in itself. This wasn't a secret realm, but a pocket realm, a place much smaller than a whole secret realm. The end of the tunnel was a rift in the void that led them here. The Mortal Realm had many such entrances to different secret realms, and Wei knew a few of them.

"How is this possible?" Chen Du stepped backward. "This is different from I thought."

Wei first saw a road made up from cracked black marble, and then he saw a large withered wooden hut that wouldn't even save one from a heavy downpour. It was quite large, and specious and a couple miles away from the entrance. Looking around, he sensed the immensity of the pocket realm. No, it wasn't a pocket realm, but a secret realm itself. They could only access a U-shaped area from the secret realm door, and the boundaries of the area were sealed by an array formation.

A line of white trees stood guard behind the array formation as if to prevent humans from going to other side.

"So many snakes." Chen Du cried, his body shaking.

A continuous rustling sound bombarded their ears, and Wei saw hundreds of snakes lurking behind the line of white trees. There were hundreds, if not thousands, of snakes roaming around the medicinal plants scattered in the plain field. Plain, at least, compared to the unending thick forest a few miles beyond the open field. Maybe the open plain would be better called a thin layer of forest.

At a distance he saw a lone mountain, but it was miles away, so he could only make out a silhouette of it.

When he moved closer to the array formation, he saw something astonishing.

The white trees were part of the array formation, and they prevented anyone from crossing the line of trees. A few energy pockets were created next to a few white trees that had Qi Crystals lined inside that acted as the energy source for the array formation.

So, first he had a road, surrounded by an array formation, then a line of white trees, and then an open field with medicinal plants scattered and hundreds—if not thousands—of snakes roaming around those medicinal trees, and then the forest started.

It was as if humans began encroaching in this realm, and someone set up an array formation to stop them. Yes, it felt like this instead of the other way around.

"These are White Bone Trees." Wei moved closer to the branchless, leafless white trees, but an invisible energy barrier obstructed his divine sense, so he remained on the edge of the black marble paved road.

Then he saw blood. Patches of red glittered on the backside of the White Bone Trees, like a massacre had occurred recently, but someone had cleaned up the corpses. The blood looked fresh, and Wei couldn't guess whose it was.

"This is—" Chen Du grabbed his throat and turned away.

Wei sighed. This brute seemed soft inside. Just the sight of blood made him retreat.

Squatting down, Wei scanned the jade boxed circles around each tree. An extra energy barrier protected the Qi Crystals that powered up the array formation. Qi Crystals were a higher type of currency than Qi Stones, and one Qi Crystal could be traded for hundred high quality Qi Stones. The thing was, the Mortal Realm didn't have Qi Crystals, so someone from the Martial Realm had set up this array formation. And by looking at the arrangement of the trees and Qi Crystals, it was a Devil Suppressing Array Formation. The White Bone Trees were demon trees that could only be found in a demon region, and these trees restrained their powers. Planting these trees at the source points, someone had created a perfect Devil Suppressing Array Formation, an Earth Grade array formation.

But why would a tiny sect in the Mortal Realm need a Devil Suppression Array Formation in a pocket realm? Couldn't they just ask someone to destroy the entrance?

"Every day, this array formation will open up, and we have to water these plants," Chen Du muttered. His face was pale, and he avoided looking at the ground. Instead, he looked into the distance where the medicinal plants grew in a huge number. "I can't believe there is a Five Petal Life Herb present here as well."

"Why is it called the Snake Rearing Chamber then?" Wei stared at the medicinal fields, unable to gauge the mystery behind this place. From a glance, he could identify a few rare herbs. There was a Red

Foul Heart Berry as well. It could increase one's healing potential, but at the expense of one's heart blood. It could even kill a Heart Blood Realm cultivator. Well, Wei wasn't foolish enough to eat it as his heart blood was more precious than his blood pearls.

"Because there are millions of snakes hiding in these fields, and when the array formation is opened slightly, their poisonous breaths overwhelm the whole area. We can only eat Poison Repelling Pills and water these plants," Chen Du said. "The task scroll said this."

"What else was mentioned in that scroll?"

"Every twenty days, the snakes go crazy and attack the array formation, so we have to water the trees and prevent it from shattering."

"Is that why the blood is splattered everywhere?"

"The scroll also said that sometimes a few snakes can escape through the cracks in the formation, and that would be our end if we are not careful enough."

Wei arched his brows. "It's just a snake. What can they do to us?" He probed for more information. Although this place had poisonous air, he needed real poison to form his Poison Pill Clone. He might need to get those snakes to bite him, or extract poison from them some other way.

"The weakest snake is in layer one of the Foundation Realm, and there is a rumor that there are snakes here which are in the Marrow Cleansing Realm as well."

"Interesting." Wei sneered. "Senior apprentice brother Chen, do you know why we have to water these plants? It's obvious that we can't go in and water those herbs. Do seniors from the sect visit to gather herbs sometime?"

Chen Du shrugged. "I don't know, but I know one thing. No one can get through the array formation. Those medicinal plants are like beauties we can only look upon and not touch."

Wei chuckled. This brute had described his previous life perfectly. Wang Zia, his previous life's goal, was like this. He could only look upon her, not touch.

"One of the seniors once told me that this place was an herb garden for our sect a thousand years ago, but then something happened, and a snake Spirit Beast emerged from the end of this place, and all the snakes charged out of this place. The Divine Fragrance Palace was almost wiped out that year, but some unfathomable expert came and set up this ancient array formation, sealing those snakes. From then on, our sect has followed this practice of watering these plants daily for unknown years. And we don't water them with normal water. Instead, we use Qi Water that we prepare daily. That's why we, alchemy cultivators, are sent inside this ghostly place."

This confused Wei further. Although the White Bone Trees were on the other side of the array formation, the water they poured would still reach the roots from underground. But doing that would weaken them, and in decades—if not centuries—they would collapse. White Bone Trees hated water, so it was a sure-shot way to weaken them. Then why were they weakening the White Bone Trees?

If they wanted to strengthen the array, they needed to replace the Qi Crystals with better quality ones.

And an ancient array? What a joke. Wei chuckled inwardly. This was a trash array in his eyes, and he had spotted ten glaring mistakes in one glance. If the array carver hadn't skimped on the quality of the Qi Crystals, no one could break this formation.

"We should relieve the two junior apprentice brothers living in the hut." Chen Du pointed at the hut built at the end of the road. It was big enough for a party of ten to live peacefully.

Wei frowned, realizing a glaring mistake in his preparation. If he had to create Qi Water and poison pills by himself, he needed a beast flame, and he had nada. In his plan of survival, this was a fatal flaw.

Chapter 29

Fox's Breath

Things went awkwardly when Li Wei and Chen Du met the junior apprentice brothers they had to relieve from duty. Those two poor souls shone like the morning sun after a dark night when they saw Chen Du and Li Wei. Those two senior apprentice brothers wanted to leave right away.

Looking at their skeletons in human skin condition, Wei frowned. A deep frown. Those two had lived in the chamber for twenty-one days, and they were barely making it with rationed dry food and Poison Repelling Pills. Their skins had turned char black, and their bodies showed high necrotic damage.

That was kind of depressing. Wei didn't think their conditions would be this bad.

This place had affected their body's vitality, and if not given a good amount of health replenishing elixirs, they might not survive for long.

Wei handed them two Fragrant Green Potatoes, and they left with joyful smiles. Maybe it was their first sweet in many days. Seeing them dragging their feet toward the tunnel entrance under the bright light from an unknown light source, Wei wondered if the Divine Fragrance Palace treated their sect disciples good enough for him to join this sect.

"This place looks more frightening than I thought." Chen Du gasped, his eyes flashing with horror. "Those two were punished for some crime, and I bet they won't repeat that crime ever." He shivered.

"Senior apprentice brother Du, they faced direct poison breath from a snake. That's why they look like dead people. If we're careful, then we don't have to worry about this," Wei answered, staring at the medicinal field. The previous caretakers had watered the White Bone Trees for the day, so Wei and Chen Du had ample time to prepare for the next day. But one problem still remained: he needed a beast flame.

"Yes, that should be it." Chen Du tapped on his chest over his gray disciple robe. "Holy heavens." It seemed like a ritual for him. "Junior apprentice brother, let's drink some tea my girlfriend prepared first, and then we can hand over our asses to this poison." He set down the big bottle he carried on his back. At the glance, it looked like it could store at least a few liters of water. "Chi'er has prepared more than enough for both of us, but given the poison air kicking its ass, we'd better drink it quick."

"Tea?" Wei asked, surprised and shocked. How could this brute use two totally different words in one sentence? Tea was like heaven, and he'd used it in the same sentence with ass. Damn this unruly brute. Wei wanted to smack his head until he fainted.

"Yes, Chi'er loves making tea. She even has many books with her. Look, she gave me one too." He pulled a thick brown book from his clothes and showed it to Wei.

"Senior apprentice brother Du, as we have some time," Wei glanced at the book and then said. "I'll make a trip outside and come back."

Chen Du's brow furrowed. "Junior apprentice brother Wei, why do you want to go out? Afraid already? Don't bail on me."

Wei smiled sheepishly. "No, I'll come back. I don't have a beast flame, and I need to grab one for myself."

Chen Du rolled his eyes. "How did you enter the sect without a beast flame? Or did you lose it after joining?" he asked.

Wei rubbed the back of his neck. "I entered through a back door. Anyway, I'll be back in a jiffy." Li Ti had told him that every disciple could get a beast flame, and he intended to do that. Then he also needed an excuse to collect his blood. After getting poisoned, he was collecting his own blood as it had a hint of the poison in. That would be useful in future.

"So, you haven't even collected your disciple token yet?"

Wei's neck jutted up. "How do you know that?" Although he got his template from Tang Sia, technically he hadn't got it from official channels.

Chen Du chuckled, his broad frame shaking. "If you had, then you'd have received a beast flame for yourself. The sect gives one along with the disciple token. So, you're still not a full disciple of the sect, and yet you're sent here. How hateful."

Wei nodded. Indeed, he wasn't a disciple yet.

"First drink this tea, and then I'll give you something."

Wei nodded and lifted a glass. It was a nice tea, a soul-calming tea. After half an hour, they finished half of the tea in the bottle.

"I hate to waste it." Chen Du stared at the half-filled bottle, and then threw it away.

"Then don't." Smiling Wei grabbed the bottle and threw it inside his storage ring without Chen Du noticing anything.

"Take this." Chen Du flicked his left hand, and a docile yellow fire floated on his palm.

"Senior apprentice brother. This . . ."

"Just take it. It was given to me by the sect, and if you go to the Administrative Hall, they will give you a similar low-tier Bronze Grade beast flame. This will be better than that because it was refined by me."

Wei's mood cheered. This was an unexpected gain. As for the low tier of the beast flame, he would find a new one once he saved his life. This flame should be enough for him to reach early completion of the Pill Clone Alchemy Art.

"Then I won't be courteous, senior apprentice brother Du." He extended his palm, and that fire jumped on his palm. As soon as the flame touched his arm, he felt a distinct connection with it. Refining a beast flame was an easier job after it was taken out of the beast's core, and having been tamed twice—first by the sect and then by Chen Du—it acted docile and accepted Wei as its new master.

System: A new organization detected. It has host's imprint on it.

Quickly, Wei sat cross legged and revolved his pure qi as per Pill Clone Alchemy Art. It had a method to refine a beast flame, and it was quite easy. In ten minutes, he had refined the flame, and it entered his palm and shot toward his dantian. Soon, a tiny fox lay next to the pool of pure qi.

"This flame is?"

"It's Fox's Breath. A common low-tier beast flame. It's low maintenance and obeys your commands easily. If you continue nourishing it with your wood qi, it will grow and may become more powerful than a mid-tier Bronze Grade beast flame."

Nodding, Wei took out a metal alchemy furnace from his storage ring. Before walking into the sect, he had brought this cheap furnace from a roadside shop to hide his Gold Grade cauldron. Furnaces and cauldrons were used for the same purpose, but anything of the lowest quality and crude was called a furnace, while exquisite things were called cauldrons. A high-grade cauldron could have many good things, like array carvings, inscriptions, and built-in heat sources. Furnaces were used for roasting anything and everything.

At his wish, his beast flame jumped to the bottom of the furnace and started heating the metal base. Soon the metal turned bright red, and the temperature reached one hundred forty degrees. A charred smell shot out of the furnace, and when he poured some water into it, it instantly reached boiling temperature.

"Good furnace." Chuckling, Wei commanded the beast flame to reduce its intensity. With his divine sense wrapped around the beast flame, it was easier to control the flame, and soon he got the furnace temperature down to seventy degrees and maintained it for three minutes. "This is a good flame. I like it."

Today, he planned to reach early completion of the Pill Clone Alchemy Art, and for that he had to vaporize a bowl of water in one breath's time. Xue Qi's inheritance had the cultivation art along with some tips to achieve that, and he was following them.

It was time to make the water go poof. After changing the water, he started fresh and continuously increased the heat, but when he reached one hundred eighty degrees of temperature, his beast flame stopped responding.

Why did it stop responding?

He commanded it to reduce the heat, and the beast flame weakened a little.

Once again, he increased the heat, but the beast flame turned stubborn after the temperature hit one hundred eighty degrees. There was a hard ceiling for temperature, and this wasn't enough for the water to vaporize in one breath. But the fire only achieved one hundred eighty degrees max, and no matter how much he cursed or shouted it wouldn't go beyond that.

Fifteen minutes later, he gave up as the beast flame in his hand grew weaker. Now he had to wait a while until it replenished itself in his dantian.

With his thumb, he wiped sweat from his forehead. This was exhausting.

"Are you practicing the Nine Lotus Alchemy Art?" Chen Du sat on a wooden chair someone had placed outside of the hut. There was a large barrel filled with Pure Water behind Chen Du, and they had to convert it into Qi Water. Wei was going to use it to train his Pill Clone Alchemy Art. But before that, he had to initiate the Pill Clone Alchemy Art.

"Sort of. But this beast flame is too weak to achieve any fire control."

Chen Du shook his head. "You should start with wood qi control. For us alchemists, wood qi is the most important thing. Fire control is important, but not as much as wood qi control. The herbs we use react to wood qi, and the more wood qi you pour into your herbs, the better quality pill you will concoct."

Wei frowned. "Senior apprentice brother Du, does herb quality improve if we pour wood qi in them?"

"Yes. It does to a certain degree. It plays an important part in deciding the rank of our pill."

Wei had a revelation. "So, if I pour my qi into my beast flame, I can achieve a higher temperature."

Chen Du nodded.

Wei couldn't help from smacking his own forehead. Why hadn't he thought of this? It was all because of his array cultivation process. In array carving, pouring more qi into the array diagram could damage it. One had to have fine control over the qi, and he was thinking of alchemy the same way.

Suppressing a smile, he sat in a lotus position and recovered his condition by slowly revolving his qi through the foundation qi path. As he had already used his Essence Burning Art, he would need twice the amount of qi to break through to the next layer, so he only focused on getting to his peak condition.

Half an hour later, he once again started heating a bowl of water, but this time his beast flame roared like a tiger and wrapped around the furnace, vaporizing the fire in an instant.

"Arr, what are you doing?" Chen Du furrowed. "Your fire should never touch the sides of the furnace. It can damage the herbs that are floating in the upper part of the furnace."

Wei licked his lips. It sounded reasonable, so he reduced the flow of pure qi in the beast flame, but then the temperature dropped drastically.

"Junior apprentice brother Wei, what are you trying to do?"

"I have to vaporize this water in a breath's time."

"This won't work. Only a low-tier Silver Grade beast flame will have enough explosiveness to do this job. If people could pour an unlimited amount of qi into their beast flames, why would anyone search for higher grade beast flames? Do you think no one thought about this before, that they all failed because you can only achieve a max temperature of two hundred degrees with a low-tier Bronze Grade beast flame?"

"What if I use a higher grade furnace?" Wei asked.

"The issue is with your process. Even a higher grade furnace would fail if your fire source reaches the upper sides. You can't let your fire touch the sides at any cost."

Stopping, Wei stared at the furnace. Chen Du was right. Even if he used his Gold Grade furnace, his fire would touch the sides and ruin his pill. This issue could only be solved using a high grade beast flame.

Or he could make the upper side of the furnace reject the extra heat by using arrays. Carving a Heat Proofing Array on the upper side would stop the furnace from going kaboom.

But that would be cheating.

Cheating wouldn't help him reach early completion of Pill Clone Alchemy Art level one.

Damn, why was this so hard?

"What a trash flame. Human, did you kill a lower-level sibling of mine to get that flame?" A little fox jumped on his shoulder and peeked at the yellow flame flickering on Wei's hand.

Chen Du fumbled and dropped on his ass. "Holy heavens, did that fox just talk?"

"Are you trying to get me killed?" Wei sent a divine transmission. If she talked in front of others, he would be in big trouble, and she would be in a big-big trouble.

"Oh, you know how to use mind transmission? Why was I wasting my energy on talking?" A message came back, and the little fox rolled her eyes while scratching her whiskers. "It's so tiring you know."

"It's called divine transmission." Wei sent. "I almost forget Spirit Beasts are born with a powerful soul and divine sense. Little fox, talk like this if you don't want people hunting you."

"Human, if you give me some Twisted Vitality Fruits, I'll upgrade that flame for you."

This time Wei stumbled backward. "Can you really do that?" he shouted.

Chen Du stumbled backward. "Junior apprentice brother, what's going on? Why are you shouting at me?" He pulled his sword out and held it in front of him from his seated position.

"Of course, I can. Don't you trust me?" the little fox answered through divine transmission.

"Senior apprentice brother, it was me talking in a woman's voice." Wei jumped to his feet and picked the little fox up too. "This is my pet.

Isn't it cute?" He rubbed his cheeks on her head, and she beared her fangs at him, scratching his face red.

"Let's do this. I'll give you ten Twisted Vitality Fruits daily if you upgrade the flame to Silver Grade." Wei smirked. This was going to be fun.

Chapter 30

Finding a human body

A black body floated above Alchemy Ascension Peak where multiple humans moved around. A few days ago, the black body had received a creator's command and the divine power to kill a human—a human it could now sense when it closed its eyes. It didn't know why it could sense the human. It only knew it had to kill that human. But when it looked at the humans below, it understood that it had to grow stronger to kill the target human. It didn't know why, but a desire arose in its soul to grow stronger quickly.

For the next few days, the black body grew stronger by devouring animals around the target's scent. It even gave itself a name: Creator's Command Soul Devourer. It was its first ability, and the strongest one.

However, though it grew stronger by devouring souls, no matter what it did, it couldn't reach the power level of the target. Whenever it tried to reach its target, it felt dread inside its soul and backed off.

One day, it suddenly stopped sensing its target. The human had vanished like it had moved away from this place. They called it the

Mortal Realm. It found this basic information in one of the special animal souls it devoured. It also realized it needed a strong body to carry out its order of killing the human.

One day, it found a human body to possess after it devoured its hundredth soul. From its birth, it knew its own abilities, and soul devouring and soul possession were among them. The stronger it grew, the more abilities it gained. When the divine light birthed it, it could only devour souls, but now it knew it could possess them, so that's what it did.

The human Creator's Command Soul Devourer chose to possess struggled manically, but faced with the creator's power, the human failed and Creator's Command Soul Devourer took control of the human's body. Others called this human Wang Fantai. It was a nice body, and it had many friends. Friends it could continue to devour. But it also knew it couldn't devour everyone, as that would raise suspicion in other humans.

Using the new human body, it tried searching for the target. However, it didn't have any information on the target yet. But Creator's Command Soul Devourer would wait. It had nothing but time. It only had one desire: to obey the divine command imbued in its mind at the time of its birth.

But with its human body, it gained memories and a nasty thing called emotion. It hated its name now, so it renamed itself Soul Devourer Demon. It sounded manly.

Chapter 31

Xue Qi's real identity

After an hour of mumbling and fumbling, Chen Du lifted the bucket filled with Qi Water and vanished down the paved road that went through the two medicinal fields. The Qi Crystals flickered, and he started pouring one bowl of Qi Water on the White Bone Tree base. Seeing Chen Du's terrified expression, Li Wei decided to fix this array before going back. He didn't like the way Divine Fragrance Palace handled this thing, exposing people to poison.

Once Chen Du vanished, Wei conjured the beast fire in his palm. It was time to upgrade it. Observing the yellowing ball of fire exuding a warm current throughout his arm, he felt ecstatic. He'd been waiting for this moment ever since the little fox told him she could upgrade the beast fire the previous evening.

Walking around the small hut under the bright light that hadn't changed for the last sixteen hours, he searched for the little fox that had vanished fourteen hours back with his comfy and thick bed roll.

She had literally hijacked his bedroll under the pretense of a young fox lady needing privacy and pampering.

When she did that, he was like, what the fuck was going on? And what privacy? She practically went around naked everywhere. He'd had to sleep on the ragged old bedroll he'd carried since his Old Martial City days, which hadn't been all that restful, and the always-on daylight made him exhausted mentally on top of that. At least the bedroll had reminded him of his good old carefree days. Having no cultivation was good sometimes. Instead of poisoning or random attacks, he'd only had to suffer his stepfather's kicks and punches.

Wei wondered how Li Sua had made his breakthroughs. A few days ago, he'd gone to his grandfather's grave and saw Li Sua there. The bastard had broken into the Marrow Cleansing Realm and had a pure Bone Manifestation that could produce bone wings.

Anyway, he soon heard snoring and found his target.

Seeing the little fox sprawled on his bright white bedroll, he had the urge to kick her hard. Her dirty paws had left prints everywhere, and if Fei'er was here she would be pissed off. She hated dirty things.

After five minutes of cursing and luring her with fruit, she finally got up.

"Little fox, if you upgrade this, these ten Twisted Vitality Fruits are yours." Wei placed ten tiny red fruits that had thick vines going from their stalks on the rough wooden bench that told a story of hundreds of years of wear and tear in its scratched lines.

"Wow." Walking closer to the bench, she sniffed the thick vines exuding the fragrance of vitality. A greedy look flashed through her eyes as she scratched her whiskers.

Heaven knows what she liked so much about those fruits. They tasted like any normal fruit out there, a bit sweet and a bit sour.

"Little fire, come in." The fire jumped in her mouth like an obedient child, leaving Wei bewildered. No, it was like a kid running toward candy, or in Chen Du's words, a boy running toward a jade beauty. That guy, half of his jokes lingered on the border of shamelessness. He wondered how he'd gotten a girlfriend with that kind of attitude. Yes, that average-faced voluptuous woman Wei had seen with him was his girlfriend Chen Chi. That guy had followed her into the Divine Fragrance Palace.

Well, he couldn't fault their looks. They, in fact, matched each other in ugliness . . . sorry, averageness.

The little fox burped after two breaths, and with her burp a bright yellow flame shot out. When it landed on Wei's palm, he could feel it moaning inside his soul. Being his beast flame, he had an innate bond with the flame, and he could sense its mood. Right now, the beast flame was more than ecstatic. It was moaning like it'd just had an intense . . .

"What did you do with it?" he asked, staring blankly at the beast flame.

"I let it devour a bit of my own innate flame." She gulped one fruit and sprawled on the stone bench, staring at the rest. "These fruits are a blessing of the heavens, and I'd trade them any day for a Dragon Healing Wood."

Wei stopped looking at the beast flame. "Did you say you let this flame devour some of your innate flame?" Many beasts developed innate flames inside their beast core, and those could be extracted as a beast flame. But once extracted, the beast would die.

She nodded.

"Are you crazy? Why are you harming your life source?" He paced around, rubbing his forehead. A beast core was the life source of a beast, and beast flame was birthed inside the beast core. Damaging a beast flame was like damaging a beast's life source. If he had known what she intended to do, he wouldn't have let it happen.

Wei's face fell as he realized he had broken the mother fox's trust. "Miss Jiya. I don't know why or how you followed me, but your mother has trusted me to take care of you. By doing this you've made me break that trust." The little fox had offered him some Seven Tailed Fox's Blood Essence, and by doing so she had formed a bond with him. A bond of friendship, a bond of companionship, and he always took care of his friends. But now he had harmed her beast core, and this put him in a bad mood. A very bad mood.

"It's just a beast core. Why are you making a fuss about it? I'll recover once I meditate in front of the Flame Dragon Tattoo inside that palace."

"What nonsense are you talking about?"

She gulped another fruit and moaned like she had touched the heavens. "Don't disturb me. Let me relax."

With one swipe, he stored the remaining Twisted Vitality Fruits away.

"Human, what is the meaning of this? We had a deal." She bore her fangs and swiped them in the air, glaring at him.

Wei took a long breath, calming his nerves. "Miss Jiya. If you want to work with me, we have to clear up a few things. First, tell me where you are living inside my body, and what nonsense are you talking about?"

She touched her whiskers. "What do you mean, where? I'm living inside the Specter's spirit artifact."

"What Specter?"

"Lord Xue Qi. Did you already forget her?"

He shook his head. "What is a Specter?"

She shrugged. "You're too young to know such things. Xue Qi is a Specter."

Wei rolled his eyes. She didn't know what a Specter was either. How cute. "When you said you can heal your innate flame, did you speak the truth?"

She rolled her eyes. "Of course. Why would I waste my innate flame on you otherwise? There's a place inside the spirit artifact that is helpful to me. I've already used it and benefited."

Calm permeated Wei's heart. If she could heal the damage, then it was fine. "But how did you end up with her?" When he'd left the valley, the mother fox had said nothing about this.

"I don't know." She rubbed her nose. "When you left, she asked me to live inside her spirit artifact and cultivate. At first, I was locked in a room and couldn't visit any other place. But some days ago, the seal vanished and I could move around freely."

Wei gasped. The Alchemy Comprehension Tower was a spirit artifact and had a separate space, but he didn't think Xue Qi had one as well. "What kind of places are there?"

"There's a palace, but most of the rooms are locked. Outside, there's a medicinal garden, an alchemy room, and a storage room. But I can only access a couple of rooms and the medicinal garden. All the fruits in there are trash. They taste so weird. There are so many large trees that looked weird. One even looked like a dragon and scared the shit out of me."

A tremor passed through Wei's mind. A medicinal garden? No wonder Xue Qi had taken the Three Leaf Asoka Tree when they found it. She must've taken it inside the spirit artifact.

Suddenly, things made sense. A spirit artifact could be stored inside one's soul, and now he realized why he couldn't find it at all. Xue Qi was using his unborn soul space to store that artifact. After she died, the seals inside the artifacts started vanishing. Although he hadn't conjured a manifested soul space, it still existed around his soul, he just couldn't access it.

"Did you see a brown-colored dragon-shaped wood, or a gray-colored dragon-shaped wood inside that medicinal garden?" His heart started racing. Dragon-shaped trees were few, and he knew of two of them.

"I won't tell you."

"Come on, you need to explain things or you can forget about these." He displayed tens of Vitality Twisting Fruits on his palm.

Drool leaked from her mouth when she saw those fruits. "If you give me ten, I'll answer your question."

He handed ten fruits to her. These were common fruits, and he had barrels full of them inside his storage ring.

"Brown. There were ten of them, but I burned them to light a fire."

Wei dropped on his ass and frothed at the mouth. That . . . It was blasphemy against the heaven and earth. No, against the entire universe. It was indeed a Dragon Healing Wood. Dragon Healing Wood was a supreme herb, an Earth Grade herb that could help a wood cultivator to jump from the Refinement Realm to the Boiling Blood Realm in one shot, and this little thing had burned them to light a fire. If a high-level alchemist heard this, he would fry this little fox alive in a frying pan.

Did the heavens have eyes or not?

"There is still a stalk remaining, and if you give me ten more fruits, I'll get it for you."

Wei's brain burst with activity. A stalk of Dragon Healing Wood. That was better than anything. "Yes, please get that for me." This was his chance to soar through the skies, and he was going to use it wisely.

Chapter 32
Regressing into qi Refinement Realm

A stalk of wood lay in front of Li Wei inside a jade box, exuding strong vitality and the fragrant smell of pure wood. Simply taking it out had reduced the poison residue in a one-foot radius around it. It was a heaven-defying natural treasure for wood cultivators, and even in the Martial Realm, people would go crazy over a single stalk.

Wei still cursed little fox for using some of it as firewood. After pestering her incessantly, she'd agreed she wouldn't burn any more. But she'd also said the trees were tough like iron, so she couldn't cut them at all.

Theoretically, Wei should be happy, but he wasn't. His forehead had broken into dozens of black lines, and his heart raced like an Iron Speed Horse.

He slapped the rough ground next to him, raising a small cloud of dust. "Are you fucking kidding me?" he shouted, looking at the details of the Pill Clone Alchemy Art initiation ritual. A minute before, he was jumping and shouting for joy near the small hut inside the Snake Rearing Chamber, attracting irked looks from the little fox enjoying her fruits nearby. Because he had managed to vaporize the water in given time and that marked the pre-requisite for Pill Clone Alchemy Art initiation.

But when he looked more closely at the details of the Pill Clone Alchemy Art, his mood quickly dampened.

"Why are you shouting?" The little fox squinted at him. "Have you gone mad over that scrap of wood?"

"This is infuriating. It's asking me to burn my wood qi manifestation completely," he said in a lost voice. This alchemy art was crazy. To initiate it, he had to burn his wood qi manifestation inside his dantian and use the smoke produced to cultivate the first level. The smoke had to pass through the qi channels mentioned in the cultivation art so he could form the coating for an outer shell of the pill clone he would cultivate in the future.

That casing was the first level of the Pill Clone Alchemy Art.

This was ridiculous, if not outright suicidal. Who would burn their own wood qi manifestation? Why would he burn the wood qi lotus he'd formed through sweat and blood and regress to the qi Refinement Realm? By using his Essence Burning Art, he had already regressed to layer zero of the qi Foundation Realm.

Wait, he had the answer.

A smile played on his face. This was the perfect opportunity. He was already at layer zero, so going a bit negative wouldn't hurt him much. And the cultivation art said that the more layers he regressed, the better the result would be from the Pill Clone Alchemy Art.

What if he burned everything?

Yes, this was perfect. He would burn everything down.

"Human, why are you laughing evilly? Are you attracted by my beauty and have some lewd thoughts?" the little fox asked, pulling him out of his thoughts.

"Wait, what?" Wei scanned the little thing. Not even in dreams. "Little fox, what other fruits are inside the medicinal garden that have pure qi stored in them?"

"There are none."

"I'll give you ten extra Twisting Vitality Fruit each day."

"There are only a few, but there are many seeds available in one of the sealed rooms."

"Not a single one that might be useful for me?" Depression assailed his heart. If only he had asked her earlier and gotten all the herbs for cheap.

"One of them is good for you." She scratched her whiskers. "The Life Bestowing Grass is already fifty years old. There were many before, but when the seal vanished, many of them withered in the blink of an eye. Now only a few dozen herbs remain in the innermost section."

"That should do." Wei chuckled. This was good. "Take these." He handed her twenty more fruits, and she vanished to fetch the Life Bestowing Grass.

Ten minutes later, Wei closed his eyes and commanded his Fox's Breath to light under his wood qi lotus. A bright yellow flame settled in the pool of pure qi and began heating the wood qi lotus.

A stabbing pain shot from his dantian into his brain. It was like someone had set his meridians on fire, incinerating him from the inside, and it was painful. It was fucking painful.

Was he doing the right thing by burning something inside his dantian? He wondered, but he couldn't stop now. No one would be crazy enough to burn their own qi manifestation inside their dantian, but he wasn't just anyone. He had done many crazy things before, and he would do many in the future.

"Human, what are you doing? I sense your beast flame burning inside your body. Are you trying to die? If so, hand over the rest of your Twisting Vitality Fruits before you do."

"You bas—" Wei grabbed his stomach and convulsed. His pure qi was boiling, and it was affecting his entire body.

Now he knew what it would feel like to set your own dantian on fire. It was an ethereal object that shouldn't be set on fire. Actually, he had turned his dantian into a sauna, but consider a sauna with a thousand-degree temperature. Fire was incinerating his dantian walls, and if this continued, he might destroy his dantian and become a cripple.

If someone else was trying it, that person might die, because this was pure craziness.

But he wasn't crazy. Living for two hundred years, he had seen many things crazier than this.

"Suppress," shouting inside his mind, he pushed his pure qi around the beast flame. A thick layer of pure qi wrapped around the fire, and the temperature in his dantian instantly dropped, but it burned off a lot of his pure qi, threatening to leave him dry.

That's where the Life Bestowing Grass, which shone like the sun because of him using Yin Yang Liquid to bring its age to hundred years, came in. It was a Gold Grade herb, overkill for a Refinement Realm cultivator, but not for Wei.

Chewing it directly, he let the pure qi ram into his dantian. When a huge stream of pure qi rushed through his meridians like a bulging river, it stretched his meridians to the extreme. Soon, pure qi overflowed his dantian. This Life Bestowing Grass contained five times the pure qi of a Dantian Strengthening Fruit.

It was another suicidal act at his cultivation level. If not for his body cultivation, he would have died or become a cripple already.

Biting his lips, he continued pouring more pure qi into his dantian and commanded the beast flame, Fox's Breath, to burn hotter.

And it did.

His beast flame burned like the sun, and the pure qi shield he had formed around it burned into nothingness. Fortunately, there was an unending amount of pure qi rushing into his dantian to replenish it.

Soon, both forces reached equilibrium.

Wei persisted and watched his wood lotus qi burning into nothingness little by little. It was heartbreaking. Once he burned it completely, he would regress to the Refinement Realm, and he had to be fine with that.

But not a single thing had gone smoothly for him since reincarnating. Before he could feel joy, the Heart Devouring Poison shifted and the seal broke. A gust of pure qi rushed toward it, and that bastard poison started devouring the pure qi in a greater quantity than Wei could imagine.

"Fuck." He was in trouble. He was in deep, deep trouble.

Chapter 33

Poison Dragon vs Qi Dragon

When the seal on the poison the old man had placed broke, Wei convulsed. The heart-biting pain returned as the Heart Devouring Poison attacked his remaining weak heart blood.

Blood burst out of his mouth, and his face turned pale. He could feel his vitality draining away.

"Human, are you dying?" The little fox stopped chewing on the fruit and walked close to him.

Everything went black. The hut, the constant daylight, even the little fox's shiny eyes grew blurry. He spasmed before falling on his back. Sharp stones pricked his body through his sky-blue robe, but he couldn't do anything.

"You are poisoned." The little fox's eyes shone, and she vanished inside his body.

Wei was in no condition to care. The Heart Devouring Poison had started sucking pure qi from the Life Bestowing Grass, turning into a green dragon. With his divine sense, he could see the dragon growing larger with the help of the pure qi.

Fuck!

This was bad. No, bad times ten. The more the poison dragon grew, the fewer chances he would have to form his Poison Pill Clone. He might even die before any sort of thing happened. His plan was to initiate his Pill Clone Alchemy Art and then refine poison to form his pill clone.

Now, the chances were low. If he wanted to survive, he had to stop the poison dragon from sucking his pure qi.

But how?

His heart blood had lost its vitality, and his blood pearls could not suppress the poison dragon. In the end, he lacked cultivation. If he was in the Bone Baptization Realm of body cultivation, he might have had a better chance.

Rumble!

The wood qi finished transforming into smoke, and his qi cultivation dropped to layer nine of the qi Refinement Realm. His body ached, and he felt every muscle in his body losing power. Regression came with a cost, and he would pay it with his own power.

No, he couldn't let this happen. Wei's eyes flashed with resolute determination. This was it. Now or never.

"Begin." Using his divine sense, he pushed the wooden smoke toward the qi channels mentioned in the alchemy art. If he could reach level one in the Pill Clone Alchemy Art, he might have a chance. Now it was race against time. Either the poison dragon killed him, or he refined the poison dragon into his Poison Pill Clone.

His eyes rolled back in his skull when he realized he didn't have enough wood qi to initiate. He had made another mistake in his haste. He had started at layer zero of the qi Foundation Realm, so his wood qi manifestation was too weak to produce enough wood qi smoke. He should have used the Dragon Healing Wood to power up first and then burned it down.

Blood spluttered out of his mouth. His heart shook. He was losing it.

Would this be his end?

"Come on." Wei spat more blood. "I can't die like this."

Squinting, he looked around, and his eyes fell on the stalk of Dragon Healing Wood he had placed on a white paper. A crazy thought popped into his mind.

What if he sucked wood qi from the Dragon Healing Wood stalk and converted it into wood qi smoke? He could use his beast fire to burn it when it entered his dantian.

If he was going to die anyway, why not try dying to something crazier?

A deranged smile played on his lips, but the next moment everything went blank as the poison dragon took a large bite of pure qi. As it grew bigger, it attacked his heart blood with new vigor.

Sinking his teeth into his tongue, he woke himself up. Grabbing the stalk of Dragon Healing Wood, Wei began absorbing wood qi like crazy. A gust of fresh wood qi rushed through his arms, breaking his meridians, but he didn't care. He sucked down everything he could and pushed it toward his dantian.

And when it reached his dantian, he dialed his beast flame up to the max.

Burn, fucker! Burn!

His dantian's temperature shot up to an insane degree, but Wei didn't care anymore. If he survived, he might fix his dantian, but if he died, what was the use of the dantian to him?

Pure wood qi smoke filled his dantian, and with his divine sense, he pushed it toward the wood qi smoke already present in his dantian.

Moments passed. Wei lay on the ground. Sometimes he convulsed, and sometimes he spat mouthfuls of blood, but he continued sucking wood qi from the stalk.

After what felt like an eternity, the wood qi smoke reached sufficient density. This was it. Using his divine sense, he pushed the wood qi smoke toward his qi channels.

Wei was about to stop burning more wood qi when the poison dragon moved. It leaped at the wooden qi smoke Wei had formed.

"Damn you, fucker!" Wei's eyes turned blood red, and he moved the entirety of his divine sense to wrap around the wood qi smoke and turned it into a wood dragon.

This fucking poison dragon had bitten something he shouldn't have.

A will burst from Wei's body and entered the wood dragon. It was the will of a cultivator who had lived for two hundred years. It was the will of a loser who'd been backstabbed yet survived. It was the will of a young man who walked on the path of laziness.

And this fucking poison dragon was trying to stop that will from succeeding.

Wei chuckled, and the wood dragon attacked the poison dragon.

An epic fight took place. Two dragons, one green and one brown, attacked each other. Wherever they went, they thrashed his meridians and internal organs.

"Eat this." The little fox appeared next to Wei and pushed a blue fruit into his mouth. It tasted cold and bitter at first, but it soon transformed into pure blue energy and headed toward Wei's heart.

Even almost dead, Wei recognized that fruit.

Ice Reincarnation Fruit.

It was an Earth Grade fruit that could cure most poisons found in the Martial Realm. Heart Devouring Poison was child's play in front of it.

Where did the little fox got this? Was it inside the medicinal garden she'd mentioned?

Fuck! He felt cheated. If she knew there was something like this, why did she let him suffer so much?

She was an evil little fox.

The blue energy from the Ice Reincarnation Fruit dashed toward the poison dragon.

Sensing the impending danger, the poison dragon moved away from it. But the blue energy continued chasing it.

Wei sneered inside his mind. What would this bastard would do now?

Ignoring the poison dragon, Wei pushed his wood dragon into the qi channels that would form his alchemy qi path and started the Pill Clone Alchemy Art incantation. Alchemy qi path was different than his cultivation qi path. The wood dragon flew through a set of qi channels and left small dragons in every one, forming the alchemy qi path in its entirety. It coated the channels with a thin layer of wood qi. This was the first step of the process. Next, it would form the outer shell of the pill clone.

Finally, a smile appeared on Wei's lips. He was getting rid of the poison dragon, and his pill clone would finally form.

Then something happened, and the poison dragon flew into his alchemy qi channel, chasing the wood dragon.

Fuck!

Chapter 34

Hybrid Pill Clone

When the poison dragon entered Li Wei's qi channels, his entire body shook violently.

Excruciating pain shot through his qi channels, and he fainted for a moment. It was his willpower that shook him awake, and he suppressed his internal injuries. Slapping his palms on the rough ground near him, he looked upwards at the eternally bright sky of the Snake Rearing Chamber.

This fucker. What did it want?

"Are you trying to kill me?" he asked the heavens, but no reply came. A weird silence prevailed around him.

The blue energy tried to enter his qi channels, but they'd been torn apart by the poison dragon, so it rushed toward his heart.

But if he didn't finish off the poison dragon, what would happen to him when the effect of the Ice Reincarnation Fruit ended?

Was he going to die?

It was as if the heavens didn't want him to live.

"Then I'll go against you," he roared, still looking at the sky.

The poison dragon caught up with the wooden dragon and attacked its tail. This time, Wei had forgotten what pain meant as he was beyond it.

Desperation spread through his heart as the poison dragon bit into the wood dragon. It grew stronger with every moment.

Then his dantian shook. A small amount of a golden-black liquid leaked from the carcasses of the Yin Yang Worms lying inside his dantian. That drop of golden-black liquid shot into his qi channels and merged with the poison dragon. The poison dragon burst into green light and merged with the wood dragon.

At the same time, the blue energy from the Ice Reincarnation Fruit reached his heart blood and began replenishing it. In a breath's time, it replenished his heart blood, and then the remaining blue energy split apart into blue rays and shot for his injured internal organs. It healed his dantian and even a tiny hole on the carcass of the worms that he hadn't noticed before.

That hole must have been an effect of him burning the wood qi he'd absorbed from the Healing Dragon Wood. Craziness did have advantages at times.

Wherever the blue rays touched, he healed. His internal organs healed like they had suffered no injuries. Best of all, his meridians were remolding, growing stronger with each passing second.

This was insane. He knew there was a healing effect to Ice Reincarnation Fruit, but he had never eaten one himself, so he didn't know it had a miraculous effect like this. This fruit was too rare to appear even in the Martial Realm. So, all he knew about it was its name and some effects.

Fucking crazy!

His mind shook when he noticed things happening in his qi channels. The poison and wood dragons had merged with each other and the golden and black liquid drops. As a new entity, they traveled through his qi channels, leaving behind a coating of green, brown, and gold.

With a thought, he directed his divine sense to stop, but nothing happened. His divine sense was out of his control. Even the wood dragon was out of his control now. Everything was happening on its own. Wei had been reduced to a spectator.

Why? His divine sense was his, so how did he lose control over it? And why the fuck was this alchemy art revolving on its own?

Unless . . .

His heart shuddered. There was only one answer. This alchemy art had reached a heaven-defying legendary grade. It was a higher grade art than his Five Elemental Way and Blood Essence Body Cultivation arts.

Every cultivation art was divided into grades: Bronze, Silver, Gold, Earth, Human, and then the highest grade, Heaven grade. But that wasn't the end. Being an Array Master in his previous life, he had touched upon something greater than Heaven Grade, but he didn't understand it fully. And this alchemy art was better than Heaven Grade because only a legendary-grade art could have its own mind.

Breath after breath, the hybrid dragon continued revolving through certain qi channels, and then finally the moment arrived when it entered his dantian.

Wei held his breath. This was the moment when the pill clone would be formed. The alchemy art mentioned that at level one only a casing would be formed, but after this strange mutation, he wondered what would happen.

A thick stream of green and brown energy separated from each other, and two casings appeared inside his dantian.

Om!

A strange fluctuation emerged from his dantian and spread throughout his body, and a new set of information entered his mind.

System: Information interface detected. Downloading information.

System: Yin Poison Pill Clone and Yang Wood Pill Clone formation successful.

Intense pain shot from his soul as his divine sense tore into three parts and two parts shot toward the pill clones. For a moment, he felt like he would die of the pain, but it vanished the next moment, and then he felt a connection with two new bodies. Although his divine sense was divided into three parts, he didn't lose it. With a thought, it could come out of any pill clone and merge with his original, but he had to keep it inside the pill clones to cultivate them and strengthen t hem.

Wow!

System: Host's body cultivation has reached layer eight of the Foundation Realm.

Wait what? Wei spread his divine sense through his body, and he was out of breath. He had reached layer eight of the body Foundation Realm. His Shaoyin of Kidney had been opened, and he had 1,840 blood pearls moving through his blood. And what about this message? The system had never sent a message when he broke through before.

System: System's compatibility with the host's body is increased. System can assess host body's situation in new ways.

"Junior apprentice brother, what happened here? Why is your pet lying dead?" Chen Du's voice pierced his ears, and he opened his eyes to look at the little fox.

Covered in blood, she lay on the ground, unconscious. His heart sunk to the bottom of his stomach. What had happened to her?

Chapter 35

Concocting a real pill

Seeing the little fox covered with cuts and lying a puddle of blood, Li Wei's heart sunk to his stomach. He hadn't been frightened when he'd hung between life and death a few minutes ago, but right now he shivered in fear.

Thoughts of death permeated his mind, and he shivered with doubt. What if she was dead?

In the bright daylight, Wei carefully observed her illuminated cuts. The more he saw, the deeper his heart sunk into the endless abyss of dread. Blood leaked from the cuts, merging with the gray, lifeless soil.

Grabbing the scarred wooden bench for support, Wei tried to get up, but his legs shook and he fell down. The mother fox had trusted him with her safety, and he had failed her big time. Emotions choked his heart, and he couldn't breathe for a moment.

"Junior apprentice brother, are you all, right?" Chen Du pulled out a bottle of some weird fragrance and rubbed it on his neck and hands.

Wei scowled. That bottle of perfume smelled irritating, and he had the urge to smash it against the wall. "Is there anyone here besides us?"

"No," Chen Du said in a serious tone. "It doesn't look like snake bites. Something sharp sliced through her skin. Check her pulse, she might be alive."

Wei crawled over to her, but he couldn't steady his shivering hand.

"Let me do it." Chen Du squatted next to Wei, sweat pouring down his forehead, his face devoid of any color. "Look at her wounds. The poisonous air has already charred them, so it must have happened at least an hour back."

Wei's chin jut up. That was approximately when she'd fed him the Ice Reincarnation Fruit. Did something happen to her after that? But how was that possible? Who could come here and hurt a cute little fox like her? This was insanity. Only a beast would hurt a cute little fox like her.

Chen Du touched her neck. "She is alive."

His soft voice sounded like heaven's music. Like a dam holding them back had broken, his emotions surged toward her along with his divine sense. She was indeed alive. Half-dead, but still alive.

Wei's shoulders eased, but guilt occupied his mind. How could he have missed her peril with his divine sense? He couldn't even check her pulse. What had happened to him? Was he too weak to see someone close to him dying in front of him?

The choking emotions he felt were odd and strange. Even when his grandfather died, he hadn't felt this down.

"Senior apprentice brother Du, do you have a healing pill on you?"

Chen Du shook his head. "It won't work. Humans and beasts are different. Wait, I know a pill recipe that might help her. I also have ingredients for the basic version of it. But that recipe is only for common animals or Ferocious Beasts in the early Refinement Realm. Is your pet a Ferocious Beast?"

Wei nodded. She was Spirit Beast, of course, not a Ferocious Beast. But he didn't want Chen Du to know that.

"Then it only has a low chance of working." He sighed. "If only we had the rare herb that could advance this recipe to new tier and help her. I just saw it on the other side of the array formation. What a pity."

"What herb?"

"Five Petal Life Herb."

Wei's eyes shone brighter. "Senior apprentice brother, what recipe is it?"

"It's called a Beast Rejuvenating Pill, and it's only a Silver Grade pill, but once an alchemist told me it could save any normal pet with one breath left."

Wei frowned. The little fox was a Spirit Fox, so even the strengthened version of the recipe might not work for her. But this was his only chance to save her, and he would take every chance the heavens presented him.

"Senior apprentice brother Du, I'll head to the other side and get some Five Petal Life Herb." But wait. Wei remembered something and pulled an herb out of his storage ring. "Is this the same herb?"

Chen Du shivered. "How did you get it? It's extinct from the Mortal Realm. How did you get it?"

"I got it from the Alchemy Comprehension Tower," Wei answered. He'd gotten quite a few herbs there, and he thanked the heavens for not giving him the time to sell them at auction. He'd been planning to do that soon. If he had, he would have never forgiven himself in this life.

"I've got the other ingredients. But . . ." Chen Du smiled.

Wei's face hardened. "Senior apprentice brother, can I trouble you to concoct that pill for me?"

Chen Du dropped on his ass as if he'd lost the last thread of support that had helped him squat. "I wish I could, but going out there has taken a toll on my mind, and if I try to concoct anything now, I'll fail for sure."

Wei stared at Chen Du's color-drained face and shivering body. There was even a hint of black on his nostrils. He suffered from poison infusion and was in no condition for concocting pills. Forcing him would yield poor results. And Wei couldn't take any chances with the little fox's life.

Maybe it was time to man up and concoct his own pill.

"It's okay, senior apprentice brother Du. You should take a Poison Repelling Pill and rest. But can you give me the recipe and ingredients?"

"Take them. They are useless to me." Chen Du handed him a bunch of ingredients. "I gathered them for my own pet, but he died before I could concoct anything. Unfortunately, I only have one set of ingredients. So, if you fail . . ." A heavy sigh slipped from him. "Be careful with the pill. Although it's only high grade Bronze Grade, its difficulty is unbelievable."

Wei was touched to see a soft side behind this brute of a man. "Take your rest, senior apprentice brother Du. I'll take care of the watering task tomorrow." He could feel the poisonous air entering his body, but his Yin Poison Pill Clone was sucking it away instantly. This kind of poison had no more effect on him.

Taking the ingredients, he placed them on a white paper before taking a deep breath. It was time to experiment and realize the power of his Pill Clone Alchemy Art.

But first thing first, he bandaged the little fox using his limited nursing knowledge to stop her bleeding. Of course, he couldn't do it properly, so Chen Du helped him, but he went into the hut as soon as they finished. Chen Du was exhausted.

Placing the ingredients in front of him, he poured a drop of Yin Yang Liquid on each of the five herbs and produced five portions of ingredients with one hundred years of age each. It was his first time concocting a real pill, so he had to have some room for failure.

After producing five sets of ingredients, he closed his eyes and meditated on the pill recipe. It was a high-tier Bronze Grade pill, Lesser Beast Rejuvenating Pill, and wasn't part of Xue Qi's inheritance. It required five herbs and three steps. Two of them were herb processing steps.

Then there was an advanced recipe, Beast Rejuvenating Pill. It used the sixth ingredient, Five Petal Life Herb, and that changed the recipe grade to mid-tier Silver Grade. The difficulty went up exponentially, and the process looked complex.

Could he really do it? Well, he had no other option, and to his merit, he had once concocted a Gold Grade pill in dream space. This should be fine, right?

"System, match these ingredients with other pill recipes and find any similar processing methods."

System: Starting analysis of ingredients.

Silence prevailed in his mind while he assessed the properties of the ingredients. The ingredients surprised him. Two of them were yang type, and one was yin type. Mixing them would be hard. Well, he didn't have to find a solution as the remaining two ingredients fell under catalyst type ingredients.

System: Found one processing method for Five Petal Life Herb. Mixing it with Qi Water can improve the solvency of the petals, thus improving the merger with Purple Threaded Grass.

Wei frowned. "But it is explicitly mentioned here to not use Qi Water in the recipe. What's the chance of success?"

System: The processing method is used in a Gold Grade pill, and the chance of success is more than 50%.

Wei nodded. He would trust Xue Qi's inheritance more than Chen Du's recipe.

"Simulate the pill recipe for the success of using this new processing method."

Simulation. An unknown word to him, but after he merged with a Soul Stone in the Alchemy Comprehension Tower, the system had awakened a simulation function. It was a wonder of nature that allowed the system to predict a new path for his alchemy. Just knowing what it did, he had many thoughts. This was the greatest wonder of the system. It would pave his path to the Houtian Realm for his body cultivation.

Anyway, if could simulate processing methods for a Gold Grade pill, then what was a Bronze Grade pill by comparison?

It should be easy.

Indeed, it was.

System: Simulation finished. Success chance with original recipe: 27%. Success chance after incorporating new processing method: 35%.

Wei scoffed. Just thirty-five percent? Was that a joke? What kind of pill recipe only had a twenty-seven percent success chance? What if he failed at all five attempts?

No, he had to have more than a fifty percent chance of success. He couldn't let the little fox's life hang on a pill recipe's low chance of success.

"System, simulate the whole recipe."

The system went silent for the next thirty minutes. In the meantime, Wei kept tabs on the little fox's condition. By heaven's grace, it didn't deteriorate. She was breathing weakly, but nonetheless, she was breathing.

And that was important.

System: Simulation finished. Three recipes simulated based on the same ingredients. Success chances are 51-59%. More data required for further simulation.

Good. Fifty-one percent was better than the thirty-five percent he'd gotten earlier.

Looking behind him, he found Chen Du snoring inside the wooden hut. With his divine sense, Wei checked on Chen Du's condition. The brute was in a deep sleep. Wei doubted even a music instrument playing next to his head could awake him.

Good for Wei.

Pulling his Gold Grade cauldron out, he let his beast flame preheat it to forty degrees. Looking at the shiny cauldron, he regretted not setting up a few arrays on it in advance, but now wasn't the time.

First, he had to prepare the Qi Water, and there were barrels of Pure Water next to him. Pouring some into the gold cauldron, he began heating it, and when it was to temperature, he then started pouring . . . Wait, he was at layer nine of the qi Refinement Realm, and he had no wood qi.

Fuck! How could he be so negligible?

His gaze moved to the little fox's body, and he spotted her convulsing in pain. The choking emotions returned to him, and he felt like his soul would leave his body if he failed to protect her.

Chapter 36

Yang Wood Pill Clone take action

Li Wei sat near the wooden hut in the Snake Rearing Chamber, staring at the cauldron and the set of ingredients. His face twitched as he went over the pill concocting process. Foul winds blew from the direction of the array formation, prickling his already rotten mood. Looking at the many requirements, he wondered if he chose the wrong path. If he had entered the Heavenly Firmament Sect, he would have become an elder with his current knowledge of arrays, but here he was stuck in a rotten place. The worst thing was his companion, the little fox, was dying and he couldn't do anything to save her.

Being helpless was the worst thing in the world, and it all boiled down to one thing.

Wood qi.

Without his wood qi, he couldn't convert Pure Water into Qi Water, and that was just the first step. Pill concocting also required wood qi, and he had none.

Staring at the medicinal fields at the other side of the array formation, he rubbed his sweaty face, but no solution came to mind. The bright light always shining overhead only dampened his mood further. Light was supposed to be bring hope, but it only brought him despair. Despair over his weakness.

Why wasn't there a solution? Why wasn't he strong enough to protect the people around him?

No, there were a few solutions. If he charged into the qi Foundation Realm, that would be best, but he didn't have a source of pure qi to do that. That fucking poison dragon had consumed all of the Life Bestowing Grass, and he would require an enormous amount of pure qi to break through again. That wasn't possible in the next half hour.

The other option was to get a Wood Qi Conversion Artifact that would convert his pure qi into wood qi. He could carve it himself, but he had no materials, nor had he enough pure qi to do that. He was doomed in that sense too.

There was a small piece of Dragon Healing Wood remaining in his storage ring, but it was useless to him unless he reached the qi Foundation Realm and re-formed his wood qi lotus.

His gaze jumped to the little fox laying on the scratched wooden bench. She looked like she would die anytime, and her white bandages had turned red. Some blood had dripped on the wood, staining it red too.

Was he going to let her die just because he had no wood qi? Was there no other option?

Something stirred inside his mind, and part of his divine sense shot into the Yang Wood Pill Clone. A stream of pure wood qi rushed out of it and reached for his hand.

This.

Wei's brows shot to his hairline, and then a smile broke on his lips. This damn little thing.

"Thanks buddy." He'd forgotten this part entirely. If the Yin Poison Pill Clone could store poison, then the Yang Wood Pill Clone should be able store wood qi as well. And technically speaking, this little thing had its own consciousness. Of course, it was his own divine sense divided, but as he reached higher levels in his Pill Clone Alchemy Art, these little things would develop their own consciousnesses.

This was no less than a magical effect. Theoretically, no one could extract or sense wood qi from any of the wood qi treasures until they reached the Houtian Realm.

Pulling out the tiny piece of Dragon Healing Wood he had left, he started absorbing wood qi from it. Streams of wood qi entered his hand, and the Yang Wood Pill Clone absorbed it greedily. Soon it shone with a bright golden-brown light, and a thin stream of golden lustrous wood qi floated out of it. So, it couldn't store wood qi like the poison pill clone, but it could extract it for him and provide him a pure source of qi. Just sensing it, Wei's pores went crazy. This was the purest of wood qi anyone could cultivate, and this would benefit him a lot in the future.

No, this would be a turning point for his wood qi cultivation.

This would be exciting. Could he also form other pill clones like this?

Bright sunlight streamed through the broken door over Chen Du's face, disturbing his deep sleep. The fragrant smell of pure wood qi rushed into his nostrils, and he opened his eyes. With the always shining skies in this place, he couldn't tell if it was day or night.

When he tried to get up, exhaustion washed over him and his body urged him to go back to sleep, but the fragrant smell attracted him. Being a wood cultivator and practicing alchemy for years, he had grown accustomed to the slightest changes in wood qi, and the one he smelled was too pure to be real.

Pushing his palms on the rough ground, he got up and dusted off his dark gray robe before walking out of the wooden hut.

The same fragrance of pure wood qi blasted his face when he stepped out.

"Holy heavens." He screamed in his mind when he saw two ingredients floating in the air, slowly merging under the influence of golden wood qi. The next thing he saw surprised him even more.

Junior apprentice brother Wei sat in front of a shiny golden cauldron—a different one from the cheap furnace he'd had before. Golden wood qi gushed out of his right hand and entered the cauldron while a thread of golden wood qi rushed out of his left hand and processed two yang-property herbs in the air.

How was it humanly possible? How could junior apprentice brother make herbs float in the air and process them with just his golden wood qi?

And why the hell did his wood qi have a golden color?

Glancing downward, he let his wood qi appear on his palm, and it looked . . . dead. Nah, it wasn't dead, but compared to what the junior apprentice brother conjured, it was worse than dead.

Alchemy had many requirements, but wood cultivation and wood qi quality were the two most important requirements every sect checked. The quality of one's wood qi depended on one's Spirit Root, but alchemy art had the biggest impact on one's wood qi. Chen Du had a mid-tier Silver Grade Spirit Root, but his wood qi quality was only at Bronze Grade, and he would have to reach a higher level in the Nine Lotus Alchemy Art to improve it.

Looking at junior apprentice brother Wei's wood qi, it seemed to be Gold Grade, but junior apprentice brother Wei had said he'd entered the sect from a back door.

How was that possible? If his wood qi was Gold Grade, his Spirit Root had to be at least Gold Grade too, and what sect in the State of Zin would dare to decline a Gold Grade alchemist? Any Gold Grade Spirit Root genius would be directly recruited as a core disciple of the sect. He had heard that Fairy Fei had a high-tier Gold Grade Spirit Root, and she had been made a personal disciple of the sect master. Junior apprentice brother Wei should at least be a personal disciple of a great elder, if not the sect master.

Then what was he doing here? And how could he process two herbs at a time?

Chapter 37

Beast Rejuvenating Pill Success

Golden wood qi shot out of Li Wei's hand, entering the golden cauldron and imbuing the Five Petal Life Herb simmering in the Qi Water while the Three Yin Petal and Pure Yang Fruit merged with each other in the air with the help of a wood qi envelope.

Sweat entered his eyes, prickling them, but he couldn't shift his attention from the herbs floating in air. This was his fifth try. He couldn't afford to fail. All his previous tries had ended in failure, and he was getting more nervous with every passing second.

The Yin Poison Clone inside his body absorbed the foul, poisonous air surrounding him through his pores, creating a vacuum of poisonous air around him. Because of his greedy Yin Poison Clone, a pure air bubble had formed around him, so he dared to mix two herbs in the air.

In previous failed attempts, he had failed at mixing these herbs as they required a room temperature cauldron, and he didn't have a cooling material to cool down his cauldron. So, the system had simulated this method of merging herbs in the air, referencing a similar herb processing method from Xue Qi's inheritance. Well, it became possible with his awesome Yang Wood Clone. It was like having two extra hands. He had to admit, Xue Qi's inheritance was top class, and if it wasn't for her dream of becoming an alchemist he might have died already. The Yang Wood Clone had awesome abilities. Not only could it refine a piece of wood in his hand and convert it into wood qi, but it could also do it with every piece of wood in a certain radius. He realized that when he sensed the piece of Dragon Healing wood lying on the ground next to him, and at his will, the Yang Wood Pill Clone began refining the Dragon Healing Wood. Of course, the rate at it which it refined it was lot less than when refining an object in his hand, but it was awesome to have something like this

Wei's divine sense noticed Chen Du getting up and watching him from the hut door with wide-open eyes. He looked astonished. Any other time, Wei would have prevented him—or anyone, really—from learning his secrets, but he didn't care for now. He was on the next-to-last set of herbs and he couldn't fail. Every moment he wasted, he put the little fox in danger. If he had a choice, he would have walked out of the Snake Rearing Chamber, but it wasn't possible since the old man had sealed the entrance.

"You can come close and watch, but don't disturb me," Wei said without moving his eyes from the ingredients in the air.

System: Merge efficiency reached 98%. Merge complete.

He poured the merged ingredient into the cauldron and closed the lid. Wei had asked system to monitor the ingredient merge this time and alert him at the best possible merge moment. He'd never thought of using this method before, but this time he tried it. After all, the system could monitor many things inside his body. Why not outside?

But there was a catch. The system said it would shut down for some time afterward, as monitoring the area outside of his body used too much power and that would put him in danger.

Wei went ahead despite the danger. After suffering from the Heart Devouring Poison, he had vowed to not utilize the system to the extent that it compromised his own body monitoring again. That had almost cost him his life last time. But the stakes were too high now. He had to succeed, so he broke his rule.

System: System is undergoing hibernation. Time to awake: 2 hours.

Emptiness took over his soul as if he had lost contact with something important.

Shaking his head, he focused back on the pill. This was the final moment, and he had to maintain a sixty-degree temperature until all the herbs inside merged together and formed the pill nucleus.

Rumble!

Two minutes passed in a blink, and the cauldron shook violently. The nucleus had been formed, and he could sense its movement using his divine sense. Now the pill would go through the Alchemy Breath process, where it would attract the essence energy from heaven and earth and condense into the final output.

Heaven and earth's essence energy rushed inside the cauldron, fusing with the pill nucleus and forming a coating around it using the remaining materials inside the cauldron.

One breath.

Two breaths.

Three breaths.

. . .

Ten breaths.

The pill recipe mentioned it would take ten breaths' time to form the pill, but his pill continued to absorb essence energy. In fact, it increased twofold.

Fifteen breaths.

. . .

Twenty-seven breaths.

Om!

Like a giant beast sucking a large pool of water in an instant, the cauldron sucked in huge amount of heaven and earth's essence energy. For a moment, Wei felt like heaven hated him, as there was no essence energy remaining inside a ten-foot radius around him. It was utterly devoid of essence energy, and that left him miserable.

Boom!

The cauldron shook, and the lid shot up before a dark black pill the size of an year old baby's closed fist jumped out and hovered in the air for a moment. A white translucent line flashed over the pill before he grabbed it and fed it to the little fox.

The little fox shuddered, and then her injuries started healing. Her labored breathing eased, and he could feel the danger on her life subsiding slowly.

Wei finally let loose his breath and relaxed a little.

"Wait—" Chen Du's words remained in his mouth. He rushed to the cauldron and peeked inside. "Three more pills. What a waste." Chen Du's face fell in disappointment.

"Senior apprentice brother Du. What are you doing?" Wei's fingers reached for his sword. If Chen Du tried to steal his cauldron, he wouldn't mind killing him.

Chapter 38

Alchemy Realms

Li Wei's fingers brushed his sword's cold metal hilt, and his shoes firmed his posture on the dead gray soil. His eyes watched Chen Du's actions, shoulders loaded with the explosive strength to attack anytime.

He was ready to kill if Chen Du showed any interest in his secrets.

Chen Du shook his head in disappointment. "Junior apprentice brother Wei, did you see the white line? Did you know that was a rank three pill with a pill line?" He bent over the cauldron and pulled three more pills out of it and threw them toward Wei. "These are all common pills, but the one you fed to your pet was a pill line rank three pill."

"What does that mean?"

"Holy heavens. Why can't people read a little about their profession?" He sighed with regret. "You missed a great chance to study it. Each third rank pill is a heaven's blessing, and you can gain enlightenment by studying it long enough." His shoulders dropped as he turned back. "What a waste. I just wanted to have a look."

Wei relaxed and loosed a breath. This brute was disappointed by something different from what he'd thought. In fact, if he'd had to fight, he would have suffered a lot. He was exhausted. Concocting a pill for four straight hours had left him drained, and he had also lost a major cultivation realm, so his body was in a bad shape. Fighting would only make it worse.

Sitting next to the little fox, he checked her condition and found that her internal veins had healed up. Her heart was in better shape, and she was out of danger. But she hadn't recovered yet.

"Junior apprentice brother." Chen Du turned toward him. "No. I should call you senior apprentice brother Wei as you've already reached the Pill Adapt Realm. In our profession, a person's seniority is decided by their profession realm. You're an ass-smacking genius."

"Pill Adapt Realm. Is that similar to Array Adapt Realm? And what about this ass-smacking genius. Do you like asses that much?" Wei rolled his eyes. What kind of language was that?

Chen Du nodded and sat on a nearby boulder. Pulling a Poison Repelling Pill from his pouch, he pushed it into his mouth. His face still looked pale. "Yes, we alchemists have similar realms. First there's Pharmacist. Anyone who can mix an herb powder can be called a Pharmacist. Then we have Pill Apprentice; once you concoct any low-tier Silver Grade pill you can become a Pill Apprentice. Pill Apprentice is further divided into three stars, and you gain one star for every tier in the Silver Grade pill." He paused to take a breath. "Then we have Pill Adapt. A Pill Adapt can concoct a low-tier Gold Grade pill. But people also treat anyone who can concoct a Silver Grade pill with rank three quality a Pill Adapt. It has nine stars in it, but I have little information on it. Then we have Pill Expert, but I don't know the requirements. There may be other realms, but I'm not aware of t hem."

"How many pill ranks are there?" Wei picked the second pill that had formed in the cauldron, but it had no pill line, nor had it the luster of the first pill.

"Five. The one you're holding is a rank two pill. Rank one is the basic, rank two has better efficacy. Rank three is the top-quality pill in the entire State of Zin, and only a few alchemists can concoct one. Only our sect master can concoct those in our sect."

"What are pill lines?"

"The white line formed on your pill was a pill line."

Wei remembered seeing a white translucent line on the pill. "What does that line indicate?" Asking this question made him realize he knew too little about alchemy. Although he'd eaten many top-grade pills in his previous life, for him they were just pills. He didn't care about their quality. Now he understood there was much more nuance to alchemy—maybe even more than there was in arrays.

But why was this knowledge missing from Xue Qi's inheritance?

"Pill ranks define the pill's efficacy, and pill lines define the pill's toxin level. A rank one pill has forty percent efficacy of the herbs used, rank two has fifty, and rank three has sixty." He took a deep breath, trying to don a sage's mantle. "Pill lines indicate the pill toxin level. Every unranked pill has sixty percent base pill toxin level, and every ranked pill has forty percent base pill toxin. A single pill line means less pill toxin."

"Does that mean a pill line would increase the pill efficacy?" Wei asked, wondering how little he knew about alchemy.

"No. They are two separate things, and doesn't add together to define pills. The pill toxin level indicates how soon you can eat the next pill. But even that differs from pill to pill and depends on pill efficacy. Common healing pills, for example, can be popped like candies, whereas complex cultivation-increasing pills need time to absorb the efficacy and process it."

"Make sense."

"So, every pill across all grades has a base forty percent pill toxin level. One pill line indicates ten percent less pill toxin. Two pill lines indicate twenty percent less pill toxin. Three pill lines indicate thirty percent less pill toxin."

"That makes sense." But Wei was shocked. The Foundation Expanding Pills he'd eaten had one line on all the pills. Was that why he could eat them like candies? It must be.

"Are there four pill lines as well?"

Chen Du nodded. "Yes, there are. That's called a pill matrix. Some say they are rarer than even rank five pills."

"Then what are rank four and five pills? With seventy percent and eighty percent efficacy, they would be too awesome to consume."

Chen Du shrugged. "I don't know. I've heard no one mention rank four or five pills, nor do the textbooks have any information on them."

Wei looked at the medicinal fields and considered his future path. Alchemy was a treasure trove, and he had so much to learn from it. But before that he had to break through to the qi Foundation Realm again. Without it, he wouldn't be able to concoct pills on his own. There was only a small piece of Dragon Healing Wood left, only enough to help him concoct a few more batches.

"Senior apprentice brother Du, you should leave the watering work to me from now on." There were medicinal ingredients present behind the array, and he had plans to get them.

"No. We will alternate every day. That is appropriate—and call me junior apprentice brother going forward. That's appropriate too. If anyone hears you calling me senior apprentice brother, they will spank my ass until it is black and blue."

Wei chuckled. "Let's just call each other brother. How does that sound?"

Chen Du nodded. "Sounds good to me."

Wei sat in a lotus pose next to the wooden bench where the little fox lay. First, he had to cultivate and recover, then head behind the array to find the medicinal ingredients for the little fox.

Growl!

A wail slipped from the little fox's mouth, and Wei's heart jumped to his throat. The little fox convulsed, then threw up a lot of blood.

Chapter 39

Devil Suppression Array

Seven days passed like the blink of an eye. Li Wei stood on the marble path, staring at the energy flow of the Devil Suppression Array Formation. Today, he had to break it and enter the medicinal garden. From here, he could see Five Petal Life Herb swaying over the wind, calling him. It was one of the ingredients he needed to make another batch of Beast Rejuvenating Pills. After he fed her the rank three pill with the pill line on it, the danger to the little fox's life had subsided, but her internal organs were still in turmoil. He had used the remaining three pills to stabilize her health.

But that wasn't enough. To get her completely out of danger, he needed more Beast Rejuvenating Pills enforced with Five Petal Life Herb, and it was on the other side of the array formation.

So, for the last seven days he had studied this array formation and came to a conclusion. Today, he had to break through this array formation no matter what. For the last seven days, when he wasn't studying this array formation, he was learning basic alchemy techniques from Chen Du and practicing them. With continuous practice, Wei had gotten much better at flame control and processing of herbs. Although he had a better inheritance, some of the processing methods and tricks Chen Du taught him were priceless. Despite chasing behind a skirt and joining an alchemy sect, that brute Chen Du was good at alchemy theory.

Wei shifted to his right, moving over the marble road behind an energy influx he had detected just now. For the last seven days, he'd kept coming here to deduce the source points so he could open a door to get in. No two arrays had the same source points, so one had to comprehend and analyze to find the source points. Without finding the source points, one wouldn't be able to break through an array.

One couldn't reach Array Master realm without learning array breaking. Well, it wasn't an official requirement, but one had to be proficient in all aspects of arrays. When he was stranded in a secret realm for ten years, he'd had to break a complex array formation to get out of that messed up realm. For seven years, he'd studied nothing but the source points, and the next two years were spent breaking it. The first year, he'd spent exploring the realm. It was there that he had found the Blood Essence Body Cultivation Art in a remote cave behind a skeleton.

The Devil Suppression Array Formation in front of him wasn't that complex, and the creator had done lousy work. Especially by using White Bone Trees. If the creator had instead set up proper formation poles using Brass Wolf Iron and high-quality Qi Crystals, the array formation wouldn't be leaking. White Bone Trees could be used to save money, but in the end, they would wither away once their vitality was sucked up by the array formation.

Squinting, he studied the white lines of wear and tear on the White Bone Trees. There were too many. Because of the insufficient Qi

Stones used and the ritual of pouring qi water on the trees, the array formation was sucking even more life from these trees. At most, they would survive for a hundred more years—and that's if the sect stopped watering them. If he had some Qi Crystals to reinforce the energy source, he could reinforce it for four hundred more years.

But that would be the best he could do in his current condition.

Staring at the Qi Crystals, he pondered the reason behind the Divine Fragrance Palace's decision to water the White Bone Trees. Were they fooled by someone? Or were they doing it on purpose? How could a higher-up not know about the weakening of the array formation? If they continued watering the White Bone Trees, they would destroy this array in a few years.

In the end, Wei couldn't guess what stupid reason the sect had. This really made little sense.

Another possibility was that Chen Du's story was false. Maybe there was something else behind this array, and the sect sought to weaken the array formation and reach the other side. But if they really wanted to break the array formation, they could do it by inviting a super expert from the Martial Realm. It wasn't impossible for experts from the Martial Realm to come here, but it was quite costly.

Whatever.

"Little fox, don't worry. I'll make sure I get the ingredients required to heal you." Staring at the other side of the array formation, he pulled out ten Qi Stones and arranged them in a pentagon shape. They were all low-quality Qi Stones, so he needed two for each point. Using a Seal Severing Array, he was planning to form a slit in the Devil Suppression Array and walk to the other side. This was one of his self-created arrays from his previous life, a toned-down version of a Seal Breaking Array. The Seal Breaking Array was a complex Earth Grade array that was mainly used to break through the strong seals protecting ancient tombs or treasure sites. It used the profound strength of heaven and earth's essence energy to weaken the seal and then destroy it in one go. It was a destructive array, while the Seal Severing Array used the weakness of the sealed barrier and formed a temporary passage point.

For the last seven days, he had studied the energy flow of the array formation using his divine sense, deducing the weakest point of the seal barrier. As expected, it was near one of the source points that connected with the formation pole. Array formations were different from normal arrays or formations. It used the best of the two worlds, but it also carried their flaws. Flaws that could be only perceived through constant study. One common thing Wei had found about array formations was that their weak point always lay around the place where a source point connected to the formation pole.

Arrays had source points, and formations had formation poles. Array formations had both, and the energy flow connecting them would always be in a weird flux because of the change in energy frequency. This wasn't a widely known fact. Only a few people knew about it, including himself. It required study of the energy flow using one's divine sense, and unfortunately many array cultivators lacked patience. They chased after money and lost sight of the focus and beauty of the array studies.

Sighing in his heart, Wei pulled out his array brush and started carving the array near the weakest point of the Devil Suppression Array Formation.

Connecting the Seal Severing Array's source point at this weakest point, he would redirect the flow of the Devil Suppressing Array Formation's energy and create a portal for himself.

He moved his brush like a painter, quickly completing the array diagram and forming the source points. Once the source points were formed, he carved power points and placed Qi Stones on them. This was quite a simple array. The Seal Breaking Array was a Three Fold Array and even he had needed to spend at least half a day carving it on the highest grade material at his peak.

The array jolted his memories. Whenever a new secret realm was found, or an ancient site was discovered, people used to contact him to buy a Seal Breaking Array. They used to present him with treasures and gifts—some crazy clans even sent a few of their daughters to lure him. Well, he never accepted their daughters, but their treasures, yes. He took them all and then spent them on good things for Wang Zia. That bitch never refused his gifts. Maybe she also accepted gifts from others.

Heaven only knows what she'd had in her mind. She could have annulled their engagement and ran away. Why the fuck had she killed him?

But if she hadn't killed him, Wei wouldn't have reincarnated and gotten to live his life again, see Fei'er, and maybe repay some debts he owed a few friends from his previous life.

When the Devil Suppressing Array Formation was at its weakest moment, Wei activated the Seal Severing Array and opened a portal that would let him walk through. As soon as the portal opened, poisonous air blew across his face and his Yin Poison Pill Clone stirred inside his dantian in happiness. Jumping through the portal, Wei quickly set up a Small Sealing Array that prevented poisonous air from leaking through the portal. If he allowed the highly poisonous air to leak unrestrained, Chen Du and the little fox would die. The Common Poison Repelling Pills they had wouldn't save their lives, so he had to seal the opening from the other side.

After setting the array, he turned toward the other side of the array formation and his eyes remained wide open. Thousands of eyes stared at him from the medicinal fields, and they had a strong sense of contempt directed at him.

They were all snakes, and they were about to attack him.

Fuck!

Wang Zhang was sitting in a meditative state when the Energy Sensing Compass attached to his waist buzzed with activity. But by the time he opened his one eye, it had gone silent. He stared at the compass, trying to deduce if it had really buzzed or not. It was a natural treasure his father had given him to monitor the array formation inside the Snake Rearing Chamber, and it buzzed when the array formation was at its weakest. That was the time when poisonous air flew out from the other side, and he could send a thing or two to other side.

"It's too early to weaken." After thinking for a moment, he opened the seal to the Snake Rearing Chamber. It was earlier than expected, but he would check on it anyway.

When he walked through the door, vibrations ran down his legs. The Energy Sensing Compass went crazy, and it flew toward a large hole in the array formation. Thick smoke covered the entire area, and he couldn't see anything, yet he ran behind the Energy Sensing Compass. It was a treasure given to him by his father, and he couldn't lose it.

Wang Zhang's face darkened when he spotted the hole in the array formation, and he instantly turned back to get out of there. The array formation was open, and he had to report it to his father, great elder

Jiang. After waiting so many decades, the Wang clan would finally achieve the glory they deserved.

But before he could step out of the door that led to outside, fear gripped his heart. Something was coming at him, and he had no time to dodge it.

"Wood Symbolic Shield," he shouted in his mind and circulated his wood qi into his meridians, triggering a protective martial skill. It was the Wang clan's famous protective martial skill that had saved his life countless times.

Something heavy crashed into his back, shaking his internal organs despite the shield. Sweat trickled down his back. What if he hadn't used a defensive martial skill?

He would have died.

"Black-patched human, I've finally found you. Now die." Two fist-sized eyes stared at him before a pair of sharp fangs emerged from the smoke. They were coming for him, and they wanted blood. His blood.

There was no option anymore. Pulling the Blood Expansion Pill, he gulped it down.

Chapter 40

Thousands of snakes vs one man

Toxic winds blew over his face, swaying the leaves and branches of the medicinal trees, and from those branches tiny tongues slipped out and in. Out, then in, like a knife constantly stabbing Li Wei's skin.

System: Foreign environment detected. Environment is harmful to the host's body. Breathing is not recommended.

Wei gulped, and his mouth went dry. He wasn't sure if it was from fear or holding a breath. But he didn't dare to release that breath for fear of attracting the attention of the thousands of pairs of eyes lurking within the shadows of the trees.

There were unlimited snakes. More than he could count with his divine sense. And his divine sense had picked up another troublesome matter. A big hole of Cold Artic Snake Pit was close. Those bastards would freeze him to death if he disturbs them, so he had to make his way around and avoid them.

But first he had to deal with the unending tide of the snakes.

Seeing those snakes from the other side of the array formation was totally different from seeing them from ten feet away, ready to leap at his throat at any moment. Although he didn't fear snakes in general, seeing tens of thousands of them slithering around the trees wasn't pleasant.

If he'd said he was fine, his drenched back and shivering legs would betray his real condition.

Shit! He was freaked out inside. Even when facing death, he never feared it. But now, he hated these snakes. He hated all the snakes in the world. Why did they look so terrifying all of a sudden? They were everywhere. Every single branch within the medicinal forest was covered by a snake or two. They slithered around, hissing at him. They were coming down, converging to come at him.

He shifted his left leg slightly and turned to run, but then he spotted some Five Petal Life Herb not far away and his willpower firmed once more. In his mind, he could see the little fox lying on the bed, unable to get up. To save her, he needed this herb. There was also some Purple Slithering Fruit, used for curing blood diseases, nearby. And a Yin Yang Healing Vine.

Wait. A bunch of Yin Yang Healing Vines. Could he use them to produce the Yin Yang Liquid he would soon run out of?

No. He couldn't run away. He had to at least get his hands on the Five Petal Life Herb for the little fox before he hid his tail between his legs and took a U-turn.

All he had to do was to leap across these little snakes, grab a bunch of Five Petal Life Herb, and run. Even if some snakes bit him, he would heal.

A sharp pain bit into his foot, and he realized he had let his guard down. A snake had emerged from the ground and bit through his shoe. Poison burned through his blood stream, and he couldn't hold his breath anymore.

Jerking his leg, he kicked the snake away and took a deep breath. The poisonous air assaulted his nostrils, burning his windpipe as it reached his lungs, but his Yin Poison Pill Clone sucked in all the poison that his lungs had inhaled. It even sucked in all the poisonous air that had touched his body. In a breath's time, a one-foot area around him was devoid of poison. A clean air bubble had formed around him.

Wow! How could he forget about his trump card? Wasn't he immune to poison?

Maybe not. But at least he would survive this.

System: Analyzing host's body condition along with poison concentration in the surroundings and building a database for Yin Poison Pill Clone tenacity.

Yes, how could he miss that? This was only the first level of Pill Clone Alchemy Art. As he leveled up, it would develop new abilities. Currently, his Yin Poison Pill Clone could absorb poison for him—well, at least anything that touched or entered his body.

Now he just had to make a beeline for the Five Petal Herb and he would be done with this poisonous nonsense.

Zap!

One of the little snakes couldn't wait anymore and leaped at Wei.

Zap! Zap! Zap! . . . Zap!

All Wei's plans shattered like a house of glass. Dozens of snakes leaped at him, and he couldn't dodge them all. Actually, he was too afraid to dodge. Cowardly. But thinking about something and facing it were totally different things. He was about to activate his body cultivation when the Yin Poison Pill Clone inside his body stirred violently. It slammed against his dantian walls as if it wanted to get out and latch onto these snakes.

How could Wei let it run rampant inside his dantian? He suppressed it using his pure qi, but in doing so he missed attacking the snakes and one of those little bastards attached itself to his neck.

"Fu—" Another one latched onto his nose. Then one stuck to his forehead, almost biting his eyes. Covering his eyes with one hand, he squatted down. The last thing he wanted was to let one of the snakes latch onto his private parts.

A big snake, as thick as his arm, bit into his ass cheek, giving him an unforgettable pain of his life.

Poison entered his blood, rampaging inside his meridians and squashing his vitality. Poison was the nemesis of vitality, but his blood vitality was strong, so it began to fight the poison.

As if someone had poured lava inside his body, his blood began to burn, and add to that hundreds of snakes biting every inch of his skin. Other than his eyes and private parts, nothing was left intact. In ten breaths' time, he had turned into a bloody green demon.

He was about to regret his decision to come to this place when a moan echoed from his Yin Poison Pill Clone. He swore, if his pill clone could shout, it would sound like a moan. It shook profusely and a strange energy spread through his body, sucking all the poison from his blood like cold water leeching the heat from a hot surface.

Om!

Calm spread through his body, and the poisoned bits didn't feel that bad. Without the poison, his blood vitality surged and his wounds began to heal instantly. A common snake bite was nothing for his cultivation, and he was whole again in no time.

The snake bites turned into small irritations that had no power to harm but were still irritating. But looking at the excited moans coming out of his Yin Poison Pill Clone, he endured and sat down, letting the snakes have time of their lives.

Of course, he didn't remove his hand from his eyes or expose his crotch to the little bastards.

Ten minutes passed, and the snakes that had attached to his body dropped off, and then another batch of snakes leaped at him, but even they couldn't harm him. Other than some tiny puncture wounds that healed rapidly, nothing changed.

As the time passed, the color of his Yin Poison Pill Clone that had the shape of a pill casing slightly changed. From a faint green, it changed into a little darker shade of green. As mentioned in the Pill Clone Alchemy Art, pill clones would advance slowly and display different properties. Poison clones would change color, and wood clones would show a qualitative change in the wood qi they refined. As long as he kept letting the Yin Poison Pill Clone absorb poison, he should be able to upgrade it.

Rumble!

The onslaught stopped. An indescribable feeling gripped his heart, and when he spread his divine sense, his heart sunk to the bottom of his stomach. A snake that could swallow an entire tiger in one gulp was coming at him, and all the small snakes had slithered away in fear.

The giant snake raised its head and shot for his head.

Fuck! This damn bastard wanted to bite off his head.

Chapter 41

One man vs thousands of snakes

A mouth that could fit a whole tiger inside it came for Li Wei's head.

Wei gasped, looking at the dagger-sharp green teeth shining in the bright light, sending a chill across his bones. The rotten smell from the snake's mouth unleashed hell on Wei's nose from a ten-foot distance.

This bastard wanted to take a bite of his head and gulp him down.

Even though a snake's bite wouldn't threaten his life, if he lost his head he would die a bloody death. Until he reached a cultivation realm where he could regenerate his head, losing his head would be a no go.

No way. A complete no go.

Blood Earth Force Divine Art!

Wei shouted inside his mind, activating his life-saving divine art. Blood energy swirled around him, forming an impenetrable shield that could withstand an attack from a late Bone Baptization Realm cultivator with ease. So, what was this snake?

Two pairs of sharp teeth struck his Blood Earth Force shield and then, like glass shattering on stone, the pair of teeth crumbled under immense force. Wei couldn't look into the bastard snake's eyes, but he bet the snake was in a panic.

The Yin Poison Pill Clone in Wei's dantian moaned in excitement when a drop of poison fell on his blood shield and was absorbed inside his body instantly.

"You have something useful for me, but first let me punish you a little." Smirking, Wei punched at the snake's coiled body next to him.

His fist pierced through the air, hitting the snake and sending it flying away. A breath later, it crashed into a tall tree and dropped unconscious on the ground. If this large snake's poison could stir his pill clone from a distance, then how beneficial would its poison be for him?

The small snakes that had circled around Wei slithered backward, fear flashing through their eyes.

With long strides, Wei reached the large snake lying unconscious, but he wasn't sure how to get the poison out of the snake's mouth.

"System, is this snake recognizable?"

System: Accessing database.

Large Buffalo Striped Snake

A rare species with a useful poison property. This snake's poison can be used to create an antidote that can treat common poisons.

There was no anatomical information in the system's storage function. So how was he going to extract the poison? With the general knowledge from his previous life, he knew that most Ferocious Beasts stored their poison in their beast cores, but some had a poison sac or a special compartment behind their teeth to store poison. Was there any option but to kill this snake and dissect it?

He didn't want to kill these snakes—at least not the ones that were no threat to him. Because he had promised Rual'er not to hurt snakes. He'd been like this in his previous life too, and that's why Rual'er, the beast princess, fell for him. Sure, he had killed some people and beasts, but he did it only to save his life. Then too, he'd only killed certain people, leaving behind many loose ends that had bitten him later in l ife.

However, he had changed in this life. When killing people, he didn't hesitate anymore, and he pulled the weeds from the roots, but there was no enmity between him and these snake beasts, so he didn't want to kill them unless they were a direct threat to his life.

"Let's try this." Wei opened the snake's mouth and inserted his wrist before pressing it down. Although he didn't know the position of the poison in the snake's body, every snake, no exceptions, bit and poisoned others using their teeth, so the source of poison should be connected to the teeth.

The broken teeth sunk inside his skin, releasing a stream of poison into his blood.

Smiling, he closed his eyes and let the poison enter endlessly. It burned at first, but when his Yin Poison Pill Clone took action, the pain vanished, replaced by ecstasy.

When the poison stopped entering his body, he lay the Large Buffalo Striped Snake's head on the ground and scanned his surroundings. He was still surrounded by thousands of snakes, but they weren't taking any action. They were probing him from a distance. When he spread his divine sense, he found most of them were in the Refinement Realm and might not put even a dent on his skin.

Thinking about it, he picked a couple of Refinement Realm snakes and let them bite his other arm. They couldn't. Their teeth scratched against his skin but couldn't penetrate. At most, they left tiny white scratches over his skin after a fierce struggle. One of them even broke its fangs.

It made sense. As Wei progressed in his body cultivation, the tenacity of his body had increased and common weapons failed to leave a mark on his body. Only high-tier Bronze Grade weapons could threaten him. Although Blood Essence Body cultivation didn't make his skin and muscles as tough as steel, the essence energy accumulating inside his blood nourished his muscles, bones and skin, and this nourishment improved his body composition by a degree.

What about the early Foundation Realm snakes?

He picked a couple and let them bite him. Their teeth sunk into his skin after some struggle. So, the current realm still had some effect on him. The large snake he had knocked out was peak Foundation Realm, layer eight to be exact, so its broken teeth could also sink in his body.

If he wanted to get a lot of poison for his pill clone, he had to find all the Foundation Realm snakes in the surrounding area and make them bite him.

"Let's start with that." Patting his chest to remove dust, he changed into a new robe and tore away his sleeves. After making sure he had plenty of skin exposed, he spread his divine sense around and marked all the Foundation Realm snakes in a three-hundred-foot radius.

Suppress!

He unleashed the aura of a layer eight body Foundation Realm cultivator from his body and every snake in the Refinement Realm slithered away in a hurry. While qi cultivators used manifestations of energy like Bone Manifestation, body cultivators cultivated an aura after reaching the Bone Baptization Realm. Of course, Wei couldn't bring out his true aura— he was still in the Foundation Realm—but by tainting his divine sense with his body cultivation, he achieved a similar result in a shallower version.

A smug smile popped on his face when he saw the thousands of Foundation Realm snakes around him. Now he was going to suck them dry. Previously, it was thousands of snakes against one man, but now it was opposite. One man was going to instill fear inside thousands of snakes.

Chapter 42

Little young master

Fan Ji swirled around the King Vitality Tree's top branch and basked in the bright daylight. It was a rare occasion to get this much daylight. In the depths of the Beast Origin Realm, where he'd lived his whole snake life —ten years to be precise—daylight was a luxury. Once every month, his father allowed his guards to fly Fan Ji to the top of Heaven Penetrating Mountain Peak and enjoy the view. The daylight provided warmth as well as nutrients to his body and helped him grow quicker.

And here at the edge of the Beast Origin Realm, every one of his clan members could climb a tree and bask in the frigging daylight. The best thing? The daylight never vanished. What a wonderful life they enjoyed. If only Father didn't prohibit him from coming here, he would have lived here forever, but he had less than ten days left to enjoy the daylight before he had to go back into the depths of the Beast Origin Realm.

"Young master, let's go back," a Three Eyed Snake said in a polite tone as he slithered around the bark of the King Vitality Tree. His huge body nearly covered the entire lower portion of the tree.

"Leader Ninth, I just frigging got here, and you want me to go back? Why?" Leader First to Leader Ninth were their clan's nine leaders, and they all worked under his father's command.

"Little young master, a human has broken through the Barrier Sealing Formation of the White Bone Trees and is killing our clan members. I'll head to the outermost edge and deal with him. I can't leave you unprotected in this area. This servant requests you go back to Leader Eighth's territory and enjoy the scenery. You might meet little Fuishui and play with her."

"A human?" Fan Ji's eyes shone with a strange light. "I've never seen a human, only heard about this two-legged beast. My father told me it is the most fascinating beast in the universe. Take me with you when you kill him. I want to see what kind of beast this human is." His father called humans the most despicable beast, and he wanted to see it for himself before it was killed by his clan leaders.

Leader Ninth almost dropped from the tree. "Little young master. Why are you joking with your servant? You, above all, shouldn't see a human. These humans have strange powers. They can even capture us and force us into strange contracts. And I've heard this human is very powerful, so I can't take you there."

Fan Ji was about to say something when one of their clan members, a Large Buffalo Striped Snake, slid his way from the outer edge, carrying a strange five-fingered print on his body. When he opened his mouth, Fan Ji saw his broken teeth.

How could he be missing teeth? Who dared to bully a friend of Leader Ninth? He had high standing in this area and just yesterday had bragged about going against Leader Ninth once. Did he fall in a pit or what?

"Brother Buffalo, what happened?" Leader Ninth slid forward, greeting the Large Buffalo Striped Snake in his way.

"Leader Ninth, this brother of yours failed to kill that human. He is too strong and vicious." Blood dripped from his broken teeth.

"The human did this? That bastard. How dare he try to kill you, my sworn brother." Leader Ninth circled around the Large Buffalo Striped Snake, but he couldn't find any other injury. Because other than the handprint on his body and his broken teeth, the Large Buffalo Striped Snake looked well.

Just a little dispirited.

"No." The Large Buffalo Striped Snake coughed. "He could easily have killed me, but he only sucked all my poison out. These broken teeth are the result of me biting a strange shield around his body. He is too strong for us."

Fan Ji shuddered. That human had sucked in the Large Buffalo Striped Snake's poison? The Large Buffalo Striped Snake was the most vicious snake for Foundation Realm cultivators, and its poison could even threaten Leader Ninth despite him being in the Bone Baptization Realm. If this human had sucked away the Large Buffalo Striped Snake's poison, that meant he must be a very, very powerful beast.

"What? Sucked your poison? How vicious." Leader Ninth roared furiously. "That human must die. Every human must die. They massacre us once every twenty days and then pretend they are good people. But is this human the same one Fuishui is searching for?"

Fuishui. Fan Ji's mind wavered for a moment. It had been years since he last saw her.

"No. This human has no eye patch." The Large Buffalo Striped Snake curled around the King Vitality Tree's branch, replenishing his might. This tree was the best for their clan members to recuperate quickly. "He vanished after sucking hundreds of our brothers dry. He took some herbs with him. But those herbs are useless for us."

"What are the casualties?" Leader Ninth asked, his voice becoming heavy.

Fan Ji's heart grew heavier too. For the last two years, every twenty days, these humans massacred thousands of their brothers, enough to thin their lower-level population. If this continued, they might lose all the lower-level clan members in a year or two. Worse, these lower-level clan members couldn't enter the inner area of the forest. Without a stronger bloodline, they would inevitably die in the inner areas of the forest. Here, at least they could retreat in time and save their lives, and yet thousands of them died every twenty days. Still, it was better than millions of them dying in one go.

Fan Ji wished his father could come here and wipe out every human that dared to barge into this realm, but he couldn't. Nor could the first few leaders of his council because of the array formation that protected the Heart Garden of this area.

"None. That's the strangest thing. He didn't kill anyone. Not even the lowest level clan member. Even when those little ones bit him, he threw them away without harming them. The only thing he did was suck everyone's poison. It's the most insulting thing someone has done to me in the last fifty years, and I'm embarrassed to say that I'm no match for him."

Leader Ninth curled around a large boulder before speaking out. "Guards."

Three Giant Two Fang Snakes came out of their holes. "Leader Ninth, please order."

"Heed my command. Ask all our brothers in the Refinement Realm to comb the outer edge of the area in the next two hours. That human might have released Beast Berserk Venom, and we can't afford any more casualties."

Fan Ji's mood dampened. He had heard about this venom from his father, and everyone above the Bone Baptization Realm feared it, so not even Leader Ninth or Leader Eighth dared to go into the outskirts of the Beast Origin Realm.

If only that human hadn't arrived, he could have enjoyed more time in daylight.

"Little young master, go back to Leader Seventh's territory. We can't keep you here anymore. I'll head to Leader Eighth and discuss our next action."

Fan Ji nodded, but he wished to kill this human and make sure he didn't come back again. This was a rare opportunity for him, and he didn't want to waste it just because a human had trespassed in the Beast Origin Realm.

This human seemed like a filthy evil character, and he'd better confirm it with his own eyes. But how could he get away from Leader Ninth?

Chapter 43

Secret Herb Garden

Li Wei made his way through the tall trees that grew in the open plain. He hated to admit it, but he had lost his way while sucking those snakes dry, and he hadn't found the array formation even after moving through the trees for two hours.

Then he'd seen the lone mountain in the distance and decided to go there. From the mountain, he should be able to figure out which direction to go to reach the array formation.

When he reached the lone mountain, he crashed on his ass at the edge of a medicinal garden in exhaustion and astonishment. How could this place be so different from other places in this pocket realm?

Like a greedy, hungry beggar, he sucked in a lot of fresh air devoid of poison.

Wei glanced at the expanse medicinal herbs swaying in front of his eyes in the north wind. They reminded him of one of the holy lands of the super sect he'd once visited in his previous life. Just the medicinal aroma exuded from the plants made him feel like he could break through in his qi cultivation.

It was that good. Or should he say holy?

In a one-mile-square area, a curated medicinal garden stood erect at the base of the small mountain. This was the lone mountain he'd seen when he first visited this pocket realm, but he'd never thought it would hold such a secret at its base. A water spring originated in the middle of the mountain slope, and flowed down into the medicinal garden slowly, as if someone regulated the flow to water the plants all year long.

Another strange thing he saw was tens of thousands of low-level snakes swirling around the herbs, but there was no foul air around the garden. Although he didn't worry about poisonous air anymore, it was good to breathe in fresh air once in a while. How could such a place exist in the realm of snakes?

The open plain he'd seen filled with various medicinal plants was nothing in front of this behemoth of herbs swaying in front of his naked eyes. If the sects outside knew about this place, they would go mad. It was equivalent to a holy land of a super sect in the Martial Realm.

"How could this place exist in the realm of snakes?" This was inconceivable.

This was a different place than what he had seen from the other side of the array formation. This was the true heart of the medicinal fields he'd seen from the other side.

"Could there be a Divine Transcending Mud Vine growing here? Doesn't it require constant rain?" For the first time, he opened his mouth and asked himself. A black vine swirled around a thin, giant tree. It was a Divine Transcending Mud Vine, a rare Earth Grade herb that only grew in the rain forest in a special area in the Martial Realm.

A special skin care cream used this vine as an ingredient, and that cream had many women going mad in the Martial Realm. Once, Wang Zia had wanted this vine, so he had shelled out all his savings to buy a single piece of this herb. It was that ridiculous, and he had been that ridiculous.

Well, he knew the ingredients required for the face cream, and in this life, it hadn't been invented yet. Maybe he should hoard the ingredients after entering the Martial Realm.

Then he spotted a Green Shoot Bamboo Tree growing in a corner. It was excellent material for making arrows and could pierce even an iron wall when carved with an Edge Sharpening Array. Well, he couldn't borrow a bow from Tang Sia. That was bad. But he could collect this bamboo to make few arrows for his use. He had plans to use the Giant Killing Bow Divine Art in the future, so he'd better collect as much materials as he could.

Yes, he'd better collect the bamboo tree.

He took a step inside the garden but retreated immediately. Thousands—no, millions—of snakes leaped at him when he took a step inside, and he'd recoiled in fright. As soon as he stepped back, the snakes retreated.

That was frightening. Really frightening. He had been fighting snakes all day long, but they were just in the thousands, if not tens of thousands. But here there were at least a million snakes, and as far as his divine sense could spread, all he saw was snakes. Agreed, low-level snakes, but he didn't dare to go in.

Well, did he really have to go in? He could muster the courage and barge his way in, but he was exhausted from the constant fighting and poison sucking, and he had to get back to the little fox.

Rubbing his subtle beard, he thought about it, but then decided to enter the garden. He was exhausted after sucking thousands of snakes dry of their poison, and he had gotten what he'd come for, so he would go back and concoct a Beast Rejuvenating Pill for the little fox. Along with Five Petal Life Herb, he also got a few Vitality Breaking Thorne, Yang Food Carcasses, and Red Foul Heart Berry.

But before that, he would set up a Blood Marker Array for the future. He would definitely come back in a few days and see if could find a way to get some of those precious herbs.

Chapter 44

Blood Sacrifice Arrays

Sitting at the edge of the secret herb garden, Li Wei washed his dirty face with cold water and then tied his long black hair into a neat bun. Glancing at the burning sky, he thanked the heavens for giving him a storage ring. If he didn't have it, he might look like a dirty beggar out of a mud pit.

Drinking a lot of cold water, he placed the water skin on the grass plain and rubbed the back of his neck. It had been a long and tiring journey, and now after getting rid of the nasty poison—and benefiting from it—he wondered why he kept facing troubles that made him stretch beyond his limits. That was totally the opposite of his dao, but things just got messed up a lot, and he was under constant pressure from life-threatening events.

Within the long shadows that extended from the huge trees at the edge of the secret garden, he extended his feet and stretched his legs before pulling a piece of crafting paper out of his storage ring. Actually, listening to the birds chirping, he could have taken a good old nap, but he resisted the urge and brushed his fingers against the rough crafting paper. It was low-quality crafting paper, a gift from Tang Sia. Since he hadn't paid her, it was a gift. Suddenly he recalled the lie he'd told Sun Hua about Tang Sia being his girlfriend. Sun Hua was so shocked when he'd pulled that prank on her.

He sighed.

Who would have dared to attack her inside the sect? Could it be the Wang clan? They had a nasty habit of doing bad things, and he wouldn't be surprised to find their name behind everything. Now he realized why Tang Sia hadn't been able to do anything when she became the sect master in his previous life, and the sect had actually declined under her leadership. Well, he had no interest in helping her now. For now, he was done with the Divine Fragrance Palace. After he left this place, he would leave the sect and find his own path to study alchemy. There was no redemption for the sect. For Fei'er, he would take decision based on her progress inside the sect. She was different, and maybe the sect was the best place for her.

Pushing all those thoughts aside, he focused on the crafting paper in front of him. This secret herb garden was a gold mine for any alchemist, and he had so many things to collect from here.

"System, access the memory of Blood Sacrifice Arrays."

System: Accessing database to extract Blood Sacrifice Array information.

A list of ten arrays appeared, and along with them a beast girl's, Rual'er's, memory surfaced from his subconscious. Her delicate look, her dainty lips. She'd looked like a doll, but when she was angry, she turned into a goddess of war. Without her opponent knowing, she would pull out her bow and start shooting deadly arrows that could wipe out an entire army. She had a nickname from doing that, actually. Goddess of Blood Rain.

She was the strongest archer he'd ever known, and she had even tried to teach him a few things, but they had drifted apart. These arrays had been a gift from her. In the Martial Realm, these arrays were taboo because they originated from demonic cultivators, but beasts worked with the righteous and demonic sides simultaneously, so it wasn't surprising that she had knowledge like this. For Wei, there was no black and white when it came to arrays. As long as they increased his comprehension of arrays, he studied them.

Unfortunately, he couldn't use taboo arrays out in the open, but here he could. One of those arrays was called Blood Marker Array. It was a simple array that could leave a marker on a certain place using one's blood. It would act like a beacon as long as the array carver came within a fifty-mile radius of the marker. Sure, there were some other similar arrays that didn't need blood, and one could even buy a marker talisman, but Wei didn't have access to any of those right now, so this was his choice. There was another use to the blood marker, but that would leave Wei crippled, so he had no plans to use it. With the blood marker placed, he planned to come back to this place in the future and harvest the herbs for himself. There were too many awesome herbs to ig nore.

The only issue with this array was it was one of the largest array diagrams, and he would have to give his full attention to it. So, he quickly set up a concealment array around himself and poured a drop of blood on the middle of the crafting paper where he planned to start the diagram. Gazing at the paper, he judged the places where the four quadrants of the array would go and marked them with a charcoal stick. Even for him, setting up landmarks beforehand would prove useful.

Dripping his bristle brush inside the beast blood bottle, he drew his first stroke on the paper and then the second and the third. Stroke after stroke, he filled the first quadrant, and intermittently, he poured blood on the paper at the source points in the array. The entire array was like a painting in itself. Beasts, trees, and whatnot were present in the array.

Minutes passed and then hours, but his right hand moved over the white craft paper like a painter moving his brush on a canvas, lost in the art itself. A sense of calm spread through his mind, making him enjoy the feeling he loved the most. The feeling of carving. In this life, he hadn't gotten back to this feeling, but today he did. To celebrate his state, even the air around him seemed to become stale in itself. All the tension and worry vanished from his mind.

Unknown to him, something stirred around his neck, and a thread of red entered his body from the Primordial Blood Palace. Unaware of the change, Wei continued carving the array in peace. It had been days since he'd found such a peaceful environment where he could just carve an array and enjoy it to the fullest. A smile hung on his face as he reached the end, and when he lifted his brush, a wave of tiredness suddenly struck him. But that didn't stop him from grinning with a wide-open mouth.

A bloody red light pulsed through the array when Wei completed it. It had exceeded the expected grade and reached high-tier Silver Grade from its original mid-tier Silver Grade limit. In fact, the grades were not set in stone and gave general guidance to average array cultivators. So, when someone called an array a low-tier Silver Grade array, it actually meant that an average cultivator's array had a high chance of coming out as a low-tier Silver Grade array.

Wei wasn't an average array cultivator in his previous life, nor was he one in this life. With his abundant experience, divine sense, and comprehension he could easily lift the tier of an array to the next level. For this array, he had used his own blood, blood filled with so much vitality that it could enhance anything, so the array being upgraded by a tier wasn't a surprise.

Getting up, he dug a long hole in the ground and placed the crafting paper inside, then poured a vial of his corrupted blood on it. When he was poisoned, he had collected his corrupt blood, and that was sufficient to act as a power source for this array for weeks, if not months.

Suddenly he saw a light flickering next to the hole, and when he dug it there, he found a Fallen Star Rock.

"Wow, this thing." He remembered Wang Zia needed this rock in his previous life. It was quite rare in Mortal Realm and he could use it in some arrays, so he grabbed the five-pound heavy piece.

Now it was time to go back and concoct pills for the little fox. Although Chen Du was there to take care of her, he felt heavy she wasn't with him. However, before he took off, a cute animal dashed at him and snatched the corrupt blood bottle from him and then drank it

.

It was a purple mink, and she was so cute that Wei tried to stop her from drinking his corrupt blood, but he could only grab her corpse. She was as dead as anyone could be.

That was a bummer. Looking at her cute face, Wei felt disappointment in his heart, so he picked her body up and carried it back with him. He would find a good place to bury her. At least that would save her corpse from being mutilated by other beasts.

Chapter 45

Beacon of Hope

Chen Du watched over the furry brown fox lying on a soft bedroll inside the wooden hut. From outside, she looked fine and only a couple of bandages remained covering her. Most of the scars were gone, replaced by new tender fur.

But he knew she wasn't doing well. The pills brother Wei fed her only alleviated her injuries, and she would need better pills or more of the Beast Rejuvenating Pills brother Wei concocted.

Sitting in the corner, he poured a couple of ingredients into the furnace and started processing, but his gaze darted to check on her. Despite brother Wei saying she was a normal beast, Chen Du knew she wasn't. She had to be a high-tier Ferocious Beast—there was no way a Beast Rejuvenating Pill wouldn't save a normal pet fox unless it was completely dead.

From the way he treated her, Chen Du knew she wasn't a contract beast either. Brother Wei cared deeply about her. His family had once had a pet dog they loved. He was injured once, and Chen Du's mother had cried for an entire night. For two years, his mother had tried everything to cure him, but in the end he'd died. It was one of the reasons Chen Du had searched for a beast healing recipe and found the Lesser Beast Rejuvenating Pill recipe in an old book belonging to a friend's clan.

Fire crackled below the furnace, pulling his attention back to refinement and his reason for joining an alchemy sect: to save his little sister, Daiyu'er. She had been bedridden since she was ten years old, and when no alchemist they knew could cure her, he'd joined the Divine Fragrance Palace hoping to save her.

But so far, he'd not only failed to find a cure, but he'd also failed to join a faction inside the sect. He was reduced to cannon fodder in the end.

Then he'd met brother Wei, and something had changed inside him.

Glancing in the direction brother Wei had left this morning, his emotions grew complex. What kind of person was Li Wei, and how could he have so many secrets? First the Gold Grade cauldron, then gold-colored wood qi, and then the Five Petal Life Herb—one of the rarest herbs in alchemy. It was used to treat life-threatening disease in cultivators, and brother Wei had used it on a lowly beast. That proved how reliable brother Wei was. At first, Chen Du had only envied him for his prowess and genius alchemy, but now he respected him as a person. A person who treated his beast companion as family would never be a bad person.

Maybe brother Wei could help him heal Daiyu'er's disease. Thinking about her, his heart shuddered. Was she okay? Since coming to the Divine Fragrance Palace a year back, he hadn't been able to return to the clan for a visit. He loved her a lot, but he'd found no cure for her. For the last five years, he'd read every alchemy book he could get his hands on to find a cure, but he'd found none. It drove him to join the Divine Fragrance Palace, but the Wang clan had pushed him into the

Waste Disposal Faction, and now he had to fight his way out of this whole mess.

He rubbed his face, unable to control his emotions. What if he died here? What would happen to Daiyu'er? His mother would die if Daiyu'er didn't survive, nor would he be able to live without her. When he'd walked into this poisoned hell, he'd lost all hope. One day of watering, and he'd almost given up on saving his life or saving Daiyu'er.

No, he couldn't give up on this. If brother Wei could do this, why couldn't he, Chen Du? Granted, brother Wei had a heaven-defying fate, and he was a genius when it came to alchemy. His alchemy art was out of this world, his golden wood qi was extraordinary, and his comprehension was . . . Holy heavens, Chen Du had no words to describe it.

But Chen Du had perseverance and patience. If he could walk away from his clan's tradition of array cultivation, he could find a cure for Daiyu'er too. What if he begged brother Wei? Could *he* find a cure for Chen Du's little sister?

Maybe he could. The pill recipe Chen Du had given him was an impossible task. It was an ancient recipe, and no one knew the correct form of it. He had happened upon it in an old book and had asked numerous alchemists about it, but everyone said it was impossible to concoct an ancient pill recipe. They said one needed a high-tier alchemy art and special wood qi. They said only great elders from an alchemy sect might concoct such a pill, so he'd had to shelve it in his memory to research in the future.

He'd only given it to brother Wei to ease his heart. Giving up was heart-crushing, so he'd given brother Wei hope so he would try, fail, and then feel a little easier about the loss.

Chen Du's heart trembled. Was he doing same for Daiyu'er? He had been trying hard for the last five years, but failing again and again. Did he treat it as a way to ease his heart?

No. It couldn't be. Brother Wei had completed an impossible task. He'd even concocted a rank three, one pill line Beast Rejuvenating Pill. Yes, he would try harder and succeed. Brother Wei had arrived as a beacon of success in his life, and he would follow it to the end.

"Brother Du, what are you doing? Are you trying to burn down the entire hut?" Brother Wei's voice pulled Chen Du from his ruminations, and then he spotted fire coming out of the cauldron. It had almost reached the ceiling of the wooden hut.

Ass!

Su Pan paced outside of the small stone chamber while constantly checking on the jasmine incense burning in the corner. He'd lit it shortly after sending a message to master Jiang. Now it was almost completely burned, but master Jiang wasn't here. Had he given up on his son? Granted, Wang Zhang was a despicable criminal, and he'd only gotten a pardon because of master Jiang, but he was still master Jiang's son by blood.

Stopping midway across the chamber, he glanced at the closed stone door. Wang Zhang lay inside, being treated by one of the Wang clan elders. An hour ago, Su Pan had been heading toward the Waste Disposal Faction to check on their month's pill usage when he saw Wang Zhang trudging out of the Waste Disposal Building in a dire state. Covered in cuts, he was on the verge of death, so Su Pan had picked him up and brought him here, knowing his true position. Despite being a criminal, he was the master's son, and Su Pan ought to save him for his master, if nothing else.

"Who did this?" Master Jiang's thunderous voice struck his ears, and he turned around to greet his master.

"Disciple greets master." Su Pan bowed.

"Pan'er. What happened to my son? Why is he in this condition?" Master Jiang shivered, his face as dark as a poisoned person's face. Without warning, he kicked the stone chamber door open and rushed in.

"Master Jiang, the treatment—" Su Pan stopped when he saw master Jiang pull a Jade Dew Marrow out of his storage ring.

He gulped. In his decades as an alchemist, he had only read about this heavenly elixir in books. It could save a person below the Boiling Blood Realm from death, no matter their condition. But it would also shorten the person's life by half.

No one could get their hands on this elixir because it was made from the Jade Boned Ant's Marrow, a Boiling Blood Realm Ferocious Beast that was too rare to find out and about. Only ancestor Wang had a few drops of this elixir in the entire Wang clan, and master Jiang was wasting it on his criminal son. Even if he saved Wang Zhang now, Wang Zhang could only continue to guard the Snake Rearing Chamber. The Jade Dew Marrow wasn't worth a father's love for a guard.

The dew worked like a charm. Wang Zhang, who couldn't even take a calm breath before, opened his eyes and stared at his father.

"Father . . ."

"Zhang'er, tell me who did this to you."

"Father . . . portal open. We can go in." He muttered a few more words before falling unconscious again. However, this time his unconsciousness was due to exhaustion and not because of the dire injuries he had suffered.

Master Jiang got up and turned around. "Su Pan, you always showed a filial attitude, and now it's your time to ride high heavens with the Wang clan. Prepare the princess. We are going somewhere."

Chapter 46

Tea Ceremony

Fire leaped at Li Wei when he entered the wooden hut, nearly burning the subtle beard he'd grown since entering the Snake Rearing Chamber. Ducking down, he avoided the fire, and his gaze darted to the corner where he had laid the little fox on a soft bedroll. His heart eased when he saw her sleeping peacefully.

The fire was yards away from her, and she wasn't in any danger.

"Brother Du, what are you doing? Are you trying to burn down the entire hut?" he shouted, irritated at the brute lost in his thoughts. What the fuck was so absorbing that he forgot there was a little fox lying in the same hut. Wei didn't care if he wanted to burn himself, but if the fire had touched a single hair on the little fox's body, Wei would have roasted Chen Du alive.

Chen Du stared at the furnace in shock and then looked at Wei foolishly.

What the heck was wrong with this brute? Waving his hand, Wei conjured a water barrel from his storage ring and emptied it on the burning furnace, quelling the furious fire instantly. Smoke rose from the red-hot metal of the furnace wall and cracks appeared. That furnace was a goner, and judging from the smoke coming from inside, the inside herbs were a goner too.

"Brother Wei, why are you naked?"

Wei stared at Chen Du. That was the brute's first thought after this mess? No explanation for the fire, no apology.

His forehead tingled, and he wanted to kick Chen Du's ass for his negligence, but he let it go. Exhaustion assailed him in the wake of the intense fight. Not that it had been supremely difficult, but when thousands of snakes bit one, one tends to feel exhausted. Right?

Ignoring Chen Du, Wei donned a new robe. Thanks to Fei'er, he had enough robes that he could discard one every day for the next two months. And they all were made of the finest silk material, soft and comfortable. They even smelled like her.

"Forget about it. I got the ingredients." Wei pulled the Five Petal Life Herb from his storage ring and smiled peacefully. By the blessing of the heavens, he had obtained three stalks of Five Petal Life Herb, enough for fifteen batches of Beast Rejuvenating Pills.

"You really went behind the array formation?" Chen Du cupped his mouth, his gaze turning weird.

Wei smiled. "Brother Du, this is for you." He handed a Purple Slithering Fruit to Chen Du. It was a low-tier Gold Grade fruit that could help one while advancing to the Bone Baptization Realm. He had found two of them, so he gave one to Chen Du. If it wasn't for Chen Du's recipe, the little fox might have died already.

"Is that . . ." Chen Du clawed at the fruit like it would vanish from his gaze. "This is . . ." Drool formed at the corner of his mouth. "Holy heaven's ass. This really is a Purple Slithering Fruit. But how could you . . ." He stared at Wei like he was a god. "Brother Wei." He bowed his head. "I can't express my gratitude, and I won't be courteous enough to reject it, so I'll keep it." The fruit vanished into his robes.

Wei chuckled. "Brothers shouldn't be courteous to each other." He patted Chen Du's left shoulder. This brute wasn't a pretentious bastard, and that's what Wei liked about him.

"Brother Wei, this is a big haul. If you sell this fruit, it will definitely fetch you a good price. I bet you can get at least a thousand low-quality Qi Stones for this fruit. And if you refine it into a pill, then the price will skyrocket."

"You do whatever you like. I've got one more." Wei displayed his own fruit. It wasn't even one hundred years old yet. Once he used his Yin Yang Liquid on it, it would be two hundred years old, and then the price would grow exponentially. Thinking about the Yin Yang Liquid, his thoughts wandered around the Yin Yang Healing Vine he'd spotted in the inner area of the medicinal garden. If he hadn't had to rush back to the little fox, he would have harvested them. But no worries, he would go back soon. For the poison and for some Yin Yang Healing Vines.

"Brother Du," Wei said, now solemn. "Please continue looking after the little fox for a while. I'll concoct a new batch of Beast Rejuvenating Pills." With the ingredients in his hands, he ought to concoct the pills and help her recuperate as quickly as possible.

"Brother Wei, you've gifted me this fruit so I can't be stingy with you. I'll share this tea with you." He pulled a small flask from the pouch he carried with him and poured a purple-colored liquid into the two glasses. "This is Lasting Kashaya Tea my girlfriend prepared. This is the best tea she has ever brewed, and it tastes best when served hot."

Wei squinted when the intense, bitter smell wafted out of the purple tea. One whiff of the fragrance, and Wei's mind went calm. Calm as a meditating buddha. Calm as still water. Calm as a dead person.

"Where did you hide it? Why didn't you share it earlier?"

Chen Du smiled sheepishly. "Brother Wei, we only knew each other on surface at that time..."

Wei chuckled.

Closing his eyes, he bowed lightly to the teacup. It wasn't a bow to the tea, but to the person who had made this tea. This was indeed Lasting Kashaya Tea, a tea made from the last leaves of a Kashaya Tree. A Kashaya Tree was a common long-lived medicinal plant used for multiple things, including in tea making, herb processing, and so much more. But even this long-lived tree would die one day, and when it died all its leaves fell like a rainfall. The last five leaves of a dying Kashaya Tree had no medicinal properties, but they did have a strong sense of death and the calmness after death. If one used the last five leaves to make tea, it was called Lasting Kashaya Tea, and it was said to help a person achieve a trance state that could give him the sensation of peace after death, and one would never fear death again.

Of course, this was only true for mortals. If a cultivator drank it, he could achieve a special calmness in his cultivation and comprehend things that were hard to comprehend. But only a few had the good fortune to find the last five leaves out of the thousands of leaves falling, and the process for making this tea was quite difficult as well.

Thinking about the tea, Wei remembered a tea ceremony senior brother Jiang Jai had taught him once, the Tea Soul Ceremony.

In his previous life, he had always thought about learning tea making, and senior brother Jiang kept talking about this Tea Soul Ceremony. Senior brother Jiang was a fellow sect member from the Firmament Sect who excelled in tea making, and Wei had often enjoyed tea with him. It was a noble art, and Wei had always wanted to learn it but never had time. Maybe in this life he could start with the Tea Soul Ceremony and walk on the path of tea making. There was an inheritance lying around Old Martial City for tea making, but he could always start with what he learned from senior brother Jiang first.

But before that, he had to enjoy this tea.

Taking a deep breath, he brought the cup to his nose and inhaled the aroma. Then he slowly raised the cup in the air, thanking the heavens for the fine tea, and then the tea maker, before taking the first sip. The first sip was important, too. Letting it slowly enter his stomach, he savored the taste. When it was inside his stomach, he let the taste settle in with closed eyes and enjoyed it until it subsided in a few breaths' time. Like this, he enjoyed the remaining tea as well.

This was how senior brother Jiang had made him enjoy every tea. It had a deep meaning of respecting the heavens, respecting the tea maker, and respecting the tea. By following it, one would earn the right to drink and enjoy the tea. Without this ceremony, one would only be drinking fragrant water and nothing else.

"What a fine tea. Chi'er keeps amusing me with all her tea making." The brute Chen Du gulped it down like he was drinking a roadside tea.

Insolent. Suppressing his anger, Wei slowly savored his tea, enjoying the mental solitude it brought with it. For a few breaths, he forgot everything else. All the worries he carried on his shoulder vanished, letting him free.

Click!

Something clicked. This was part of his dao of laziness. Seeking the sense of freedom.

Pulling his Diary of Dao of Laziness out, he jotted down the third rule.

1) Never cry. It takes you on the path of revenge, and you have to work hard to do that. Instead, eliminate anything that can make you cry.

2) Make everything shabby. Having nothing to protect means you can be as lazy as you want to be.

3) Seek freedom. That's the ultimate goal.

He savored the tea for thirty breaths, and then he closed his eyes to prepare his mind for pill concoction. He didn't really need to do anything, as his mind had already reached the calm state needed for pill concoction.

But with a calm mind, he sensed the intricacies of the concoction in a new light. This was a process, and he had to think about it as a process.

Wei paused, opened his eyes, and looked at the ingredients he'd placed in front of him. They were all jumbled up. To concoct a Beast Rejuvenating Pill, he first had to prepare Qi Water, and he'd prepared it right before it needed it last time. Well, he could have prepared it in advance for all the items.

He would do that now.

There was another thing he noticed. The last time he'd merged two catalysts, he'd had to do it in the air and, although it had worked with the help of the system, it used excess wood qi. If he had another cauldron at room temperature, the wood qi consumption would be halved. Last time he was pressed for time, but now he had some time so he could carve a Temperature Regulation Array, a semi-permanent solution, or a cheap Temperature Draining Array like the one's he asked Wu Xiodia to sell to the Divine Fragrance Palace. Or a little better Temperature Morphing Array.

But after giving it some thought, Wei prepared to go ahead with the Temperature Regulation Array. First, that would be a semi-permanent solution, and it would prove useful in the long term. Second, he would carve it on the cauldron itself. The many recipes he had seen required the finest temperature control and . . . Wait. He would need to carve it with his own qi as it was a Gold Grade array. That was a problem, because he had regressed into qi Refinement Realm.

Could he use wood qi? Glancing at the tiny piece of Dragon Healing Wood, he decided not to go there. He couldn't waste any resource on other things.

So, a cheap Temperature Morphing Array it was.

In the next half an hour, he carved a Temperature Morphing Array that could be activated using a low-quality Qi Stone.

Glancing at the tiny thumb-width piece of Dragon Healing Wood remaining, Wei calculated he would only need a quarter of it for the next batch of pill processing thanks to the Temperature Morphing Array. That meant he had four chances to concoct pills, and he had to succeed at all four tries this time.

With the calm mind, he began concocting the new batch of pills.

Chapter 47

Saving female snake

Chen Du watched brother Wei concoct pill batch after pill batch. He waited for a batch to appear with a pill line, but it didn't happen. So far, he had concocted three batches comprising four, six, and five pills in each of them, but they were all rank three or rank two at most. When brother Wei started the third batch, Chen Du nearly stopped him, but he didn't. Brother Wei was a genius, and Chen Du wanted to see how much longer brother Wei could carry on.

Brother Wei didn't disappoint, amazing him once more. For a Pill Adapt, two consecutive batches of mid-tier Silver Grade pills was treading into awesomeness territory. Any alchemist would be long spent before that point occurred, but brother Wei performed three batches in a row and looked like he could do another one if he pushed himself. This was just amazing. How could the Divine Fragrance Palace miss out on a prodigy like this, consigning him to the Waste Disposal Faction? They must have gone mad when they recruited brother Wei. And what brother Wei had told him about coming through the back door, that had to be a lie. Chen Du knew it was when he'd pulled out his real beast flame, a Silver Grade beast flame, after borrowing a low-tier Bronze Grade beast flame from Chen Du.

Brother Wei may have been trying to hide his secrets, but he got busted when his pet was injured. Maybe it was a good thing that the little fox had gotten hurt so Chen Du could see through brother Wei's disguise of pretending to be a pig to eat a tiger.

Long live brother Wei.

But this time, brother Wei left Chen Du disappointed when he didn't refine his herbs in the air. Chen Du had been looking forward to witnessing that technique again to see if he could learn something of it. Too bad, brother Wei had used an array to reduce the temperature of the cauldron. If Chen Du guessed correctly, it was a Temperature Morphing Array, and it hadn't been there before.

Had brother Wei carved it himself?

Chen Du shuddered at that thought. It was a high-tier Silver Grade array, and one needed to be a Three Star Array Apprentice to carve them. Was brother Wei a Three Star Array Apprentice too? He'd passed through the array formation and came back intact, and since they were still alive, he hadn't broken open the array formation. If he had, they would have drowned in snakes by now. Was he really a Three Star Array Apprentice too?

No way. Brother Wei must have carved it beforehand and Chen Du missed it. Becoming a Pill Adapt required so much effort. How could brother Wei also become a Three Star Array Apprentice? In fact, array cultivators were rarer than alchemists, and they required support from a sect like the Heavenly Firmament Sect. And these sects had stringent requirements. Despite the Chen family serving the Heavenly Firmament Sect for centuries, they only got four slots for recruitment and only one might be accepted into the sect. And it was the only array sect in the five nearby kingdoms, whereas there were two alchemy sects. No one dared to provoke them.

Brother Wei couldn't be a stray array cultivator as well. He only knew one stray array cultivator who had reached the Array Apprentice realm, and he was Wu Xiodia from Old Martial City. When he'd passed the exam through the Array Master's Guild, there was a small commotion in the nearby cities. If brother Wei had been a stray Three Star Array Apprentice, he would have known about it.

And brother Wei was just seventeen years old. How could he be proficient in both professions? It was impossible. He must have had some contact with an array cultivator to get this Silver Grade array carved on his Gold Grade cauldron. This brother Wei wasn't a simple person.

Suddenly, the air grew stale, and all the essence energy from the surroundings was sucked into the cauldron.

Chen Du straightened up, not daring to make any sound. This was the same phenomenon that had occurred when brother Wei produced that one pill line, rank three pill. Was he going to do it again?

Chen Du gasped when the third batch went for more than twenty-five breaths of congelation process once more. The first two batches had only taken twenty-two breaths. The excitement rushing through his veins reached a new height when the pills reached twenty-eight breaths.

This was it. His heart thumped. Brother Wei was going to create another one pill line pill, and Chen Du had the good fortune to observe it twice. This was just awesome.

Chen Du's muscles tensed. Any more and he would lose his sanity. His eyes stuck to the cauldron, not daring to blink as well. He wanted to see the endowment of alchemy dao when the pill took form. When a pill obtained a pill line, it attracted a thread of an alchemy law, so every lined pill was treated as a treasure. If one could observe it, he or she might get some insight into alchemy.

Lightning zapped for a tiny second when the congelation reached the thirty-ninth breath, and a fragrance that could drown an immortal spread out of the cauldron.

Had brother Wei performed another miracle and concocted a two pill line, rank three pill?

Chen Du couldn't hold it in his heart anymore. He dashed forward to check the cauldron. To his shock, there was only one line on the dark translucent pill, but there were two in the cauldron.

Chen Du watched brother Wei in a daze, as if watching a beautiful girl dancing for him. Brother Wei was sweating like a pig, but it seemed artistic to Chen Du's eyes.

Brother Wei stopped after the third batch. He was sweating profoundly and seemed dull as his actions had turned sluggish.

Chen Du poured the last of the Lasting Kashaya Tree for brother Wei. By gifting him with the Purple Slithering Fruit, brother Wei had won Chen Du's heart. He was a person with a big heart who could pass through the array formation outside and return after facing millions of snakes.

Brother Wei was like a god of fortune.

Brother Wei's face turned grim, and then something huge crashed outside of the hut, startling Chen Du so much that he nearly dropped the last of the Lasting Kashaya Tree.

"Brother Du, feed this pill to the little fox. I'll check what's happening outside." Brother Wei rushed outside with a stern face, and by that face Chen Du guessed whatever happened outside wasn't good.

Li Wei was drained as fuck when he finished the third batch. For the third batch specifically, he'd concentrated hard to make the merging process as smooth as possible, and his efforts were rewarded with two one pill line Beast Rejuvenating Pills.

It was repeatable. That was his thought. For the first two batches, he'd wanted to concoct another rank three, one pill line pill, but he'd failed. With the system's help, he'd kept simulating during the third batch and he succeeded, proving his hypothesis. It was repeatable.

However, the process had drained him like a leech sucking one's blood. He had overestimated his own endurance, so when his divine sense had picked up a giant beast heading toward them, he'd reacted sluggishly.

Jumping to his feet now, Wei dashed outside. Whatever the thing was, he couldn't ignore it. A strong sense of danger had attached to his skin when Wei sensed the thing with his divine sense.

Wei stepped out of the hut to discover finger-thick fog blanketing the area. This was new. The fog restricted his senses, but it couldn't keep the stench of poisonous blood inside the fog from him entirely. It was as if the fog was comprised of that blood. It was thick and so poisonous that it corroded his skin upon touch. Thankfully, his Blood Essence Body kicked up his healing, and his skin went back to normal.

Strangely, the Yin Poison Pill Clone inside his body wasn't excited about this poison. It only purified poison he came into contact with and didn't show any willingness to absorb it on its own. The purified air bubble from before had shrunk to a few inches from the feet radius previously, as if poison pill clone had its stomach full with poison it had already absorbed.

A huge tail shot at him, and he jumped to his right to avoid it. Extending his divine sense, he remained vigilant and soon got his first glimpse of a giant snake head moving through the fog with no hindrance. The snake head was as thick as a fat buffalo, and the body spanned nearly a twenty-foot area. Hundreds of cuts littered the entire body, bleeding everywhere.

The blood mixed with the fog, and the fog thickened.

This was a strange innate ability he had never seen before.

"Human . . . give me the pill." A fist-sized pair of eyes stared at him from the fog, and an arm-thick tongue flickered from the mouth that could gulp him down. Triangular green scales covered the snake's head, extending toward a sword that cut through its neck area. The snake was losing life, and it wouldn't survive. If this snake was at its peak, he might have trouble fighting it, but right now it didn't pose a threat to him.

"I guess you slipped out when I opened the portal, but who injured you?" Wei asked, wondering if he should suck its poison or not. Given his pill clone's disinterest, he might just skip it.

"Human, give . . . m . . .e healing pill, or I'll take it fro . . . m you . . . r . . . corpse." The voice trailed off and the fog dissipated, revealing the sorry-figured Double Headed Fang Snake. It was a peculiar species of Ferocious Beast, and this one was a Spirit Beast. This species only produced females, and they always had a second small head attached to their main head, hidden under the green scales. The sword must have penetrated the second head, so it was bleeding like a buffalo with a cut throat.

"You are welcome to try. We'll see if I can sever your second head faster than you can kill me," Wei said, staring into the snake's dimming eyes.

"Despicable human," A pearl-sized tear rolled from the snake's left eye. "You are all same. You or that black-patched Wang Zhang killed my father, and now I'm dying by your ha . . . nd . . . too." Her giant head dropped like a stone. "I . . . cur . . . se . . . you. You . . . wi . . . ll . . .

die like my little br . . . others . . . and . . . sis . . . ters die every . . . twe . . . tey . . . da . . ." She trailed off with a wheeze and remained down like a broken kite.

Wei frowned. First, he didn't like being associated with the Wang clan, and second, he remembered the blood he'd seen near the White Bone Trees when he first observed the array formation. It had looked like the day after someone had cleared the corpses from a battlefield.

"Li Wei, save her." A feeble voice echoed from behind him, and when he turned, he saw the little fox standing there.

"Little fox, you've recovered!" Dropping to his knees, he pulled her into his embrace. She had endangered her life for him, and he'd given a promise to the mother fox that he would save her. If anything had happened to her, the guilt would haunt him for the rest of his life. "Thank heavens, you are all right."

"You stinky Li Wei, let me go. How can you embrace a young girl like this? Don't you have any manners?" She purred near his ear, sending warmth into it. His heart filled with warmth, too.

"I'll protect you," he said in a choked voice. She was like a little sister, and he would definitely protect her.

"What a shameless man, hugging pretty girls like they are cabbages."

"Girl? Where's a pretty girl? Show me." He looked around, teasing her more.

"You moron. How can you not see a beautiful girl in your arms? When I shift into human form, I'll the prettiest girl in the entire world. But give me some Twisting Vitality Fruits first. I'm so hungry that I'm dying from hunger."

Wei chuckled. No matter the age or species of girl, she would always think about looking pretty. Well, Fei'er was different. She always made sure *he* looked good by feeding him a lot and sewing him nice robes.

Speaking of eating, he had lost weight again. When would he get back to his chubby self?

"Li Wei, save her. She is a good girl too," the little fox asked once again.

Turning back, he stared at the snake lying on the ground. The giant snake had shrunk to its original size, and she was now just a five-foot long, arm-thick Spirit Beast with no cuteness like the little fox.

"She tried to kill me. How can she be a good girl?"

"It's my intuition. She has been lying outside of the hut for six hours now, but she didn't attack Chen Du after sensing me. She came here, driven by her injuries, when she smelled your fresh pills' aroma."

Wei's heart did a somersault inside his rib cage. "What did you say? How could she have been outside the hut? I checked our surroundings when I came back, and other than the three of us, no one was there."

"It's her innate ability, her fog. It's special, and it can hide her presence from anyone. When she came near the hut, she momentarily lost her fog and I sensed her."

Hearing the little fox, Wei struggled with complex emotions. On one hand, he was grateful toward this snake girl for not attacking Chen Du and the little fox. If not for Wei, they might not be opponents of the snake girl. On the other hand, she'd attacked him, and what about her injuries? Who gave them to her?

He was conflicted. After living for two hundred years, he couldn't trust a person who just momentarily acted kindly. The world was different. It wasn't just black and white. Most of the time, it was gray, and a darker shade of gray at that. What if she attacked them in the future?

"Do it," the little fox said. "Trust a woman's gut. It's shockingly good. If my mother hadn't had a good gut feeling about you, do you think you would have survived?"

Without thinking anymore, Wei pulled out the second rank-three Beast Rejuvenating Pill with a pill line. While he extended this pill to the snake girl's mouth, his hand shuddered. His mind told him it would be a waste to feed it to a stranger, but his heart listened to the little fox and let go of it.

"Little fox, hide inside the spirit artifact. Someone is coming." Wei stared at the door of the pocket realm. It was opening, and he wasn't sure who was on the other side.

Chapter 48

The real culprit

Wang Rong rushed behind Wang Joji through the dark tunnel leading to the Snake Rearing Chamber, dragging his heavy body with thin legs. The long dark passage irritated him, but a light awaited him at the other end. Brushing his fingers along the dark tunnel wall and sensing the rough stones, he made some calculations. For years, he had heard about this place from his father, great elder Jiang, and many others. But uncle Wang Zhang guarded this place like a precious treasure, so no one could come here.

But today he would because uncle Wang Zhang was injured and bedridden, so Wang Joji guarded this place instead. Wang Joji was a member of Dark Shadow Force, and he wouldn't deny Wang Rong—the future head of Dark Shadow Force—entrance.

"Senior brother Rong, I beg you not to wander too much. If anything happens to you, or this act of ours is exposed, I'll be in trouble. Big trouble." Wang Joji complained as he placed a key in a door. Sensing the energy covering the door, Wang Rong guessed this was the door to the secret realm.

Behind that door lay his main reason for coming here. Chen Du. That waste. If he'd wanted to, he could have killed Chen Du openly when he'd fought with that trash Wang Fantai, but that bastard Li Wei had somehow stumbled upon him and he'd lost the chance. Actually, he thanked Li Wei in his mind because he needed to kill Chen Du discreetly, and there had been too many people at the competition. It would've caused issues for him. The Su clan had specifically said that Chen Du's death should be discreet, and only then would they hand over the low-tier Gold Grade beast flame, Flood Dragon's Roar. Once he obtained that beast flame, nothing would stop him. He would burn Ki Fei alive, and no one would be able to do anything about it.

Just the thought of it made him chuckle. "Brother Joji, don't worry. He's just a Foundation Realm brat. Killing him will be easy." His fingers brushed against his storage ring that uncle Jiang had gifted him. In the ring, he had plenty of things that he could use to kill Chen Du, including his bow, arrows and talismans. With the ring, it was so easy to carry things around.

"Senior brother Rong, your words put me at ease." Wang Joji laughed, trying to butter Wang Rong up.

Bastard. Wang Joji had only a few more hours to live. How could Wang Rong, the future head of Dark Shadow Force, allow a rule breaker to live?

"Senior brother Rong, I heard that bastard Wang Fantai killed brother Gong and he was close to you."

Wang Rong cursed under his breath and almost punched Wang Joji. Why was this bastard reminding him of this infuriating topic? "Wang Fantai is a bastard. I only left him alive because he keeps that bitch Kai Kai away from me." He chuckled, but inside he smoldered with rage. Wang Fantai had suddenly turned aggressive and killed his lackey Wang Gong. When he'd wanted to execute Wang Fantai for it, great elder Jiang had stopped him for some reason, so now he could only sulk to himself. Once he left this shitty place, he would teach Wang Fantai a lesson.

The door to the secret realm finally opened, and Wang Rong choked as he inhaled rotten air that sent a shiver down his spine. An intense itch emerged from his warm skin which began to turn darker and darker.

This was bad. He was sensitive to poison, and this reaction meant there was poison in the air. Reaching into his robe, he grabbed a high-tier Silver Grade Poison Extinguishing Pill and quickly ate it.

Sitting on a nearby rock, he regulated his breathing, and after five minutes of slow cultivation, the itching stopped and his skin regained its normal hue. “That was close.” He rubbed his throat, still feeling a phantom itchiness.

“Senior brother Rong, I warned you not to come here. This place is poisonous, and I could have killed that Chen Du for you. My layer nine Bone Baptization Realm cultivation is enough to steamroll him.”

“Brother Joji, I mean no insult, but I like to take my own revenge. I joined Dark Shadow Force to take it to a new level. How can I depend on others for a small task like this? That brat insulted me, and I can’t let it go. If he dies here by natural cause, my reputation will take a hit, so I’ve to kill him with my own hands.” Wang Rong smirked. After he finished this work, he had plans to kill Wang Joji too.

His principle was simple - do not leave any witness behind.

“Senior brother Rong, do you know who the other person sent here with Chen Du is?”

Wang Rong shook his head. He didn’t know, nor did he care.

“It’s Li Wei. The one our clan wants to kill. If you kill him too, great elder Jiang will be happy about it.”

“Li Wei?” Wang Rong frowned. This guy’s name had so much legend behind it. “Brother Joji, this Li Wei is not simple, and you must be ready if we meet him inside here." He remembered the warning from elder Su Pan. This guy wasn't as simple as he seemed.

"Senior brother Rong, are you talking about some other Li Wei? This guy might be dead already. Shadow Twelfth easily poisoned him. If it wasn't for the master's orders, she would have killed him easily."

Wang Rong nodded, but he wasn't sure Li Wei was a weakling. That day, he'd bumped into Li Wei, and at the same time Shadow Twelfth had attacked him. Was he distracted?

Who cared? "Let's ignore him and kill Chen Du. If we see him, just kill him as well," Wang Rong said in a calm voice. "We must hurry, as great elders Shun and Shuntao are coming as well."

Wang Joji touched his nose and adjusted the black cloth he always wrapped around his mouth. Between that, a dark hood, and his always-cloth-wrapped slender body, he looked like the perfect assassin. Actually, he was a good assassin. Compared to him, Wang Rong only had low cultivation. But Wang Rong was famous for his alchemy skills, and he had confidence that he could defeat any alchemist from the Destiny Mirror Sect. In the year-end alchemy competition, he planned to challenge several Destiny Mirror Sect youths and defeat them all in a single match. That would be only the start. Later, he planned to kill Ki Fei too and remove an obstacle for the Wang clan. Great elder Jiang kept saying that Ki Fei was a nuisance, so he would remove that nuisance and gain attention from all the elders.

And that would start with the beast flame he would soon get from the Su clan.

Li Wei walked out of the concealment array with deep creases covering his forehead. So, this was the story behind that girl's attack. The Wang clan was behind it, and that meant these two were going to die here today. But he hadn't expected Wang Shuntao and Wang Shun to come here. Why were they coming here? What was the Wang clan's plan for this secret realm? Wei remembered Wang Shuntao, a fatso with a stomach bulge wider than a baby elephant's body.

Whatever the plan, he would thwart it before escaping from here.

Chapter 49

Trap

Sneaking behind Wang Rong and Wang Joji, Li Wei circulated essence energy from his surroundings, refilling his blood pearls at an accelerated rate. Cultivating Blood Essence Body always filled him with bliss. The vitality surging through his body also affected his mind and mood as well.

Circulating his pure qi simultaneously, he applied a thin layer of pure qi below the soles of his shoes, suppressing any noise that might arise from his shoes hitting the cracked marble road. With the rotten poisonous smell in the air, he didn't have to worry about alerting them with his smell. An issue could arise if they looked back, and stick-legged Wang Rong did just that while walking toward the hut.

With his divine sense wrapped around them, Wei managed to sneak behind some debris lying in the corner and avoided detection.

Wang Rong moved his gaze around and then turned forward to head toward the wooden hut standing lonely at the end of the walkable area.

Chen Du was in there, and so was the little fox, but Wei wasn't worried about them. They were inside a concealment array, and these two didn't have the capability to detect them.

“Brother Joji, do you think someone is following us?” Wang Rong asked, once again looking over his shoulder.

Wei frowned. This guy seemed to have developed an extra sense related to danger, but that only made things more interesting.

“I don’t see anyone. If those two trashy disciples are here, we will hear them from miles away.” He paused and glanced at the hut. “There’s the hut. Let’s just burn it and finish them off quickly.”

Wei rubbed his metal storage ring. If they really tried to burn that hut, he wouldn’t mind burning them, and he had the perfect thing with him to do it—a Dantian Burning Yang Beetle. It was a beetle he had found in the courtyard of the Waste Disposal Faction.

Wang Rong’s face twitched with disgust. “Brother Joji, do you want to announce our visit to this place? Did you forget some elders are coming here tomorrow? If they found out we were here, what would be the result?”

Wei bit his lower lip. There were more elders coming? Good. Either he had to run after killing these two bastards, or he had to set something up to surprise the Wang clan.

Maybe he should do both. There was the Cold Arctic Snake Pit he had seen on the other side of the array formation. If he could somehow bring those snakes here, the Wang clan would get a nasty surprise. And they deserved it. They’d been targeting him from the start, and it was time to return the favor. Too bad he didn’t have enough firepower to just roll over the entire clan. The Wang clan was a behemoth in the region, so he had to take things slowly. But the stronger the opponent, the tastier winning would be. The victory should linger on one’s tongue like a fine tea.

Wang Joji gasped. “Senior brother Rong, who else is coming? Am I going to get in trouble for allowing you inside?”

"Of course not." Wang Rong patted Wang Joji's shoulder and smiled. "They won't even know what happened here. Did you see the snake corpses on the side of the road? We will mutilate Chen Du's and Li Wei's corpse and throw them among the dead snakes. Everyone will think they fought a fierce battle and died."

Astonishment overflowed Wang Joji's face as he cupped his hands and bowed. "No wonder you're a prodigy of our clan and I'm just a lowlife. The way you think is beyond my grasp."

Wang Rong shook his head, but he couldn't hide the smirk on his face.

It was funny watching him smirk now because when Wei attacked, the smirk on his face would vanish like water evaporating from a hot surface. Quick and dirty.

"Brother Joji, I'll scan inside area while you check outside area," Wang Rong said as they stepped through the door.

"Senior brother Rong, that sounds good. I admire you for taking risk for your brothers. You're the best."

Wei rolled his eyes. He might see this Wang Joji lick Wang Rong's shoes if he didn't attack them soon. How much buttering up was he planning on doing? Wang Rong needed to hurry up and get in the hut so Wei could take care of Wang Joji first.

Although Wei's qi cultivation had dropped back to the Refinement Realm, he could still hold off against a peak qi Bone Baptization Realm cultivator with his body cultivation, and he could tire his opponent before killing him. Well, this was the baptization of battle for him.

Wang Joji didn't make him wait too long. He soon walked out of the hut with a wide smile on his face and headed around to the back of the hut.

Wei sneaked around the hut, keeping track of Wang Rong with his divine sense. Wang Rong pretended to look around inside, then pushed his nose to the wall to peer between the cracks in the boards, checking on Wang Roji.

He was still suspicious. Interesting.

Well, Wei could just change his plan and kill Wang Rong first. It didn't matter who died first. They had to die anyway.

With his pure qi still wrapped around the soles of his shoes, he crept into the hut and saw Wang Rong frozen in front of the wall, his fat nose pressed to the wall.

Taking a knife out, Wei slowly moved forward, but suddenly he realized something was off. His divine sense was wrapped around Wang Rong, but there was no movement from him. There was no heartbeat, nor anything that resembled to a live human being.

The hairs on his neck stood up as he sensed something dangerous coming at him. Throwing himself to the right, Wei planted his left hand on the ground and threw the knife toward a figure concealed in the darkness. This was a trap, and the thing stuck to the wall wasn't Wang Rong, but something else. A thick arrow struck the ground where he was a moment before and froze a foot-wide area around it.

There was an archer between the two bastards, and Wei didn't know who it was.

Chapter 50

Archer

Swoosh!

An arrow cut through the air and brushed past Li Wei's ear, drawing blood. Wei's heart thumped like a drum. If he hadn't jumped away, it would have pierced his throat, and there was no coming back from that.

Damn this archer. A bitter taste covered his tongue when he remembered Rual'er's fierceness. Archers were difficult to deal with, and one of these bastards was an archer, and Wei was standing ten feet away from him. That was practically begging him to shoot him. Of course, that fucker would try and put a hole through the challenger's forehead.

Fuck! This was a bad day. First that female snake, and now an archer. He wished he had never joined this fucking sect.

The next arrow didn't give him much time to think, so he rolled across the rough ground, and a piece of metal stabbed through his robe. It wasn't an incoming sword but rather a knife Chen Du had carelessly left on the floor. That fucker.

Bright light reflected from the broken window and Wei tensed. A shiny gray sword came at him, and Wei was forced to get to one knee and lift his own sword to match the trajectory of the incoming sword. But defending from the worst possible position only resulted in the opponent's sword running over his shoulder, drawing more blood. Fighting with invisible opponent was tougher than he expected.

Well, blood wasn't a problem, but the icy effect the sword left behind in his shoulder was. It was the same feeling he'd had when the girl who'd poisoned him had stabbed him. These bastards from Dark Shadow Force were all proficient in ice arrays.

Cursing, he threw himself to the left and shattered the ice wrapped around his wound. His knee scraped over the rough ground, and he cursed violently as he rolled around, avoiding the sword chops aimed at him. Thank the heavens, he could at least detect the trajectory of the sword with his divine sense, and even dodge the arrows right before they hit him. If not for his divine sense, he would be dead by now. But soon he rolled into a barrel Chen Du had filled with Qi Water for experiments.

Fuck! He wished he could pull Chen Du out of the dark corner he hid in and kick his ass until it turned black and blue. Wei was trying to not go that direction, but Chen Du's littered things were causing him trouble.

The sword came slashing at him again, and Wei had nowhere to go. Pushing his right hand on the ground, he twisted his body in an insanely abnormal way and avoided the strike, but the sword shattered the wooden barrel and Qi Water washed over Wei's body.

Cursing Chen Du profusely, he rolled and rolled, avoiding the chops from the swordman. If that wasn't enough, he also had to deal with the arrows coming for him, and each fucking arrow was laden with ice energy array that instantly froze the place where it landed. If one of them struck him, his movements would slow to a crawl.

It was quickly growing impossible to maneuver in the forty-by-forty space, which was littered with trash thanks to Chen Du, and avoid a sword and arrows at the same time. Damn that bastard. Wei was fighting for his life, and that brute was sitting in a concealment array in the corner. Wei hoped he would be bitten by a snake once or twice, or for the sword to slip from the swordman's hand and stab Chen Du's back.

He deserved that.

"Brother Rong, use that special arrow to stop this rat from jumping around." The swordsman spoke for the first time, and Wei saw the veil over those two lift. They had used some special talisman or an array to conceal themselves from his divine sense, and their voices came from a separate location too, but with his divine sense he caught the source quickly.

Now he knew who the fucker was who was shooting arrows at him. It was Wang Rong. What kind of fucking talisman were these guys using? It must have been a high grade one, otherwise even a Houtian Realm expert wouldn't be able to hide from him.

Distressed, Wei pulled two more knives out and threw them at the archer, Wang Rong, hoping they would at least distract the bastard for a moment or two so he could launch a counter-attack on the swordman, Wang Joji.

The first knife hadn't even reached the blurry figure when a sword sliced out of the shadows and sent the knife flying away with a clinking sound.

"Senior brother Rong, you were right. There was someone spying on us, but he ended up being this trash. There's no fun in playing with him. I think we wasted our Shadow Movement Talisman."

Wei had been waiting for this moment for so long. Taking advantage of their distraction, he jumped to his feet and stomped on the ground while throwing a bottle of poison at Wang Roji.

It was Mad Elephant Stomp, activated with his entire cultivation base of layer eight body Foundation Realm, and he unleashed an earth-shattering wave at Wang Joji.

Wang Joji stumbled and nearly fell, but before the poison bottle crashed into him, an arrow shattered it into pieces.

That was what Wei had wanted. Smirking, he evoked his Yin Poison Pill Clone, and it controlled the poison powder rushing toward the ground. It stopped falling like it'd suddenly gained life of its own and leaped at Wang Joji, wrapping around his face and entering through his nose.

"Fuck! What is this thing?" Wang Joji shouted, scratching at his face. "Poison, senior brother Rong! Please give me a Poison Extinguishing Pill, else I'll die from this."

Wang Rong pulled a pill out of his robe and threw it toward Wang Joji, but Wei had no intention of letting Wang Joji eat it, so he swung his sword at Wang Joji, trying to distract him. The poison wasn't much lethal, but it would incapacitate Wang Joji if he didn't eat a good poison resistance pill, and that's what Wei wanted.

"Li Wei, you're courting death." Shouting, Wang Rong shot an arrow at Wei. This arrow was pristine white, and there was an intricate pattern marked on it. It must have been the special arrow Wang Joji had mentioned, but whatever. Could it possibly break through his Blood Earth Force Divine Art shield? Once he got access to gravity times three, he could reach middle completion, and then he would be invincible among his peers.

Activating Blood Earth Force Divine Art, Wei lunged forward, ignoring the arrow. He used his entire force to attack Wang Joji who was gulping down the pill, but his foot rolled over trash left by Chen Du, and he missed.

Fuck! Wei was going to smack Chen Du black and blue if he survived this.

Struggling to his feet, Wei attacked Wang Joji with his full force, but by that time Wang Joji had gulped down the pill and his grim face had already lightened. He raised his sword to defend. "Trash, that's the last mistake of your life."

Wei smirked. "I could say the same." Letting the arrow stab into his Blood Earth Force Divine Art, Wei raised his leg at lightning speed and stomped on Wang Joji's foot, and this was done using Mad Elephant Stomp.

A tremor ran into Wang Joji's leg, and Wei heard bones cracking inside his body. Wang Joji froze before rolling on the ground as the entire bone structure inside his body collapsed with one strike.

This was fun, but before he could laugh, an arrow penetrated his Blood Earth Force Divine Art and pierced into his back. Although only the mere tip made it through, that was enough to spread ice over his back, and he ended up spurting blood. A lot of it.

Wei chuckled. It was painful, extremely painful, to have your back covered in ice. But breaking someone's entire skeleton using Mad Elephant Stomp dwarfed the pain. It was awesome as fuck, and he was going to do it again and again.

Now it was Wang Rong's turn.

Chapter 51

Absorbing Beast Flames

Wang Rong grew frightened when he saw Wang Joji topple like a broken tree. How was that possible? That trash had just stomped on Wang Joji's foot, and he'd collapsed like a house of cards collapsing under strong wind.

"You! What did you do to him?" Wang Rong pulled out a Polar Ice Arrow. It was enhanced with an ice-attributed array that could be used with his mutated ice-attributed Spirit Root. "Never mind, trash. It doesn't matter how you incapacitated brother Joji. Today you'll die."

Li Wei chuckled like a mad person. He was crazy, really crazy, and Wang Rong regretted not believing this man was a monster and thinking he could kill him with one strike.

But he wasn't a coward. If Li Wei could kill a layer one Marrow Cleansing Realm cultivator, given a bow and the right arrow, he could too.

Putting the Polar Ice Arrow back in his quiver, he drew a very special arrow instead—a Boom Box Arrow. A weird name, but it was one of the most powerful arrows he had in his arsenal. It was a low-tier Gold Grade arrow filled with explosive powder, and it could level an entire mountain and easily kill a layer one Marrow Cleansing Realm cultivator. Maybe even a layer two.

"Li Wei, you'll regret meeting me today." Biting his lips, he nocked the arrow and pulled back the bowstring. His beast flame climbed onto the arrow, lighting it slightly. With his beast flame leaving a mark on the arrow, Wang Rong could detonate it whenever he wanted. Because he had no flame-attributed Spirit Root, he had to use his beast flame.

"Gah! What the fuck are y—" a fierce pain echoed through his ass, and he felt his entire body numbing, and his control over his body waning rapidly.

The bow and arrow dropped to the ground, and Wang Rong toppled over like a dead man. Until the end, he didn't know who had stabbed the paralyzing poison inside his body.

"Chen Du, you fucking idiot. I'm going to kill you," Li Wei shouted before Rong slid into unconsciousness, but he didn't understand. Where had Chen Du been hiding? He had looked around, but he hadn't seen anyone else in the room.

Li Wei gasped. He was too close to death. The arrow Wang Rong pulled out could level up the entire hut and a twenty feet area around it. Even Rual'er had an arrow like this.

When Wang Rong dropped, his heavy body slipped out of the dark veil concealing his presence. A knife coated with a pitch-black sticky substance poked out of his gut. It smelled disgusting, like a rotten corpse hidden in a dark wet cave.

"Brother Wei, I did good, right?" A wide grin covered Chen Du's face, displaying his eagerness for praise.

Fury burst in Wei's mind, and he dashed forward, intending to smack that bastard's face. "Chen Du, you fucking idiot. I'm going to kill you." But before he could reach Chen Du, he slipped on a cork lying on the floor and plopped on his ass hard. "Fuck you, Chen Du. Why did you leave so many things lying around in here?" It pained his heart. Humiliation. Shamefulness. Insanity. A myriad of emotions flashed through his mind. Was he destined to die from slipping on something cast aside by Chen Du? If it wasn't for these things, Wei would have killed Wang Joji sooner.

Pushing his hand on a clean surface, he got up and headed outside; the taste of defeat lingered in his mouth. "Get the fuck out of here." Without looking back, he plopped his ass on a stone cube and began cultivating Blood Essence Body. The frigid ice Wang Rong had used was a special type of ice and couldn't be melted the normal way. He could burn his beast flame intensely, but that might damage his meridians as the liquid ice could slip into them. Instead, he chose the biggest advantage he had. Slowly, he pushed his blood pearls toward the wound, and when the blood pearls crashed against the frigid ice energy, it had no other option but to melt away. The ice was aggressive, but his blood was more aggressive, so he quickly overcame the coldness induced by the ice arrow.

"Brother Wei, you seem angry. Are you hurt badly?" Chen Du carried the little fox in his hands, holding her like a child.

That calmed Wei's heart, and the creases on his forehead vanished along with his anger. "Brother Du, can you expose your beast flame for me?"

Chen Du nodded, and a yellow-white ball of docile fire appeared on his hand.

Wei's brows arched as he stared at the ball of fire. When the beast flame came out, his own mutated beast flame, Fox's Breath, stirred inside his dantian and urged him to let her devour the flame on Chen Du's hand. He'd had the same feeling when Wang Rong had mounted his own beast flame on that arrow. Fox's Breath radiated an intense love-hate emotion from his dantian, and he was shocked by it. There was no record of one flame devouring another flame.

Was it because he could devour beast bloodlines? But those things were totally different from each other. Weren't they?

Suppressing the flame in his dantian, Wei stared into Chen Du's eyes. "Brother Du, bring Wang Rong out. I'll help you refine his beast flame."

"You mean—" Chen Du looked into the hut where the two bodies lying inside could be seen from the doorway. "He has a mid-tier Silver Grade beast flame, Salamander's Oath. How can you give that to me?"

"Yes, you can have the mid-tier Silver Grade Salamander's Oath, and I'll store the other's flame for myself. That one is a low-tier Silver Grade beast flame."

Chen Du's legs trembled. "Brother Wei, why would you give me a higher tier flame? You killed them, so you earned it."

Wei smiled. He hadn't forgotten the day Chen Du had given him his own flame. Of course, Chen Du had obtained a new one, but the gesture was important, and Wei believed in people who had generosity in their hearts and not just fake smiles on their faces. "Take it. I have my own uses for a low-tier Silver Grade beast flame. But I also want the one you're using now." Wei wanted to devour Chen Du's mid-tier Bronze Grade beast flame before allowing his Fox's Breath to take a chunk out of the low-tier Silver Grade beast flame.

When Chen Du brought Wang Rong out, he stabbed his fingers into Wang Rong's stomach wound and pushed his divine sense into his dantian. It was generally impossible to access another cultivator's dantian, but with physical contact and an unconscious body, he had a way to do that. Of course, that was only possible because he had a divine sense that transcended the Mortal Realm and Wang Rong was paralyzed by Chen Du's poison. Wrapping his divine sense around the beast flame, Wei wiped away Wang Rong's soul imprint and cleared it for another refinement. There were other ways to do that, but divine sense was best when it came to dealing with things related to the soul.

Wang Rong jolted awake and opened his eyes with a crazed expression. The removal of the soul imprint must have awoken him. "You—What are you doing with my—no, you stole my beast flame! I'll—"

Wei pulled his hand out of Wang Rong's stomach, letting loose a spray of blood.

"Don't worry, you won't die." Wei paused. "For now." He smiled and tossed the ownerless flame to Chen Du. "Absorb it far away from here." He didn't want his own beast flame to attack Chen Du for another beast flame.

"My beast flame!" Wang Rong coughed but couldn't move his body as he was still paralyzed.

Wei stomped his foot on both of Wang Rong's arms and crushed his bones, then repeated the same with his legs so he wouldn't dare to attack again. "That's for trying to kill Chen Du in the alchemy competition and harboring evil thoughts about us. Now I'm going to plant a special bug in your dantian. Consider this repayment for the Wang clan."

"Li Wei," Wang Rong wailed from the bottom of his stomach. Wood and ice qi leaked from his body; he was losing control of his own qi. "Please, let me go and I'll ask them to let you go. Please, Li Wei. I beg of you."

Wei cleaned his bloody hand with fresh water, then cursed himself. He'd just get it bloody again putting the beetle inside Wang Rong's dantian.

Damn. He glanced at his clean hand and then put it back into the hole he had just made into Wang Rong's stomach.

"Li Wei, please, don't cripple me. I'll be your slave if you want. But please let me go."

Wei paused and looked in Wang Rong's eyes. "Wang Rong. Answer one question and then I might let you go."

Wang Rong nodded, his breath quickening. "Yes, ask me anything. I'll even sell information on my mum if you want. But please let me go. I'll run far away from the sect and never return."

Wei's face hardened. "Should I kill you and leave your mutilated body near the dead snakes, or should I burn your corpse? Answer wisely."

Wang Rong gulped before crying out loud, but there was no escape from this. There was no humanity in that bastard, and Wei didn't like leaving loose ends behind.

Not anymore. But Wang Rong was still useful to him, so he would let him live a little longer.

Wei pulled the little green beetle out of his storage ring, and a warm scent spread around the bug, easing everyone's mind for a moment. "This is a Dantian Burning Yang Beetle, and it feeds on wood qi. It will form a cocoon when exposed to pure yang energy, and when it hatches, the cocoon explodes, generating a steady stream of fire so the beetle can complete its fire baptization." Wei paused, and knocked Wang Rong out and put the little green beetle inside Wang Rong's dantian. With his divine sense wrapped around it, he easily pushed the beetle in without triggering the dantian's defense mechanisms.

When he let go, the beetle ran amok like a child set loose in a land full of candy. For the beetle, the wood yang energy inside the dantian was like candy.

Wang Rong's body jolted up, his eyes opened and he wailed like someone stabbed a knife in his heart.

Ignoring Wang Rong's shouts, he pulled his hand back out and cleaned it again with fresh water. "Do you know the interesting thing about this beetle? If its cocoon is disturbed by a powerful fire, it will undergo mutation and suck all the fire energy from outside into itself, then explode with double the intensity. It's a self-destruction mechanism. A barbarian tribe once used it to destroy their enemies by sending warriors grooming these beetles inside their dantian. They were heroes of the tribe, and today you'll become a hero too. Consider changing jobs and be proud," Wei said in a determined voice. The Wang clan had no redemption. They had used their powers to harm countless innocent people and beasts, and they deserved punishment for it.

And this was just the start.

Chapter 52

Setting up traps

Sweat crawled through the creases on his forehead, reaching his brows and then dripping down to his nose. Raising his arm, Li Wei wiped his forehead with his sleeve, then continued digging the pit. For four hours he'd been at it, but he had only reached thirty feet underground, and the target was forty feet farther down. With dirt falling on him from the sides, he looked more like a gravedigger than a cultivator with a decent cultivation base. Some of the dirt had even gotten into his mouth, dampening his mood and taste.

Pausing for a moment, he sighed and cleaned his mouth with fresh water before gulping down a mouthful. The Wang clan was coming, and he had to reach the Cold Artic Snake Pit a few feet away from his current position.

Placing the leather water skin aside, he cursed the Wang clan for planning to send more people to the Snake Rearing Chamber. If they weren't coming, he would have walked out of this place and found a comfy bed to sleep in. Well, if he'd had a key, he would have walked out of this place, but Wang Rong didn't know about the key, and Wang Joji had died from internal bleeding and Wei couldn't find the key on his body. Tipping his head back, he stared up at the irritating bright sky that stung his eyes like needles. If he could change one thing about this place, he would introduce a day-night cycle. That would make things so much better.

"Li Wei, how much time are you going to waste doing this? I told you I can do it faster." The little fox appeared next to him, forcefully cuddling against him in the tiny space. Placing her front paws on his knees for balance, she licked her whiskers. Her injuries had half healed, and she looked much better, but how could he let her work on such things in her condition?

Wei rubbed her furry head. "Don't worry, I've got this. Tell me more about that female snake. Why did you ask me to save her?"

She scratched back of her ear, but it was difficult for her to reach there, so he reached over and scratched it for her.

"I just felt like it. I wanted a pet of my own, but she refused. She's got a big ego. Much bigger than your fat friend."

Wei rolled his eyes. A Spirit Beast wanting a pet. Damn. The world was so wrong.

"Little fox, you shouldn't act on impulse going forward. What if she'd attacked you inside the spirit artifact? She is stronger than you, and you're in a weakened state."

The little fox giggled. "Don't worry. Inside that place, I'm the queen, and no one can overrule my authority unless the original owner, that Specter, comes back."

Wei sighed regretfully, thinking about Xue Qi. That would remain his one regret in this new life, and he didn't want to regret anything in this life.

"Watch me, Li Wei." The little fox pulled out a green fruit and munched on it before vanishing from his sight. She was too fast.

When a stream of dirt and stone slammed into his face, he realized she was digging the tunnel ahead of him. Her front paws moved like a twister, carving a way forward. It was fabulous to watch, but he was worried she would get hurt.

"Fuck! Stop it. Don't do that," he shouted and pulled her back.

"I'm helping you, dummy. Don't you want to tunnel to the snake pit?"

Wei gulped. Just thinking about entering the snake pit made his mouth go dry and sent a shiver across his bones. "Do you want to die? If you end up opening a way into the nest, we will definitely die." He rubbed his forehead. "Do you think I can fight against hundreds of snakes that can freeze everything in a fifty-foot radius around them?"

"But you're digging a tunnel to them, aren't you?" She looked at him with confusion.

"Yes and no. It's called a Cold Artic Snake Pit for a reason, and no one goes in their pit. No one. I said no one."

"But they are just layer five Foundation Realm Ferocious Beasts. Why are you worried about them?"

Wei shook his head. Although she'd lived in Ten Beast Valley, she hadn't seen these particular snakes. "That's where you're wrong. They are layer five, but there are six hundred of them. Remember, quality is not always better than quantity. Although they are quite weak, they can perform a combination attack, and with their numbers they can easily kill a layer one Marrow Cleansing Realm cultivator. Even a layer two or layer three Marrow Cleansing Realm cultivator would be hard pressed against them."

The little fox stopped munching on the fruit and stared at him with wide eyes. "Six hundred? Are you kidding me?"

Wei shook his head. "No, and that's not the scariest thing about them. The scary part is their ice poison. Despite not being lethal, it can slow down movement, and they can superimpose their attacks to form an icy ground that would block a cultivator's qi when touched, and that would be certain death for many cultivators."

"Then why are you opening a tunnel to their pit? Are you really suicidal like that human girl said?"

Wei almost flipped. "Who?"

"Sun Nuan, that shorty who moved around you like a mouse." She sounded irritated.

Wei arched his brows. That was Sun Nuan for sure. She loved to talk with others and tell them how suicidal Wei was, or how much pain he loved. Damn it. "Don't worry. I'm not suicidal, and I've got a plan. I'm going to use these snakes to attack the Wang clan force that is coming in a few hours." One trap was already set, and he was planning to use the pit as the second trap. The Wang clan would be in trouble—big trouble—this time.

"Li Wei, I don't understand a single word you're saying. Talk some sense, and give me more Vitality Twisting Fruits. This little one hasn't eaten them in years."

Wei snorted coldly. This little fox had exhorted twenty fruits from him as soon as she woke up. Years? It hadn't even been ten hours. "These snakes lay eggs to reproduce, and I've found a bunch of eggs below their pit. I'm going to use those eggs to invite them to our side and set up a trap for Wang clan." With his divine sense, nothing could be hidden from him.

"Ah-ha, that's why you dug a shallow pit next to the entrance. I thought you were planning to roast some Dragon Skin Fruits in an underground fire. Those taste awesome, but mother never let me eat one raw." She churned her lips and made a pitiful sound.

Wei chuckled. What a joke. Of course, Mother Fox wouldn't let her eat Dragon Skin Fruits raw. They were full of essence energy, and anyone below the Houtian Realm would burst if they ate one.

"But I sneaked one out." A human-head-sized fruit appeared in front of him. "Can you cook this for me?"

Frowning, Wei snatched it and put it into his storage ring. "Do you want to die? I'll make a soup of it for you later."

She made a weird sound and looked away. "Anyway, if we had a map I could dig an exact path, and I'm way faster than those snakes."

Wei's eyes shone. She was right. The little fox was much faster than him when it came to digging tunnels, as she could dig through the soil in a much better way than him.

"If I give you exact directions as you dig, can you do that?" Wei asked.

"Of course. You can always depend on me." She patted her mouth and smiled.

"Then let's do this." With his divine sense, he implanted a map in her head, and at the same time he readied himself to scan everything around and ask her to come back in case of danger. This was going to be an interesting trap for the Wang clan.

Well, they had it coming. They shouldn't have attacked him in the first place.

Chapter 53

Disappearance of a prodigy

"So, Wang Joji died, and no one cared to worry about that," Wang Jiang said, tapping on the chairs arm.

"Yes, force leader. He was just an ordinary member, and the news didn't even reach my ears. The elders at the clan soul tablet house treated it as a normal thing and let it go."

Wang Jiang grabbed his teacup and crushed it. "A soul tablet broke that belonged to a person guarding Snake Rearing Chamber, and you're telling me this only after Wang Rong has gone missing?"

Wang Jutong lowered his head and said nothing. How could he say anything when the prodigy had gone missing, and it wasn't the normal going out to fool with girls. This was different. One day he was in his courtyard, and then he was missing.

Wang Jiang slammed his fist on the stone chair, crushing it under his force. "How could you come and tell me that my personal disciple is missing? Do you realize what has happened? He was the future leader of Dark Shadow Force." Everyone was focused on him. He was their hope of defeating Ki Fei in the next competition. How was Wang Jiang going to tell the Wang ancestor that the pupil he doted on was missing?

This was unacceptable.

"Did you activate the Blood Imprint Location Tracker?" It was a Spirit Artifact that could track the location of a person whose blood it had archived inside.

"Yes, force leader." Wang Jutong lowered his head farther. "But there is no response. This can only happen if he is out of this realm, or de—"

"Impossible." Wang Jiang shook his head. "He can't be dead. Who saw him last?"

"Wang Fantai saw him heading toward the Waste Disposal Faction."

Wang Jiang frowned. "Fantai?"

"Yes, force leader."

Wang Jiang stroked his beard. Wang Fantai. There was something wrong with that kid, but he had recently shown promise. Enough that Wang Jiang had let him go even after he'd killed another clansmen. That dead disciple was a trash one, and Wang Jiang only believed in bright disciples.

"Wang Joji was guarding the Snake Rearing Chamber, wasn't he?"

"Yes, force leader."

Wang Jiang's lips twitched. Something was off, and he wouldn't feel right until he checked on it himself. "I'll go with the Shun brothers to the Snake Rearing Chamber."

"But force leader, that is overkill."

"No, Wang Rong is as important as the treasure from the Heart Garden. What's the use of making the elder generation strong if your young generation is nothing but trash?"

Wang Jutong cupped his hands and bowed deeply. "I understand, force leader. I'll make preparations."

Chapter 54

Soul Orb

Annoying bright daylight poured into his eye when Wang Zhang opened the sealed door. The fog had vanished, and he could see the chipped black road that needed maintenance, but today the black path was covered with patches of blood. It must have been the result of the fight between him and that motherfucking snake. How could that bastard sneak-attack him? If it had the guts to attack, why didn't it come from the front?

His face twisted in pain upon recalling how he'd survived. A Blood Expansion Pill. If he hadn't eaten that pill and raised his cultivation by five minor layers, he would have died. But he knew how much harm that pill had done. It had raised his cultivation by six minor layers in one breath but at the cost of ten years of cultivation. After the effect ended, he'd not only fallen to layer two of the Bone Baptization Realm, but his cultivation would remain stagnant at that level for the next ten years.

That was a heavy enough price to pay, but he'd also failed to kill that motherfucker and had to run away with his body covered with wounds. He'd been on the verge of death, and the pill had extracted blood essence from all over his body. If his father hadn't fed him the Jade Dew Marrow, he might be dead now.

He growled inwardly at his father. The Jade Dew Marrow had saved him, but at the cost of fifty years of his life. So, now he only had fifty years of life remaining, and he might never reach the Marrow Cleansing Realm in this life.

Fuck! He rubbed his face.

His father was here in the Snake Rearing Chamber with them. This wasn't the original plan. Wang Zhang was supposed to take one hundred Wang clan juniors with him, along with two great elders, but his father and a couple more elders had joined too.

Something was off. Was it because of that motherfucking snake?

Hatred ran through his bones, and it demanded the life of that bastard motherfucker snake. Today he would bathe in that snake's blood and then murder thousands of others to offer as a sacrifice for his own loss. With the portal open, no snake would be spared. He would kill them all.

His fingers brushed against the orb he always carried inside his storage ring. He had pulled it out to collect the souls of those nasty snakes all day long. He would be their nemesis. Even though the portal was open, so he didn't need the orb, he would still use it and collect snake souls.

He hated everything in the Snake Rearing Chamber, and his heart would ease only after killing them all.

Snakes were the worst, and he hated them.

"Zhang'er, where's the portal?" his father Wang Jiang asked with a furrowed brow that sent a shiver down his legs.

Wang Zhang stared at the array formation, but there was no sign of the portal. It was as if it had never existed.

"Father—"

"Zhang'er, there'd be better a good explanation for this, or I won't be able to save you from the ancestor's fury this time." His father rushed toward the array formation and checked it with another Energy Sensing Compass. "Strange. There was a fluctuation around this place, but there's no evidence that a portal was opened." The furrows in his brow deepened, so deep that there was almost a crease on his forehead.

The deeper the crease, the deeper the fear Wang Zhang felt. Ancestor Wang would kill him for this. The last time, he'd almost done it. If it wasn't for his father pleading for him, he would be dead already. This thing was a secret the Wang clan had kept for decades. If something went wrong, he would suffer a fate worse than death.

Wang Zhang rushed to the Devil Suppressing Array Formation and checked it from one end to another, but there was no gap or no opening. How could that happen? Had he seen it wrong?

"What a joke. It seems like little Zhang made a mess once again." Wang Shun spoke in a conceited tone. "I wonder what the ancestor will take away from little Zhang this time?"

Wang Zhang's blood rushed to his mouth, and he spurted a mouthful of it. This was insulting. The twins Shun and Shuntao had always hated and mocked him. But Wang Zhang couldn't dispute it. He wasn't only weak in cultivation, but he was stationed here to guard the Snake Rearing Chamber while the twins enjoyed everything he was supposed to enjoy. "Father, I will take a heaven and earth vow that I fought with a giant snake and there was a portal."

His father ignored him and called to everyone that had followed them. Excluding Wang Zhang and his father, there were forty-nine more people. Ten of them were elders from the Wang clan, three great elders including his father and seven inner sect elders. The remaining forty members including himself were people groomed by the clan, and they were here to reap the benefits of the Heart Garden on the other side of the array formation. It was a well-kept secret, and the other thirty-nine didn't know about it. There was princess Hua as well, an almost mature girl with all the soft softs figure he longed for.

"Form groups of five, and search for anything suspicious," Wang Jiang said.

"Brother Jiang, why are you asking disciples to roam around? Shouldn't we ask little Zhang questions for fooling us?" Wang Shuntao asked arrogantly, his bulging stomach bouncing a little as he forced his words.

Wang Zhang frowned. These two bastards. Wang Shun and Wang Shuntao. They had been promoted to great elder a few years back. Wang Shun's cultivation was only a little inferior to his father's, but after being promoted they were arrogant toward his father because they were brothers, and they could overpower his father when worked together.

"Brother Shuntao, don't worry about it too much. We must stay here for twenty days, as the soul orb is almost filled. With the princess's blood, we will open the portal and achieve our goal in the Beast Origin Realm." His father spoke in a calm tone, but Wang Zhang could see the fury behind his clear eyes.

"We agree with brother Jiang's words. Let's wait, everyone," Wang Shun replied.

That bastard. Wang Zhang cursed inwardly. How could those two ignore his father's seniority and call him brother? How presumptuous.

Wang Zhang's gaze darted to the fifty-second person they had brought with them: Sun Hua. Her cultivation had been disabled, and she looked so innocent and ravishing that he wanted to play with her, but he couldn't in his condition. Ancestor Wang had cut off his manhood, so even if she stood naked in front of him, he could do nothing.

However, ancestor Wang had also promised to restore him with a Vitality Restoring Pill if he guarded the Snake Rearing Chamber for decades and performed his job of collecting souls, making no trouble. Now, if only his father didn't discuss his failure with ancestor Wang he would get that pill. Maybe his father should die once the portal opened, and then he would finish his task. Wang Shun and Wang Shuntao should die too, then the world would really become peaceful again.

Then the discarded princess would be his plaything . . .

"Why is she here," Li Wei muttered, moving his fingers to the sword when he saw Wang Zhang staring at Sun Hua with lecherous eyes. The unending lust lurking in Wang Zhang's eyes disgusted Wei.

Sometimes he wished he didn't have a divine sense that could see people's expressions despite their backs being turned. Especially the kinds of expressions Wang Zhang had on his face as if he was stripping Sun Hua naked with his eye.

Wei wished he could cut open the dog's remaining eye right away. But that moment wasn't too far away, so he stayed his hands and waited for the right moment. First, he wasn't a match for the Wang clan lineup, and second, he didn't think Sun Hua would come with these people, so he had to be prepared to save her. But when these guys talked about using Sun Hua's blood, his mind went into overdrive. This could be an issue. But why was she here? Tang Sia had said she was attacked, that she'd put her somewhere safe. If that was the case, how did she end up in the Wang clan's hands? Was Tang Sia part of the Wang clan now?

There was another question. How did these bastards get their hands on a Soul Orb?

A Soul Orb was a tyrannical artifact used by demonic cultivators to collect the souls of living things. These orbs were used by a society called the Way of Demons from the demonic empires. Demonic cultivator was a broad term consisting of many types of people. Some practiced ghost arts, some practiced wicked rituals, and some cultivated a slaughter path. There were many more, but a peculiar group called themselves the Way of Demons, and they used souls for cultivation. Human souls. Soul Orbs were invented by them. It was a taboo thing in the righteous world, and yet the Wang clan had one. By their discussion, Wei understood the Wang clan used it to store Ferocious Beast souls.

When he thought about it more, it made sense. The puzzle pieces finally fit together. The blood he'd seen around the White Bone Trees, the female snake cursing him for killing snakes every twenty days, and the Wang clan's closeness to Sun Hua. Suddenly he remembered Wang Yungun's face when Tang Sia was about to expel Sun Hua. She was panicked. Was this the reason? Was Sun Hua a sacrificial object from the very beginning?

This answered one question for him, why the Wang clan watered the trees. They were trying to weaken the array formation, combining it with the Soul Orb to open a way to the Beast Origin Realm.

But he couldn't guess why the Wang clan had entered the Snake Rearing Chamber to start with.

And the main question: Why had the Wang clan collected snake souls for decades? If they desperately wanted to open a path through the array formation, they could have done it by some other means. With the resources and control they had in the Divine Fragrance Palace; it shouldn't be impossible for them to break an Earth Grade array formation.

Something was missing. There seemed to be a big conspiracy, but Wei couldn't put a finger on it.

"Father, there were two juniors living inside this place. What should we do with them?" Wang Zhang asked, his intact eye scanning the wooden hut.

"Kill them. The Soul Orb would love some human sacrifices as well."

Wei chuckled and looked at the two clowns sitting behind him. They were inside a concealment array, so no one could detect them inside this formation.

"Elder, there's a pit here, and I can see a Sun Glaring Tree at the middle of it," a disciple shouted, and Wei's chuckle expanded into a broad smile. The first trap was activated.

Chapter 55

First Trap

Wang Zhang heard a disciple shouting in excitement and charged forward.

A treasure?

That might save his life. If he'd said he wasn't anxious, he would be lying. His survival depended on this mission, and he had already messed up many things. Any further failure would see his head mounted on the clan's entrance gate. Just thinking about it made his ass sweat. But if they found a useful treasure at this place, that would ease his burden. That would be awesome.

As he rushed forward, a thought struck him. How could there be a tunnel here, and a treasure lying inside? Wasn't it too good to be true?

Three elders rushed from behind him, and a few disciples circled the tunnel entrance while a few more headed inside.

Could it be a trap? No way. Who could set up a trap here? Those powerless trash, Li Wei and Chen Du?

It was impossible.

A disciple shouted, "Snakes, there are snakes inside. Hundreds of them."

Wang Zhang relaxed. Snakes were fine. It wasn't a trap. Maybe they'd come after his fight with the giant snake and made a small nest. He must have missed the tunnel because of the fog. They would serve nicely for his Soul Orb.

Turning back, he rushed to his father. "Father. There are snakes in the pit. This is proof that the portal was actually open." He couldn't hide his smile.

"Zhang'er. There might be some truth to your words after all. This many snakes couldn't sneak through a weakened array formation." His father nodded at him.

"Maybe someone placed them there as cover." Wang Shuntao smiled smugly, staring at Wang Shun.

Wang Zhang gritted his teeth. That bastard. If he ever reached the Marrow Cleansing Realm, he would carve all the fat from Wang Shuntao's stomach and feed it to Wang Shun and then kill them both.

"Little Zhang'er. Don't be too happy. What if that pit is a trap?" Wang Shun added to the mockery.

"Great elder Jiang." An inner sect elder came to meet them. "The pit is filled with a few hundred snakes, but they are all layer five Foundation Realm Ferocious Beasts. We are thinking about killing them. Please give orders."

"Kill them and retrieve the herb. It might save little Zhang'er's life today." Wang Shuntao orders, smiling, a smug smile that hurt Wang Zhang at his weakest point.

Wang Zhang growled inside his mind and looked away. He had nothing to do with these bastards. The elders would take care of things now. Their combined power was enough to kill thousands of peak Foundation Realm experts, and these were only mid-level snakes. Nothing serious.

A minute passed, and a wail pulled Wang Zhang's attention toward the tunnel.

Wang Zhang saw a layer of ice covered the cracked black ground, and two disciples lay dead on that, their blood flowing out of their broken heads. Finger thick icicles had pierced through their bodies and they were falling on the ground, painting the ice in red.

Before anyone could react, a flurry of icicles shot from the tunnel, piercing the twenty-two disciples clustered outside. They didn't even get a chance to defend themselves.

It was a clusterfuck. A massacre. It reminded Wang Zhang of his own massacres he carried out every twenty days. This time, he was losing his clan members, and that didn't feel good.

When the dust settled, only four elders remained standing, and their condition wasn't good. A few icicles had managed to bypass their defensive artifacts and bore into their bodies.

"Morons. Get back!" Wang Jiang leaped in the air, drawing his sword. "That's a Cold Artic Snake Pit. Stay back." His sword shone with a bright brown light, and everything around him grew silent. But he was too late. The elders couldn't defend against the next barrage of icicles and dropped dead, spilling enough blood that the ground looked like a painting of blood ice. It kind of looked surreal.

Twenty-six people were dead, and no one else could do anything. If this wasn't a trap, then it was very unfortunate for the youths who'd died. Or fortunate for Wang Zhang who hadn't gotten close to the tunnel.

His father unleashed an attack, destroying the area around the tunnel, and hundreds of white snake corpses flew through the air.

But he wasn't done, and he unleashed a flurry of attacks, destroying everything in his path. The place where the tunnel mouth had been wasn't there anymore. Instead, the mutilated corpses of white snakes lay around.

A few snakes jumped out of the pile of dead snakes and sent a combined ice attack at his father. Filled with multiple icicles the attack packed enough power to send shivers down Wang Zhang's legs, but his father swung his sword, and the icicle fell to pieces before it even travelled a few feet in the air.

"You motherfucking beasts, you dare to kill my clan members? I'll wipe you from this realm." His father's sword swung in a repeated movement, and every time it moved, it cut through the remaining snakes.

Wang Zhang felt a rush of fighting energy toward his heart. Watching his father was like watching an idol, but it also reminded him that he could never be this good. He would always remain a criminal to the Wang clan.

His father danced on the bed of ice and cut through the horde of snakes, but in doing so the frozen sculpts of the Wang clan members shattered into pieces. But no one could blame his father. They were all dead, turned into icy black sculptures even before they could see anything beyond the array formation.

Wei laughed inside his mind. If he could, he would have walked next to the Wang clan's people and laughed while pointing at them. Twenty six out of fifty-one Wang clan members were dead, and four of them were inner sect elders at the peak of the Bone Baptization Realm. That was a powerful lineup. Enough to destroy a county, but they'd died like ants.

If only low-level qi Marrow Cleansing Realm bastards were there. They might have died too.

But he couldn't have everything, right? The second trap was still there, and more of them might die there.

Wei's gaze fell on the old man with the half-missing ear. He was more powerful than he seemed. With his layer six qi Marrow Cleansing Realm cultivation, he had destroyed the snake pit like crushing candy under his shoe. The sheer power his sword strikes produced could cut Wei in half. For now, Wei had no trap that could kill him, and it was impossible to kill all three Marrow Cleansing Realm cultivators including him.

"Li Wei, that was an awesome plan." The little fox appeared next to him, munching on a Twisted Vitality Fruit. "Are you planning to kill them all, or are we getting out of here?"

Wei's gaze fell on Sun Hua who lay next to where the elders sat. She was unconscious and innocent, and his heart grew hesitant. How was he going to save her? Could he be a demon and leave Nuan'er's sister behind?

But he couldn't save her with his own powers.

What should he do? There was pain in his heart. The pain of conflict, and he didn't know what to do.

The only option he could think of was to take her and pass through the array formation and seal it up again. Because he didn't know to unlock the sealed door leading out, and that he had to find out from one of these jerks, and he wasn't sure if he could keep her and himself alive until that happened. But if he chose to go beyond the array formation, what would he do later? He had been there once, and there were thousands of snakes, if not millions. He could survive using his

Yin Poison Pill Clone, but what about the others? He wouldn't have just Sun Hua to worry about, but also Chen Du. It would have been so much easier if he could put them inside the spirit artifact.

So much easier.

Damn, why was this so complicated? Why couldn't it be simple?

Chapter 56

Clusterfuck

Wang Zhang couldn't stomach seeing the young generation of the Wang clan being massacred like that. The hope of the Wang clan had been eliminated by half in one moment. It didn't take more than that. A mere moment, and their lives slipped away. They were brought here to gain experience. led by three great elders. They weren't supposed to face any trouble. But they'd died like commoners.

It was trouble. Too much trouble for his father.

Wang Zhang rubbed his forehead. His scalp tinged as he thought about the repercussions of these events. Ancestor Wang would be so pissed off because of their continuous failures.

This time, his father might lose his position as leader of Dark Shadow Force. Shun and Shuntao had been trying to knock him down since they became great elders, and this would be the perfect chance for them to do it.

Rubbing his cheeks, he tried to find a solution. But there was none. Actually, there was one. If Shun and Shuntao died and his father captured the secret treasure on the other side of the array formation. This should prevent any mishap from happening with his father. But how would he kill those brothers? They were too strong for him.

Yet only if both things happened would calamity would be averted. Otherwise, they might just stay here and never go back as explaining these things to ancestor Wang would be impossible.

"Brother Jiang, why didn't you stop them from going there?" Wang Shuntao got up and looked around. "You should take responsibility for this and step down as leader of this expedition. Brother Shun is more capable of leading us." His threatening gaze rolled through everyone. "What do others think about this? Brother Shun is almost as powerful as brother Jiang, and he has good battle experience. He won't let these slip ups like these happen."

Wang Zhang couldn't hold it in anymore. "Nonsense. It was you, Wang Shuntao, who told the elder came asking for order, to go fuck himself." Removing his father from his position. What nonsense. Did he think everyone here was a one-year-old child or what?

"Zhang'er. Stand down." His father got up. "I'm not so weak that I need my son to fight my battles." He wiped the snake blood from his face with a clean pink cloth. "Wang Shuntao, you're free to go back to ancestor Wang to get your brother reinstated as the leader of the expedition. Until you get the seal from ancestor Wang, shut your mouth or don't blame me for being merciless." Wood qi and ice qi leaked out of his body and covered a feet radius around him.

Wang Zhang smiled. This was his father, his idol. When it came to arrogance, no one could beat him. His mother had told him that he once went against ancestor Wang over something and didn't back down despite threat of imminent death.

Wang Shuntao's face twitched abnormally. The leader position belonged to his brother, but when Wang Zhang's father had joined the expedition, leadership had passed to his father due to his higher rank. "If you're going to threaten us, I don't have anything else to say. But this is wrong, and every death will be on you."

His father sneered. "Wang Shuntao, don't make me go into what is right and what is wrong. We both know who gave the order to that elder to kill those snakes. Whatever happens, we three share equal responsibility, so shut your mouth and find a solution to the matter at hand. There might be other traps waiting for us."

Wang Shuntao cupped his mouth. "So, you already knew this place would have traps, and yet you didn't inform us. Are you sabotaging our mission? Heavens have mercy on us."

Wang Zhang picked up a stone lying on the ground and nearly threw it at Wang Shuntao. That bastard. How could he make such nasty claims?

"Wang Shuntao, that's nonsense. Don't spout baseless accusations. If I wanted you all killed, I wouldn't have joined you in the first place."

"And that is even more suspicious. Why is the leader of Dark Shadow Force joining us on this mission? Are you trying to steal our achievements? Ancestor Wang has allowed us to go in and procure the item because we performed meritorious service for the clan. Now we have you bossing us around, ready to take the reward for our hard work."

Wang Zhang crushed the stone in his hand. What nonsense was this? Why were they going against each other rather than finding the culprit? Now he wished he could put them to death.

"I came here for Wang Rong. He has been missing for the last couple of days, and he was seen coming here."

"Rong'er? What is he doing here?" Wang Shun spoke for the first time. Wang Rong'er was his blood nephew, so he would definitely panic upon hearing about his disappearance, but this cheered Wang Zhang. If Wang Rong was dead, then Wang Shun and Shuntao would suffer great heartache, and that would make him happy.

An elder came running toward them. "Elder, we found the corpse of Wang Joji, the guard."

They fought among themselves like dogs while Li Wei enjoyed munching on the Green Fragrant Potato Chen Du had roasted. Wei loved them raw, but after roasting, the flavors exploded inside his mouth.

"Brother Wei, they found Wang Joji's corpse." Chen Du sat cross-legged near the fire. "Holy heaven's ass. This is exciting. They have reached your second trap."

Chuckling, Wei checked on the Burning Yang Beetle. It was still in cocoon phase, and he could make it explode anytime. Thanks to Wang Rong's bow and arrows.

"Stay behind. I'll check on this." The old man with the half-missing ear headed toward Wang Joji's corpse.

Seeing his stiff walk, Wei couldn't help but grin. By killing half of their youths, he had left a strong mental effect on them. And when he killed the other half, they would shatter under the mental pressure. Wei wasn't boasting about this; he had learned from real-life experience. Mental pressure was a bitch. A mortal felt mental pressure the same as a king, and both could crumble under it.

In the Martial Realm, there was a kingdom called the Shattered Bone Kingdom, and its king was infamous for his cruelty and capability to go against stronger empires and not lose an inch of his land. While claiming territory, he'd provoked a novice cultivator with strong willpower. That cultivator had turned into a Poison King in the future. After gaining enough power, the Poison King put pressure on the Shattered Bone Kingdom by killing officials one after another. Over ten years, he killed every imperial clan member one by one, including the king's ten sons and five concubines. The Poison King was lower in cultivation, but by using mental pressure he turned the king into a cowardly puppet. One night, the king killed himself, and the kingdom had collapsed.

Of course, Wei wasn't killing them one by one, but he was using a similar tactic on the Wang clan elders.

And Wang Joji's corpse was the second trap.

Wang Zhang followed the old man with the half-missing ear, but raising his hand, the old man stopped everyone at a hundred meters' distance. He was cautious, and Wei had expected that.

But he couldn't prevent the next clusterfuck Wei was going to cause.

Chapter 57

Poison

A fire burned near Li Wei while he lay with his head on a stone and his eyes on the drama unfolding outside of the concealment array. The roughness of the stone provided an eerie feeling to his head, but he was focused on the characters in the drama.

The old man with half an ear missing inspected Wang Joji's corpse, and his eyes widened as he looked more into it.

Wei had thrown the corpse between the dead snakes and mutilated it. It wasn't the best job he had performed in his two lives, and he still felt uneasy about it, but those bastards were planning to do the same to him and Chen Du. Wei had just used their plan on them.

The world was unfair, but what could Wei do to change it?

"That Wang Joji, he must have fought a brutal battle with the snakes and died with them. Poor soul," one of the elders said to another, and everyone else nodded—except Wang Zhang, the man with the eye patch who had guarded the Snake Rearing Chamber's entrance when Wei first arrived. His face twitched, and his eyes burned with suspicion.

Wei tapped on the rim of the water skin he held. Even if Wang Zhang knew it was a trap, what could he do?

A black shadow floated over Wang Joji's body, and Wei used his divine sense to watch the scene unfolding. The man with half missing ear was performing some ceremony with dead Wang Joji. Being in the concealment array let him snoop on anyone and everyone in range. The old man with the half-missing ear was Wang Jiang. Wang Zhang had called him father. Wang Jiang was using a black medal to project the last memories of the soul into an illusion mirror, but right now nothing appeared in the mirror. It was a similar technique to a Soul Searching Talisman, but Wei had taken care of it. He didn't want the mistake he'd made with Du Su to repeat here.

Wang Jiang frowned when the black shadow showed nothing but a bright yellow sun vanishing. "Someone has concealed the memories. I can only see the beast flame vanishing from his body. There's nothing else we can learn here."

"Those bastard snakes. First, they cut brother Wang Joji to pieces and then stole his beast flame too. How vicious," someone whispered in the crowd.

Wang Jiang picked the mirror up and raised his hand to stop the clamor. "It was not done by a snake. A snake can't wipe out one's soul. This is a very advanced technique," he said in a grim tone while looking at Wang Shuntao.

"Brother Jiang, don't try to make it sound mysterious," Wang Shuntao replied, his stomach flab bouncing as he talked. "The proof is in front of us, and yet you're redirecting blame elsewhere?" Wang Shuntao stepped forward and placed one hand on his stomach and pointed the other at Wang Jiang. "Brother Jiang, don't forget the ancestor is watching everything through his spies. You'd better not force others with your fake narrative."

"Shuntao'er, shut up. Don't insult brother Jiang. Although he was wrong, we can't blame everything on him. He is baffled too," Wang Shun said with a smirk.

Politics. No clan was free of politics and throat-grabbing villains.

Surprisingly, Wang Jiang didn't react. "Someone has set a trap for us." He crushed Wang Joji's head and kicked the remains of his torso away. It bounced over a mutilated snake corpse before landing in a small pit.

Wei scoffed. Along with the torso, the sword was kicked away too. This wasn't going according to plan. He wanted someone to pick up that sword, so he had kept it next to Wang Joji's torso, but if no one picked it up, how would his second trap work?

That would be a bummer.

Maybe he had to use the divine sound again and influence a disciple to pick up the sword.

But then one of the disciples turned back and reached for the sword on his own. Picking it up, he hid it inside his clothes when no one was looking.

That's it, boy.

"Brother Wei, congratulations. You can spring your second trap now."

Wei nodded. "Not yet. I have to wait for the perfect moment." But it didn't take long for that moment to arrive.

The disciple who had picked up the sword walked back into the crowd and pretended nothing had happened.

Smiling, Wei activated his Yin Poison Pill Clone and released the poison that coated the sword. It floated around and then spread like pollen, landing on a few disciples' exposed arms and necks. It was a peculiar poison he had obtained from a bunch of snakes on the other side of the array formation. It was called Skin Rotting Snake Poison, and it was only deadly for Foundation Realm cultivators. The elders and others wouldn't even feel it. When it landed on the skin, it started rotting the skin and muscle membrane. Once it reached the person's blood, it would spread everywhere and then they would inevitably die.

It was kind of a cruel method, but it was the best Wei had. Only this poison could work in pollen form; the others required different methods of transportation.

In ten minutes, five disciples started scratching their necks and arms. Soon, they realized the itch wasn't stopping even when they peeled their skin with their scratching. They took some pills, but the itching continued, and before an elder took it seriously one of them had died, his skin turning charred black. If they were fed a Silver Grade Poison Repelling Pill, they might have been saved, but no one noticed it

.

Two more died before an elder identified the poison and sent everyone away. He gave two pills to the remaining two disciples, but their lives were worse than death as they would need extensive treatment. They were crippled.

The irony was, Wei too had been called a cripple in his childhood, but things had taken a different turn now.

"Brother Wei, that's gruesome," Chen Du complained.

Wei shrugged. "It was them or us. Would you choose to lie mutilated among those dead snakes or to kill these bastards who plotted against our every step?"

"I'd kill them with a clean sweep." Chen Du answered.

Wei chuckled. "Brother Du, you can't be too soft when dealing with your enemy. Being vicious when needed is part of your strength. One day, you'll understand this." He sighed. It had taken him two hundred years to understand this, so he couldn't expect Chen Du to understand it from the get-go. Some people were nicer in their hearts, and it took them years to harden up and realize one mistake could endanger their entire family.

It just wasn't worth it.

"Father, I think someone is setting deliberate traps for us." Wang Zhang was the first one to realize what was going on and speak out.

"Little Zhang'er, who could that be? Your imaginary friend who opened the portal? Or the imaginary snakes that attacked you?" Wang Shuntao said with mockery.

Wei watched the disciples move away from the three dead and two barely alive ones. They weren't ready to gain a contagious disease if there was one.

Wei sighed. That was a bummer. If someone else had picked up the sword, he'd had another surprise hidden. But it was impossible for now.

A disciple with green eyes rushed toward Wang Jiang and said, "Elder, we found senior brother Wang Rong lying unconscious inside the hut. He is quite injured and missing his legs."

Wang Jiang jumped to his feet and rushed toward the wooden hut.

Wei chuckled inside his mind. Thirty-one were dead, and only twenty people remained.

The third trap could be activated now, and this time his target was Marrow Cleansing Realm cultivators.

Chapter 58

Devastating blow

Wang Zhang's heart contracted inside his rib cage as he looked at the rotten corpses. Their black skin and the nasty smell coming from their bodies irked him—not because he cared for them, but because they had lost three more promising youths and two were almost dead. The strange thing was, no one knew how it had happened, and no one was trying to figure it out. They were afraid of the poison spreading, so everyone maintained a strict distance from the corpses except his father.

But with a glance at his father's face, he knew the situation wasn't good.

His gaze jumped to the two disciples lying on the ground, their skin turning darker with every moment. They were dying too, and no matter what pill they fed them, they weren't improving. Watching their skin slowly succumbing to necrosis, many disciples had thrown u p.

The uncertainty of the cause made everyone ill at ease. Tension bolstered their anxiety. The pressure was mounting, and no one knew what would happen next. It was like they'd walked into a death maze instead of the Snake Rearing Chamber. This could lead to everyone's death, and for the first time, Shun and Shuntao were silent. In fact, no one was talking. No one dared to talk. They just moved in circles, avoiding going anywhere.

One of the elders sent to patrol returned with a grim face and approached Wang Jiang. "Elder, we found senior brother Wang Rong lying unconscious inside the hut. He is quite injured and missing his legs."

"Rong'er is found?" His father's face lit up, and a bout of jealousy swelled inside Wang Zhang's heart. Wang Zhang was the legitimate son of his father, but he'd never gotten such a reaction from his father. It wasn't fair, but nothing was fair in this world. One day, he would like to see his father having the same expression for him too.

But what the heck was Wang Rong doing inside the Snake Rearing Chamber? Wang Joji had been tasked with guarding the chamber, so he might have walked in and died, but Wang Rong?

Did his father come here to look for Wang Rong? It made sense now, and it also made him wonder if Wang Rong had been drawn here to get his father here. Was this a trap for his father from the start?

An ominous feeling spread through Wang Zhang's heart, and he wanted to stop his father from checking on Wang Rong.

"Yes, force leader. But his condition is bad."

"It doesn't matter, as long he is alive." His father jumped to his feet and dashed toward the hut. He covered the mile distance in a jiffy. The hut was in the same rundown condition Wang Zhang remembered. For dozens of years, it had been like this. Disciples came and went, but they cared only for their own lives rather than the hut they lived in. If it wasn't for the poison in the air, the hut would have turned into a nest of insects and spiders.

Considering the previous experience, Wang Zhang hung back and didn't enter the hut. Even if it was a trap, he wasn't worried about his father. He was a layer six Marrow Cleansing Realm expert, and not many could set up a trap that could hurt him.

But the question remained. Who had set up traps? Could it be snakes from the other side? Maybe a Spirit Beast with intelligence like humans? Or was it those two trash disciples who had entered this place? Li Wei and Chen Du. After they went in, Wang Zhang never heard back from them. They didn't even come begging for more Poison Repelling Pills like the others before them.

Could those two behind these traps?

Nah! It was impossible. Those trash were in the Foundation Realm. How could they set up traps like the ice snakes in the pit? It was impossible. It had to be a Spirit Beast from the other side. They had grudge against the Wang clan. After all, Wang Zhang had killed tens of thousands of snakes. Those nasty fucking animals. How could they hurt the Wang clan? They deserved to die.

He was pulled out of his ruminations when his father re-emerged from the hut with a grim face. His eyes settled on the elders. "Get him out and put him in a clean place and start healing him."

Wang Zhang moved closer. "Father, is he all right?" He didn't care what happened to Wang Rong, but he had to display some empathy for a fallen comrade.

"No. He isn't. All his meridians are broken, and his beast flame has been stolen." His tone was lower than Wang Zhang had ever heard, and he realized how shocked his father was.

"Who did this to Rong'er?" Wang Shuntao roared and rushed into the hut. Five minutes later, a couple of elders carried Wang Rong out on a makeshift stretcher.

Wang Zhang stared at the people taking Wang Rong away. Wang Shuntao and Wang Shun followed him with dread leaking through their faces. Wang Rong was their nephew, so crippling Wang Rong was a slap to their faces, and it felt so good.

Whoosh!

Something shot past him from far away, and before Wang Zhang could process what it was, it hit Wang Rong's body and exploded like a miniature sun. Seizing the opportunity, Wang Zhang pushed a disciple standing between him and Wang Shuntao and prevented Wang Shuntao from running away. At the same time, he leaped backward, avoiding the explosion. And having Wang Shuntao's elephant-like body between him and the blast shielded him perfectly.

However, that didn't prevent the fierce winds from hitting his body and sending him flying away. The wind sliced his body with a hundred small cuts, drawing blood from everywhere. When he crashed to the ground, he looked more like a bloody hound than a human.

"Fuck you," he cried and pulled out a healing pill and popped it into his mouth. Thank heavens he'd had a two-man buffer in between him and the explosion. If he hadn't pushed that disciple onto Wang Shuntao, he might have suffered more.

Was he dead?

Wang Zhang lifted his head and crawled out of the small pit he had created and saw Wang Shuntao lying on the ground. His right hand was missing, bone deep cuts ran over his entire body, and his left eye was missing, yet his chest heaved up and down.

Fuck! Why wasn't he dead yet?

Wang Zhang grabbed his chest. If there hadn't been two people in front of him to take the brunt of the explosion, finding even a single one of his limbs afterward would have been impossible.

When he looked around, all he saw was shattered bones and mutilated limbs. Other than Wang Shuntao, no one who had stood near

Wang Rong was alive. Nine people had died, including four inner sect elders. Now only twelve people remained including Sun Hua.

His throat tightened when he saw his father on his knees, roaring at the skies. The blow the Wang clan had received this time was unrecoverable. No one could save them now.

Yet, Wang Shuntao was alive. Fucking bastard.

His father's roar sent a chill across his feet, and he closed his eyes and concentrated on his cultivation. His father was pissed off, and when he found the person or beast who did this to the Wang clan, he would die a thousand deaths.

But before that person or beast died, he should at least kill Wang Shuntao once and for all.

Chapter 59

Chase

The little fox jumped out of the spirit artifact, followed by the female snake whose lingering slashes spoke to her grievous wounds. Compared to her twenty-foot-long body in its expanded state, she looked like a tiny child in her five-foot-long body. Yet her shiny blue eyes that looked like the depths of a sea sent a warning sign to Wei's core.

As soon she appeared, she hissed at Li Wei and Chen Du.

Frowning, Wei brushed his fingers against the sword lying on the ground next to him. If this snake attacked, he wouldn't mind driving his sword through her.

The little fox raised her paw and slapped the female snake. The snake went rolling away. Raising her head, she growled before moving away and curling herself around a stone lying next to the fire Chen Du had lit to roast some food. The fragrance still lingered in the air.

This was the big benefit of a Major Isolation Array. It concealed everything, scent, voice, energy fluctuations, and nasty snakes. It was good enough to camp in an enemy area and eat a nice meal while listening to their enemy's plans, but it had a major flaw: it couldn't hide them from everyone. If a Marrow Cleansing Realm cultivator came too close, he might discover them. If Wei hadn't regressed to the qi Refinement Realm, he could have carved an Illusion Concealment Array, a two-tier array, to hide them from anyone below a Houtian Realm expert, but he wasn't there yet. Nor he had predicted there would be so many people he had to kill.

"Snaky, you haven't thanked Li Wei yet for saving your life." Brushing her whiskers, the little fox sat next to Wei and rested her head on his lap. Wei brushed his fingers around a bare patch on her forehead. After she had suffered for him, she had lost half of her fur, but it was growing back.

He rubbed her forehead and glanced at the female snake expectantly. A thank you was due.

"Thank you, human."

"Snaky, say it nicely."

"Human lord, thank you for saving my life."

"Call me Li Wei."

"You can call me lady Fuishui." Raising her head, she looked in his eyes. "I'm a Spirit Beast, better than you filthy humans. Don't forget to respect me."

Wei shrugged. He didn't even want to talk to the arrogant snake. If it wasn't for the little fox, he would have let her die.

"Brother Wei, your third trap was a major success. Where did you find that beetle?" Chen Du took a bite of the roasted boar he had just prepared.

Wei moved his fingers over the little fox's furry head. Her fur was the softest, and comfortable, but it was still thin. "I found it inside the sect. In my run-down courtyard at the Waste Disposal Faction."

"Holy heavens. I can't believe these beetles live inside the sect. They almost killed a Marrow Cleansing Realm cultivator. That's fascinating."

Wei sighed. "Almost. Wang Shuntao had the lowest cultivation of the three, and yet he survived. No matter how low level they are, Marrow Cleansing Realm cultivators are tough nuts to crack. At least he's missing a hand now, so his battle prowess will take a big hit."

The little fox nestled close to his sky-blue robe and made herself comfortable while Wei watched the Wang clansmen forming a close-knit circle. Wang Jiang wasn't ready to let them move, or Wei would have sneakily killed a few more. Only eleven Wang-people remained, and he could definitely kill the seven below the Marrow Cleansing Realm.

"Brother Wei, are there any more traps you left for those bastards?"

Wei chuckled. "Do I look like the son of a sect leader? Those traps were improvised tactics, nothing more. If I had enough materials, I'd show you what an actual trap would look like. With a proper array formation, it wouldn't be difficult to kill them all." A regretful sigh slipped out of his mouth. In fact, there were a few low-level arrays he could set up to separate and kill them one by one, but he hadn't had enough time to prepare nor the materials required to carve them. Most of his time had gone into gathering the eggs from the Cold Artic Snake Pit and then luring those nasty snakes to this side.

"Human, you've sacrificed my clan members to kill people for your revenge, and I can't accept that." Fuishui stared at him.

"You're free to walk out of this concealment array and do whatever you want," Wei said sternly. Even after saving her life, she accused him unnecessarily.

No, he wouldn't let that happen.

"Despite that, I thank you because these humans have killed hundreds of thousands of my clan members, and even if I must sacrifice tens of thousands of my clan members, I want them all dead."

Wei tapped on his nose. This Fuishui, she was changing her colors faster than a reptile. Well, she was kind of a reptile.

Heaven knows.

"Brother Wei, when the news of forty-two Wangs' deaths transmits outside, I want to see the Wang elders' faces. I recognize a few of those who died, including Wang Rong, and they are the elite of the Wang clan's young generation. This is a big blow to their foundation."

Yes, it was a huge loss to the Wang clan. Six of their inner sect elders and thirty-four young disciples had died, and that didn't even include the two people he'd killed before them. Even if they reproduced and made new members every month, they wouldn't get back to the peak of their current talent in a hundred years. He wished he could kill the entire Wang clan. Not that he enjoyed killing innocent people, but he didn't believe in anyone from the Wang clan anymore. They had again and again proved that they would do anything to attain their goal, and the Soul Orb was a prime example of that. By killing thousands of innocent snakes and filling their demonic soul orb, they had gone past redemption.

"The big blow will be when we kill the three Marrow Cleansing Realm cultivators, but in our current condition that's impossible." Wei wished he could do more, but he had limitations. With his three traps, he had done the maximum damage he could do to the Wang clan here and now. That was it. His cultivation was too low to take revenge on the entire Wang clan.

"Li Wei, what are your plans now? Let's get out of this place and find some of those Twisted Vitality Fruit trees you promised me. This place sucks." The little fox growled.

Wei chuckled. This vegetarian glutton. All she thought about was food.

"Let's watch them for now, and once we get a chance, we will save Sun Hua and get the hell out of here," Wei said, staring at Sun Hua lying near the hut under the supervision of Wang clan elders. After his third trap, everyone had gone crazy. They were watching every place like the killer hid there, but they couldn't find Wei even after an hour of searching.

He was safe. For now.

Or not. His divine sense picked up a fat person limping toward them. It was Wang Shuntao.

Dread spreading through Wei's bones. Why the fuck was this bastard coming at them? Did he notice something? Were they about to be discovered?

Chapter 60

Revealed

Flicking his arm, Li Wei threw a stream of water to douse the fire. The concealment array could hide everything from low-level cultivators, but it couldn't hide smoke and scents from a Marrow Cleansing Realm coming close to the array.

"Everyone. Hold your breath and don't move. Someone is coming," he sent through his divine sense to all three of them. An Illusion Concealment Array could have saved them even if someone walked through the array itself, but a Major Isolation Array only hid them in plain sight. If someone walked through the array, they would be discovered right away.

Another Wang clan elder roamed around the hut, looking for them, and Wei realized this would not work. The Major Isolation Array couldn't hide them forever. Sooner or later, they would be discovered by someone. If they wanted to live, they had to get out of this place and then get the fuck out of the sect as well. After what he had done to the Wang clan, they wouldn't welcome him with open arms.

But the question was, how would they escape? Five hundred feet's distance lay between them and the door that led to the outer tunnel. Ten Wang clan members stood in between, ready to strike. Even if he somehow made it through using his movement art, what about Chen Du and the two Spirit Beasts? He wouldn't let the little fox get into trouble.

"Little fox, get ready to go back to the spirit artifact on my signal."

She nodded.

At least she would be safe in the spirit artifact.

"Can you take Chen Du in with you?" he asked, hoping she would say yes.

She shook her head. "Only dead people and beasts can go inside."

Wang Shuntao limped closer. Although he hadn't recovered his missing hand, and thick cuts sprawled across his entire body, his vitality had recovered back to normal and his qi seemed to have recovered as well. This was bad news for Wei. Even in his weakened state, it would be difficult to kill this bastard.

Wang Shuntao walked to the edge of the array, scratching his belly. A piece of meat juice stained the corner of his mouth, and he licked it with his tongue. He stood at the edge of array, close enough that Wei could have extended his hand and slapped him hard.

Everyone in the array held their breath as the flab of meat lowered his pants to take a leak.

Fuck! Dread filled Wei's heart. He quickly cupped the little fox's eyes. She was like a little kid who knew nothing about the cruel world. Exposing her to such things would be tainting her innocence. Even he turned around to avoid a sight he might not forget.

But Chen Du wasn't so fortunate, and a jet of urine shot for him, turning his face pale like he faced certain death. It was indeed a death sentence. Death by drowning. Wang Shuntao was in the Marrow Cleansing Realm, and he might drown Chen Du in a river. The higher the cultivator realm, the higher one could piss if they wanted to.

Wei couldn't look at Chen Du. He wouldn't even wish this kind of situation on his worst enemy. In his previous life, he had once seen a lunatic in the Martial Realm who killed his opponents and then pissed on their dead bodies. He was a water-attributed cultivator, so he literally drowned them in his piss.

It was disgusting, but he was famous as fuck. Many girls thought it was a manly thing to do and wanted to marry him. He had a cult following.

Heavens, there were so many weird things in this world.

However, Fuishui leaped at Wang Shuntao when the jet of water moved at her. Thick fog covered the area, and everything turned gloomy.

Wang Zhang stared at the irritating daylight and cursed it openly. Standing under this light made him sweat, and when sweat broke out under his eye patch, it burned like someone had poured a furnace full of hot water into his eye socket.

He hated this sweat, and he hated those snakes, he hated the bastard that had killed all the Wang clan people so everyone had to stay out in the sun and couldn't rest in the wooden hut. For the last five hours, they had checked every single corner of the Snake Rearing Chamber, not leaving anything behind, but they didn't find anything other than snake bodies. There was no trace of the one who'd fired the arrow, and there was no trace of those juniors either.

Sitting there, he wondered what happened with those trash juniors, Li Wei and Chen Du. Did they go to the other side of the array formation and get killed by the snakes?

Could it be possible? It was indeed possible. That bastard snake had attacked him—nearly killed him. Given the cultivation levels of those two juniors, they must have been killed and eaten by that giant snake.

Fuck! Was he wasting his time looking for those two bastards? They were already in deep trouble, and he wasn't sure how his father was going to handle all of this. Being the supreme cultivator and leader of Dark Shadow Force he would be held responsible for this. And if he was implicated, then Wang Zhang would face death for starting all this. He was the one who'd said the portal was open.

Fuck! This might just end with him having to lose his life. Pushing his fingers through his long hair, he turned to leave. This was frustrating. His injuries itched from inside, and the high-grade healing pills had gone to that fatso Wang Shuntao.

Why didn't he die?

A wail came from behind him, and when Wang Zhang turned around, he saw Wang Shuntao running out from behind the wooden hut, holding his crotch with his left hand. Or what was left of his manhood?

Behind him two juniors surfaced, and he knew those two. Li Wei and Chen Du. Those bastards.

What was he doing behind the hut? Why was he bleeding a bucket full of blood from his crotch?

Wang Shuntao pointed at Wang Zhang, then at his crotch before stumbling and crashing face-first on the ground right next to Wang Zhang. What the fuck was he trying to say? Was he mocking Wang Zhang because he'd had his manhood cut off? Was this a new way of insulting him?

These brothers. A tremor passed through his legs. Lava exploded inside his mind. Since the day he'd faced his punishment, these brothers had been going too far while mocking him and his father. This was too much to handle.

"Great elder Shuntao, don't go overboard. Just because you have power doesn't mean you can mock me openly." Unable to restrain his anger, he kicked at great elder Shuntao's gut. He couldn't hold it inside anymore. Today, he would kill this bastard once and for all.

Wang Shuntao wailed and then lost consciousness completely.

"Brother Shuntao!" Wang Shun came running. "You bastard, what did you do to my brother? How could you?"

"Insolent brat. We're attacked by a mysterious entity, and you're busy playing pranks with brother Shuntao?"

Wang Zhang chuckled inwardly. As long as his father was here, these brothers couldn't touch him.

"Zhang'er, go. Quickly kill those bastards. We can't let this humiliating scene leak out. How will brother Shuntao show his face to his fiancée after losing his . . ." Wang Jiang shook his head. "Maybe you can take care of her after the ancestor gives you that Vitality Restoring Pill."

Wang Zhang chuckled lightly. "This unfilial son will listen to father and kill those bastards quickly and come back to receive your next command." Maybe he was worried for nothing. The treasure was more important than these death's and ancestor would probably understand the reasoning. It had to be this, otherwise he wouldn't be in any mood to joke after losing forty-two members of Wang clan including the ones came here before. And although his father looked down on him, deep down his father loved him. Otherwise, his father wouldn't have wasted the special elixir on him.

Once the portal opened, he would do everything in his power to kill these two brothers. Then only things would be right for him.

Chuckling, Wang Zhang charged at the juniors. He was going to kill them in one sweep. "Junior, if you stop and accept your death, I'll leave your corpse intact." He was in a good mood now, and he might even show mercy by not chopping them into hundreds of pieces and feeding them to ants. He didn't know where these juniors came from, but he knew he had to kill them to quell some of the anger inside every Wang clan member's heart. He'd never suspected those trashy juniors could kill all of the Wang clan members who'd died, but they had appeared at the wrong time and in the wrong place, so they had t o die.

"Die, you trash." Wang Chenlei swung his six-foot-long great sword at the juniors. A sword image shot from his sword, traveling toward the huge junior with the long sword on his back. It was so fast that the junior had no time to react.

The thin junior, Li Wei, moved like lightning and pulled the sword from the huge junior's back and intercepted Wang Chenlei's blow with ease. He didn't stop there but took the initiative to counterattack Wang Chenlei.

"You're courting your death." Wang Chenlei swung his great sword horizontally, unleashing his ultimate move.

Wang Zhang shook his head. He'd missed an opportunity to vent his fury. With Wang Chenlei's layer three Bone Baptization Realm cultivation, the junior might not have a corpse left at all. He was one of the fiercest warriors of the Wang clan and known for his viciousness. Using his full force attack on a junior was overkill.

What a shame. Wang Zhang was looking forward to killing them himself.

Wang Zhang slowed his pace when Wang Chenlei's sword reached the thin junior. That junior was a goner, and he didn't want to get blood and flesh splashed over his body. And if it reached his face, he would regret it big time.

Blood splattered, but not from the thin junior's body.

Wang Zhang froze and rubbed his eyes.

How could it be possible? How could the junior cut through Wang Chenlei's sword and make a huge wound on Wang Chenlei's body instead? It was inconceivable.

But the undulation of power he sensed from the junior's sword told him something different. It was a genuine strike, and Wang Chenlei's bulging eyes and painful cry said the same.

Something was wrong here.

The junior didn't stop. Picking up momentum, he jumped on Wang Chenlei's shoulder and sliced his sword through Wang Chenlei's head like cutting through tofu.

Was it that easy to cut through the Wood Symbolic Shield Wang Chenlei had swiftly activated? What if he, Wang Zhang, had faced that strike?

He would have been dead.

Wang Zhang stepped backward. That junior was too strong, and he wasn't a match for him. But how could it be? How could a peak Refinement Realm cultivator cut down a layer five Bone Baptization Realm cultivator like he was a piece of soft tofu?

How?

"Junior, you're courting your death." Wang Jiang charged forward; his fist enveloped in brown energy. It was his father's famous attack skill, the Sacred Wood Sutra. It could fight across minor layers, and with his father's cultivation of layer six of the Marrow Cleansing

Realm, that thin junior should burst like a bubble. The kid was really a goner this time.

Chapter 61

Dragon Fist of Pain

That bastard Chen Du had one job, and yet he'd made a mess out of it. After the female snake attacked Wang Shuntao, they had to run. So, Li Wei had asked the little fox to hide inside the spirit artifact along with Fuishui. All they had to do was make it to the array formation without provoking the ire of the Marrow Cleansing Realm bastards. Wei had kept his Seal Severing Array active so he could open it on whim and pass through the Devil Suppression Array Formation a few more times. His immediate plan was to get to the other side and then make a big plan to save their asses—and Sun Hua's too.

It was a simple plan, to quickly cross the three hundred feet between the hut and the Seal Severing Array. But Chen Du, the clumsy bastard, had crashed into the water barrel and attracted everyone's attention. Heck, even if he hadn't done that, he probably wouldn't have made it all the way to the array without attracting attention anyway. Instead of lifting his legs while running, he kicked the soil, raised clouds, and scratched his shoes over the pebbles like a hundred-foot-tall animal trampling a fragile piece of soil.

How could one be so clumsy while running?

Wei cursed, but when he saw the sword image shooting at Chen Du's throat, he couldn't hold back. He'd used his Basic Movement Skill and charged forward. In the end, he'd had to paint his sky-blue robe with blood. So many robes he had ruined in a day. Fei'er wouldn't be happy when she found out his rate of robe ruining greatly surpassed her rate of robe sewing.

"Junior, you're courting your death." Wang Jiang charged him, unleashing killing intent with his layer six qi Marrow Cleansing Realm cultivation base. His fist glowed with thick brown wood qi. The intense aura his attack exuded was so thick that Wei's forehead throbbed in pain. Taking that fist head-on would be suicide; his head would explode into pieces.

Yet with Chen Du right behind him, he couldn't dodge it or Chen Du would explode into oblivion. But he had no confidence in defending against this attack even with the strongest of his powers. Even if he had reached level two of his One Sword Strike, he might not have had any chance of defending his life.

Staring at the fist coming for him, he stiffened. It was like watching an avalanche rushing toward him with nowhere to hide. Even with his entire strength he might remain like an ant in front of the real power.

This was bad. In that single moment, his brain processed all his options, but there was nothing that could allow him to go against a layer six qi Marrow Cleansing Realm expert's full-power fist attack. Wei lacked good martial skills, and his Five Elemental Weapon Art required him to be in the qi Foundation Realm to practice it. This was one of the biggest predicaments of his current life.

His eyes twitched when he sensed an impeccable connection with the wood qi surrounding his opponent's fist, as if he could refine it into his own wood qi. The thought came from his Yang Wood Pill Clone, and it was exhilarating.

Fuck! It could even sense wood qi from a ten-foot distance.

Maybe he could still survive this. Smirking, Wei activated his Blood Earth Force Shield Divine Art and pulled his elbow back to accumulate all the force he could from his body.

Dragon Fist of Pain.

An undulation of physical energy surged from his body, shooting toward his right fist. One hundred blood pearls rushed to his right arm, exploding into more power. Hundreds of tiny meridians in his right arm exploded under the onslaught of physical force. The blood pearls exploded too, moving more physical force through his right arm.

It was going to fuck him up, but he had no other option. Meeting his opponent's fist was suicide, and not meeting it would end Chen Du's life.

At least this way he had a one percent chance of survival.

Small meridians around his wrist burst internally, shooting blood out all over his arm. Immense pain shot through Wei's arm, and he wished he could just abandon his arm and run away. Every time he used this fucking fist art, he regretted it and wanted to kill that bastard Chang Ziang who had created this crazy first art. Why did he only look for the gate of pain, not the other gates? The human body had twelve gates, and that bastard could have used any other gate like the gate of joy, but he was a narcissist who enjoyed self-injury. It suited his personality, but it was torture for Wei.

More! Wei shouted in his mind. This wasn't enough to counterbalance the attack aimed at him. Even after weakening his opponent's wood qi, he still lacked a little. He wasn't a match for it.

Unless he poured more power into the Dragon Fist of Pain, and he could only do that by burning a few drops of his heart blood, but he didn't know if his body could support it. If not, he would lose his arm completely, and it might never grow back without a heavenly elixir. The Dragon Fist of Pain was one of the more bizarre divine arts he had seen in his previous life. One could extract more physical energy from one's body, but doing it might harm their limb permanently. In fact, he had thought about limiting the power of the attack, but in this case, he had to go beyond his capacity.

Was he ready to do that? If he didn't, he and Chen Du would die.

Whatever. Fuck it! Wei extracted more physical energy from his body and poured it inside his right fist. Tiny cracks spread across his arm bones and soon enlarged into big cracks before the bones crumbled under the pressure.

Air cracked and time froze when their fists met.

Like two dragons clashing their fangs, their fists clashed, sending an undulation of power in all directions. Wei's clothes tore apart, and hundreds of tiny injuries appeared on his body, cut by the air blades that resulted from their fists clashing. Blood leaked out, and he turned into a blood demon. Or at least looked like one.

But Wei had no presence of mind to assess his injuries, because the bones and muscles in his right hand had been shredded by the physical shock that had traveled through his arm.

Then Wei was sent flying back and crashed into Chen Du. The powerful physical force carried Chen Du with him, and they only stopped when their bodies slammed into the Devil Suppressing Array Formation's energy barrier, spitting mouthfuls of blood.

However, before he was sent flying back, Wei noticed the old man's lips curling downward and his forehead wrinkling when he looked at the drop of blood that appeared on his knuckle. He must not have imagined a tiny junior would be able to withstand his full-force attack, much less injure him.

Wei chuckled and threw up more blood. His injuries were heavier than those he'd received from Wen Shang, the Destiny Mirror Sect elder he'd fought, but because of his improved body cultivation, he didn't fall unconscious right away.

However, he did sway on the edge of consciousness. The line was so thin that he could fall to either side.

"Junior, you must be that Li Wei everyone is talking about. No wonder you went against Wen Shang and killed him." The old man pulled his fist back and drew a clean pink cloth from his pouch and wiped the drop of blood from his knuckle.

Wei bit his tongue, trying to remain clearheaded. He was still ten feet away from the Seal Severing Array, but his condition was terrible—worse than he realized, even. Bursting his blood pearls had put his body under inhuman stress, and he couldn't even lift his hand or move his body. He would need a month or two at least to recuperate from this injury.

His right hand was . . . maybe a goner forever. There was no hope of reviving it unless he obtained a Golden Healing Pill or an equivalent quality pill.

Wang Jiang walked toward them. "I underestimated you, and now I know how you, mere trash, could go against Wen Shang. You were hiding body cultivation, something only a few cultivate in the Mortal Realm." He stroked his half-cut ear. "I'm impressed, junior. But you must die. Rest assured; I won't mutilate your corpse. Instead, I'll burn it here."

Wei's eyes grew heavy, like someone had tied a ton of weight to them, and it was getting difficult to keep them open. Was he really going to die here? But more than that, was he going to listen to this jerk's self-righteous talk?

Chapter 62

Grim Time

A blood-covered Li Wei stared at the half-eared old man walking toward him spurting righteous nonsense. He hated such bastards the most. "Kill me if you have to . . . or get—" He coughed up more blood, then used the last of his energy to shout, "Or get lost!" Bastards who lectured their opponents, trying to be righteous before killing, made him sick. Why waste their breath and talk uselessly? Not everyone would reincarnate and remember who killed them. Just kill and be done with it.

"Junior, you disappoint me. Even on your death bed, you remain arrogant. Did you feel like an almighty god after killing a trash elder from the Destiny Mirror Sect?" The old man sneered. "Then I'll become a god killer today." He stepped closer.

"God killer." Wei chuckled, spitting out some pieces of his internal organs. There was blood all around him, and he couldn't guess if it was all from him or if some was from Chen Du who lay behind him. He seemed to be in the worst condition.

"Arrogant junior. I'm helping you by sending you to the maker. You should thank the heavens for dying by my hand."

Wei stared into the old man's eyes, unafraid. It was just another death. What was to fear about it? Other than the regret of leaving Fei'er behind, he had no regrets. Maybe it was good. This way he would meet his grandfather again. In this life, he'd failed to achieve his goal, but not everything had gone wrong. At least he'd gotten to spend some time with his grandfather and mend their differences, and he cherished the moments he'd had with both his grandfather and Fei'er.

"Sacred Water Shield Talisman." Chen Du's feeble voiced came from behind him, and a blue shield of water enveloped him.

"Sacred Water Healing Talisman." Another talisman was slapped on his body, and healing water qi rushed into his body, pouring blessings from the heavens. It was a healing talisman, and a high grade one too. The healing water qi mended his internal organs rapidly, and new strength sprouted in his body. It only healed him to twenty percent of his peak, but it was enough for him to move his body.

"Leave your life behind, juniors." Another fist attack came, but this time Wei didn't counterattack. Instead, he raised his left hand in front of him and burned twenty blood pearls, activating enough energy to use the momentum of the attack and fly toward the Seal Severing Array. Of course, he took Chen Du with him.

"I said leave your lives behind." Wang Jiang charged them, aiming to kill them in one go.

Wei's heart raced like an Iron Steed Horse as he pulled a Qi Stone from his storage ring and activated the Seal Severing Array.

A portal opened, and he pushed himself through it along with Chen Du's unconscious body. With his left hand, he smashed a Qi Stone on the portal, disturbing the energy flow. When the energy flow was disturbed, the Devil Suppression Array pulsed intensely, and everything in a five-foot area was blasted apart. Wei felt like a mountain had crashed into his chest, and he spat more blood. By this time, he had no idea how many buckets of blood he had spat. If it wasn't for his Blood Essence Body, he might have turned into a dried corpse.

After breaking a tree in two, he crashed into the soil and then everything went quiet. Deathly quiet. There were no snakes nor any living thing other than him and Chen Du for a mile around them.

Before his eyes closed, he spotted Wang Jiang climbing out of a pit. He had been blasted too, but he had only suffered superficial injuries. In fact, if Wei hadn't had the protection from the Sacred Water Shield Talisman, he might have been torn into tiny pieces by the blast. The Seal Severing Array had redirected the energy flow and fooled the target array. Dissembling was a complex process, and he'd just broken it with his hands, attracting backlash from the target array.

But at least it had saved his life.

"Wang Jiang, let me tell you a secret." Wei coughed blood, but he spit it out and used all of his energy to push the words out. "I killed them all, and I'll wipe out the entire Wang clan someday. Wait for me." And then he lost his conscious.

System: A foreign substance has invaded host's body. It is attacking host's heart blood. It is recommended to remove the foreign substance within the next four hours.

Wang Zhang watched the high-octane action with his only eye widened to the limit. How was it possible? Was this junior Li Wei a reincarnation of the devil? First, he'd killed Wang Chenlei in one shot. He'd cut through Wang Chenlei's head like it was tofu, and he didn't even flinch when the blood splattered over his face. Could he be a blood demon himself?

Then junior Li did a thing that was impossible. Just impossible. How could a peak Refinement Realm cultivator go against a layer six Marrow Cleansing Realm expert? Although he didn't win, he'd walked out of the fight alive.

And then he'd done another impossible thing. He'd opened a portal in the Devil Suppressing Array and walked through it. So, when Wang Zhang had seen the open portal the day before, it had been opened by this junior.

Even "impossible" sounded insufficient. It was just . . . inconceivable.

When the dust settled, he reached the pit his father had crashed into with long strides. His father lay in the pit with blood leaking from the corner of his mouth, looking miserable in tattered clothes. However, other than tattered clothes and disheveled hair, he looked fine.

"Father, are you all right?"

His father replied with his action by climbing out of the pit.

But suddenly he heard something from the other side of the array formation. It was junior Li Wei's words, and they fell on his ears like someone poured lava in them. "Wang Jiang, let me tell you a secret." Li Wei coughed up a mouthful of blood, but he didn't look like he was dying. "I killed them all, and I'll wipe out the entire Wang clan someday. Wait for me."

Wang Zhang felt like a mountain was crushing his soul. The threat from junior Li Wei struck directly at his core, and for a moment, he forgot to breathe.

A palm pressed his shoulder, and he was pulled out of the trance.

It was his father. "Shake it off. That junior used some powerful soul technique to rattle your soul." From his pouch, he produced a new dark gray martial robe and donned it. "You were right, Zhang'er. There was a portal, and we missed it completely."

Wang Zhang nodded. What could he say? That junior Li Wei had taken all the wind out of his lungs? That junior was too fierce.

"He won't live to see tomorrow," his father said in a calm voice.

"Brother Jiang, you couldn't even kill a mere junior. What a shame." Wang Shuntao laughed crazily. After losing two organs, he seemed to have gone crazy. His bleeding had stopped, but two missing limbs wouldn't grow back easily. He was going to suffer the same fate Wang Zhang had suffered for years. It would tear him up inside, and Wang Zhang would watch happily.

"At least my father fought with him, Wang Shuntao. You just stayed back like a coward." Wang Zhang chuckled in the same manor that Wang Shuntao had chuckled at his father. If that bastard was crazy, then Wang Zhang was the father of crazy. He could see his own image in Wang Shuntao. Wang Zhang too had gone crazy for days when ... Well, seeing his enemy going through the same pain calmed his own anxiety for some odd reason. He liked it this way. Everyone should feel what he'd felt for years. That way, they would know the wrath of the heavens.

"Nephew Jiang, you're courting your death," Wang Shun shouted and charged at him.

His father sneered. "Do you think you can fight me just because I suffered a minor defeat?" He raised his leg and kicked Wang Shun, sending him flying away.

"Don't go overboard, Wang Jiang. I won't tolerate this." Wang Shuntao drew his sword with his remaining hand. "Don't try to humiliate my brother. We can still beat you half-dead."

His father's face grew dark, darker than Wang Zhang had ever seen it before. "Wang Shuntao, did you miss the part where he opened a portal and vanished to the other side?"

Wang Shun got up from the ground and brushed his clothes clean. "Wang Jiang. Don't spout nonsense. I bet that was an illusion cast by you. I see through your actions now. You'll be answering to the elder council once we get out of this place."

"Would you believe it if that junior had killed your brother as well?"

"Nonsense. I'm standing here alive. Even missing a limb, I'm capable enough to kill him, unlike you," Wang Shuntao mocked.

Wang Zhang's father slashed with his sword before Wang Shuntao could react. A brown beam shot out of the sword and cut through Wang Shuntao's body, separating his head and torso. "Do you believe me now, or should I say he even managed to kill you?"

Panic dashed through Wang Zhang's veins. Why had his father killed Wang Shuntao? That would alert the elders of the clan, and they would use the soul tablet to find out who had killed Wang Shuntao. After all, Wang Shuntao was a great elder, and his death would be a big loss to the Wang clan. More of a loss than all forty people who had died today. They would definitely investigate it properly.

"Father, why—" Wang Zhang didn't complete his question before his father swung his sword again. Another brown beam shot from the sword and struck the secret realm's door around five hundred feet away from them. It cut through the door, rendering it unusable. Now it would take at least a few weeks to repair. That meant they were stuck here until then.

"We wait until we can use the Soul Orb once more, and then we kill those juniors. They might even die before we have the chance. But first we must obtain the treasure we seek. That's our priority," his father said in a calm voice and then walked toward the hut.

Wang Shun dropped next to his brother's corpse, his eyes burning with fury, but he didn't do anything. It was as if he overwhelmed by the things that had happened. Well, without his brother's power added to his, he couldn't do anything to Wang Jiang, so he was as good as dead.

Wang Zhang stared at the two juniors on the other side of the array, lying on the ground in a pool of blood. They were half-dead, and there was an army of snakes rushing toward them. They would not survive for long.

Chapter 63

Fearful predator

The dust settled, and Chen Du opened his eyes only to spit up a mouthful of blood. It made him dizzy, but the tiny stones poking into his torn back jolted him back to consciousness. They sent shocks of pain through his muscles, but he couldn't muster enough energy to sit up and clean his back. Instead, he thought about his current situation. After brother Wei had saved him and fought with the scary pointy-nosed Wang elder with a half-missing ear, they were blasted to the other side of the array formation. From his lying position in the open area, he could see the medicinal gardens swaying in the north winds.

Wait, what happened to brother Wei? Was he dead? He sat up, his eyes scanning around in search of brother Wei.

Ahh! Pain pulsed through his body, reminding him of his own grave situation.

He fell back and coughed up more blood. A lot of it. Even after using the Sacred Water Healing Talisman, his injuries hadn't healed completely, so he could only guess what brother Wei's condition might be. Brother Wei had taken the attack head-on. He might be dead.

But a few breaths later, he saw brother Wei lying next to a tree, not far away from him. He looked awful.

Taking a deep breath, he pushed himself up and stood. The first thing he did was check on brother Wei, and that gave him a sense of relief and dread at the same time. The relief was that brother Wei was still alive, but his condition was . . . What could he say? Was there a word for worse than the worst?

Brother Wei's right arm was no more. Well, it was there, but it was a mass of flesh and blood. There wasn't a single spot on his body that looked intact. Just looking at him, one would expect he would die anytime.

"Brother Wei." Chen Du tried to wake him, but there was no response. Other than weak breath, there was no other sign of brother Wei being alive.

A rustling voice attracted Chen Du's attention, and his heart tried to jump out of his rib cage when he saw thousands of snakes, if not tens of thousands, slithering toward him. Each of them looked crazy, and they were coming to kill them.

"Fucking assholes. Why are they coming toward us?" Cursing, he stuffed a bunch of Poison Repelling Pills in his mouth and a few in brother Wei's mouth too. Granted, brother Wei might not need it. While on the other side of the array formation, he had seen brother Wei with a strange air bubble around him that filtered poisonous air. Actually, he doubted poison affected brother Wei at all. Even right now, he smelled no poison around brother Wei's body. His body was covered in a pure air bubble.

This was one more reason to get brother Wei back on his feet. If Chen Du wanted to survive, only brother Wei could perform that miracle.

Sighing, he pulled two talismans out. One was a Sacred Water Healing Talisman that he slapped on himself, and the other was a true life-saving talisman his father had given him for an extremely life-threatening condition. A Divine Life Replenishing Talisman. It was a Gold Grade talisman, and his entire clan only had a couple of them. He was going to use it now.

Holy heaven's ass, what other choice did he have? If he wanted to survive, brother Wei must survive. With brother Wei's unending stream of miracles, they might have a chance to get out of this shit.

Looking at the shiny talisman in his palm, his mind wavered, but then he saw his sister Daiyu'er's face in it. For her, he had to survive. Even if it meant wasting a Gold Grade talisman, it was fine. Taking a deep breath, he slapped it on brother Wei's chest.

A golden light enveloped brother Wei, shining brightly as it reached inside his body, and then the injuries on brother Wei's body began healing rapidly. It happened so fast that Chen Du stepped back from him. With wide eyes, he watched brother Wei's bones re-attach, his muscles and tendons merge together, and his right arm form back to a shadow of what it originally was. In a few breaths' time, brother Wei became flawless except for his right arm.

Brother Wei's right hand had healed a little, and the bones had reformed, but the muscles and tendons remained in a mushy state. Unfortunately, Brother Wei remained unconscious, and there was no change in his weak breathing pattern.

Chen Du stretched his hands. The Sacred Water Healing Talisman had restored him to almost perfect condition, but he didn't have the guts to fight the snakes that were still advancing slowly toward them.

From the unending sea of snakes, a giant viper moved forward. It was as thick as a grown adult's waist and at least ten feet long. When it opened its mouth, the light reflected on its two shiny fangs. It was terrifying. Chen Du's heart did a somersault and bashed against his ribcage as if it would crack open his chest and run out. His throat grew parched when the python got within ten feet of them.

"Brother Wei, if you don't wake up now, we are in trouble. Or just send that female snake out and ask her to stop this attack."

No response came. Brother Wei remained unconscious. If his breathing hadn't stabilized, Chen Du would have lost all hope. But what was the use of hope when their death stood ten feet away from them?

Chen Du closed his eyes when the giant snake approached a five-foot distance from them. He readied himself for a cruel death. Maybe he shouldn't have challenged Wang Fantai and come here. After discovering the Wang clan's secrets, there was no hope of survival.

A breath passed. Two breaths passed. Five breaths passed, but nothing happened. Was he dead already?

Slowly, he cracked open his eyes and saw himself surrounded by an unending stream of snakes. They lingered at a five-foot radius, not moving an inch closer.

What was wrong with them?

Of course, he was happy that they didn't attack, but why did they look like frightened kittens instead of fierce predators. Surprisingly, they all stared at brother Wei. Did brother Wei have some relationship with them?

"So that's what a human looks like." Fan Ji perched atop a Three Leaf Asoka Tree, the tallest tree present at the edge of the Beast Origin

Realm. From here, he could see the White Bone Trees, the energy barrier that covered them, and the despicable humans on the other side of the array formation. One man had a black eye patch covering his right eye, and he was the one who sparked intense fear in all Fan Ji's low-level clan members' hearts.

Seeing him there, Fan Ji wondered if he was here to kill his clan members again.

He returned his eyes to the two humans surrounded by thousands of his clan members. The tall one looked afraid. A sword lay beside the smaller human lying at his feet, but instead of picking it up he sweated profusely.

Unfortunately, all the low-level snakes of his clan feared the man lying on the ground, so they didn't move an inch forward. They only encircled the humans and did nothing.

Fan Ji gazed at the unconscious man. He wore a tattered sky-blue robe, and his right hand was in a bad state, but he was the one whom his clan members feared right now. He was the one who'd sucked thousands of his clan members dry the day before. As per his clan members' report, that human was a demon. They'd said he'd chuckled when hundreds of snakes bit him all over his body.

A true evil.

He had to die for humiliating Fan Ji's clan members. For walking through the array formation. For making Fan Ji retreat back into the depths of the Beast Origin Realm. If this human hadn't come, Leader Ninth wouldn't have forced him to go back right away.

Anyway, he'd sneaked away from Leader Ninth and came here to see the terrifying humans with his own eyes.

"Young master, we should go back. The humans are dangerous, and Leader Ninth will get a fright if he finds out you came to the edge of the

Beast Origin Realm," one of the guards accompanying him, a Three Colored Python, said.

"Don't worry about Leader Ninth or Leader Eighth. They are busy searching for little Fuishui." She had gone missing after the portal opened. Did she go to the other side of the portal? Was she all right? If she'd been hurt, he would destroy the entire human population. It was their fault little Fuishui had become like this. Distant.

He glanced at the human with the black eye patch. Little Fuishui hated him the most, because when he'd first used the mysterious smoke, Leader Fifth, little Fuishui's father, had gone mad and killed thousands of clan members, then killed himself in embarrassment. He hoped little Fuishui didn't make any such mistake. "Ask our brothers to attack the humans together. The fearful human predator is unconscious, and this is our best chance."

"Yes, young master. I'll try that." The Three Colored Python shook his head, releasing a high-pitched soundwave that traveled through the air, and every brother snake in the vicinity trembled in fear. They all turned their heads toward the tree where Fan Ji sat.

"Young master, they are afraid," the Three Colored Python said.

Fan Ji roared, an innate ability that came through his royal bloodline. When he roared, every low-level snake lowered their head and listened to his command. "My brothers, heed my command and kill that human. He is at the weakest point of his strength."

Everyone nodded, and Fan Ji smiled inside his mind. This was his chance to shine in front of his father. If he could kill those nasty humans, everyone would praise him, and his father might let him come here more frequently and enjoy the daylight.

"Kill them both." His sound transmitted through the air, and all his clan members leaped at the humans. Fan Ji watched with satisfaction as his clan members overwhelmed the humans.

Chapter 64

Divine Life Replenishing Talisman

A strange golden energy entered Li Wei's body, healing him rapidly. Warmth spread through his body and moistened his dried-up meridians, healing them and generating new blood all over his body. He could sense everything, but he kept drifting between the edge of sanity and darkness. When his back had crashed into that tree and broke it in two, one of the splinters had pierced his lower back, and his body was mending around it now. Technically, he should get it out of his body first, and then heal his injuries, but he couldn't do anything as he couldn't move at all.

System: External healing energy detected. Taking host out of hibernation mode.

The warmth spread through his body, and he could sense the energy re-attaching his bones, mending muscles, and healing his meridians. If this continued, he might survive.

Surprisingly, when the warmth reached his right arm, which he had lost hope of healing anytime soon, he felt a connection with his right limb. This was awesome. After using the Dragon Fist of Pain and overusing his physical force, he had lost his connection with his right arm. It was a goner, and he might not have found a solution before concocting a Gold Grade pill himself. But he knew that was a distant dream, and his cultivation progress would be slowed drastically. For a body cultivator, losing a limb meant grave trouble. Even if they grew the limb back in the future, it would always remain weak compared to their other body parts.

So, one couldn't lose their limb completely. But he'd had no other choice if he wanted to save his and Chen Du's lives. The situations he fell into always stopped him from using the selective output theory he wanted to try, and he always had to go beyond his capacity.

Damn!

However, somehow he could feel his right arm again, and his body was healing rapidly. Blood pearls were generated and rushed through his body, healing the injuries the strange energy missed. His blood pearls had grown beyond 1,000, and this was good, but there was an issue with his heart blood. It wasn't generating again because of the ice qi that Wang Jiang had sent into his body when their fists clashed.

Finally, he could sense his surroundings, and when he spread his divine sense, he saw a large viper leaping at his head, Chen Du right next to his body, and an army of snakes surrounding them on all sides.

Fuck! This was bad.

With his left hand, he grabbed Chen Du's sword which lay next to him and swung it vertically.

"Don't." A large snake appeared in front of him and blocked his sword, then defended against the viper's strike. Who was this giant snake?

The viper convulsed in the air and changed direction to drop on Wei's other side. After hitting the ground, it slithered away from the large snake.

"Li Wei," the large snake said in a low, feminine voice only he could hear. "If you want to survive, you'd better abduct the tiny snake, little young master Fan Ji from the Three Leaf Asoka Tree out there." She landed next to him.

What was going on? Why was this female snake asking him to abduct another snake?

Abduct.

Really?

His divine sense spread toward the Three Leaf Asoka Tree in a beam shape, instantly reaching five hundred feet's distance. In a beam shape, his divine sense could reach beyond its normal limit of three hundred feet. On the tallest branch of the tree, he spotted a tiny snake that could fit in his pouch staring at him. The tiny snake had a lustrous black body covered in green scales. It looked quite ordinary. So ordinary that he couldn't determine the species. Even the system had no answer about the species of the tiny snake.

"Are you sure? There's a Three Colored Python curled below it. Don't you think he seems more useful?" Wei asked, staring at the female snake. He recognized her now as the one he had saved by feeding her a rank three, one pill line Beast Rejuvenating Pill at the little fox's request. When he'd fought Wang Jiang, the little fox had taken her inside the spirit artifact, but she'd been smaller—at the time.

"You impudent fool, how can you speak of the young master like that?" Fuishui shouted back at him. Her arrogance had no bounds.

"Brother Wei, you're finally awake." Chen Du's muffled voice echoed in his ears, and then he saw the sweat-drenched brute sitting next to him, his face as pale as white paper.

"Did you heal me?" Wei asked, unable to determine what exactly had healed his right arm. Although it wasn't completely healed, it was much better than losing it. Given time, his Blood Essence Body would show its magic and heal it completely. In fact, he could feel the muscles growing on his bones as the blood pearls rushed through his right arm.

"Yes, I used a Divine Life Replenishing Talisman." Chen Du wiped his sweaty brow with a clean cloth from his pouch. "Brother Wei, what are we going to do now?"

A Devine Life Replenishing Talisman. Wow! No wonder it had pulled him back from a dire situation. It was a Gold Grade talisman, but where did Chen Du get it? Talisman cultivators were a rare breed, and he didn't think the Mortal Realm would have a talisman cultivator who could refine a high-tier Gold Grade talisman.

"Are you two even listening to me?" Fuishui shouted at them. "If you let the little young master walk away, you will die at the hands of the other leaders. They bear a deep resentment toward every human in this world, and they will definitely kill you. If you want to take revenge on the Wang clan, you must capture young master Fan Ji. If you want to survive, this is your only chance."

"Let me do it." The little fox appeared next to him, brushing her whiskers while snacking on a fruit, and then leaped at the Three Leaf Asoka Tree like it was just a foot away. She flashed through the air and quickly grabbed the little snake in her mouth and returned.

Wei squinted. If he wasn't wrong, this was the little fox's divine ability. Although they lived together, he didn't know about her blood linage or how many tails she had manifested.

Suddenly a commotion took place in the army of snakes surrounding them. They started making a strange noise, and the Three Colored Python enlarged into giant snakes that matched the Fuishui's large size.

This was bad. The Three Colored Python had layer three Bone Baptization Realm cultivation, and Wei was no match for it in his current state.

But he need not fear them. With a thought, he pulled the little snake they had abducted earlier, and when the Three Colored Python saw the little snake, it moved backward, averting the current danger.

Wei sighed. He was safe. For now.

Chapter 65

What the future holds

The north wind swirled around Li Wei as he sat atop a three-hundred-foot-tall Wild Oak Tree, holding a strange-looking, heart-shaped yellow fruit in his hand and listening to the sound of the wind. It had a strange rhythm that harmonized with his heart, forming a tune of its own. Staring at the expansive forest spread in front of him, Li Wei considered the last month. The entire month had been kind of dramatic. Getting poisoned, cultivating two pill clones while almost losing his life, and then wiping out an elite Wang clan party with some tricks. Now he was on the other side of the array formation, sitting atop a tree with a bleak future ahead.

After a while, the north wind reduced in intensity, and a gentle breeze rubbed against his skin through the sky-blue robe he wore, lifting his mood. The robe always made him feel like Fei'er was with him. Just one thought of her, and his frustration vanished.

Should he be afraid in this strange land, a land filled with snakes and beasts he didn't know about? That Purple Mink he'd grabbed near the secret herb garden, he had never seen one like it before, and he suspected there would be more such beasts in this land.

But why should he be afraid of anyone? He was baptized by so many troubles over the two hundred years of his previous life, and he had learned to move ahead without stopping. This was just another test in his path to his Dao.

Suddenly something floated out of his body and wrapped around his neck. The sudden entrance of that thing startled him, but his divine sense told him it was the Purple Mink he had found near the secret herb garden.

Lifting its head, the mink squealed in his ear as if to thank him for saving its life, and then it wrapped around his neck and went silent. It looked like a thin purple shawl wrapped around his neck. This was surprise. How had it survived?

First, Wei scoffed and thought of pulling it away from his neck, but when he studied it further with his divine sense, he relaxed. It was a common animal. Not even a Ferocious Beast. It couldn't even scratch his skin with its entire might. Patting the adorable mink, he chuckled. The mink wasn't afraid, so why should he be?

In his previous life, he had spent many years in more dangerous places than this. He had seen beasts that no one could even imagine and survived them. This realm was nothing when compared to that. This was just a step to overcome in the path of his dao, every step meant to baptize him for his future endeavors.

Yes, this was just a step in his path of laziness dao.

And he should look at it positively. He was still living with all his limbs intact, and he had learned so many new things while going through the month's worth of troubles.

Then he pulled out the bow he'd got from Wang Rong. It was a high-tier Silver Grade bow, and it would help him hunt in this forest.

Archery was something he'd always wanted to try, and he had even gotten some lessons from Rual'er in his previous life. She had even taught him a bow type divine art. Maybe he should practice it now that he had the time, and a good bow. Or he could focus on the defensive arrays a little more. He was lacking defensive skills. Wind Mountain Defensive Array was a good one to practice.

Everything he'd suffered had enabled him to charge toward his goal like a bull. And the first step was to eat the fruit in his hand.

But he didn't want to eat this fruit.

His face twitched as he stared at the bitter fruit in his hand—Red Foul Heart Berry. The last time he'd passed through the array formation, he'd picked a couple of those to make a few pills, but he didn't expect he would need to eat one. Just bringing it near his face made him think of a basket of overripe fruit about to go waste. It gave him a bad taste, and he didn't want to eat it, but it was crucial for his survival. That bastard Wang Jiang had pushed ice qi into his heart when their fists collided, and it had clawed at his heart blood. On top of that in overusing blood pearls while activating Dragon Fist of Pain he had burned through some of his heart blood. Heart blood wasn't something that could be easily replaced like a blood pearl, and Blood Essence Body couldn't replenish his heart blood.

The ice qi still remained in his heart and was attacking his heart blood. If he lost all his heart blood, he would die. Even his blood pearls couldn't fight against the remnant ice qi. So, his only option was this fruit. The fruit was a precious poison used to kill Heart Blood Realm cultivators. In Heart Blood Realm, one's heart blood became their primary energy source, and this fruit, once consumed, sealed the heart blood. After that, a slow death awaited the target.

Heart blood was the source of one's vitality, and this fruit could kill a qi Refinement Realm cultivator in a month's time without leaving a trace behind. The cultivator would lose his vitality and then one day he would turn into dust. But Wei was different than normal cultivators. Every drop of his blood surged with vitality, so he didn't have to worry about dying due to loss of vitality.

He brushed his fingers against the uneven skin of the fruit. Despite being a perfect poison for him, it would also affect his cultivation, and he couldn't lose too many of his blood pearls going forward. Whatever he did, it had to be within a certain limit, else he would tip the balance and might even die. Eating it would solve his current problem, but it would result in some side effects, but his priority was to solve the problem of the ice qi and unseal his heart blood.

Closing his eyes, he let the vast scene disappear from before him and popped the fruit into his mouth, letting the bitter taste spread across his tongue.

His Yang Wood Pill Clone sprang into action the moment the fruit entered his mouth, separating the wood element out of the fruit. The fruit dissolved into two streams of energy. One went to his dantian, and the other shot toward his heart like a child seeing her mother after a long day of separation. The strange energy wrapped around his heart blood and instantly cut it off from the ice qi clawing at it. The ice qi clashed at the strange energy but couldn't do anything about it.

System: Foreign substance detected. Host's vitality stream is drying up. Time to dry vitality energy: 5 years. Recommended to remove the foreign substance from host's body.

As expected, Red Foul Heart Berry had sealed his Heart Blood.

The entire process took merely a breath's time, and Wei didn't feel anything. That was how people killed a Heart Blood Realm cultivator. But this fruit was impossible to find, and normally it could be only found in the Martial Realm.

Sighing loudly, he rubbed the collar of his robe, feeling Fei'er's presence on his robe. Her beautiful face floated in front of his eyes. What was she doing right now? Maybe sewing new robes.

"Stay safe, Fei'er," he whispered, brushing his finger against the purple mink wrapped around his neck. By provoking the Wang clan, he had put a target on himself, and he didn't want Fei'er to get dragged into this mess. Well, he wished she could accompany him here, to the top of this tree. She would definitely love the view. When she was ten years old, she always pestered him to take her to the top of the Big Dipper Tree, but he never had.

Thinking of her reminded him of Sun Nuan, the other kindhearted girl he knew, and those thoughts moved on to Sun Hua, Nuan'er sister.

How would he face Sun Nuan if something happened to Sun Hua?

He glanced at the glaring sunlight and focused his gaze. Two things were clear. First, he had to get stronger, fast, and save Sun Hua. And second, the Wang clan had to be wiped out from this realm.

But before either of those, he had to find a way to remove the ice qi from his body, then remove the seal placed by the Red Foul Heart Berry, and then find a way to kill everyone from the Wang clan still camped out on the other side of the array formation.

Tip! Tip!

Water droplets as big as a piece of peas dropped from the ceiling outside the cell, forming a surreal atmosphere for the girl inside the prison cell. A girl in dark gray clothes pressed her face to the rusted metal bars. Stretching out her tongue, she had found just the right spot to collect droplets on the tip of her tongue. It bruised her face whenever she collected water like this, but she really didn't care. Who would see her as long as she remained imprisoned here? And the one she wanted to show her face to was far away from here, so she cared not at all about the rusty brown metal bruising her face. It could recover in a day with a healing pill.

For the next ten minutes, Sun Nuan collected the water droplets that tasted like the most delicious meal she had ever eaten. It beat the chef from the palace hands down. This wasn't how it was supposed to happen, but once she hadn't been given water for three days and she'd had to set her pride aside and drink drops like this.

But today she was glad she'd gone through that suffering because this water was magical. After ten minutes of catching these water drops on her tongue, she wouldn't feel any thirst or hunger for an entire day. It also helped her refill her wood qi faster than before. This was a dark underground prison, so essence energy density was at its lowest, and she roughly needed ten hours to fill her dantian completely. It heavily restricted her practice time.

However, after she drank this water, she could refill her qi in just four hours. That was miraculous.

When she first realized this, she wondered if it was similar to the water big brother Wei had used to swiftly age plants to hundreds of years' age. That was a heck of a mysterious liquid. Heck, big brother Wei was the biggest mystery she had seen in her entire life. If only she could collect this water in a big barrel and give it to big brother Wei. That would be awesome. Unfortunately, she had nothing to store water in, and how was she going to give it to big brother Wei? He might be thousands of miles away, and she was stuck inside this prison.

Crossing back to her stone bench, she sat cross-legged on it and cultivated silently. When she felt the sizzle around her index finger, she opened her eyes. A thin layer of golden wood qi wrapped around her finger, and when she swung it, it shot out of the finger and struck the stone bench, leaving a scratch behind.

She had finally done it. A path that she had glimpsed a few days ago had become clearer. She had finally stepped through the level one peak completion of Wood King's Sword. At this level, she could shoot a sword through her fingers. Of course, the sword image she'd shot before was nothing but a fragile qi attack, but she had formed the foundation. Going forward, she would get better at it the more she practiced this martial skill. If big brother Wei was here, he would be so happy with her progress.

It was all thanks to the treasure senior Xue Qi had given her. Senior had told her that it would allow her to increase her alchemy knowledge with greater comprehension, but Sun Nuan had never thought she would use it to increase her comprehension of a martial skill. She was getting close to learn the Essence of Comprehension of Wood King's Sword level one peak.

"Senior Xue Qi." She cupped her hands before her chest. "Please forgive me for using this treasure for a martial skill. Once I get out of this place, I'll spend years with you learning alchemy, but for now please forgive me and let me use this for martial skills. Only if I can become strong can I accompany big brother Wei, so I'll make good use of this." She wrapped her palm around the treasure tied to her neck and felt a connection with senior Xue Qi. A warmth radiated through her heart, and she sensed a powerful will entering her body. She had to do this. For big brother Wei, for her mother, and for her sister.

Thinking about her sister, her fingers reached around the pendant the queen had given her a month back. "Hua'er, how are you doing? With that pendant, she could sense her sister's emotions. Until now, she hadn't felt anything. That was a good sign, so her sister was good.

As she thought about her loved ones, her determination reached a new state, and she walked toward the metal bars. To get out of this place, she had to cultivate harder, and the mysterious water was her best friend.

Chapter 66

Epilogue

On a landscape far away from the Mortal World, a man with a short beard opened his green eyes, shooting a red light toward the jade-coated roof of his secluded cave. The rocky bed he slept on broke apart under the immense pressure his body released, but the man didn't fall. Instead, he floated in a relaxed position with his arms crossed behind his head, a few feet above the rocky ground that spread throughout the cave.

"The Primordial Blood Palace has produced the first blood servant already?" Shock evident in his eyes, he swept his immortal sense through his entire body, but there was no connection established with the blood servant.

"Who has picked up the Primordial Blood Palace and formed a blood servant? Strange. It can't be trash of the family. It has to be someone very powerful." Closing his eyes, he tried to divine his own location, but the Primordial Blood Palace hadn't reached the level where it could connect with him for him to divine his location. It had only reached level one.

Now the blood servant had to take over the owner's body and then start the process of producing more blood servants.

It was too low level right now.

There were many levels, and he could only feel the vague sense of his artifact. This wasn't enough. He might have to wait at least a hundred more years until the Primordial Blood Palace reached the required level.

Closing his eyes, he once against went into meditation. With his cultivation sealed, all he could do was meditate on the Soul Mandate Law.

The next book is available for purchase

Beast Origin Realm (Path of Lazy Immortal Book 4)

If you want to receive a bonus scene and extended epilogue from book 2 and 3, sign up for my email list below.

Sign up for my Wuxia Sect to get latest update, and sneak peeks.

Patricia's Wuxia Sect

Chapter 67

Cultivation Realm Index

Realms of cultivation in the Mortal World (Body and Qi cultivation share the same names)

Mortal Realms (Where a person's body is still considered a mortal body.)

Refinement Realm

Foundation Realm

Blood Baptization Realm

Marrow Cleansing Realm

Boiling Blood Realm

Heart Blood Realm

Houtian Realm

Xiantian Realm

Violet Palace Relam

...

Meridian List for the Blood Essence Body Cultivation Art

Lower body Constellation

Refinement Realm (Earth Constellation) - 1) Yangming of stomach 2) Taiyin of spleen

Foundation Realm (Water Constellation) - 1) Taiyang of bladder 2) Shaoyin of kidney

Bone Baptization Realm (Wood Constellation) - 1) Jueyin of liver 2) Shaoyang of gallbladder

Grades of everything (Divided into three tiers. Low, mid, high)

Bronze

Silver

Gold

Earth

Human

Heaven

...

Array Realms

Array Carver Realm

Array Apprentice Realm

Array Adapt Realm - 9 Stars

...

Alchemist Realms

Pharmacist

Pill Apprentice – 3 Stars

Pill Adept - 6 Stars

...

Martial skill completion levels

Early Completion

Middle Completion

Late Completion

Peak Completion

If you like cultivation novels, don't forget to check below facebook groups to find out more books in cultivation genre.

Western Cultivation Stories

Cultivation Novels

Milton Keynes UK
Ingram Content Group UK Ltd.
UKHW031642281024
2423UKWH00026B/131